# Knight's World

*Kenneth D. Hammond*

ISBN: 1974647323
ISBN 13: 9781974647323
Library of Congress Control Number: 2017913196
CreateSpace Independent Publishing Platform
North Charleston, South Carolina

# Contents

| | | |
|---|---|---|
| Chapter 1 | Surviving My First Week | 1 |
| Chapter 2 | A Bank Robbery | 8 |
| Chapter 3 | Guarding a Train | 13 |
| Chapter 4 | Flying Squad | 18 |
| Chapter 5 | Winter Snowstorm | 25 |
| Chapter 6 | Heavy Response | 30 |
| Chapter 7 | River Pirates | 36 |
| Chapter 8 | Queen's Protection Detail | 42 |
| Chapter 9 | Siege | 50 |
| Chapter 10 | Inspector | 55 |
| Chapter 11 | Mysterious Death | 62 |
| Chapter 12 | Petty Thefts on the Docks | 71 |
| Chapter 13 | Murder in a Mage Shop | 77 |
| Chapter 14 | Corrupt Constables | 83 |
| Chapter 15 | Missing Children | 88 |
| Chapter 16 | Ransom | 93 |
| Chapter 17 | Princess in Disguise | 100 |
| Chapter 18 | Blackmailed Nobles | 113 |
| Chapter 19 | Smugglers | 122 |
| Chapter 20 | Home Invasions | 129 |
| Chapter 21 | Random Killers | 136 |
| Chapter 22 | Tracking Train Robbers | 143 |
| Chapter 23 | Knight Inspector | 151 |
| Chapter 24 | Mouse in the Treasury | 161 |

| Chapter 25 | Sinister Cousin | 169 |
| Chapter 26 | Army Supplies Missing | 178 |
| Chapter 27 | Missing Maid | 188 |
| Chapter 28 | Dead Minister | 197 |
| Chapter 29 | Raiding Lords | 207 |
| Chapter 30 | Murdered Guard | 216 |
| Chapter 31 | Hunting a Fugitive | 225 |
| Chapter 32 | Gunfight in the Nursery | 234 |
| Chapter 33 | Duke of Knight | 245 |
| Chapter 34 | Wizards Do Not Die | 255 |
| Chapter 35 | Death of the Constable General | 265 |

## Chapter 1

# Surviving My First Week

I HAD WORKED in a shooting-and-fighting gallery from the time I was ten. My grandfather was the one to talk me into becoming a constable, which had not been hard. I read books in the evening, mostly on science or magic. These books ranged from religious spells to sorcery or witchcraft. They all could be either good or bad, depending on how they were used. The constable academy was six months long, and only a third of us finished.

I was twenty and looked in the mirror and straightened the dark-blue uniform and adjusted the wide belt. The new Sharp twelve millimeter was heavy but felt right on my hip with the three cased cylinders in front of it. The billy on my belt on the left hip was also new and weighted. The two cases on the back of my belt were for the new restraints.

I climbed the steps up out of the basement apartment and headed down the street. At the corner I nodded to the constable walking his beat. I caught the streetcar and rode across the city and stepped off as we went passed the port constable station. I checked my pocket watch as I walked to the main doors, and I was still early. The morning briefing was with a warning of dock gangs starting a war.

I glanced at the older man who was my partner. He had five year strips on his left sleeve and two wound strips on his right. He also had two valor medals under the constable shield on his chest. We walked out of the building together, and he glanced at me as we turned for docks. "My name is Winston."

I nodded, and he glanced around.

"You listen to what I tell you: keep your eyes and ears open and your mouth shut."

He nodded to the pistol on my hip.

"Remove the thick retaining strap and put a thumb loop on it. Look for one of the lower-thigh holsters but make sure it has an upper- and lower-leg strap so you can run."

I glanced at his and nodded again. "Okay."

Winston turned down a street, and I turned with him. He slowed a few moments later. "Look at the youth across the street and in front of the apothecary."

I glanced at the store and the youth, and Winston nudged me. "Go around through the alley to the back of the store. The rest of his gang will probably be loading a cart."

I nodded and turned to cross the street and go back to the corner. Once I was around the corner, I began to walk faster. At the back of the building, I turned in at the service alley. I could see a hand cart behind the apothecary with two men loading it. I stayed beside the buildings in the shadows as I walked, and they did not see me until I was almost to them.

One turned and saw me and reached to his waist. I took a couple more steps as I pulled the billy and lashed out. The long wharf knife he was pulling out spun away when I hit his wrist. I jabbed into the other man's stomach when he turned, and he folded. I glanced at the door when I heard yelling and a struggle. I quickly put restraints on both men and through the spokes of a wheel.

I moved to the door as Winston pushed three young men out. He smiled and pushed them to me. "Not bad, kid."

I slipped the billy back into the ring and turned the men and pushed them against the wall. "The shop owner?"

Winston shook his head. "Beaten and tied up."

He turned to toss two restraints as he headed back into the shop. "I will call for a wagon and the doc."

I secured one and turned to the next, and he suddenly twisted and lifted a foot to kick. I snapped a kick out and into his thigh, and he yelled as he fell. I shifted to the side and shoved the last one back into the wall. "Stay there."

I turned and knelt and turned the man on the ground onto his stomach. I yanked his arms back and put the restraints on him. He glanced back and sneered. "You are dead."

I pulled him up and shoved him into the wall. "I will let my bill collectors know."

I pulled a couple of cords from a pocket and tied the last man's wrists. I moved the first two I had captured and shoved them against the wall as Winston returned. I began searching them, and Winston cleared his throat and said, "Check that last one's right ankle."

I found a small slim knife and took it before going back to searching. Winston made a list of everything that had been put in the cart before moving it inside. We pushed the men down the alley when the constable doctor arrived. A barred wagon was waiting, and the officer replaced our restraints on the men before leaving. An hour, and we stopped at a small diner.

While we ate I wrote up the report on the men. Several hours later Winston glanced around; we were just off the docks in a group of fish warehouses. I looked around and felt uncomfortable like someone was watching me. I undid the retaining strap on the pistol and moved to the side beside a tall fish trash bin. Winston stood still, and then he was moving just before several shots were fired from a shadowy doorway.

I do not even remember drawing my weapon, but I aimed as three men moved out. Winston ducked into another warehouse as they kept shooting. I fired, and one went back and down as I cocked the pistol and aimed again. The two men left were still firing at the doorway Winston had gone through, and I shot another in the chest, and the last realized I was shooting at them.

He turned, and shots from the doorway Winston had gone through made him spin and fall. I moved forward and pulled my mage whistle and started blowing it. Any and all constables near us would hear and come running. They would also call it in, which meant even more constables would know. The last man was on the ground, writhing around as he screamed, while the other two were still.

I holstered my pistol as Winston joined me and knelt to put restraints on the man; the other two were dead. It was not long before a few more men appeared and moved toward us as they pulled knives. Six constables ran around the corner behind them, and they pulled billies. Ten minutes, and there were two dozen constables and a wagon.

An hour after that, we were back in the station and writing reports while the night commander waited. Firing a weapon was a big thing, and a constable inspector was back at the warehouses and looking everything over. The man who was still alive was in the same gang as the ones we had arrested earlier. Winston slapped my shoulder when we left, and I headed home.

I walked all the way and checked my street as I headed for my apartment. Once inside I threw the door bolts and the two locking bars. My first day, and I had already shot and killed someone. What was worse, the gang had a contract out on Winston and me. I washed and got a new uniform ready before lying down to sleep. I was up six hours later and dressed in regular clothes.

I dropped the dirty uniform off at the cleaners and went to the fighting gallery to exercise and practice shooting. It was afternoon when I walked back down my street and nodded to the constable. I glanced around the street as I walked and slowed when I saw the two boys. They were trying to blend in but did not wear the type of clothes for this area.

I looked around again before going down the stairs. I turned my body as I unlocked the door, but instead of just opening it, I slammed it open. I pulled a knife from the small of my back as I stepped in. The man behind the door yelled, and the one on the other side of the room lifted a gun. I threw the knife as I lunged back into the door, which slammed into the man once more.

The knife struck the man in the throat as the gun fired, and I felt a searing pain in my left shoulder. I caught the other man's wrist as I took another step. He had grabbed the door, and I twisted and spun as I stepped back and yanked. He came out from behind the door and yelled as he was thrown into a wall. I let the wrist go and snapped a kick behind his knee as I grabbed his hair.

I continued into him as he dropped the gun he carried. As he went down, I slammed his head into the wall. I reached onto a shelf to shove books aside and grabbed a pistol. I spun and aimed at the door as one of the two watchers appeared. He held a knife and froze as he looked in. I growled, "Drop the knife and get on your knees."

He looked away from the man with my knife in his throat and at me before dropping the knife. A minute later a constable was in the doorway with his pistol in his hand. I gestured. "Watch for the other one behind you."

He glanced back and lunged to the side as I heard a shot. The boy in the doorway dropped, and I heard the constable fire three times. I moved forward and checked the screaming boy as the constable got up. He went to check the other boy he had shot before returning. I was holding the other boy down and applying pressure to the bullet wound in his back. "The other one is only unconscious."

He crossed to put restraints on him and search him. I turned and started to lift my pistol when three more constables came down the stairs. I turned back to the boy and set my pistol on the floor. "The boy is going to need the doc." I gestured to the side of the room. "My call box is in the corner. You might want to check on my partner too." A couple more constables arrived including a sergeant. They took over with the boy as I stood and moved aside. "I need to check my duty weapon."

The sergeant gestured, and I began to search my apartment carefully. They had not touched anything, which was good. I sat at my table and began to write a report before the constable inspector arrived. I got word they had tried to kill Winston, but he had been with four other off-duty constables. When I left later, my door had all new locks, and the beat constable walked me to the streetcar.

All the constables were more alert as they realized the dock gang had declared war on us. As it grew dark, Winston and I had only a few responses, which were mostly misunderstandings. We were in an area known as the dark. Most of those who lived there were oriental and were respectable. We stopped to have dinner in a small family diner.

I glanced at Winston when I saw the two lads watching us. He smiled. "Different gang."

I looked at them, and the older lad shifted before strutting to us. I shifted and moved my hand under the table. He grinned as he stopped beside the table. "Word is the Dock Boys have added the constables to their war."

I glanced around as Winston leaned back and smiled. "People make dumb mistakes."

The lad grinned. "That is true. Last month they were trying to muscle in on us and wanted to go to war." Winston waited, and the lad looked around and said, "They have a collection and opium-distribution house at Saint George and Michaels. The place was an old clothing shop and has two escape routes. One is over the roof and through the cathedral of Luke, and the other is a hidden door into the laundry on the other side." He looked at Winston. "They have a major gang meeting in two hours and plan to send kill teams for the constable commissioner and all your commanders."

He smiled and turned to walk away, and I looked at Winston and asked, "Think we can trust the information?"

He snorted as he drained his cup of tea. He stood, and I quickly followed and put a silver coin on the table for the meal. He walked to the kitchen door and smiled at the owner and cook when we stepped in. I used the call box and told the desk sergeant what we had been told. The sergeant passed it to the lieutenant who told the commander who called the commissioner.

He was the one to call a magister and give the word. Not that the commander was not already pulling everyone in. Sixty constables armed with double-barrel shotguns converged on the shop, the cathedral, and the laundry. As much as I wanted to be one of the first, we were sent around to the back with two other constables and two sergeant constables.

The back door burst open, and four men started out with weapons in hand. The two sergeant constables fired, and the men screamed as they went down with lead shot in their legs. I moved to one while Winston took another, and the other two constables went to the last two. I took the weapon the man had dropped and hit him with the butt of the shotgun when he started to kick out.

I yanked him onto this stomach and put restraints on him as constant shots sounded from inside the building. I searched him and yanked him up as he cursed and pulled him as I moved back. Six men were suddenly coming out and firing almost blindly. The man in front of me grunted and folded as several shotguns went off, and I lifted mine and fired both barrels.

I changed hands and pulled my pistol, but the men were down writhing or lay still. I knelt to check my prisoner and looked at the stomach wound. I grabbed the back of his shirt and pulled him back and away from the door. It was only a couple of minutes before all the buildings were clear. Everyone in the gang was either dead or in custody.

Those who were not there would stay in hiding or leave the city. Only four constables were injuries, and the material recovered showed that the information had been correct. How they got most of the information about where the commissioner or commanders lived was unknown. The next three nights were very quiet and peaceful.

CHAPTER 2

# A Bank Robbery

I MISSED WINSTON before I even left my place to take the streetcar out to the southwestern constable station. After only four months, I had been assigned my own beat. Mostly it was stockyards or wooden houses close to them. I had been out to check in with the day commander, and he had given me an address. It was for a small house just inside our patrol area.

My beat was part stockyard and part shops, including one of the major stock banks. There were a lot of pubs and taverns that would open around midday, so mostly I would be walking around and through the shops. I smiled and nodded to people and stopped to meet and talk to the shopkeepers. Close to midday I had two cattlemen bothering a woman outside a shop.

When I walked up, they barely glanced at me before ignoring me. That was a mistake, and I pulled my billy and jabbed one man in the side and stepped as I brought it down on the other's head. He dropped, but the first had snarled and turned as he yanked at a pistol. I brought the billy down on his wrist and jabbed into his gut before hitting him on the side of his head when he folded.

I glanced around to see everyone watching before I knelt and put the restraints on the two. I got the information from the woman before I used a corner call box. The one I had struck in the wrist was yelling and complaining that I had broken his wrist. I had checked and removed any weapons the two had and gave them to the constable guarding the wagon when it arrived.

They were charged with public mischief, and one of them with attempted assault with a weapon on a constable. During lunch I ate in a small diner and wrote my report. I handed it off to the afternoon runner as I began moving between the shops, the pubs, and the taverns. That became my routine although mostly it was breaking up public arguments and disputes.

It was a week before anything major happened. I used alleys and backstreets to move between areas. It was late afternoon when I came out of an alley beside the bank. It was on the corner, and the front door faced into the intersection. I glanced toward the intersection and saw a man standing with a wide-brimmed hat pulled low and holding a double-barrel shotgun.

That rang bells, and I pulled my weapon and stalked toward him. Before I reached him, I saw a second man dressed just like him and also carrying a shotgun. I was almost to them when one turned and saw me. He jerked the shotgun up, and I reacted and lifted my pistol and fired. The bullet struck him in the throat, and the other man spun as he lifted his shotgun.

I extended my pistol and fired from only a couple of paces. The bullet struck one eye, and the back of his head exploded. I pulled my whistle and blew as I moved to the door and tried to open it from the side. Several shotgun blasts ripped it apart, and I spun and kicked out. The door crashed open, and I shot another man aiming a shotgun in the chest.

I shifted back to the side as more blasts ripped through the other door and into the space I had been in. I started through the door and shot a man pulling a pistol in the gut. Several people were on the floor as I went right and fired at a man behind the counter. Several shots followed me and struck the wall after I went past. I ducked down behind the end of the counter with my back to it.

I began removing the cylinder and pulling a full one from my belt. I slipped the full one in and dropped the other on the floor. I twisted back to the front area and aimed before firing at a shotgun-wielding man running toward the door. I spun and leaned out the other side as several shots tore up the front edge of the counter. I fired and cocked and fired again at the head of another robber at the other end of the teller counter.

He went back and down, but there were several more shots that struck the counter from a back doorway. I had to aim and wait before a man leaned out and I fired. He spun back and into the other room, and I came to my feet and started over the clerks on the floor. I was heading toward the office and the vault area when a man stepped out as he lifted a shotgun.

I dived to the side as I fired, and when I hit, I rolled to the wall as I cocked my pistol. I hit the wall and held the pistol straight out and over my head as the man staggered and I shot him in the chest. He dropped the shotgun and fell back into the doorframe before tumbling to the floor. I came to my feet and moved along the wall while watching the vault doorway.

I shifted when another constable came through the front door, and I gestured to him. "Get the people out!"

He nodded and started moving the people who were still on the floor. I moved to the doorway and peeked in before yanking back as a shotgun fired. The area of the doorway where my head had been was ripped apart, and a man yelled, "Try anything, and I kill the clerk!"

I glanced at the door as several more constables came in. "Put the weapon down and give up!"

One of the constables went around and came up on the other side of the doorway. He peeked in and yanked back as the shotgun fired again. The doorframe splintered, and I growled, "One more shot, and we come in shooting!"

The other constable grinned and glanced at the others as they split up and moved toward the office door in the corner. One peeked in and jerked back before there was a shot. They shifted, and one peeked and pulled back, and there was another shot before the first constable spun and fired. He moved in with the other constable following, and I looked at the constable on the other side of the vault doorway.

He grinned and peeked and pulled back, but there was no shot. The other two constables came out and headed to us, and I took a breath and switched hands on my pistol. I let it lead as I looked into the room, and the robber was behind the clerk with his pistol to his head. I aimed as I stepped in and to the right, and the other constable followed and went left.

I continued to aim. "You are trapped. Just put the weapon down. No one has been hurt, so it is just robbery."

He shifted as he tried to keep the clerk between him and both of us. "How about you leave and let me walk away."

I smiled and shook my head as I inched closer and further to the right. "That is not going to happen. You are leaving this vault one of two ways."

He shifted and half turned as the other constable stepped more to the left and another stepped into the doorway. "Stay back, or I kill him."

I looked at the sweating clerk and frowned at the bulge under his left arm. I looked at the robber as I changed hands on the pistol and turned sideways and extended it. "Go ahead. I am counting to three, and if you are still holding the weapon, I will kill you."

He shifted and ducked behind the clerk. "I will kill him!"

I took a step closer. "He was helping you rob the bank. One."

The clerk gasped, and the robber jerked and looked from me to the other constables. A fourth had stepped in, and the robber licked his lips. "I do not—"

I took another step closer and cocked my pistol. "Two."

His eyes darted around as he tried to step back, but he was at the back wall. "W…wait."

I took another step and was less than a pace away. "Three."

He gasped and dropped the pistol. "No!"

I reached for the clerk and put the barrel between his eyes as I pulled and stepped back. The other constables swarmed the robber as I spun the clerk and shoved him against the wall. "Hands on your head."

I started searching him and took the hidden pistol from under the left arm and another smaller one from the middle of his back. I pulled one hand at a time down and put restraints on before I put my pistol away.

I turned and pushed him to another constable at the door. "At least a couple will live to see the magister."

I glanced around and walked out to find a chair and sat. One of the others hit my shoulder. "An inspector will need your weapon, and the commander will need the report."

I nodded as I took a breath before standing and moving to the office. I looked in at the dead man on the floor before crossing to the desk. I took a sheet of parchment and walked out. I sat to one side at a clerk's desk and started writing. A few of the others were doing the same thing along the counter. The commander walked in and looked around while ignoring the bank manager.

He gestured, and a constable moved to pull the manager away. The commander walked around and looked into the office and then the vault. He walked up beside me and glanced over my shoulder before giving it a nudge. "Finish and let the inspector look it over. The clerk was a little reluctant to talk, but the other one has been talking nonstop, so we have them both." He looked around the room. "On the charge sheet, annotate nine counts of murder."

I stopped and looked at him. "But—"

He chuckled as he started around the counter. "This is a bank constable, and robbing a bank is a capital crime, which means any death that results from it is charged to the men robbing it."

I looked after him as the others chuckled, and I shook my head before going back to writing. The investigator was the same one from my last shooting. He looked at each of the dead closely before picking up the empty cylinder I had dropped. He took the other constable's weapon and slipped it into one of several pouches before coming to me.

He ignored the pistol I held out and took the report and read it. He gestured to the chair when he was done looking around. "I need the room." The others walked out, and he took my weapon. "You killed eight men this time."

I nodded. "I did not have a lot of choice."

He smiled. "Ashton, when we kill, something happens to us inside. With each life we take, a little of us pulls back. Normally I do not stick my nose in, but you are still very new. This time it was justified and maybe the next time, but you could just as easily begin to think using your weapon is the solution." He sighed and looked across the room. "You need something to do when you are not working. Something that does not involve weapons or violence. I think I will be recommending a change for you."

I shifted in the chair. "What change?"

He looked at me. "Something away from people to give you time to relax and think." He turned and started for the door. "I am glad it was not you on the floor."

CHAPTER 3

# Guarding a Train

I SHIFTED THE heavy belt on my shoulder with the six large cylinders on it and glanced around as I walked into the train yard. I nodded to the other two constables and set the new revolving shotgun on the table with our water jug. "When is it due in?"

The other two men were Constables Adams and McOwens. McOwens growled, "An hour."

I nodded and glanced out at the yard before frowning. "I thought there were more yard lanterns?"

Adams sighed. "Broken today by a gang."

I shook my head and lifted the shotgun. "We going to use the same positions?"

They nodded, and I started for the other end of the yard. The other two would take the two towers that looked over the yard. The train brought a single car of raw silver ore for the mint and normally had six guards on it. It would sit in the yard until it was unloaded in the morning, but the six guards would not stay. I hesitated when I reached the spot I had been using and went past it to an empty train car.

I sat in the dark and listened to the night sounds as I waited. With the broken yard lanterns, the train yard was very dark. When the distant train's light brightened the yard, I frowned. Shadows slipped into hidden niches, and there were quiet sounds and the crunch of gravel. Normally I would move out so they could see me, but I stayed in the train car and waited.

When the train went past and stopped, the guards did not wait and jumped off. They walked away without even glancing around or looking for us. I watched the men who worked for the train company as they began shutting it down, and finally after almost an hour, they left, and quiet returned. It was almost another hour before I heard the distant sound of a struggle.

I started to move when I heard a voice from where I had been the night before. It was male and hissed, "He is not here. Spread out and keep your eyes open."

I shifted the heavy shotgun and waited, and the shadowy figures of four men moved passed. Another joined them from the direction of the west tower. "They are dead."

My eyes narrowed as the men looked around and started for the train car with the silver. I dropped out of the car and knelt as I lifted the shotgun. "Constable!"

They spun, and two fired—one before he even lifted his weapon. I returned fire, and they all jerked as the buckshot hit them. I cocked the shotgun and fired twice more until they were down and screaming. Of course that was when I heard all the other men yelling as they ran toward us. I fired a last chamber as I stood and backed to the train car.

I removed the spent cylinder and dropped it as shots were fired at me. I went between the cars as I pulled another cylinder and slipped it into the shotgun. I turned and moved over the connection and then down between several cars before coming out. I glanced back in the dark before looking at the entrance tower. I hesitated before I started running.

I was on the stairs when they began to fire at me and charge closer. I felt a burning, stabbing pain in my leg and ignored it. I swung up and into the tower to see constable McOwens in a pool of blood. Bullets were impacting with the wood of the tower as I checked him and tried the call box. It was dead, so they had cut the line somewhere. I looked at the siren and started cranking it, and it began to scream.

The tower shook with an impact, and I stopped and heard an axe hitting one of the supports. I looked around before grabbing McOwens cattlemen's rifle and slinging it with my shotgun. I pulled the belt of cylinders off his shoulder and put it over my head and under my right arm. I undid his duty belt and stripped the holster and knife. I tucked the pistol under the belt in the small of my back and the spare cylinders in my shirt.

I looked out the door and took a breath; the tower had four guide cables going from the top of the tower and out to poles. The poles were anchored but were much lower than the tower. The one I was looking at went out and over the silver train. I rushed and leaped as I swung McOwens duty belt over the cable. I caught it as I came down and swung before I began sliding down the cable.

I was away and in the dark before they could get a shot, but a few still fired. I slid down and gained speed as I dropped, and when I started over the silver train, I let go. The car was still several paces under me when I dropped, and I landed and rolled before catching the far edge and swinging over. I was in the middle of the car and above the doors, and when I swung down, it was open.

I dropped and landed in a crouch as I pulled my pistol. Two men spun, one with a double-barreled shotgun and the other with a pistol. I shot the man with the shotgun in the chest before cocking the hammer and firing at the other man who was stumbling back. I moved to them quickly and took their weapons before starting to shift cases of silver to use as cover.

I knelt as men rushed out of the night and started shooting into the train car. I lifted the shotgun the man had tried to use and fired. Two men went down screaming, and a couple more staggered away as the rest dropped. I took my shogun off and aimed as I leaned out and fired into one of the closest men. He jerked and began thrashing around while screaming, and I cocked the gun again.

I pulled back as the sides of the car splintered when bullets struck. I turned and began shifting more cases to the other door. I heard voices outside it and stood beside it in the dark shadows. The door was yanked open, and men fired blindly into the car. I shifted and brought the shotgun barrel up and fired into the group and cocked and fired once more.

Several were down, and some were screaming, while others only moved spasmodically and died. I turned to the other door as I changed the cylinder. I moved to the front of the car as they began shooting into the sides again. I looked up at the roof hatch and grinned. I used a few cases and reached up to remove the locking pin and shouldered the shotgun.

I lifted the hatch quietly and climbed up and out. I closed the hatch and moved forward. I looked down between the car and the fuel car and climbed down. I pulled the shotgun off my shoulder and moved to one side as I cocked it.

I leaned out and pointed it and fired at a group of men beside the car. Two went down, and the others yelled as I pulled back and went the other way.

I cocked the shotgun again and leaned out the other side and pointed the barrel as several men looked in my direction. I fired, and one fell, and the others jerked and staggered back. I dropped off the train and onto the ground as I cocked and fired again, and one of the men dropped while the other turned to flee. I spun and moved into the darkness in front of the train as I replaced the cylinder.

Several lanterns entered the yard, and a dozen more came from two other directions. I heard the constable whistles, and I pulled mine and blew as I knelt. It was not long before light fell on me and a constable stepped out. "Where are the others?"

I stood. "Dead."

I started walking back down the train as even more constables arrived. I set my shotgun in the open door to the car and winced at the pain in one leg. I looked at it as a constable held up his lantern. I could see the hole and blood and remembered the pain while I was running up the stairs of the tower. I grabbed the shotgun and sat and watched as dead and wounded men were brought together.

This time it was a constable commander with a detective inspector who questioned me. The attackers were from one of the largest gangs in the city called the three-strike gang. With the death of two constables as well as all the other deaths, the commander was recommending a citywide collection of everyone we knew was in the gang.

I was finally put in an ambulance since the doctor had left with the most severely wounded. I stretched out and set the shotgun and rifle I still had to one side. I shifted and moved the second pistol out from the small of my back and put it beside my leg. A few blocks from the train yard, there were shots, and the ambulance jerked to a stop.

I cocked the pistol as I sat up, and the back door was jerked open. Two men were in the doorway and held pistols. One lifted his. "You are a dead ma—"

I shot him in the chest and cocked the pistol as he went back, and I shifted before firing into the second man. I was moving off the narrow cot as he fell, and I cocked the pistol. When I reached the door, several men were already running away. I pulled my whistle and blew as I slowly stepped out and went to check the driver and helper.

They were both dead on the seat, and I looked around as I pulled my own pistol and tucked the other away. It was morning, and I glanced at the hospital door and relaxed when it opened. Winston grinned as he crossed to the bed. "Hey, kid."

I smiled. "Lost your way?"

He leaned against the bed. "I thought I would check on you before I started."

I nodded as I shifted the pistol under the sheet. "What is going on?"

He snorted. "Panic in the street. The two men you killed when they attacked the ambulance were the head and second man in the three-strike gang. There are a few trying to bring everyone together, but we have been hitting them in every hideout we find. A lot of the other gangs have been providing us with locations, so they are really screwed."

I grinned. "I really feel for them. Any word on when I can get out?"

Winston glanced at the door. "A detective inspector was talking to the doctor when I got here."

I growled and finally yanked the sheet off. "Look in the closet for my pants."

He chuckled. "Not me—the nurse did not look very friendly."

The detective inspector from the train yard walked in and glanced at Winston. He looked at me. "The doctor says you can leave but you are not to do any walking for a few days." He smiled. "The commissioner is sending a carriage for you. As far as we can tell, the gang does not know who you are." He sighed and shook his head. "This is your third time under fire. I do not agree with the last constable inspector. From what I heard and saw, you are thinking before using your weapon. I recommended you to the commander and the commissioner for the flying squad."

I looked at Winston, and he grinned. "You get to police horseshit."

# CHAPTER 4

# Flying Squad

I LOOKED AT the large estate before heading to the stables for my horse. Both the mayor and the duke had given me awards, but the best had been the estate the constables had seized. It had thirty acres of land inside tall stone walls. It was divided by wooden fences into grassy areas for horses. I had two women with children living on the estate; they took care of the house and stayed for free.

Of course we had a large chicken coop against the back wall and two cows they milked. What we did not use they could have and sell. They also took in laundry and did work as seamstresses. One of the lads even looked after the two horses I had bought. I saddled the horse and slipped the short revolving rifle into the boot before swinging up.

My flying squad patrolled the area to the north and west of the city. It was mostly estates and large manors. I rode out of the stable and down the drive before climbing down to open the gates. I led the horse out and closed the gate before climbing back up. I headed toward the edge of the city and the small constable station. I hitched my horse at the rail with a dozen others before going in.

Only two dozen constables were on the flying squad, so the station was not large. I checked in with the sergeant and sat in the briefing room with some of the others. After the briefing ended, I joined Edward Dover at the door. He was an older man who walked with bowed legs and a large moustache. He was also my riding partner and had been teaching me.

He grinned as we headed for our horses and rode out. Our patrol was one of the farthest away, and we passed the two constables we were relieving before we reached the area. Most of the estates out there had someone at the gate to welcome guests or turn them away. As we passed each gate, we stopped to see if everything was okay.

It was just before noon when we approached the MacGibbins estate. Three men on horseback were arguing with the attendant, and one kept waving a short whip. We rode up just as he growled and spurred his horse and leaned out to strike the man. I was closest and brought my billy up and out as my horse leaped forward.

I brought the billy down on the wrist of the man with the whip, and he screamed as the bones broke. I let my horse hit his as I caught his fancy jacket and yanked. He twisted and grabbed as he came off the horse and crashed to the ground while yelling. I swung down while Edward moved between me and the other two, and I knelt to turn the man and put restraints on him.

I yanked him up, and he glared. "Do you know how I am?"

I smiled as I started pulling him to the estate gatehouse. "A criminal under arrest for attempted assault."

He choked, "Arrest!"

I accepted the call-box handset from the attendant and dialed. I shook the man when he began to struggle. "This is Constable Knight. I have one in custody for attempted assault at the MacGibbins estate."

I listened and nodded when the desk sergeant said he would send the wagon. I hung up and glanced at the two men still arguing with Edward before pulling my prisoner to the side. "Sit."

He spit on me, and I kicked his feet out from under him and spun at the sound of a pistol hammer cocking. Mine came up as I cocked it and fired into one of the men who was just starting to aim at me. He twisted and fell as Edward pulled his weapon, and the other man froze with his half out. I recocked my weapon. "Get down!"

The other man was screaming on the ground, and I shifted and kicked the one in restraints as he tried to pull his pistol. I stomped on his ankles, and he screamed as Edward swung down with the other man. He searched him and took his weapon as I knelt and searched my prisoner. I went to call in for a doctor and report what happened.

I got a statement from the attendant while we waited. He had called into the estate to let Mr. MacGibbins know what had happened. The constable inspector arrived while the doctor was checking the man I had shot. The other two were already on their way back to the station to see a magister. The inspector looked at the weapons and checked with the doctor before speaking with Edward.

I knew they would probably send me somewhere else. The inspector walked to me as I fed my horse a carrot. "You were very lucky, Constable." I blinked, and he smiled. "From what everyone says the man you shot not only had his weapon cocked but was aiming at you." He glanced at Edward as he joined us. "Just so you know, these three are wanted for questioning in several armed robberies. They were working to the east and forced their way into the estates by pretending to be wealthy sons of nobles or merchants." He glanced at the doctor as the man was loaded into the ambulance. "This time they will not see freedom for several decades." He sighed and turned to his horse. "Stay safe."

I watched him ride away and looked at Edward who grinned. "We tend to have more incidents where we have to shoot someone."

I grinned and moved to swing up into the saddle. The rest of the shift went smoothly with only one stop to help find a lost child. When we returned to the station, the night lieutenant handed both of us a bottle of aged whiskey. "From Mr. MacGibbins."

Edward grinned as I nodded my thanks and went to do the shift report before going home. I gave the bottle to the women to sell, and I ate dinner before walking around the estate and then exercising. I sat in the study to read about new magical forensic techniques before going to bed. It was midafternoon of the next day when we heard the screaming.

We kicked our horses into a run and turned in at the next estate. The attendant had seen us and yanked the gates open. This was the Marabel estate, and he was one of the city barons. When we reached the front of the manor, we swung down and strode to the door. I used my fist to bang on it, and after several moments, a footman yanked it open. "Do not—"

He froze as I shoved him in and followed. "Who is screaming and why?"

He swallowed. "The lady is."

He pointed up the stairs, and Edward started for them as I looked at the lad. "Gather everyone in the manor. No one leaves; call the gate attendant and tell him to lock the gates."

He nodded as I went after Edward, and we found the woman in what looked like a child's nursery. A man was holding and comforting a woman. From the door I could see the bloody crib. Above it on the wall was a message written in blood. It read, "Your child for mine."

I caught Edward and moved into the room to the man and woman. The child was missing, but blood was everywhere. I pulled them out of the room and gestured to Edward. "Call the lieutenant. We need the constable mage and Detective Inspector Carter. We also need the whole flying squad."

He nodded and turned to run down the stairs as I turned to the man and woman. The man was staring almost blindly back into the room, and I cleared my throat. He looked at me. "I want them dead."

I shook my head. "I doubt if the blood belongs to your child. There was no sign of spatter in the crib. Whoever they are, they are still close—the blood is still wet."

He stiffened as his wife turned to look at me and sniffed. "Are you sure?"

I nodded and gestured to the stairs. "We need to leave the room for the constable mage and Detective Inspector Carter. All the constables on patrol are on their way, and we will find the culprits."

I moved them downstairs and saw Edward still on the call box. I left them in the study and went looking for the servants. I had them hold up their hands while I checked them carefully, especially under the fingernails. None had seen or heard anything. I returned to the room upstairs and bent to look at the floor carefully. I saw a couple of drops of blood by the door and went out into the hall.

I barely glanced at Edward when I saw another drop of blood in the hall. After that there was a single drop at the door into the servants' stairs and another at the bottom. The stairs ended in the basement, and Edward brought a lantern as I hunted on all fours. I found another drop and then several on the outer steps leading out of the basement.

Now it became hard as I stayed on my knees to look through the grass. We were fifty paces away from the manor when several of the other constables arrived. I straightened and looked at Edward. "They need to spread out and search to the southeast. One should ride ahead to the river ferry; it does not cross for another half hour."

He nodded and yelled as I went back to looking for blood. I was off the lawn and found a boot print and stood as I looked at it. When I had it pictured in my mind, I looked in the direction it had been heading. I started walking and found a few more before Edward brought our horses. He followed and marked the boot prints. "The lieutenant has called the commissioner."

I glanced at him, and he shrugged.

"We have fifty men coming to help."

I nodded and pointed to a clear area. "Ride ahead to look there."

After that we leapfrogged, and within an hour, we were miles away when the direction turned. I looked around to see several roads and growled as I straightened, "He saw us patrolling and searching." I gestured to the last track. "This is fresh. No more than a few minutes." The crowd of constables looked around as I gestured. "Spread out and start checking the field borders and the culverts under the road."

I swung up onto my horse as they did as I asked and kicked my horse into a run. I knew about a small bog not to far away, and it would be a good place to hide a body. I saw the man a moment later as he looked over his shoulder. He was on the very edge of the wet bog and turned to lift a squirming child who began to scream. I pulled back on the rains as I pulled my rifle and swung down.

Edward kept going as I cocked the rifle, aimed, and shot the man in the back. He staggered and turned before going to his knees and dropping the child. I cocked my rifle as he fumbled a pistol out and cocked it and aimed at the child. I fired, and his head snapped back before his body went back and into the bog. I stood and went after my horse as Edward leaped off his horse and swept up the child.

All the other constables converged on us as I rode up while Edward was checking the screaming child. He smiled and looked up at us. "She is fine."

I sighed and nodded before gesturing. "You can take her back while I wait for the inspector and fish the body out of the bog."

He snorted as one of the other constables held his horse while he swung up. "Leave the bastard."

I smiled. "The doctor or his attendant do not deserve that."

The constables laughed as they turned to head away. I swung down and removed the bridle.

"We will be here awhile, so you might as well browse."

I pulled the body out and sat to wait and think. I was thinking of the three men from the day before and the estate they had been at. It was not long before Detective Inspector Carter arrived; the doctor was behind him. I gave him my statement while the doctor and his assistant checked the body before loading it into his wagon.

Detective Inspector Carter had already talked with several of the constables including Edward. He smiled when I finished. "Better the man than a child. Head back and get with your partner. I will need the written report before you get off." I nodded, and he looked at the bog. "I will have the Marabels look at the body to see if they know what this is about."

I caught my horse, and we rode back to the estate together. Edward was waiting when we got there, and we left. I told him I wanted to check on the MacGibbins estate. He grinned and said, "Thinking the rest of the gang might decide to hit there and take a little revenge?"

We kicked the horses into a trot and then a gallop. As we approached the estate, we slowed to walk the horses. Edward growled when we did not see the attendant, and I swung down and strode into his small shack. I found him on the floor and knelt to check him before standing. "The attendant has been beaten."

I used the call box and then went to open the gate and swung up into the saddle. We kicked the horses into a run, and I pulled my rifle out before we reached the manor. I had already cleaned and reloaded the spent cylinder. We both dropped out of the saddle as we pulled the horses to a stop. I tossed the reins over its head and followed Edward to the open door.

When we stepped into the house, we heard loud talking from the parlor and more from upstairs. I gestured to the parlor, and Edward nodded before starting up the stairs. I moved to the parlor and brought the rifle up to my shoulder and cocked it as I stepped into the doorway. "Constable!"

Two men with pistols spun, and I shifted and aimed as one lifted his. I shot him in the head and cocked the rifle and aimed at the other man.

He quickly dropped his weapon, and I gestured. "Turn around and move to the wall."

I heard two shots and hesitated as I went forward and put restraints on my prisoner.

I looked at the frightened people in the room. "Everyone okay?"

Some looked a little bruised and ruffled, but they all nodded.

I turned my prisoner and shoved him to the door. "One of you go use the call box and tell the constable station we need the doctor and the prisoner wagon as well as the inspector." I shoved the man out into the hall. "Edward!"

I heard him a moment later. "Here!"

I waited, and finally he appeared at the top of the stairs, pushing two sullen-looking men. A man followed him with a women who had her dress torn. I hissed, "Were we in time?"

Edward glared at the men. "Barely." He gestured. "I had to kill two upstairs."

I nodded and glanced back into the parlor. "Another is in there."

We shoved all three prisoners against the wall, and while he watched, I searched them. I took knives and two small hidden pistols off them before moving to the door. Four constables were riding their horses up the drive hard and slowed when they saw me. I waved and turned to go back in, and it was not long before the place seemed crowded with constables.

The prisoners were taken out to wait for the wagon as Edward and I sat in the kitchen to write our report. The doctor ignored the dead to check the hurt and injured people first. Detective Inspector Carter only grinned as he sat to read our report.

# CHAPTER 5

# Winter Snowstorm

I BRUSHED THE light sprinkling of snow off and straightened my long coat. I glanced at the new sergeant strips and grinned before leaving the changing room. The year and a half with the flying squad had mostly been boring with flashes of action and excitement. I had tried for and passed the test to be a sergeant and received the three officer recommendations I needed.

I was assigned to the commerce district of the city after I was promoted. I nodded to the lieutenant when I came out and accepted the notes to pass on to the constables today. I went to the briefing room, and a few quieted as I went to the front. I ignored them as I went through the notes before finally looking up and straightening.

A week, and they already had me down. They became silent as I began the morning roll and then the briefing. The other three sergeants were in back and took notes. When I finished, the senior sergeant stood and cleared his throat. "The constable mage sent us a weather warning for more snow."

All laughed as they stood and began heading for the door. It was the middle of winter, and lately we had snow falling every day, so a weather warning was redundant. I put the notes away as I headed out and began a random patrol of one area. It had a dozen constables already walking it, but the sergeants were there to check and back them up.

I greeted the few people and shopkeepers who were out. It was not long before the falling snow became heavier. I caught up to a man trying to help his pregnant wife through the snow in front of a shop. He looked at me frantically. "Help!"

The woman's face was white, and she was bent and clutching her stomach. I moved closer. "The baby coming?"

The man nodded as the woman groaned, and I looked around and gestured to a shop.

I helped push the door open and glanced at the shopkeeper. "Call the station and let them know we need the doctor."

She nodded as she looked at the woman before heading to the back wall. It was an hour before the doctor got there, and she still had not given birth. The doctor grunted as he knelt and lifted her skirt; he looked and nodded. "Tell my assistant we have time to get her to the hospital."

The husband was clinging to her hand as she moaned. I went to the door and opened it to yell out. A few moments, and the assistant came in carrying a litter. By the time we loaded her into the ambulance, it was snowing harder, and we could barely see fifty paces down the street. I led the team of horses at a fast walk and finally turned in under the hospital porch.

I walked away and headed back to the area I was checking and caught four older boys trying to break into a closed shop. I walked up behind them while they were trying to force the door open and touched one with my billy. "Hands against the wall." They spun, and their faces went white; one half turned, and I growled, "If you want, I will break a few heads. Get your hands on the wall!"

They turned and leaned against the wall, and I went down the line and put restraints on and tied their hands behind their backs. I pulled them out to the edge of the street and started pushing them to keep them moving. Barely a block away, I met one of my constables who was pulling three young men out of a building. They were already restrained and sullen, and he grinned. "Are we enjoying this wonderful weather, Sergeant?"

I snorted and kept pushing the boys. "Just look at the rosy cheeks it is giving you."

He laughed as he pushed one of the men who glared. "If you were not wearing that badge—"

He grinned. "You just keep thinking that, bucko."

It took three times as long to reach the station and put the five into a holding cell. I grabbed a cup of coffee before I returned to the street. The falling snow had thickened, so I could barely see a dozen paces. I found one of my constables having a snowball fight with a dozen children and shook my head. I jerked up when I heard the gunshot. "Get these kids inside!"

I ran through the snow in the direction I had heard the shots. Two men were standing over a third while trying to break the chain on the case he had on his wrist. I pulled my pistol as I slowed to a walk and stopped. I lifted my weapon and cocked it, and the sound faintly echoed.

The men froze, and I said calmly, "Drop the pistol and put your hands on your head."

One turned his head to look back and shifted, and I smiled. "Go ahead; I have not killed anyone in a couple of weeks."

He snorted but dropped the pistol, and the other man let the case go. I waited for a few moments and glanced at the constable when he joined me. He grinned and moved to one side and forward before cocking his pistol. "I do not see hands on your heads."

They jerked and glanced at him before slowly doing as they were told. He moved in and yanked their hands down and back before restraining them one at a time.

Once they were secured, he knelt to check the man in the snow. He looked at me and shook his head. "Dead."

I lowered the hammer and put my pistol away as I moved to the men. "Grab him and the weapon and pull him into a shop. We will not get the doctor or the wagon until the snow lets up and they can see."

I turned the men and searched them and took a second pistol off one.

I started pushing and shoving them. "Pass the word to the others to start patrolling in pairs and take breaks out of the weather to warm up."

It took me a long time to reach the station, and I only found it because they had put out the large red storm lanterns. I put the two silent and sullen men in a cell and let the jailor know their crime. I warmed up before heading out and ran into the lieutenant pulling two women in. They were restrained and cursing him, and I grinned and waved before heading back to my area.

At each intersection I went to each of the corner lights and made sure it was lit and slipped the yellow lens in. I met a few of my constables as I walked, and they were putting the yellow lens on the streetlights. A couple of hours after that,

I stumbled into a half dozen kids in an alley. They were trying to light a fire and huddled together.

I pulled them out and down the street to a small diner. I paid the serving girl a couple of silvers to get them hot coco for the night and let them nap in a corner. She grinned and ruffled one's hair. "No problem, Constable."

I was barely out of the diner when I heard the yelling and shouting. I pushed into an entryway and listened before going in and up the stairs. I heard the woman scream and the sound of a fist as the man yelled and began banging on the apartment door. I pulled my billy, and it was a minute before the door was yanked open. "I told you if you came back, I would—"

He froze with his fist back, and I jabbed into his gut. He folded, and I grabbed his hair and yanked him up and spun him while shoving him back and into the room. I saw the woman in one corner, crouching and crying. I spun the man and slammed him into the wall before I put restraints on. "You are under arrest for assault and attempted assault on a constable."

He started whining that they were married and I could not do this.

I spun him and shoved him back into the wall. "Not only can I do this but I will also be making checks with your wife. If she has even one tiny bruise, I will have several men I know start paying you a visit every day." I looked at his wife. "Will you be okay, or do you need a doctor?" He glared and growled, and I slapped him with the stick. "Shut up."

She sniffed and shook her head. "I will be okay."

I yanked him to the door. "Close the door after us and keep warm."

He began protesting as I pushed him out and down to the first floor and then outside.

When I shoved him into the station, he was shaking with cold. I shoved him to one of the constable. "Put him in holding. The charge will be assault and attempted assault on a constable. He is a wife beater, so make sure the others in the cell know."

The constable grinned. "Sure, Sergeant."

I went to get coffee before I headed back outside and started back to my area. I struggled through the snow and began making my way around. I had just reached two of my constables when I heard the breaking of glass. They looked at me, and I sighed as I gestured. "One of you go around to the right. The other take the front, and I will go to the back."

The shop we were in front of was a furrier's. I expected someone very cold or freezing. What I found inside the back door was a large, well-dressed man in a long full-fur coat. He was whispering direction and telling the others which coats to take. I poked him with my billy. "Against the wall with your hands on your head."

I should have known it would not work. The man spun and yanked a large, shiny pistol from the coat pocket while yelling. "Constables!"

I brought the billy down on his wrist before he could cock the pistol. He screamed, and the weapon fell as I slugged him and then brought the billy around and into the side of his head. I heard the two constables yelling at the other men as the large man fell. I knelt and rolled him over before I put restraints on him and then began to search him.

I pulled the struggling man up and shoved him against the wall. I stepped away and bent to pick up the fancy pistol and slipped it inside my coat and into a pocket. I grabbed him and pulled him after me as he began threatening. The shop was in disarray, and one window was broken with the front door wide open. The two constables had four men out front in restraints.

They grinned, and I gestured. "I will walk them back. You two secure the shop and leave a note for the owner. I want the report before you leave, so stop in one of the diners when you warm up and write it."

They nodded, and I began pushing and moving the five men and ignoring the threats and begging and then the offered bribes. When I shoved into the station, there was a small crowd. I pushed the men to the side and gestured to one of the desk constables. "Burglary, and the big one also gets attempted use of a weapon on a constable." I pulled the fancy pistol and handed it to the constable when he came to take the men. "Also the furs they are wearing are stolen from the shop they broke into and need to be placed in evidence."

He grinned. "No problem, Sergeant."

I looked at the crowd, and most were just there to stay warm. I sighed and turned to head back out into the storm.

## CHAPTER 6

# Heavy Response

I RAN TOWARD the sound of gunshots and the constable whistle. This was the fifth time in three weeks, but I was hoping I would reach the street constable in time. A new criminal gang was organized a lot better and ran as soon as they could. I was almost to the corner when a pair of men rushed around it. I slid to a stop as I brought my pistol up. "Constable!"

They were both carrying double-barreled shotguns, but I had heard the loud reports of four shots and thought they were empty.

The men stopped and were looking around while reaching into their coats. That was not a wise move, and I cocked my pistol and turned as I aimed. "Hands up!"

They ignored me as they started to yank out pistols. I fired, and the man on the right spun and fell. I was cocking my pistol as the other man hesitated, and that was a mistake. He started to lift and aim, and I shifted my aim and fired. He screamed and bent forward; his pistol dropped with the shotgun. I moved forward as he went to his knees, still screaming.

I grabbed his hair and yanked him around and shoved him into the slush on the ground. I knelt and pulled his arms back and tied him and glanced at the constable who ran around the corner. I nodded to the constable. "Check him but be careful."

The constable growled as he moved to the man. "They shot Jim."

I finished tying the man and stood. "Is he—"

The constable nodded. "Dead."

I growled as I bent and yanked the screaming man up. "Wait for the detective inspector and watch the weapons."

The constable nodded as he stood. "This one is dead."

I pulled the other one after me as he kept trying to bend over. I went around the corner, and down the street I saw several constables around the body of another. When I reached them, I shoved the man I was pulling to one of the constables. "Search him and get the doctor to look at him."

I put my pistol away and shrugged out of my long coat and carefully covered the constable on the ground.

"Two of you mark off a ten-pace area, and someone call the lieutenant and let him know." I shook my head. "Get the detective inspector out here."

I looked around and began going to the few people who might have seen what happened. They were all afraid to say what they saw, all except an older woman. She was almost as angry at the other people as she was at the two suspects. An hour later I was sending a constable home with her and looking at the four well-dressed men watching us.

I had my long coat back and stared until they turned and walked away. I was not sure why, but I pulled my pistol and put it in the large outer pocket of the coat. My men were back on patrol, and I started off with long strides to get to the other side of the area. Barely two streets away, I saw three men in long coats step out down the street.

That was not unusual, but all three coats were open, and they had one hand inside the coat. I slipped my hand into my outer pocket and cocked the pistol as I walked closer. The men acted like they were talking but were not speaking. When I was almost to them, they turned and started to pull the double-barreled shotguns. I pulled my pistol and shot the one in the middle as I kept walking.

He went back and down as I cock my pistol, and the other two froze for a second. I fired again, and the one on the right spun and dropped, and the last panicked and fired both barrels into the snow. I reached him as I cocked my weapon and put it between his eyes. "Freeze!"

I pulled my whistle and blew as I moved around behind him. I yanked the shotgun away and tossed it aside.

I aimed over his shoulder at two more men walking toward us with shotguns. "Drop them!"

They hesitated and shifted, and one started to bring the shotgun to his shoulder. I fired, and his head snapped back, and he fell.

The other quickly dropped the shotgun and shoved his hands up. I yanked the man I was behind down on his knees. "Put your hands on your head!"

Constables ran around the corners from both ends of the street and slowed as they got closer. They looked at the men lying in the snow as they pulled the two living ones up and put restraints on them.

I went to check the men and shook my head when I stood. "Call it in. Tell the doctor he does not have to rush."

One of the men sneered. "You are dead."

I looked at him as the constable slugged him. "Speaking of dead. Attempted murder of a constable means at least twenty years, but add in the three deaths, and they might just hang you."

He looked at the other constables. "You killed—"

I stepped very close. "You tried to kill a constable. That is a capital crime, which means any and all deaths that result are attached to the crime. Three counts of premeditated murder mean death."

He licked his lips. "You can...not—"

I growled, "I can and will. I will be standing in the viewers' box to watch you hang." I turned and walked away. "Secure the scene and mark it off. The rest of you go ask around for witnesses."

The detective inspector was there before the wagon or the doctor. When he started questioning the two men, he glanced at me before smiling and turning back to them. Their faces went white at what he said, and then they were pleading and begging and telling him everything he wanted to know. The doctor arrived and barely looked at the men before loading them into the wagon.

I had two men ride in with the prisoners, and finally I turned to the detective inspector when he chuckled. He grinned. "That was perfect, Knight." I lifted an eyebrow, and he snorted. "We just got names and locations of the leaders of this gang."

I looked at the bloodstained snow. "Good we need to hit them where it hurts."

He nodded. "I am headed straight to a meeting with all the commanders and the commissioner." He gestured, and I started walking with him. "They have singled you out. Start wearing a second pistol and maybe one of those revolving shotguns."

When we reached the station, he took a horse and left as I started writing. The next shift went out before I was done, and my officers began coming in. I went to grab my bag and hesitated before reloading cylinders and pulling out a second Sharp pistol. I made sure it was loaded before I put it in the other coat pocket. My horse was in the warm constable stable and ready to go.

I did not have the shotgun, but I did have my revolving rifle in the saddle scabbard. I swung up and rode out and started for home. Two streets from the station, I saw the trap. A dozen men in short coats with shotguns were in a group. They tried to hide the shotguns with their bodies, but the long barrels could be seen. I slowed and stopped and looked back to see four men pushing a wagon across the street to block it.

I shook my head and swung down and led the horse to one side. I tied it to a hitching post as the men from both ends started for me. I reached up and pulled the rifle out before walking to the middle of the street. I went to a knee and aimed as I cocked the hammer. They yelled and rushed me, and I fired. I cocked the rifle and shot a second in the chest and then a third.

I turned to look back and pulled the pistol from my pocket and cocked it as I brought it up and then fired. I dropped the rifle as I reached into the other pocket to pull and cock the other pistol. I dived to one side just as several men fired the shotguns, and I felt the burning pain in my left hip. I rolled and came up with both pistols and shot two men.

I twisted as I was hit in the right shoulder but cocked both pistols again. The right I held at my waist and pointed and fired, and the left I extended and aimed before firing. Two more men went down, and the rest decided this had not been a good idea and turned to flee. So far I had taken down one man for each shot; several were still screaming and writhing around.

I cocked the pistols as constables came around the far corner, and the men stopped. I turned, and the three men who had run for the wagons found two constables waiting. They died as they lifted their shotguns, and the rest yelled as they tossed the guns away and shoved their hands into the air. I bent to pick up my rifle and limped to the steps of a building.

People slowly came out as more constables arrived. Of the eight men I had shot, four were dead, and the other four in serious condition. Of course the constable doctor wanted to look at my wounds first. I was in the parlor of an elderly woman who had not only insisted but also ordered me to come in. Before the doctor was finished pulling large pellets out of my hip and shoulder, the commander and the commissioner were there.

The commissioner listened as I reported to the commander what had happened, and then he growled, "Enough. Call all your constables in and hit these people. Issue shotguns and slug ammo and extra pistols for every man. If they want war, they have it."

He spun and walked out, and the old woman sniffed. "Hang the lot. Shooting at constables—the very idea…"

I grinned as the commander snorted and headed for the door. I fixed my clothing and stood with a wince and bowed to the woman. "Thank you."

She nodded, and I walked out and went to collect my horse. I thought of going home, but if the commander was calling everyone in—I headed back to the station and put the horse in a warm stall. I went inside and started cleaning both pistols and my rifle as I waited for my people to come in. I glanced up at the commander when he held out a revolving shotgun and the belt with extra cylinders.

It was just over an hour before over a hundred constables split into groups and started walking through the streets. I limped, but there was no way I was going to miss this. I held the heavy shotgun in one hand until we slowed and our commander gestured for me to lead. The large pub on the corner had only a few people near it, and they took one look and ran.

I did not even slow as constables split off to go around to the sides and back, and I walked through the front doors. Two men turned and reached into long coats as I brought the shotgun up. I fired, and one man was thrown back as one of the constables moved to the side and fired. The other man spun and went down, screaming, with a huge hole through his belly.

The few men left threw their hands up as I cocked the shotgun while walking toward the office door. The tender backed away from the bar with his hands in the air when I walked by. I did not bother knocking or trying the door—I blew the handle through the door. I cocked the shotgun again as the door swung open, and three men stood with pistols in their hands.

They did not even have time to drop them as six shotguns fired, and they went down, screaming. Constables had split off and gone upstairs, and we heard several shots as I walked into the office. I glanced at the second door when I heard shots from the back of the building. I changed the cylinder and cocked the shotgun and shot the door lock.

Bullets ripped into the door as it started to swing open. Luckily no one was in front of it, but two constables growled, and one lashed out and kicked the door. It flew open to show two men looking up from changing cylinders. We all fired, and they were jerked back and into the wall before falling. I stepped into the room to see a single well-dressed man in one corner.

He held his hands up, and I gestured. "Arrest him."

He sneered. "I have not done—"

The constables growled and surged toward him and yanked him around and slammed him into a wall. They put restraints on him and spun him to face me as the commander walked in. I stepped closer. "Listen very close. We are going to be asking the court for the death sentence. Now we already have all the names of the men in the gang or organization or whatever you want to call it."

I reached into his jacket and pulled out a slim five-shot ten millimeter.

"Guess who is at the top of the list and the first to hang?"

His face paled. "You need evidence."

I cocked the pistol and put it between his eyes. "Special circumstances. You see when an organization starts targeting and killing constables, they are considered enemies of the state and not criminals. That means we can use the testimony of one who turns queen's evidence to hang the others." I sniffed and shook my head as I lowered the hammer. "Take him away and do not let him change his pants."

The other constables laughed, and one yanked him out.

I spun the pistol and reversed it and held it out to the commander. "Thank you, sir."

He chuckled as he took the pistol. "My pleasure, Sergeant."

# CHAPTER 7

# River Pirates

I STEPPED INTO the commissioner's office and closed the door. He glanced at me. "Sergeant Knight, have a seat."

He went back to the report he was reading before shaking his head. He leaned back and looked at me.

"The doctor tells me your hip and shoulder are healed. That was a nasty business with the gang, and Her Majesty and the constable general have signed off on our action. The last of them were hung outside the royal court this morning, if you did not know."

I nodded, and he turned to look out the window.

"You have been at the heart of a lot of action. Necessary action that has saved lives." He looked at me. "I see two courses for constables. One is into the investigations, and the other up the ranks of street constables. You I see continuing to be a street constable."

I grinned. "You tend to stay closer to the people that way."

He nodded. "Just so. Now I have a problem that is and is not ours. River pirates have been hitting a lot of barges and ships; many have not been in our jurisdiction." He snorted. "Most have been leaving our jurisdiction. Anyway Her Majesty has asked me through the constable general to form a team to catch these pirates and put a stop to it, and I have chosen you to lead it."

I leaned forward. "How many constables?"

The commissioner leaned back. "The few survivors report at least a dozen men, so I will find another five men and have them contact you."

I nodded. "Do we have an idea where the goods are going to?"

He blinked. "Not as far as I know. They have not returned to the city or gone further upriver."

I was thinking of the map, and if I remembered right, it swung south for several leagues before turning west. I stood. "I will catch them, sir."

I left and headed to the docks while thinking as I walked, and first I needed to find out what type of cargo they were taking. The next thing would be to find a way to speak with a ship captain and slip onto the ship. I was thinking of using a ship as bait to trap the pirates and take them when they attacked and boarded the ship. My first stop was the closest station to the docks.

I caught up with one of the sergeants and walked with him as I explained what I needed. He grinned as he listened and glanced around. "I can find out what the cargos were. As for a ship captain, try the *Wobbly Duck* just up from pier seven. He can tell you when, how, and where to get onto the ship and hide."

I nodded. "Have you heard anything about a black market selling any of the items?"

He shook his head. "They take the ship, unload it, and then move it to the middle of the river to drift."

I walked away and headed back into the city and to my station. First was to take the revolving shotgun with a belt of cylinders out of my locker. I went to see the lieutenant to let him know what the commissioner was having me do. He grumped but nodded, and I started to leave and found five constables waiting for me. They were all still in uniform and not happy.

Clifton, Ringer, Nelson, Samuel, and Adams had one thing in common. They all grew up or came from a waterfront area and had experience with ships. I pulled them into one of the briefing rooms and told them about the pirates and what my plan was to catch them. They changed their mind quick, and they left to change and get or draw out revolving shotguns.

I headed back to the station by the docks to meet with the sergeant. He looked at the shotgun and grinned as he handed me a list of cargos that had been taken. He also gave me a list of where each ship was thought to have been when it was captured. I thought and then nodded. "Want to bet there is a new dock on the east side of the snake?"

He looked at me and then grinned. "We have a flying squad that can—"

I shook my head. "That might tip them off. If one surrenders, we will get everything out of them, including where they took the cargos. You could have the flying squad take a ride along the river a few hours after the sun rises, though."

He nodded and handed me a folded note. "That is a ship leaving in the morning with a similar cargo. The captain is Jacob Dwayne."

I glanced at the ship name and nodded. "Thanks."

I met the other five men behind the *Wobbly Duck* and briefed them as we put the shotguns on underarm slings before we went in to eat. Samuel was the one to point out Captain Dwayne. I waited for him to head for the jakes and stood to follow. He looked at me when I stepped in behind him and shifted as he touched a large knife. I grinned as I opened my long coat to show the shotgun, and his face paled.

I opened the other side to show my constable badge, and he looked up and into my face. I grinned as I leaned against the door. "There are river pirates, and your cargo is similar to what they are taking. The queen wants them stopped, and I would like your permission to sneak aboard with my men and hide."

He cleared his throat. "You think the pirates will attack my ship?"

I nodded. "We are not sure one or more crewmen aboard the ships are part of the gang. That is why we wish to hide and wait. If your ship is attacked, we will take the pirates and anyone else involved."

He grinned. "In that case, Constable, I think I have the perfect place."

We talked, and he told me how to sneak aboard and where we could hide. I let him leave first and then waited a minute before I followed. I returned to the table and finished the mug of ale before I tilted my head. We paid and left, and once we were outside, I told them what I had found out. They listened and then agreed, and we moved to watch Captain Dwayne's ship.

At midnight we moved and slipped up the gang plank and spilt up. Samuel and Adams went to the rear of the wheelhouse and sat between the rail and the wheelhouse. Nelson and Ringer split up to hide in the ropes on each side of the sail locker at the bow of the ship. Clifton and I hid under the large tarp over the cargo hatch. I relaxed and dozed until the sun began to rise and the crew woke up.

It was not long before the ship left the dock and started its trip upriver. The morning was calm, so I listened to the crew chant while rowing. It was an hour before I heard the shouts and a gunshot. I rolled out from under the tarp and came to my feet before moving to the port rail. A dozen small, fast sailboats were closing, and I glanced left and right to check my men.

The captain appeared beside me and hissed. "The damn helmsman tried to turn us into them."

I gestured my men back. "Let them board!"

I guess the pirates thought that was meant for them and that we had surrendered. I shifted the shotgun and looked at the captain. "Move your men below."

He nodded and turned to gesture to his men, and several moments later, the deck was clear except for us. We moved back from the rail so the pirates would not see the shotguns. I knelt beside the cargo hatch and waited until the first pirates came over the rail. I aimed the shotgun. "Constables!"

They froze before yanking out pistols. I shot the one I was aiming at, and I heard the other shotguns as I cocked the hammer and stood to move toward the rail.

"Surrender, or we will shoot!"

I shot another pirate as he climbed over the side while lifting a pistol. Next was the rush as several dozen pirates tried to board while others fired from the sailboats. I crouched and just cocked and fired into them and changed the cylinder to empty a second before loading a third into the shotgun. I reached the rail and fired down into one of the boats at three men with revolving rifles.

I ducked back, and the rail was splintered by other pirates in other boats. Of course that was when Samuel and Adams stood and fired before ducking back. After them it was Nelson and Ringer and then Clifton stood with me. I saw one boat trying to flee and fired at the two men while Clifton held the last three after they surrendered.

Next was the job of checking the men and securing any alive. We put all the sailboats on lines behind the ship and put the bodies in the last. The crew had returned, and the captain turned the ship to the south bank for us. It was not long before we saw the new-looking dock and a collection of buildings. Several of the flying squad were already there and grinned as we shoved the wounded off the ship.

We had not only those here at the docks but also the route to the coast and a smuggler cove where everything was sold. We had six wounded and tied up the sailboats while the captain and crew waved and left. The flying squad called in for an inspector, a doctor, and the prisoner wagon. We were not done but sat to write reports until the inspector arrived.

He was a gruff man who barely glanced at the bodies. "Sergeant Knight?"

I looked up from the report I was writing. "Sir?"

He gestured to the bodies. "Is this all of them?"

I shook my head. "We will be needing the south flying squad to accompany us to the coast. There is a smugglers' cove where they are selling everything."

He nodded. "I will make the call to get you horses."

I finished my report before I stood and stretched. "Clean and reload the shotguns and cylinders before we move out."

I started on mine as we waited, and we talked with the flying squad that was gathering. Finally, one appeared with six spare horses behind him, and we swung up and started toward the coast. It was an hour ride before we came through tall hedges to see a small collection of cottages and a long dock. I pointed to the ship moored at the end and talked with the flying-squad lieutenant.

My people rode for the dock while the flying squad spread out and hit the houses. We swung down as men yelled and started down the dock as sailors on the ship hurried to get the ship ready to move. One lifted a rifle, and Nelson and Samuel fired their shotguns. The man went down, and the others stopped and threw up their arms.

Clifton and I boarded first and watched them while the others came aboard. They moved to restrain and search them, and we went below to search. When I pushed the captain's cabin door open, a shotgun blast ripped into the door. I was to the side of the door and lifted my shotgun as I turned around the doorframe. I fired before the captain and he spun and fell as the shot hit his right side and arm.

I moved into the room and knelt to yank him onto his stomach before I put him into restraints. I searched him and pulled him to his feet before I searched his cabin. I took a ledger and shoved him out and up onto the deck. On shore we could see a small crowd of men and women with the other constables around them. Adams and Samuel grinned and looked up from the open cargo hold. "This was listed on the last ship they took."

We started moving everyone off the ship and had to send a runner for the doctor and several prisoner wagons. I also sent a message requesting a crew to bring the ship around and to the city. The prisoners were taken away later in the day, but we had to wait for the crew before we could return to the city. The pirates involved in taking the ships were hung, and the others who were smuggling the stolen goods received five years.

CHAPTER 8

# Queen's Protection Detail

I BRUSHED THE new lieutenant braid on my sleeve before walking into the commander's office. He looked up and grinned. "It looks good on you."

I grinned back. "And feels strange."

He turned to a message on the corner of his desk. "I do not have a shift for you, but you have been personally requested by the queen to head her protection detail."

I frowned. "But—"

He smiled. "She is coming here for the duke's nobles' assembly. You will have the best from each station. Her royal guards have sent a man to coordinate with you. He will give you all the information. Your people will be meeting you at the city courts in two hours."

I nodded. "I will not disappoint you."

My mind was spinning as I walked out, and a man in a royal-blue uniform stood. "Lieutenant Knight?"

I looked him over before nodding, and he pulled a packet from under his arm. "This is everything you will need. Mostly you and your people will be doing the exterior and route protection. Look over the schedule and the places Her Majesty wishes to go. If you see anything you think we need to change, let Captain MacBride know when he and the queen arrive."

He walked away, and I looked at the packet before slipping it into my shirt and going to put my long coat on. I left and took a trolley through the city to the city courts. I walked in and saw several constables turn as I crossed the large lobby. I sat in a quiet corner and pulled out the packet and glanced up as they approached. One cleared his throat. "Lieutenant Knight?" I nodded, and he turned and gestured to the others. "We are part of your detail."

I gestured to the other chairs. "Have a seat. There should be a few more coming." I opened the packet and began to read and shook my head long before I was done. I put everything back into the packet and leaned back. "Wonderful."

Several grinned. "That good."

I snorted. "Typical nonsense from an idiot who has no idea what security is or how to protect someone." When the rest of the men arrived, I stood. "Follow me."

I led the way into an empty courtroom and made sure the door was closed before I began to tell them what we were doing. Six of us met the train when it arrived, and I sent two more to watch and follow with the queen's baggage. When she stepped off, all the city nobles and officials were there to greet her. Her royal guard consisted of eight large men in fancy uniforms.

We were carrying revolving rifles with a cylinder belt under our long coats. When the guards started moving, I whistled, and one turned and then said something. Another in fancy braid looked at me before they changed direction. The officer almost looked angry as he led the queen and his guards. I was looking past him as well as scanning the crowds.

When I saw the rifle barrel above the exit they had been heading for, I reacted, "Threat!"

I shifted and brought my rifle up while cocking it and then aimed and fired. The guards were trying to cover her and huddled together as my constables fired, and one growled and snatched a guard up. "Get her out of here!"

The rifle vanished, and two of my constables rushed to the station doors. I spun and shoved guards out of my way as I let my rifle drop on the single point lanyard. I caught the queen's arm and pulled and turned to hurry her toward our planned exit. People were still yelling and screaming and running as we surrounded the queen, and then I lifted her up and into a covered carriage.

I slipped in as two constables stood on the side runners, and the last two jumped on the back. The carriage driver yelled as he started the horses off at a run. I looked at the frightened queen and the guard officer who had managed to climb in and smiled. "Relax they are behind us now."

She smiled weakly, and the officer growled, "Who told you—"

I leaned forward. "Listen very close, Captain. I am not your flunky-go-for-this boy. I do not know what training you have to protect Her Majesty, but as far as I am concerned, you are a moron. She should always have two layers of protection, close and far, and you never huddle with her to protect her. You get her the hell out of danger."

I looked at the surprised queen before looking at him.

"You and her guards maintain a clear space around her at all times and never let people surround her. You watch the crowds and any and every opening above eye level. Never use a main exit that brings her out to be exposed or makes her have to walk long distances where she would be exposed." I sat back. "You and your men will protect her in and at her rooms, but my constables will protect the floor she is on and the building. We will scout the routes she will use and provide escort to and from when she goes out. We need a list of all appointments and visitors and any servants."

He leaned forward. "You listen to me you—"

The queen cleared her throat. "That will be enough, Captain. Lieutenant Knight is correct. You have come straight from the military, but he is a constable and works with the people." She looked at me carefully. "You are more than what I expected, Lieutenant. I did not expect someone to try anything this soon, but your reputation is justified. Tell me, why did you bring rifles?"

I smiled as I glanced at the frowning captain. "In case we saw anyone in a window or on a roof. While constables normally carry only pistols, we are required to know and use both rifles and shotguns. The constables inside the Gilbert House will be carrying the new revolving shotguns."

I glanced out the window before looking at her.

"Why come here, Your Majesty? I am not complaining, but you do not normally travel."

She grinned and glanced at the captain. "We were reminded that it helps the people and gives them hope if they see us more often. We will be doing a lot more traveling, but I wanted to start off here."

When the carriage stopped, I held up my hand and moved to step out first. My constables were spread out and looking around as we searched windows and roofs. I turned and stepped to the side as the captain stepped out and then the queen. We closed in and walked to the door, and once inside two more constables were waiting with the manager.

He bowed, and we followed the constables to and up the stairs. On the top floor, two more constables were waiting and nodded their heads as the first two led us down to a suite of rooms. The door was opened, and I stepped in and looked around before the captain and then the queen. I left and had the two constables who had led us up stay on each side of the door until the rest of her guards got here.

There were another two at the other end of the hall and four on the roof. I went downstairs and used the call box to reach my men at the station. The gunman was dead, but I had them bring everything he had on him. I sat at the desk and started writing a report, and when the detective inspector arrived with all the royal guards, I gave it to him.

He read it and nodded before looking out the door. "I do not think it will end with just one."

I nodded. "I am having everything the assassin had on him brought here."

He looked at me and smiled. "You would make a good inspector."

I grinned. "Thanks."

What he had on him was only the rifle, and that was it. Even the constable mage had not been able to determine who he had been or why he had tried to shoot the queen. I received a list of the queen's expected guests and her appointments and places she was expected to go. My off-duty constables had several rooms on the top floor so when they were off they were still close.

Myself or one of the sergeants would greet her visitors and escort them up. If it was someone not on the list, we sent a note and either had him or her wait or come back. It was noon when I sent two constables on horses to scout a route to the queen's meeting at the city assembly. I checked the eight constables who would be escorting her before she came down with her guards.

My two constables returned while she was climbing into her carriage. I got a thumbs-up from one and pointed to the second carriage driver. He swung down, and a constable quickly moved to climb up beside the driver. The carriage began to move, and both my constables and the royal guards trotted beside it. The royal guards still wore only pistols, which made me shake my head.

I was riding on the running board and scanning the windows and roofs ahead. As we approached the assembly, I thought I saw someone on a roof across from the assembly hall. The driver started to argue with the constable beside him, and the royal guards who were trotting beside the carriage slowed. I looked inside as the captain shifted. "Wait until we get around to the side of the building."

He growled as he grabbed the door, "We are not—"

I saw the movement from the corner of my eye and jerked as I stepped off the carriage runner and lifted my rifle. "Threat!"

I was not the only one to fire as the constable by the driver snatched the reins and whipped the horses. This time there were men shooting from three buildings, and I knelt after one went back, and his rifle fell into the street below. I shifted to fire at another as the carriage sped away. "Team one, take the left building! Team two, the right, and team three, clear the middle!"

My constables were up and rushing for the building doors before I finished speaking, and I was left alone to return their fire. All together six men had been on the roof, and none had surrendered. One had even leaped off the roof and dived headfirst to the cobblestones below. I had the bodies pulled out and checked each of them. All they had were weapons, and that was it.

We let the street constables take over and headed back to the Gilbert House. When I walked into the lobby, the captain spun and stalked toward me. "We are going to—"

I slugged him and then grabbed his throat. "I warned you once." I shoved him back. "The next time you become a threat to the queen, I will shoot you myself."

He reddened. "You are relieved."

I smiled. "Fine. I will let Her Majesty know she no longer has the constables to protect her."

His face whitened, and he sneered. "I will ruin you for this."

I snorted. "Listen, close asshole. I do not care what you think you can do. I am a constable, and the queen's protection is my duty. Interfere again and see what happens." I turned to look at the constables. "I will be back after I speak with the queen. Do a walk around the building and look for anyone trying to sneak in."

I headed for the stairs, and when I reached the queen's suite, I knocked. A maid opened the door and then looked back. "It is a constable, my lady."

She opened the door, and I stepped into the room. The queen turned from the small fireplace. "Lieutenant."

I bowed. "They were not carrying anything and refused to give up."

She sighed. "They are part of a fanatic group that has been trying to kill the royal family for the last year."

I straightened. "Why were we not told?"

She shook her head. "I do not...I have been thinking over my appointment of the captain since we arrived."

She turned to look into the flames.

"Would you tell the captain his services are no longer needed. I also need to send a message to the palace and"—she looked at me—"please contact your commissioner and ask if he might have more men to spare."

I bowed. "I will send up a constable to take your message and take care of everything else."

She nodded, and I turned to the two royal guards beside the door. "Out."

They looked past me before turning to leave. I pulled them and the other two who had been on the outside of the room to the stairs. I looked at them before I gestured to the constables. "No guards inside the room. One of you will be on one side of the door, and one of the royal guards will be on the other."

I looked at the four guards.

"She dismissed the captain and not you. You stay to protect her and prove she was right."

They looked at each other, and one cleared his throat. "Thank you, sir."

I gestured and headed down the stairs and right into an argument between the captain and two of my men who had a man in restraints. I yanked him back and spun him. "The queen has dismissed you. Get out and do not return."

He started to hit me, and I slugged him under the ribs and then caught his fancy jacket. I slugged him several times before I spun him and yanked his arms back. "Restraints!"

I put him in restraints while he struggled and spun him as I took his weapon. "Now we take you to the train station and send your dumb ass home."

He jerked at the restraints and looked around before shaking his head at the other man my constables had caught. I frowned and turned to look at the man.

"Never mind. Call the constable mage to question both of them."

They both fought and struggled at that, and I had them tied hand and foot. I sent one of the constables up to take a message and used the call box to call the commissioner. That brought thirty more constables in an hour, and he showed up personally to talk with me. The mage who questioned the two men walked out grimly. He told us the captain had been groomed and was part of a group that wanted the royal family dead.

The other man had been sent to sneak in and poison the queen. The most important thing was the list of names he got. The commissioner took the list and grinned as he headed for the door. "You take charge, Lieutenant."

Within minutes runners were heading out, and then stations were sending squads of constables to make arrests. Calls sped out to the capital and a couple of other cities in other duchies for other traitors to be arrested. An hour later I sent scouts back to the assembly and had half the flying squads from several areas standing by the queen's carriage. This time there were no attempts, and the queen was able to have her meeting.

After it was over, she wanted to go to a fine eatery, and I had men already there. After she ate she returned to the Gilbert House, and several of the district nobles were waiting to speak with her. It was two days before a brightly dressed officer arrived from the palace. This time I was taking no chances and asked for a constable mage to question him before I let him see the queen.

He had not said anything about what I had done and, after giving his oath to the queen, came to see me. He listened as I explained how we were running the protection for the queen and made a few adjustments that made it better. Five days later the queen took my hand after making me a knight and turned to board her train.

The new captain smiled and held up my protection plans. "These will help create a more effective royal guard. Thank you for protecting her, Lieutenant."

We watched as the train left the station, and I turned to start sending men back to their stations with my thanks. The old royal-guard captain was being sent back to the capital tomorrow to be hung. The assassin was already on the way to the gallows here. The other men who had been arrested in and around the city were on trial in the capital.

# CHAPTER 9

# Siege

SILVERTON WAS AN isolated station just inside the city and out of the area for flying squads. Mostly we dealt with traffic entering the city from the country to the west. It was farms and ranches bringing their wares to market. There was also one other thing we were looking for. Recently the city had a rash of poorly made alcohol, which had caused the death of several people.

The commander of the station had taken a vacation, and the other lieutenant worked only during the day. Somehow I thought there was something off about him. It was the way he acted and sometimes disappeared. It was several days after the captain had left and the day-shift lieutenant did not show up for the morning briefing. I gave it and let the sergeants send the men out.

I went out to a checkpoint I had put up on my shift and found farmers arguing with the constables. It seemed the other lieutenant would remove the checkpoint during the day. They did not like having to wait while we checked their wagons. While several were arguing with me, I noticed two men trying to turn their wagon around.

I held up my hand to quiet the farmers and looked at the constables. "One of you go check that wagon."

They looked at me, and one moved toward the wagon. The farmers went back to complaining, but I was watching the constable. When he jerked and pulled his pistol, I shoved the farmers away. "Seize them!"

One of the men had his hand inside his jacket, and the other was starting to run. Of course he was not watching and ran right into a man riding up on a horse. The other constables rushed to help and put the men in restraints. The one had a pistol in his coat, and the other kept blurting that they were just paid to bring it in. I found the whole bed of the wagon filled with cases of illegal whiskey.

That was when Lieutenant Donald arrived and tried to send me away. I started to leave when he ordered the two men released. I spun. "No!"

I growled as I stalked back toward him, and he glared. "This is my shift."

I stepped close. "And you were late, and I was in charge when they were arrested. They will go before a magister."

He looked at his constables. "Release them."

I nodded and moved quickly as I yanked his pistol out. I spun him as he jerked and touched the pistol to his head. "You are under arrest for violation of the constable oath and attempted release of a prisoner."

He yelled for his men to get me off him as I pulled my restraints and looked at them. "One of you, go call for a detective inspector to meet us at the station. Move that wagon to the station and put those men in a cell. The rest of you, finish checking these wagons."

I yanked one of the lieutenant's arms back and up.

"Shut up, and put your hands behind you."

Once I had him in restraints, I looked at the constables as they quickly checked wagons. I pushed the lieutenant ahead of me and started back to the station. When I walked in, it was almost like the station was deserted, and only the desk sergeant and two constables were there. The constables were locking the two smugglers up as I searched the lieutenant.

I pushed him into another cell and removed the restraints before backing out. He spun and glared. "You are dead."

I snorted as I closed and locked the cell. "We will see."

The two constables sat and drank coffee while making their report, and I began mine. It was several minutes before I thought about the detective inspector. I went to the front desk and the call box and tried to call, but the line was dead. I frowned since the only time we ever had trouble with the lines was during bad storms. I went to look out the front door and jerked back and to the side.

A man had been walking toward the door with a double-barreled shotgun. He fired, and a large hole was blown in the door. I pulled my pistol as I turned back and shoved the door to fire into his chest twice. Even as he fell, I saw several wagon loads of men spilling out and moving toward the door. I moved as they fired into the door and splintered it.

I gestured to the two constables who had come running. "Guard the other doors!"

I twisted and shot a man rushing the front before ducking back as some of the other men fired. I heard shots from the side of the building and wanted to check it out but had to trust that the constables were okay. One appeared in another door and grinned as he held up a revolving shotgun and belt. I glanced out and gestured when I pulled back.

He threw it, and I caught it and dug in a pocket before tossing a set of keys. "Open the armory."

He caught the keys and turned to run to the back while I cocked the shotgun. I shifted as I brought it to my shoulder, turned, and aimed before firing. Two men were rushing the door and went down screaming. I spun and ducked to the side as bullets splintered the doorframe. There were more shots from the side, and then I heard the shotguns from inside the building.

Everything went silent after that except for men screaming in the street. I knelt and waited as the men outside moved around. They did not rush the door again, but bullets struck the doorframe again when I peeked out. A few minutes later, the one constable was back with a revolving rifle and a belt of cylinders. He stayed back from the door as he knelt and slowly shifted with the rifle to his shoulder and cocked it.

When he saw one of the men, he fired and shifted back as they fired through the door. He grinned at me as he cocked the rifle again. "One at a time, sir."

I gestured. "Try the second floor and shoot down at those on the side. The other side and back are blocked off, so either they come through a door or window."

He looked back. "Or climb up and in a window in the back or the other side."

I nodded, and he spun as he came to his feet and ran to the stairs. It was a couple of minutes before I heard the rapid firing from inside the building and hoped the constable had been in time and did not get shot. A rush from outside, and I waited until they blocked the others. I leaned out and started firing and cocking and firing and…

Those who were not hit and screaming fled toward safety.

I looked at the wounded I could see, and most were trying to crawl away while I changed the cylinder in the shotgun. The shooting from the side had stopped, and so had the shooting from upstairs. A man yelled from outside, and I peeked out to see a white flag. I snorted as he stepped into the clear. "Give us the whiskey and the lieutenant, or we will burn the building!"

I started to lift the shotgun when there was a shot from above me, and the man jerked and staggered. He looked at the spreading blood on his chest before going to his knees and then falling into the street. I smiled as the other men lifted up to shoot and another shot struck one in the head. They dropped down, and I stood and lifted the shotgun to my shoulder as I stepped out.

I started across the street as another leaned out and was shot, and I shifted and fired into one who stepped out with his weapon up. He went back and down as I cocked the shotgun again and the constable on the second floor shot another man. I was walking around one of the wagons protecting them and fired into a man who leaped up.

That was enough for the others as they yelled and threw down their weapons. I pushed and shoved them against the wagon while searching them. I pushed them back to the front door, and the constable from the second floor appeared. He took the men, and I changed the cylinder and headed to the side of the building. As I walked around the corner, I brought the barrel up while cocking the hammer.

I fired into two men holding shotguns when they turned. They went down, and I headed to the right and the stables as I lifted the shotgun to my shoulder while cocking it. I fired as a man leaned out with a rifle, and his head exploded. When I stepped into the stable, the four men there threw their weapons down and gave up. I searched them and shoved them to the side door.

Any men who might have been on the other sides had vanished. The next step was to restrain the wounded and then find and send a runner to the closest constable station. That brought a small army of constables who only grew as time went by. The wounded and prisoners gave us names and that sent large groups of angry constables out to make arrests.

Not only did our commander appear but the commissioner also came with several inspectors and a constable mage. The other lieutenant broke before they even began to question him. We got not only the supplier but also the smugglers and the merchants who were selling the alcohol. One of the magisters arrived in the afternoon to hold court in the now-crowded station.

The first case was the lieutenant who was sentenced to life in the mines. That set the tone, but those involved in the attack and siege of the station were sentenced to hang. I recommended the two constables who had been with me for a commendation of valor, which the commissioner approved on the spot. As things began to calm down, a detective inspector appeared beside me.

I glanced at him as I finished checking one of my constables just coming in for night duty. "Yes?"

He smiled and looked the constable over before looking at me. "I am Detective Inspector Mcgivens. I am the chief of inspectors."

I looked at him, and he looked around at the damage that workers were trying to repair. "You have a knack, Lieutenant. You always seem to be in the heat of it."

I shrugged, and he looked at me.

"You do know you will never make commander now?"

I blinked as I straightened. "What do you mean?"

He sighed. "How many men have you killed, Lieutenant?"

I looked at the bloodstained entrance. "Too many."

He nodded. "Exactly. Which is why when your record goes to the nobles for consideration, they will turn you down."

I looked at him. "You have a reason for telling me this now?"

He smiled. "How about coming to work for me as an inspector?"

CHAPTER 10

# Inspector

SOMEHOW I HAD only thought of inspectors who came to investigate after a death or shooting involving a constable. I glanced at the man leaning against the building and shifted the unfamiliar weight of the Sharp under my arm. He shifted and glanced at me with a smiled. "Relax, Ashton."

I snorted. "Easy for you to say."

He grinned before looking back down the street. "You will get used to carrying the pistol concealed."

I looked behind us before straightening. "Trouble."

He glanced back. "Just talk to me like nothing is happening. You are not in uniform, and they do not know you are a constable. They will go into the shop to try enforcing the protection scheme."

I nodded and sighed before I smiled. "So you said Mage Norris found the perfect woman for you?"

He grinned and then chuckled. "So he wants me to think. The last time it was a joy girl looking for a husband to hide her daytime customers."

I laughed, and the three men glanced at us and then seemed to ignore us before going into the shop across the street. Constable Detective Inspector Stern pushed away from the wall, and we started across the street. We slowed as we reached the door and listened to one of the men making threats. When I heard something smash, I started moving and walked in.

One of the men was at the door and sneered. "The shop is closed."

I lashed out and punched him in the throat while still walking. "Not anymore."

One of the other men spun to look as the first man folded and went to his knees. He started to reach into his coat as I pulled and cocked my weapon. "Pulled it, and you are dead."

He froze as the last man looked around frantically. The shopkeeper was against his counter and straightened. I gestured with my weapon. "Hands in the air before I shoot you in the knees."

They moved slowly, and Stern chuckled while putting restraints on the man I had struck. "You are a cruel man."

I moved to the first man and took the pistol from inside his coat and spun him before I gave him a push. "I do not like bullies."

I spun the other man and shoved him against the counter and started to put restraints on. He glanced over his shoulder. "You are dead."

I slugged him in the back of the head. "That just brought you another five years, asshole."

I moved to the other man who shifted on his feet.

"Want to threaten my life, scum?"

He shook his head, and when I was done, I searched both of them carefully. I took hidden knives and lockpicks and jimmies before I nodded to the shopkeeper. I shoved the men out.

"You three will be seeing Magister Davis in the morning."

They jerked, and the one in charge shifted. "We can make a deal."

I snorted as we started pushing them down the street, but Stern cleared his throat. "What kind of deal?"

I looked at him as the man slowed. "Compensation."

Stern laughed. "You do not have enough compensation."

The man glanced back as the other two hissed. "But I know where you can take a counting house for the new drug gang."

Stern nodded. "That might be worth something." He slowed and turned the man. "The problem is your two friends and the shopkeeper and the several people who saw you being detained."

The man smiled. "It was a mistake. We can take care of the shopkeeper and—"

I pulled my weapon and put it to his head. "Do you really think I am going to let you walk away?"

Stern caught my arm. "Relax." I glared, but he shook his head. "We are not going to let them harm anyone." He looked at the man. "How about a nice boat ride upriver? As for your men, they are going to prison. Maybe you can return in a year or two."

The man snorted. "No deal."

Stern grinned and spun him and gave him a shove. "Okay."

The man staggered and turned. "Wait! The counting house is in the back of the Blue Cow butcher shop."

Stern nodded and pushed him again. "Thanks. We will pay them a visit."

The man jerked on the restraints. "Get me out of these!"

My partner grinned. "Why? Besides assault, extortion, and a death threat against a constable, you just tried to bride us."

I grinned and then chuckled. "I thought I was the cruel one."

He laughed, and we kept pushing the men. "I am also telling the other prisoners he is helping us against the gangs."

When he was pushed in front of the magister, he was bruised and bloody, and so were the other two men. They were in for more hard luck since Magister Davis was not known for being lenient. I walked out with Stern and looked at the crowded morning street. "So."

He grinned. "We have two dozen constables from the docks coming to help us search the Blue Cow butcher shop."

I smiled as I stepped out with him, and we started walking. "That was why you spoke with Magister Davis?"

He nodded and patted his coat. "We have a warrant to search the shop and detain anyone inside for questioning."

I grinned as we reached the moving streetcar and jumped up onto the running board before moving inside.

He glanced at me as we sat. "Once we get there, you go around to watch the back, and I will take the front. They will have watchers who will warn them when they see the constables. Watch yourself and be ready because once they are warned, they will try to get away."

I nodded, and he shifted as he glanced around.

"Try not to kill them. We need the leader and the supplier."

I smiled as I looked out the window. "I will try not to."

An hour later I had turned down the back alley and stopped across from the back door of the butcher shop. It seemed like a long time before I heard a commotion and glanced up and down the alley. I pulled my weapon and held it beside my leg, and a moment later, the back door opened. Four men carrying large bags started through, and I waited for them to come out.

I stepped out and lifted my pistol. "Constable!"

They froze, and then one started to reach into his jacket, and I cocked my weapon.

He froze, and I gestured. "Drop the bags and put your hands up."

Another man rushed out the door, carrying a shotgun, and I shifted as I brought the pistol up. I fired as the man lifted it, and he screamed and folded while dropping the shotgun.

The men started to move, and I cocked the pistol. "Hold it!"

Suddenly a half dozen uniformed constables were rushing down the alley from each end. I heard yells and a couple of shots from inside the shop. The men let the bags fall and slowly raised their hands. One glared. "You are dead."

I sighed. "I really hate assholes telling me that."

I gestured to the constables. "Put them in restraints and search them carefully."

Stern peeked out the door and then stepped out. "Blindfold and separate them. Two men with the bags at all times." He looked at me. "We will go through the bags at the port constable station. I had one give up the drug supply house, so all the others will be going to the gallows."

I saw their faces pale, and he winked before turning to go back inside. After they were separated, a couple of prisoner wagons arrived to take them away. Thirty minutes later we were watching three constables count all the money from the bags while going through the ledger.

I looked at the first prisoner who was brought in, and Stern shook his head. "I do not know why you are bothering. We already have one who turned."

We had talked about how to play this. I shrugged. "You know Magister Davis. He would rather have two witnesses for any death case."

I looked at the man the constable had pushed in.

"You have one chance to avoid the gallows. Who is in charge? Where does the money go after the counting house? Confirm the location of the drug supply house and give us the location of the supplier and his name."

He glared, and I shrugged.

"Put him back and bring another. One will want to avoid hanging."

The constable grabbed the prisoner's shoulder and spun him, and he jerked. "Wait!"

The constable let him go, and he turned and licked his lip.

"Banker Monroe is in charge. The money goes to his bank. The drug house is Abrams Apothecary, and the supplier is Damon Clark. He refines the drugs on an abandoned estate, Thirty-Seven Trenton Street."

I gestured to the constable. "Have him write it out and then put him in an isolation cell. All the others can be placed in one holding cell."

He grinned and nodded before pulling the man out. Stern chuckled, and I glanced at him, and he gestured. "Once they finish we can go see Magister Davis with his statement. First we arrest banker Monroe and call the flying squad to raid the estate and arrest Damon Clark."

It was an hour before we closed, locked, and sealed the bags of money in a large iron money chest. We picked up the witness statement and headed to the courts' building. After that it was downtown to the Golden Reserve Bank. When we stepped in, I glanced around before looking at the bank guard. Stern shifted and opened his coat to show his badge, and the guard straightened and moved to us.

Once he stopped I looked toward the fancy paneled offices. "We are here to arrest banker Monroe."

He shifted and turned to look at the offices. "He is in his office with a couple of businessmen."

Stern grinned. "Good."

We started across the lobby, and several tellers and customers turned. I opened the door and stepped in while pulling my weapon. "Banker Monroe, you are under arrest."

The three men in the room spun, and two reached into their coats. Both Stern and I cocked our pistols, and they froze.

I moved to them and gestured. "Face the wall with your hands on your head."

The older well-dressed man cleared his throat. "You are making a mistake, constables. I am—"

I growled as I reached him and spun him to face away. "The head of a drug gang. Shut up until we ask you a question."

I put my pistol away and yanked his hands down and behind his back as he hissed, "I will have your badge."

I tightened the restraints. "You will hang by the neck until dead."

I moved to the next man and pulled his hands down and behind his back. "What is your name?"

He glanced back and sneered. "Damon Clark."

I grinned. "You just made our job easier. You are under arrest for making and supplying illegal drugs in a kingdom city."

Stern chuckled as I put my other set of restraints on him.

I moved to the last man. "Your name?"

He looked back and snorted. "I am the king."

I slapped the back of his head. "Funny man."

I accepted the restraints Stern handed me and put them on him and then searched them. I took four pistols and several knives as well as a pouch of drugs from the last man. We had to wait for a court auditor and a uniformed constable before we could leave. They were going to search the office and go through the bank records to find the money the gang had been sending.

We took them to the closest station and put them in a cell before doing up the report. We made a call before the afternoon shift change and headed out and caught a streetcar. We had to change a couple of times, and it was growing dark when we reached Trenton Street. We called in from a corner call box, and Abrams Apothecary had been raided, and everyone arrested.

When we reached Thirty-Seven Trenton Street, the flying squad was already there. Six men were in restraints, and three were already talking to the constables. One of the other constables was guarding the estate gate and grinned at us. Stern chuckled. "Now we inventory everything and take a couple of days off. Not bad for starting with a simple assault-and-extortion case."

Banker Monroe and Damon Clark were given a death sentence, and the rest got ten years hard labor. The man who had tried to extort money from the store clerk got fifteen years. His two men got five for assault and a court warning, which meant if they were ever caught again, it would be life. The drugs were destroyed, and the money confiscated and given to the royal orphans fund.

CHAPTER 11

# Mysterious Death

I STEPPED INTO the shop and nodded to the two constables. I smiled as I crossed to Constable Sergeant Harris. "What do you have?"

He turned and then grinned. "Hey, kid."

He slapped my arm and then turned to nod to the body.

"The doctor was just here and has no idea how he died. He is too young to suddenly drop dead, so I called for an inspector."

I squatted beside the body. "The doc did not want to take the body to be examined?"

He snorted. "He had a shooting and said he would return."

I nodded as I slowly shifted and looked around the body. I checked the floor and then the shelves and finally stood. "Do me a favor and go call for the constable mage on duty. Tell him I need a reading."

He nodded. "Want me to leave the constables who found the body?"

I turned to look at the two men. "Did they touch anything?"

He snorted, and I smiled.

"Okay leave one outside and the other can go back to work."

He nodded and headed for them, and I pulled out several small bags. I carefully used tweezers to pick up a small piece of notepaper and then moved to a shelf. A large can of something powdery was open, and I carefully closed it and put it in a bag. I moved to the corner where a small envelope was lying and put it into another bag. The last thing I picked up was a small piece of lace.

I went back to the body and squatted again and blinked as I looked at the fingers of one hand. I worked another small bag over the hand and then went around to do it to the other hand. I bent and looked up at his face and shook my head before I finally stood and walked to the door. The constable turned and grinned. "Solved the mystery?"

I shook my head. "I only have more questions."

I looked around the neighborhood and smiled.

"Does the owner of the sundries shop still undress in the window when you walk by?"

He blushed as he looked at me. "Um...yeah."

I laughed and turned and waved to another shop owner. He smiled and then grinned and waved back. The constable looked at me. "You from around here?"

I shook my head and turned to look back into the shop. "This was my first beat." I glanced at him. "Harris was my training officer."

He grinned and then chuckled. "And now you are an inspector."

I shrugged. "I miss walking patrols and meeting the people." I gestured. "What I do not miss is seeing someone killed."

He turned. "You think it was murder?"

I nodded. "From what I have right now, I would say a woman or perhaps a jealous boyfriend or husband of a woman." I looked at him. "I would bet on the woman."

He grinned. "I will remember when they start the betting."

It was an hour before Constable Mage Norris arrived and the doctor was back. The doctor snorted but waited as I stood behind Norris when he stepped into the shop. The hair on my arms stood up as he chanted and drew something I could not see in the air. He finally turned and shrugged. "He walked in and found a small letter. He opened it and read it and then fell and died."

I nodded. "No magic was used?"

He shook his head as he started around me. "None."

I turned and gestured to the doctor and pointed to the victim's hand. "The tip of one finger is discolored, and the inside of his nose looks like it is swollen."

The doctor moved toward the body. "I will look—"

I cleared my throat. "Wear gloves and a mask."

He looked at me. "Why?"

I shook my head. "Humor me and do as I ask. Do not let your assistants touch or breathe around him."

He looked at the body. "You are thinking it was a poison?" I nodded, and he shook his head. "Poison would make the throat and tongue swell and—"

I turned. "There was a documented case in the capital of another type of drug that was inhaled and another that was absorbed through the skin from a shirt."

He blinked. "I will take precautions."

I watched as he went to get his assistants, and they returned wearing masks and gloves. They loaded him up, and I took the bags of evidence and had the constable close and lock the shop. I walked and took a streetcar back to the central station and went down to the mage labs. I grinned at Norris. "Ready for some strange requests?"

He smiled and turned from his cluttered desk and gestured. "What do you have?"

I set the bags down. "First I need to tell you I found things on the body. One finger was discolored, and the inside of the victim's nose was swollen. I believe it is some type of poison, so be careful."

He nodded, and I touched the can of powder.

"This was open and on a shelf, but it might be nothing."

Norris stood and carried it to a long table and set it down before opening the bag. He put on gloves and lifted the can out and opened it. He held his hand over it and murmured, and the tingle was back, and it felt like static was in the air. He shook his head as he closed the can. "Nothing in the can is poisonous unless swallowed."

I brought the other bags and touched the one with the lace. "I found a piece of notepaper, a small envelope, and a piece of lace."

I looked at him. "I think the note was in the envelope, and the lace was wrapped around it."

He shrugged, and I opened the bag with the lace, and he reached in to bring it out and set it on the table. This time when he murmured tiny glyphs appeared in the air over the lace. He frowned and turned to write the glyphs down. "Perfume but with something in it."

He touched one of the glyphs. "If a person smelled this, it would speed up his heart and widen his veins."

He looked at the other bags. "Let me see the envelope."

I set the bag on the table, and he replaced the lace in the bag it had been in. He looked at me and murmured and touched my forehead. "Just in case."

I grinned. "I can live with that."

He opened the bag and set the envelope on the table, and we looked at it. "It looks like it might have a type of oil on it."

We opened it, and he shook his head. "And tiny bits of powder inside."

He straightened and then closed the envelope before murmuring a spell that made more glyphs appear. He wrote them down and touched one.

"This would be absorbed through the skin very quickly. It would cause the heart to beat irregularly and affect the lungs. It will also speed up the skin absorption by opening the pores in the skin."

He looked at the writing on the envelope.

"It looks like a lady's hand, but it was pressed into the envelope too hard, so probably a man."

The writing only had the victim's name on it, which I had noted. He put the envelope back into the bag.

"The powder inside will be on the note I think."

He put the note on the table and opened it. All it said was, "I hope this will help to change your mind about our offer."

When he did his spells, he wrote the glyphs down and touched one. "This was the one that killed him. It would have discolored the skin and been absorbed quickly. Once it reached the heart, it would have paralyzed it and killed him."

I nodded. "Would you write it out and list the three compounds?"

He snorted as he returned the note to the bag. "Of course."

I returned to the shop and began to ask the neighbors if they knew anything about a woman he might have been seeing. When no one admitted seeing or hearing him talk about a woman, I thought of the message. I was talking to the shopkeeper next door to the right, "Do you know of any offers he may have gotten?"

He looked around and then nodded. "There was a short bald man who wanted to buy his shop."

I waited, and he bit his lip.

"He has been trying to buy all the shops on the street."

I nodded. "So you know who he is."

He nodded. "He is a solicitor named Jonathan Smythe."

I wrote the name down. "Was he buying for himself or on behalf of someone?"

The shopkeeper shifted. "I think it was on someone's behalf."

I looked at him. "And you know who."

He looked around and leaned closer to whisper, "The purple merchants' guild."

I snorted as I wrote it down. "The purple merchants' guild was disbanded by the orders of the court."

He shrugged, and I turned and headed toward the courts. I stopped to make a few calls at a constable call box and had all the stations check the places that sold the drugs or chemical compounds. The office of Jonathan Smythe was on an upper floor in a building across from the court. When I stepped into the outer office, two men who were leaning against the wall straightened.

One look, and I knew they had weapons as I crossed to the desk with a pretty woman behind it. "I am Constable Inspector Knight and need to speak with the solicitor Smythe."

She smiled but did not even look at the appointment list or even the inner office door. "I am afraid he is busy. You could make an appointment and—"

I snorted and turned as the two men moved toward me. I shifted my jacket and pulled my pistol, and they froze. I gestured. "Take the weapons out slowly and drop them."

I moved to the side.

"If I were you, I would be letting Mr. Smythe know these two men will be going to jail."

She stood and moved to the inner door as the two men slowly pulled weapons and dropped them. I gestured, and they turned, and I moved up and put restraints on them. I glanced at the short bald man who walked out looking angry.

I bent and picked up the two pistols. "I had questions for you, but now you can answer them when a magister contacts you."

He gestured. "You cannot arrest these men. They are on private property."

I smiled. "They were wearing concealed weapons in the public area, which means I can arrest them. If I find out the purple merchants' guild is once more operating and that you are representing them, I will be back."

His face went pale. "I do not know what you are talking about."

I watched his eyes as he shifted and avoided looking into mine. "Right now I am investigating a murder. I know how it was done and will have the person who bought everything to make the poison. You are my primary suspect, Mr. Smythe, and given the manner of death, I would expect a death sentence."

I pushed the two men toward the door.

"Someone will talk to avoid swinging beside you."

I watched the two men as I kept them moving all the way to the nearest station. I pushed them into a cell and gestured to the day jailer. "Take the restraints off. The charge is carrying a weapon concealed."

I looked at the two men.

"Wait a day to bring them before the magister, by then I will have the name or names of the killer I am searching for."

They looked at each other as the jailer took the restraints off. I waited until he came out of the cell.

"If the purple merchants' guild is back, everyone involved is looking at ten years on a work farm."

One cleared his throat. "What if we give information?"

I looked at him and then the other man who grinned. "I will ask the magister to suspend your pending case."

They exchanged looks, and he looked at me. "The solicitor is working for the purple merchants' guild. The only one we saw was a druggist named Paulson, but there are others."

I gestured to the jailor. "Keep them separated and have them write out statements."

I left and put the two weapons in an evidence box under a pending case. I headed to the courts to see a magister and got two warrants. I headed back to the solicitor after calling the station to have a couple of constables sent to the offices and a couple to go watch the druggist Paulson. When I walked in with the constables, a couple of men were packing things into boxes.

I gestured. "Seal the boxes and call for a wagon."

I headed into the other room as the constables put the men in restraints. The solicitor was shoving folders into a large case and looked up, and his face went white.

I gestured. "Turn around. You are under arrest for violation of a royal-court order, solicitation for an illegal organization and conspiracy to commit murder."

He stammered as I started around the desk. "Wait! I…was just—"

I caught a shoulder and spun him. "You are a solicitor and know the law and what you were doing. One man is dead, and I do not know how many people you have forced out of business. The purple merchants' guild is a group of criminals who buy shops to use as a way to hide their illegal business and money."

He looked over his shoulder as I put restraints on him. "I did not—"

I jerked him to the door. "Too late to play that."

I pushed him to the constables.

"Take him and have someone come collect everything in the offices."

I looked around.

"Where did the woman go?"

One of the men cleared his throat. "She told the solicitor she was going to see someone named Paulson."

The solicitor hissed, "Shut up, moron!"

I smiled. "Separate the workers and put the solicitor in isolation."

I left and headed across town to a drugstore.

I stopped next to one of the constables watching the front of the store. "How many people are in the shop?"

He looked at me, and his eyes dropped to my open coat and the constable inspector badge on my belt. He grinned and turned to look at the store. "Only a woman, and they just put up a closed sign."

I nodded. "Warn your partner and watch the back."

He looked at me carefully. "By yourself?"

I grinned as I started across the street. "That is all I need."

I slowed when I reached the front door and kicked, and the door crashed open. I walked in and pulled my weapon. "Constables!"

In the back of the shop was a door, and I heard someone drop and break glass. I crossed the shop and went around the counter as I heard a shout and a door slam. I kicked the inner door open and started into the room before I stopped and took a step back. The druggist and the woman were looking around frantically with kerchiefs covering their nose and mouth.

I cocked my weapon and aimed. "Come out, or I shoot."

The man looked at the puddle of a black liquid on the floor and the spreading vapor before he shook his head.

I smiled as the woman clutched his arm. "Very well. We will seal the shop and wait until your poison absorbs through the kerchiefs and does whatever it is supposed to. Our mage will neutralize it later, and we can bury your bodies."

I backed up, and the woman ran toward me. "Wait!"

I caught her and spun her around before I slipped my weapon into the holster. I put her into restraints while backing around the counter, and the druggist came out of the other room. I watched him as I reached the front door and stepped out. I glanced around and saw a constable crossing the street. I gestured. "Clear all the shops next this one. We have a poison gas that was set off. Warn the men in the back."

He nodded as I turned the woman and looked at the druggist.

"What is it going to be?"

He just looked back, and I shrugged.

"Dead saves us money."

He started to move toward the door, but I pulled my weapon.

"If you come out, you go into restraints."

He glared. "The guild will free me."

I waited, and he finally gave up, and I turned him and pushed him to the wall beside the woman. I put the weapon away and put restraints on him and then searched them both. The street constables cleared the other shops, and one called Constable Mage Norris. I sent the two prisoners to the nearest station while we waited. Norris took five minutes to neutralize the poison vapor.

I searched the shop and found the three compounds as well as the paper, lace, and envelopes like the ones used to kill the shop owner. I returned to the station after ordering everything removed and the shop floors, walls, and ceiling checked. The solicitor was talking as fast as I could write and gave us a lot of names and shops they had already taken over.

The street constables who were searching the druggist shop found almost twenty thousand gold coins and twice as much silver. All had been hidden under the floor in the office. The druggist was hung for murder, and the woman got twenty years on a work farm as an accomplice and for conspiring with the solicitor and the purple merchants' guild.

I sent the names and locations of the guild members to the station commanders, and they had the street constables arrest everyone. The magister confiscated everything they had and sent them to work the mines for ten years.

## Chapter 12

# Petty Thefts on the Docks

I GLANCED AT the door when the constable commissioner stepped in. Stern was out hunting a killer, and I was trying to finish an expenditure report. I sat back. "Sir?"

He shook his head and sat in one of the two wooden chairs across from me. "I think I was wrong about you."

I blinked. "Wrong?"

He nodded. "You are an example to the street constables, but you have the knack for investigating."

I smiled. "I like solving puzzles."

He smiled. "Her Majesty has read your report on the purple-merchant business and sent a commendation."

I blushed, but he waved it away.

"Not why we do it. I came because I have a problem. Normally I would try to let the street constables catch the thieves, but they have not even caught a scent. Anyway, we have been having a rash of petty thefts on the docks. Something here, and something there, but never a lot in any one place. The street constables think it is a gang, but I am not so sure."

I looked at the door as I thought. "Value of the individual items?"

The commissioner growled, "Not cheap and not too expensive."

I nodded. "So it is a sneak thief and probably fencing the stolen items in the city."

He stood. "I hope you find whoever it is. I am getting tired of the screams of anger from the merchant guild."

I watched him leave before I returned to the report and finished it. I stood and put my light jacket on since it was raining. I stopped on the way out to drop the report off in the office for our bookkeeper. Once on the street, I took a streetcar heading to the docks. I jumped off before it got there and started to walk. I entered a small eatery and grinned as I crossed the room and sat beside Constable Sergeant Harris.

He grinned. "Hey, kid."

I waved the waitress down as I looked over his new constable trainee. "The commissioner said you were having problems on the dock."

He nodded. "Probably one of the gangs, but we have not heard anything."

I ordered soup and tea and slipped the waitress a silver coin. I looked at Harris. "Mind if I stick my nose in?"

He chuckled. "No."

I relaxed as I waited for my tea. "I will swing by the station later to look over all the reports of items stolen. It could be a single thief collecting things and then fencing them across the city."

He smiled as the trainee snorted, and I glanced at him. "Always think like them, and they will not surprise you."

I grinned at Harris. "Mrs. Miller said you were by again. She seems taken by you, and her son has been talking about becoming a constable."

He reddened. "She is a fine woman, and the lad seems to have the knack."

I chuckled and accepted my tea. "I have been thinking of just giving her the estate. She does the work of three people, she sells the eggs and milk, and now she is making butter. Ms. Givens is talking about more cows and making cheese or a larger garden."

We talked for a while before I paid for their meal and left. I went to the dock and loitered by a couple of the dock warehouses. I ignored the dockworkers mostly and watched the traffic moving past.

I glanced at three large dockworkers when they closed on me and grinned. "Long time, Sidney."

The one in the middle frowned as he looked at the other two. "You know me?"

I snorted. "I carried your drunk ass home more than once."

He looked at me closely. "Now why would you do that?"

I glanced at a lad looking around by the next warehouse. "So I would not have to arrest you and do a lot of paperwork. Besides your wife always gave me a nice cup of tea before I had to go back into the night."

The other two men shifted, and he grinned. "Constable Knight."

I smiled and straightened as the lad moved to a few small crates stacked to one side. "Time to go back to work."

I started moving as the lad walked by the crates and picked up one. He acted like he was working and turned to enter the warehouse. I did not try to follow and went around and glanced down the other side. The lad came out a side door and started to walk away. I waited and then began to follow as the lad shouldered the crate and walked into an alley.

I stopped to peer around the corner and saw him set the crate on several others. He walked away toward the other end of the alley, and I glanced around before turning the other way. I crossed the street and went into a small tailor shop. I smiled at the woman behind the counter. "Hello, Mrs. Lee. Any chance you still have a stray bolt of white silk?"

She stiffened. "We do not—"

She peered at me.

"Constable Knight?"

I stood by the window and started watching the alley. "All the wonderful shirts you made are starting to get old."

She chuckled and came around the counter. "For you I could find a bit of silk."

I smiled back at her. "Say a dozen?"

I checked the alley and stripped my coat and shoulder holster off so she could measure me. A minute, and she was back behind the counter, and I was dressed.

I glanced at her. "Have you seen any strange delivery wagons or carts lately?"

She nodded. "There is a new rubbish collector who seems to make a lot more rounds on days they are off."

I nodded and then shifted when I saw the rubbish cart coming down the street. Another lad slipped into the alley, and the cart turned in after him. I walked out and crossed the street and peered down the alley to see the rubbish man and the lad loading the crates into the cart. I waited, and the lad walked to the other end of the alley as the cart started to move.

I hesitated before I began to follow and watched as the rubbish collector made several stops along the dock front. He finally pulled up to the back of a new store in the middle of the city, called the Emporium. I watched as he unloaded the crates and carried them into the back door of the store. I checked the time before walking around to the front. I peered in a window to see the rubbish collector changing clothes.

I looked around and leaned against the wall and waited until a street constable walked down the street. He glanced at me, and I shifted and opened my coat to show my badge. I gestured, and he crossed the street to me. "Need help?"

He was grinning, and I nodded. "Call the station. Tell your commander Inspector Knight needs a warrant to search the Emporium for stolen goods. Tell him I witnessed them being stolen and brought to the store. Also ask him if I can borrow a couple of men and need a list of items reported stolen from the docks."

He blinked as he looked at the store. "Okay."

He headed down the street to the corner to use the call box. I moved to peer into the store until the constable returned.

I moved back to join him and he grinned. "The sergeant is sending a couple of men, and the commander went to see the magister."

I nodded. "Watch the back and stop anyone from leaving."

He nodded and turned a few stores down and went in. It was thirty minutes before three men with a sergeant arrived.

He handed me the warrant and a list, and I gestured. "Two of you go to the alley. I will wait a few minutes before going in. Stop anyone from leaving and come in when you hear us."

They nodded, and I looked at the other man and the sergeant.

"Everyone goes into restraints."

I had seen a couple of women, which was why I said that. We waited, and finally I pulled my pistol and walked to the door and went in. "Constables!"

Two lads spun and ran to the back as the women and an older man shifted. The man started to reach into his coat as we moved toward the back, and I growled, "Hands up!"

He licked his lips. "This is my shop, and I run an honest business."

I turned him and put my weapon away before I started putting him into restraints. "You are selling stolen goods."

He protested, and I searched him and took the concealed pistol. The constables from the alley shoved four lads in the back door, and I nodded. "Good. Here is how it is going to go. I have a list of stolen goods, and for each one, you will spend a year on one of the prison farms. Now you might say I cannot prove you knew, but I watched the theft."

I moved to the women.

"I watched the rubbish collector who brought it straight here on a day he was not supposed to be in the streets, and I watched the workers unload and bring it into this store. Then I saw it being unpacked and placed on your shelves. That is a full circle, so any other stolen goods will be an extra bonus and admissible."

I looked one of the women over.

"I am willing to bet I can find more than thirty things reported stolen. It is going to be a shame to send you away until you are old and gray."

I moved to the sullen lads.

"Now I might be willing to trade it down to a single year for everything if one of you provides us with the names of everyone involved." They shifted but remained silent, and I glanced at the sergeant. "Would you call a wagon for the prisoners?"

One of the women cleared her throat. "I will talk."

The others hissed as she blushed, and I gestured. "Take them outside. One is all we need; the rest can rot on a farm for the rest of their lives."

The other woman jerked against the restraints. "Wait! I will talk too!"

I nodded as the man and lads were led out, and I turned to listen as the two women started talking. They gave names of street thieves hired to steal from the docks. They gave the name of the fake rubbish collector and then the owner of the shop who was the one running things. They also gave up the name of a dockworker who was their spotter on the docks.

I let the sergeant deal with bringing in the ones not here and led the women out. We took them all to the station, where I had the two women tell a clerk who wrote their statement down. I spoke with a magister who agreed to my deal with the women. He sent them to work in a homeless kitchen for a year. The store owner got twenty years in the mines, and the lads ten on work farms.

The rubbish collector got ten years on one of the street-cleaning crews. The dockworker seemed to have gotten away, but we found him a week later. He had hung himself in one of the empty warehouses. I got a bonus and a raise, which was enough to pay for my new shirts.

# CHAPTER 13

# Murder in a Mage Shop

THERE ARE FEW shops constables do not go into unless they are off duty. A mage shop is one, not because they do not have problems but because they tend to handle it before we get involved. I stopped in the doorway and looked at the very nervous constable. "Where is the body?"

He gestured to the back. "Beside and behind the counter."

I nodded. "You can wait outside. Call for Constable Mage Norris please."

He nodded, and I checked the floor before moving into the shop. I was careful as I checked the few shelves and ignored the flashy displays. The floor was clean and polished with no signs of a struggle. Nothing on the shelves had been taken or moved that I could see. I squatted beside the body and started at the feet and carefully looked it over. I ignored the shiny silver dagger in the chest until I was done with my examination.

I bent to peer at the dagger closely to see tiny smudges. I looked up when someone cleared his throat. "Hey, Doc." I stood. "Any chance you can wait until Constable Mage Norris gets here?"

He smiled. "Sure. There is a nice coffee shop just down the street."

I nodded. "I will send the constable when he is done."

They left, and I moved behind the counter and to the cash box. I used the tip of my knife to lift it and look in. There was still money inside, so this was not a robbery. I moved to the door into the back and opened it and looked in at what appeared to be a work area. I left it open and moved out of the shop to wait. It was a little while before Norris rode up and swung down.

He looked at me. "Something happened to Dingle?"

I shrugged. "I do not know the victim by name."

He strode into the shop and slowed before moving closer.

I followed and cleared my throat. "Do you know him?"

He nodded while looking at the body. "His name was Edward Merlo Dingle. He was what you would call a hedge wizard."

I snorted. "Not me—I call all magic users mages." He smiled, and I pointed. "There are smudges on the dagger. I was hoping you could get something from that."

He moved closer and knelt and bent to look. "Some type of ink or dye. I should be able to get a likeness of the person who left it."

I nodded and moved to the side of the shop to watch him work. I glanced at the floor to see wire-frame glasses. I frowned before I slipped my gloves on and picked them up. "Um…Norris?"

He glanced up and then at the glasses before snorting. "Those are night glasses. They were something he specialized in."

I looked at the glasses. "As in able to see in the dark?"

He nodded and glanced at the shelf. "He used to have several pairs on the shelf."

I glanced at the place they had been. "So they took something."

I hesitated before slipping the glasses into an inner pocket of my coat. My hair stood up as he began to chant while holding a crystal. When he finished he stood. "There are no traces of magic on him. The smudge was dye."

He handed me the crystal, and I looked into it to see a man I did not know and I nodded. "Thanks."

He glanced at the body. "Find the one who did this."

He headed toward the door, and I followed and sent the constable to get the doctor. I watched as he examined the body before moving it to his wagon. After the body was gone, I went into the backroom and searched it before closing the shop. Why would someone kill the mage and only take night glasses? How had they managed it in the early morning without anyone noticing?

I started with the neighboring shops and showed the image of the man Norris created. One after another they said they had not seen him. I was on the other side of the street and across from the mage shop when I found a witness.

The shopkeeper was making scented lamp oil and glanced at the image. "I seen him. He came out of Edward's shop and got into a carriage."

I glanced across the street. "Would you recognize the carriage if you saw it?"

She snorted as she began to fill bottles. "Try the Amber Carriage Service. The horses were wearing their harness colors, and the carriage had their crest."

I got the horses description before I left and caught a city streetcar heading north. When I walked into the huge stable yard, lads were busy cleaning carriages, and inside they were grooming horses. I spoke with the owner, who told me who the driver had been, but he said he had not listed a hire. He did give me a location where the man normally picked up fares.

When I reached the area, it was in the middle of the city. Mostly banking houses crowded the street with the large mint building on a corner. Carriages lined one side of the street, and I looked for the carriage and driver who had been in front of the mage shop. Several constables were walking the street as I saw the carriage I was looking for.

I crossed the street and started toward it, and the driver saw me. He frowned and turned to look at the two constables on the walk moving toward him. Suddenly he spun and yanked out the carriage whip and snapped it over the horses. I yelled as I started to run. "Stop! Constables!"

Of course he did not stop, but it made everyone else look, including the constables on the street. The two on the walk started to run, and then two more came out in front of the carriage. One waved his arms to stop the horses as the other pulled his weapon. The driver leaped off the seat and landed on the street before he tried to run. By then I was there and dived into him and forced him to the ground.

He tried to fight as I yanked him over and onto his stomach. The other constables arrived, and his arms were pulled back, and he was put into restraints. I slapped the back of his head before I stood and yanked him up. "Why the hell did you run?"

He glared. "I did not rob the shop."

I snorted. "Rob? I am here about a murder."

His face paled. "He did not say anything about a killing."

I pushed him to the walk and looked at the constables. "Would one of you move the carriage off the street? Have someone from his company call in to have it taken away."

They nodded, and I looked at the driver.

"Where and who was the man?"

He shook his head. "I do not know who he was. I dropped him at Gilbert's stables."

I looked into his face and knew he was not telling me everything. I nodded to one of the other constables. "Take him in and lock him up. The charge is conspiracy in the death of Edward Dingle and armed theft. Let the magister know Constable Inspector Knight will be in later to give his sworn statement."

He nodded and pulled the prisoner away, and I glanced at the other carriages and drivers.

"Who knows these streets?"

One of the constables cleared his throat. "I have been walking them for a year."

I looked at him. "Which have night guards?"

He snorted. "All of them."

I shook my head. "Which would be worth robbing during the night?"

He blinked. "The streetlights stay on all night so…the side street beside the mint building does not have streetlights. The vault is on that side and toward the back, and they only have one guard. He is older and likes to step out for a pipe at night."

I smiled as I thought about the night glasses that had been taken. "And the doorway is very dark."

He nodded. "That would be the one I would pick, but they would never get into the vault."

I headed toward the mint. "Thank you."

I walked into the mint and looked around. The machines were clicking and clacking and slamming together. There was the sound of the forges and the smell of metal in the air. Two guards moved toward me, and I opened my jacket to show the constable badge on my belt.

I gestured. "Where do I find the person in charge?"

One pointed to a door in the back, and I nodded. "Thanks."

I moved through the coin presses and around caged carts full of shinny coin blanks. I knocked on the door, and a few moments later, a man opened it. He frowned as he looked at me. "This is a restricted area."

I showed him my badge and then pulled out the crystal. "Do you know this man?"

He pulled out glasses and peered at the crystal. "That is Christian Miller."

He looked at me, and I put the crystal away. "Does he work here?"

He snorted. "Not anymore. He was one of the press operators and let a defect spoil a whole pressing. We had to remelt and cut the blanks to fix the mistake. They are supposed to—"

I held up a hand. "Do you know where he lives?"

He shook his head. "The last I heard he was leaving the city to go to the capital."

I turned to look at everything before I looked at him. "Would you mind if I came back tonight and did rounds with your guard?"

He nodded, and I thanked him and headed for the door. I stopped to speak with the guards so the night guard would know I was coming. First I went to eat and then check in at the station closest to the mint. I made a call to Detective Inspector Stern and made a report of the case. I stopped by the courts to do a sworn statement in front of a magister.

I finally returned to the mint as the sun was setting. The night guard let me in and grinned. "So you think we will have some fun tonight?"

He led me to the back of the silent building. It seemed like a completely different place without the noise from the furnaces and the presses. I was not going to allow him to take his normal smoke break. My killer had already shown he would take a life, and I was sure he would try to do it again. I walked the rounds with the guard and sat with him until just after midnight.

I heard the side door lock break and gestured to the old guard as I pulled my weapon. I slipped the night glasses on as I moved toward the door. I slowed and turned to the vault instead and looked around a furnace to see four men. I lifted my weapon. "Constable!"

They spun, and two lifted weapons. I shot one, but the other fired. I felt the burning tear of a shot in my left shoulder. I twisted and then turned back as I brought my pistol up. I fired as the man was running at me, and he folded and fell to the floor. The other two men had ducked behind empty crates, but I was not going to rush them.

I aimed and waited, and one stuck a pistol over the crate he was behind and pointed it toward me. I shifted and fired as his muzzle bloomed and a bullet went over my head. He fell back, and I heard him struggling and the other man cursing. I shifted as I aimed at the crate he was behind. "Give up!"

He stuck his weapon over the crate and started firing without even looking. I shifted back, and then I saw someone sneaking along the wall. I aimed at him until I realized it was the guard. A minute later I heard the scream and ran to the crates to find the last man down. He was cringing and cradling what looked like a broken arm.

The guard nudged him with his foot and twirled his billy. "On your feet, you."

I grinned as I yanked him up and searched him and put him in restraints. I checked the others, and only the one who had charged me was dead. I gestured to the guard. "Go to the front doors and see if there are any constables."

There were, and I had them call for the prisoner wagon and a doctor. The one with the broken arm was Christian Miller. The other three were just thugs he had talked into helping him rob the mint. The two still alive got ten years on a work farm, and he was sentenced to death. Of course Constable Mage Norris did visit him before he was taken away, and he seemed to be in a lot more pain.

# CHAPTER 14

# Corrupt Constables

I WAS LOOKING out the kitchen window at Winston, or Constable Sergeant Harris, when he and Mrs. Miller kissed. I turned as her son chuckled and grinned before I set the empty teacup in the sink. "Think he will ask her?"

He nodded. "He told me he was going to."

I headed for the door. "That makes it easier. Let your mother know I am moving my things out."

He frowned. "Why?"

I gave his shoulder a pat as he walked with me. "I am giving her the estate. A man and wife need their own place."

I left and saddled my horse before I walked it to the gate and swung up. I was a little early and swung by to see one of the city clerks. I checked seized houses and grinned when I saw one out toward the stockyards. It even had a small stable and carriage house. I made a claim and went to my bank and returned to pay the tax before he wrote out the deed.

I grinned as Stern finished his story of his latest search for the perfect woman. I looked at the constable commander as he stepped in. He cleared his throat. "I need your help."

Stern sat back and gestured to a chair. "We just finished our case, so sit down and tell us what we can do."

He crossed and sat with a sigh. "We have at least one and as many as four constables gone bad."

I sat up. "Like…"

He shook his head. "I do not think it is an officer or a sergeant. I have noticed a few areas have changed in the number of arrests and the number of citizen complaints. The arrests are down and mostly petty domestic, and the few gangs or serious stuff are not there. The complaints are up about gang threats or robbery and in a few cases shootings."

I looked at Stern. "Sounds like the constables are not there."

He snorted as he stood. "Or not looking. We will look into it, sir."

The commander stood. "Try Elm or Knob Streets. Those have the most complaints."

He left as I stood and reached for my coat. "And have the most business."

Stern headed for the door. "Time to earn your princely sum."

I laughed as I followed. "Maybe you will find one of the shopkeepers with a daughter."

An hour, and we were leaning against a building and watching Knob Street. The constable had walked by when we first got there, but he was paying more attention to a sundry shop. I kept track of the time, but he did not return when he should. Four older lads walked out of another alley and headed for the shop. I straightened and slipped my constable badge onto my belt in the front. "Time to see who talks."

Stern chuckled as we watched the lads walk into what was plainly a woman's shop. We started across the street as we heard something break and a woman yell. Stern was the first through the door, and I followed as he grabbed a lad and slammed him into a wall. I slugged the next in the side of the head and reached for a third who was holding the shopkeeper.

I yanked him to the side and spun him before I hit him in the stomach. The first man I hit went down, and the second folded. Stern was moving past me to the last at the cash box. He fumbled for a pistol under his belt, and it went off. He screamed as I let the lad go and pulled my weapon. Stern was shaking his head as the lad kept screaming. "That is going to hurt for a long time."

I gestured, and the lads turned and went to their stomach. "Now you boys are looking at armed robbery, armed assault, and an attempted assault with a weapon on a constable. That adds up to twenty-five years in a mine or work farm."

I waited while Stern took the weapon from the injured lad and then came to search the others. Of course they had fancy new pistols straight from the factory.

We put them in restraints and had the shopkeeper call for a wagon and doctor. The lads would not talk and seemed calm. When the constable finally arrived, he looked from the lads to us and cleared his throat.

I smiled. "Where were you?"

He shifted. "I was helping a widow two streets over. She claimed to have a peeper."

I nodded. "I will read your report later."

I gestured. "We have this; go back on patrol."

He glanced at the lads before he turned away. Stern sighed. "Too bad about your friend. It looks like he shot his privates off."

They glared, and I grinned. "The men in the mines will not mind. They have not seen a woman in a long time."

Stern chuckled. "True."

One of the lads hissed, "We will never see the—"

The others growled, and he shut up. I shook my head. "I have news for you. We are inspectors, and our case gets priority. Your friend might get to wait a few days, but you three are going straight to the magister. I would say by lunchtime you are on your way out of the city in chains. I believe they let you have thirty minutes when you get there to write to your families."

They shifted, and I saw the prisoner wagon pull up and bent to start pulling them to their feet. One struggled, and the other two tried to kick, but we knew all the tricks. We were shoving them into the wagon when one broke. "Wait!"

I pulled him back as the others hissed and told them to shut up. Stern snorted and shoved them to the front as I pulled the one away from the wagon. "Talk."

He looked around. "I get to walk."

I shook my head and started pushing him back to the wagon and the others. "Thanks for the information."

He protested and struggled and that was enough for the others to start talking. The old constable sergeant driving the wagon grinned as the three gave us the names of four constables they were paying. They told us where their gang was and where all the stolen property had been taken. We let them talk and then sent them off with the wagon.

The sergeant would take them straight to a magister. The doctor finally arrived, and we brought out the one who had shot himself. He looked at us, but Stern grinned. "He kept his pistol in the front of his pants."

The doctor shook his head as he climbed in, and the driver got the ambulance moving. I glanced at Stern. "Do we pick them up now or at shift change?"

He sighed as he started walking. "First we talk with the station commander. After that we arrange for a strike group from another station to take the gang and the stolen property."

He looked at me.

"If they are taking money from one gang, they might be taking it from another."

I nodded as I walked beside him. "Once we have one gang, we can take them and let the gang know the constable gave us the information."

Stern grinned. "And put them in the cell next to them. I would be willing to bet they sing before the door is even closed."

An hour, and the station commander had a dozen constables from another station on the way. Stern and I met them at the house where the stolen property was being kept. Three minutes, and we had four more men in restraints. We raided the gang's hideout and captured a dozen more without a shot being fired. The station commander had called the four constables in, and they were waiting when we arrived.

I walked into the room first and pulled my weapon and gestured. "Turn around and put your hands on the wall."

They froze, and their faces went white, but Stern growled, "Turn the fuck around!"

While I watched he searched them and took their weapons. We put them in restraints, and I followed as we headed to the cells. We had mentioned the constables giving them up to the gang. When they saw them, the gang yelled and shouted and threatened. The four constables struggled as we kept pushing them toward the cells. Stern opened it, and one broke. "Wait! I...we can give you two other gangs and a theft ring!"

Stern spun him and slammed him into the bars as he pushed the cell closed. "Start talking."

One of the others cleared his throat. "We walk—"

I slapped the back of his head. "Put them in the cell."

Stern turned, and they struggled, and the first one gasped. "Okay!"

We made them write everything down separately and then put them each in an isolation cell. Of course their stories were not the same, and we got five more gangs. One gang was stealing straight off cargo ships at the river docks. Another gang was responsible for a couple of dozen home break-ins. A third gang had been robbing from the train yards. It took twelve more hours to round everyone up and bring them in.

The four constables were charged with accepting bribes, and then the magister slammed them with multiply charges of theft since they had been working for and with the gangs. Almost every gang member went to the work farms or mines for over ten years. For our work Stern and I both received an award and fancy engraved pistols.

# CHAPTER 15

# Missing Children

I GRINNED AS Stern continued talking about his night. He had gone back to the shopkeeper we had saved from the four gang members last week. So far he had been with her every evening. That whole part of the city was enjoying a period free of crime since the gangs had been sent away. Even the other constables working the area seemed more relaxed.

Winston and Mrs. Miller had gotten married the day before and almost a hundred constables had attended. He had a surprised and stunned look when I gave them the estate for their wedding gift. They had gone to the country for their honeymoon. I had a feeling another little one would be on the way by the time they got back.

We were sipping coffee with the desk sergeant before going to check a few random thefts on the north side of the city. The constable commissioner walked in, and we straightened. He hesitated and then grinned. "Since you are free I have an urgent case for you."

We sighed as the desk sergeant laughed, and the commissioner gestured and held out a folder.

"We have a dozen children missing from one of the orphanages."

We started moving, and I cleared my throat. "How long have they been missing, sir?"

He shook his head. "The girls were last seen at bed count, which was at nine o'clock. When the house mother went to wake them, their beds were empty."

I glanced at Stern before I accepted the folder. I opened it and read what we had so far and handed it to Stern. "We will find them, sir."

The commissioner nodded and turned to leave, and I waited for Stern to give the folder to the desk sergeant to be sent to our office. We left and went to saddle horses for the ride to the orphanage. I took the horses and tied them while Stern went in. After I was done, I started checking the windows and the area below them. I was all the way around in the back before I found the tracks under a window.

I checked the tracks and then the window, but there was no sign it had been forced from the outside. There was a stick stuck in the grove to one side holding it open, and seeing the dust on it, I doubted it had been moved in a long time. I knelt to look at the tracks, but there were too many to separate. I finally stood and looked in the direction the footprints had gone.

I glanced into the window before following the tracks. "Stern!"

The entire back wall was covered in ivy that hid the fence. The footprints had disappeared in the tall, unkempt grass. I began to check the wall of plants, and Stern caught up. We stopped at the corner where someone had pulled the ivy apart like a curtain. I was thinking the kids had just run away as I bent and pushed the plants out of the way.

There was a wide hole in the fence, and I slipped through. I was in the dirt alley behind the orphanage and found tracks from a large wagon. I also found a single large footprint of a man to one side of all others. Stern knelt beside me and shook his head. "They did not run away."

I stood. "Whoever this is used something to keep them quiet."

We looked around the alley, and I turned to start following it.

"We need more help."

Stern agreed and went back through the fence while I continued toward the end of the alley. I stopped when I saw the almost-hidden shelter of a homeless person. I went closer and shook the large crate, and a man jumped out. "Hey!"

I moved my coat so he could see my badge. "Kids were taken from the orphanage last night."

The man looked like he was in his fifties and glared before glancing back down the alley. He relaxed and shook his head. "I saw a bakery wagon just after midnight."

I nodded. "Could you see any lettering or a name?"

He frowned. "Brown's?"

Stern rode into the alley, leading my horse, and I tossed a silver coin to the homeless man. "Thanks."

I swung up and into the saddle. "Do you know of a bakery called Brown's?"

He frowned. "No, but there used to be one called Brownie's."

We stopped at a call box to have other constables meet us at the bakery before continuing. When we swung down and looked at the loading yard and the back of the building, it looked vacant and empty. Several constables were waiting, and one cleared his throat. "No one is here."

I moved to look in a window before I turned. I looked at the empty corral and stable before I looked at Stern. "We need to find out who the owner was and ask him a few questions."

One of the constables cleared his throat. "That would be Mr. Albert, but he died. His wife might know something."

He went to use a call box before returning.

"She sold everything to a Mr. Sonders. The only address she has is a house out on Greenish Lane, number three three nine."

I straightened and looked at Stern. "I know that place from when I was with the flying squad. It is a brothel but not doing very well."

All the constables growled as we headed for our horses.

I swung up and glanced back. "Call the flying squad."

I spun my horse and kicked it into a run to catch up to Stern. We slowed when we went through the middle of the city but did not stop. As we finally left the city, three of the flying squad fell in and rode with us. What we did not expect was Detective Inspector Mcgivens and a dozen other inspectors. When we turned in at the gate, a guard moved out into the middle of the road.

I did not stop and let the horse knock him aside. Half of the men spurred their horse into a trot as they headed for the rear of the large manor. When we reached the front doors, we heard shots from the back. I pulled my pistol as I swung down and started for the door. It was yanked open, and I dived aside as a man with a shotgun pointed and fired.

I felt the searing pain in my right thigh as I hit the ground. Shots ripped into the door as the man ducked back. I rolled and came to my feet as the others spread out to find cover. I ignored that as I limped to the door. The man leaned out again, and I fired while walking. I cocked the hammer as he jerked back, and the shotgun fired into the air.

When I reached the door, a second man was aiming at it, and I spun aside. There was the roar of another shotgun, and the edge of the door splintered. I turned back as I lifted my pistol and fired, but he had moved into the other room. The man I had already shot was on the floor, writhing around while trying to reload the shotgun. Stern reached the other side of the door and fired, and the man jerked and died.

The man in the other room spun and fired, but I had moved, and the shot struck the door again. Detective Inspector Mcgivens stepped into the doorway and fired, and the man folded and went down. Two others moved in, and Stern and I followed. We could hear more shots from the back, and the other inspectors headed through the house.

Stern and I started for the stairs with Detective Inspector Mcgivens and two constables. I backed up beside Stern to cover him, and a man suddenly jumped up. Before he could fire, I shot him, and he twisted and fell. I began to reload and Detective Inspector Mcgivens took my place. We reached the next floor, and the man I shot was curled up on the landing.

The firing at the back of the building stopped as we began to move down the hall. I yanked open a door as Stern pointed his weapon. He lifted it and gestured. "It is okay, girls."

I glanced in at the young teenage girls and slipped into the room. "Go downstairs, girls."

They nodded and almost ran out as I searched the room. I heard Detective Inspector Mcgivens and Stern in the next room with more girls as I finished. I stepped into the hall as two more girls ran out, and I gestured. "Down the stairs."

I heard more of the flying squad arrive as the other two constables yanked another door open. I limped passed as two more girls ran out. There were only three more rooms as I stopped at the next. Detective Inspector Mcgivens appeared and nodded, and I opened the door. Shots struck the doorframe, and the detective inspector fired back.

I spun around the frame with my weapon up, but the man was down. I slipped into the room and kicked the pistol away from his hand. I gestured to the two girls hiding behind the bed. "Out and downstairs."

They nodded and came to their feet and ran out, and I checked the room. When I came out, I saw the blood on Detective Inspector Mcgivens's leg. Stern was at the next door with the constables, and one opened it. It was only two more girls, and he slipped in. I gestured and Detective Inspector Mcgivens smiled as he went to open the last door.

I aimed, and he yanked it open, and I almost fired before I took a step. "Let the girl go."

The man who was inside was only half-dressed, and one girl was naked and curled up in a corner. He had a pistol pointed at the other girl while holding her like a shield. "Leave, or I kill her."

I kept aiming as I limped closer. "We are not leaving. Let the girl go."

His eyes flicked around as I entered the room. "I will kill her."

I extended my weapon as I took another step. "I am only going to ask one more time before I kill you. Let the girl go."

He licked his lips as he took a step back and turned his head. I fired, and the round exploded out the other side of his head, and he fell. I took a quick step to catch the girl and pull her away and around me. I moved to the body and kicked the pistol away while Detective Inspector Mcgivens held the crying girl. I put my weapon away and went to the other girl and picked her up.

I held her as I turned and limped out. Three of the girls had been molested, which made us want to go back and shoot the bastards again. Only two men were still alive to tell us the whole story. They had a list of clients who wanted young teenage girls; we found that list down in a study. Mr. Sonders was not the owner's real name—it was Mr. Greene, and he had been wanted. He was the one in the last bedroom.

The girls were returned to the orphanage, and we had all the stations begin making more checks during the day and at night. The constables also did a lot more, and the girls were all given new homes within a few weeks. The two men went before a magister, who sentenced them to hang. I ended up with desk duty for three weeks thanks to the three rounds of buckshot in my right thigh.

# CHAPTER 16

# Ransom

WE WERE BUSY with case after case and little time off. I had just finished a case with a blackmailer, and both he and the person being blackmailed were seeing a magister. I glanced at the door when the desk sergeant looked in. "Something?"

He nodded. "We have a young woman who was kidnapped."

Stern, like the other inspectors, was out on a case, and I stood. I got the address and went to get my horse. The estate belonged to Baron Nickols and was huge. I swung down and tied the reins to a post before I walked to the door. The doorman already had it open and directed me inside. The butler led me through to a very large study where the baron was waiting.

He was pacing back and forth and spun. "About time!"

I ignored the remark. "Where was your daughter taken from?"

He growled, "From the garden."

I nodded. "And are you sure she was taken?"

He glared. "What do you mean by that!"

I sighed. "Was there a note? Could she have gone to a girlfriend?"

He blinked and shook his head. "She did not go out the gates, and she would have told me if she were going to see anyone."

I turned. "I need to see where she was when she was taken."

He snorted and gestured to a servant. "That is not going to help. You need to start searching the city."

I looked at him before I followed the servant. In the small garden, the servant stopped, and I moved past him. First I looked around carefully before I started to walk. I glanced at the servant. "Did you or anyone else see anyone?"

He shook his head, but I saw something in the way he would not look directly at me. There was no trace in the garden, and the gardeners' gate had been raked a few days before, and there were no prints. That left the only way out back through the house or to climb over a wall. If they were carrying a struggling young woman, they would not climb a wall, so that left the house.

I turned and headed for the door. "You do know that if you lie to me or do not tell me what you saw, I can arrest you as a conspirator in the young woman's disappearance?"

The servant stiffened. "I have not lied."

I stopped in front of him. "But you have not told me everything."

He looked around. "The master had many errands and sent everyone out of the house."

I nodded. "Leaving only himself and the young woman."

He nodded. "She was gone when I returned, and he ordered me to call the constables."

I looked at the garden. "If she was taken, it was not from here." I gestured to the door. "Show me to her room."

The house was quiet as we went inside and climbed the stairs. The daughter's room was clean and orderly with her bed made and all her clothes in the closet. I found her diary missing, but older ones still there. I turned and left. Next I went through the other bedrooms and then downstairs. There was no sign of a struggle in any room, and I returned to the study.

The baron turned and growled as he held out a sheet of parchment, "A runner just brought this."

I crossed to take it and read it. It was asking for ten thousand gold for the return of the girl. I looked at the baron. "Where is the runner?"

He snorted. "I sent him away."

I shook my head. "And did anyone else see this runner?"

He stiffened. "My word is enough."

I looked at him. "First I have not found any evidence anywhere that your daughter has been abducted. There is no sign of a struggle or of anyone leaving the garden. Her room is straightened, and the only thing missing is her diary. Now you say a runner has brought this ransom demand, but you sent the runner away before I could question him."

I turned and started for the door.

"I suggest you begin collecting the ransom."

He sputtered, "You incompetent ass. I will have you broken!"

I turned at the door. "I did not say I will not keep investigating. I will find your daughter, and I will learn the truth no matter how hard you try to hide it. The crown will not pay the ransom since there is no evidence of an abduction."

I spun and left and walked my horse to the gate. "What did the runner look like?"

The guard blinked. "What runner? Oh…um…skinny kid with a pockmarked face."

I smiled. "Clothes?"

He shrugged. "Dirty with a white shirt and brown canvas pants with ragged, scuffed boots."

I nodded and pulled out a notebook. "Lets see what the baron said."

The guard shifted on his feet. "Well…I…I did not really pay attention and…"

I looked at him. "Let me put it this way. When I find the daughter—and I will—I will get answers. Those involved will face a magister on charges of abducting a noble and extortion. If they are not hung, they will go to the mines for at least twenty years. That includes anyone conspiring with them or protecting them."

The guard swallowed and glanced toward the manor. "I did not see a runner. The baron called and said to tell you there was one."

I nodded. "And the daughter? I cannot believe you had an errand away from your gate."

He shook his head. "I have not seen her since yesterday afternoon."

I swung up on the horse and rode out and then around the walls of the estate. Along the back wall in the servants' alley, I swung down and walked looking at the ground. I checked the servants' gate carefully before I continued along the wall. I finally swung into the saddle and rode to the closest station house. When I walked into the constable commander's office, he was talking on his call box.

I waited, and he glared at me. "I understand, sir, but it is obvious this inspector is incompetent or inexperienced. The baron is furious and demands we—"

He shook his head.

"No, he just walked in."

He snorted while looking at me.

"Yes, sir, I will listen to—"

He reddened.

"With all due respect, Commissioner, the baron—"

He shook his head and put the head set down.

"Talk you."

I smiled. "Since I am incompetent or inexperienced, you might want to go do my job."

He glared. "Report."

I nodded. "The baron said his daughter was taken from the garden. There is no sign, and no one has entered or left the garden unless it was through the house. The young woman's room is neat and clean, and the only thing missing is her diary. The baron sent all the estate servants out on errands, so there are no witnesses. The note delivered to the baron by the runner did not happen."

I glanced at his lieutenant as he stopped in the door.

"If it did, the runner climbed the estate wall. The guard did not see him enter and received orders from the baron to lie about him. I examined the whole estate wall and the servants' entrance, and no one has left using it this morning. The only thing I have right now is the young woman is missing and the baron is lying about it."

He shifted and turned to look out a window. "The baron said you told him the crown would not pay the ransom."

I snorted. "Ten thousand gold? With no evidence the girl has been abducted and the father lying and the servants trying to cover up?"

He nodded and finally turned to me. "You have my apology. What are you going to do?"

I smiled. "When the baron filed the abduction, he opened the door. I am calling a magister, requesting permission to use our mage to search the estate and manor for the young woman. I am also notifying the duke of the circumstances so far and giving him my recommendation. What I would like from you is a few constables to accompany me when we return to the estate."

He smiled. "For a detailed search."

I nodded. "For the basement or secret rooms or passages."

He nodded again. "Granted. I will have my lieutenant assemble a few men."

I turned and walked out and went to use the call box. While I sat and talked to the magister and the duke, I wrote the start of my report. I looked at my notes, and when Constable Mage Norris walked in, I stood. He grinned as we started for the constable briefing room. "A search for a girl's body?"

I stopped in the doorway and gestured to the lieutenant. "Dead or alive. The duke has considered my report and has already spoken with the baron. He will not pay the ransom, and the city lords who the baron called have protested."

We started for the front doors, and I held out the ransom note.

"Notice anything strange about the note?"

He accepted it and looked at it while we began to walk. "He tried to make the writing look bad. The paper was crumpled but good quality—the same for the ink he used. They spelled everything correctly, which means education."

I glanced at the constables following and then looked at Norris. "I believe the baron is behind whatever this is. Hopefully he has not killed his daughter, and we will find her hidden."

He smiled. "Once I have something of hers, it should not be hard to find her."

We walked the rest of the way in silence, and I found a runner from the magister waiting outside the gate. He grinned as he handed me the folded warrant. "The magister said to find the girl quickly."

I started for the gate as the guard moved out of his small building.

He cleared his throat. "The baron has said you are not allowed onto the estate."

I opened the warrant. "This is from a magister. It is a warrant to search the grounds and manor using any and all means to find the baron's missing daughter. You will open this gate, or we will."

He swallowed and nodded as he quickly unlocked the gate and pulled it open.

I started through and looked back. "Lieutenant, if you have a few men start with the out buildings, stables, and carriage house, I would be grateful."

He nodded and gestured, and half the men split off. When we reached the door, the butler opened it and looked at me. "You are not allowed—"

I held up the warrant. "Yes, I am. Where is the baron?"

He looked at the paper and opened the door wider. "The study."

I walked through. "Show Constable Mage Norris to his daughter's room."

The other constables spilt off as they began to search the manor while I continued to the study. The baron looked up from his desk and came to his feet. "How dare you!"

I crossed the room and dropped the warrant on his desk. "This is a warrant to search for your daughter using any and all means. Right now Constable Mage Norris is up in her room. When he gets what he is after, we will find her."

His face paled, and I pointed to the chair. "Sit and keep your mouth closed, or I will put you in restraints until we are done."

He sat slowly and glared as I moved to one side. "The duke has refused to pay the ransom. The runner never entered your estate, which means you lied. The paper is from your own stock, and so is the ink. You wrote the ransom demand. You sent your servants away, but no one has left through any other gate except the front. The guard was on duty and did not see your daughter leave."

I glanced at the wall of bookshelves as he shifted and started to open a drawer. I reached into my jacket and pulled out my pistol and cocked it. The baron froze, and I moved around and reached into the drawer where his hand was. I took the engraved pistol out of his hand and tucked it under my belt.

"Would you like to talk now or wait?"

He growled, "You will never find her."

I moved to the side as Norris walked in and looked around. He frowned. "She came in here but did not leave."

I nodded. "Could he have a mage-shielded room or secret passage?"

He nodded. "Possible."

He leaned against the wall, and finally the lieutenant stepped in. He shook his head, and I turned to look at the wall as the baron stood and growled, "Now get out of my house!"

I looked at the floor along the base of the shelves and saw scrapes. I looked at him. "Sit down before I knock you down."

I moved to the bookshelf, and his face whitened. "Do not touch my books."
I gestured to the lieutenant. "Would you put the baron in restraints please?"
I squatted and looked at the scrapes. "Norris?"
He moved closer and grinned. "A secret door."

He murmured, and I felt the tingle of magic before we heard a click. I stood and pulled, and a section of the bookshelf turned and opened. The baron started to struggle with the lieutenant, and he spun him and slammed him down on the desk. I stepped into the other room and saw the girl crumpled and tied on the floor. There was a tiny bit of blood in her hair as I went closer and knelt.

I felt her pulse and relaxed a little as I turned her over. The room held a single book case and a chair with a lamp. I picked her up and moved back into the study. "Lieutenant, would you take the baron to the station? The charge is false imprisonment, attempted extortion, and assault. We do not need to add the false report or the attempted assault on a constable."

The daughter woke in pain, but the constable doctor had arrived and began to treat her. She recovered fully, and I was able to get her statement. Her father had wanted to speak with her, and she had gone down to the study. She had her diary because she had been writing in it about her father losing money while gambling. When they entered the secret reading room, he had struck her from behind and tied her up.

Since the baron was a noble, the case went before the duke. The duke was not in a forgiving mood and notified the queen, who stripped him of his patent and sentenced him to thirty years in the mines. The city lords were chastised for interfering in constable business. The lady Madeleine was confirmed as the heir and granted her father's patent. The commissioner reviewed the case and the note of commendation from the commander.

A week later I was promoted to detective inspector. Of course we were still swamped with cases, so the celebration would have to wait.

# CHAPTER 17

# Princess in Disguise

THE PARTY HAD lasted for most of the afternoon and left a large mess for me to clean up. At least my friends knew better than to drink too much. There had also been a lot of others who had stopped by. Like all the station commanders and the commissioner, the city lords and many of the nobles who knew me. There had been gifts including a new pistol with a constable badge engraved on it.

With my promotion, I lost my partner and was going to be working on my own. I also had a new office and not one I was sure I would like. It was in the middle of the city and close to the courts building. There were only a handful of constables in the station with a lieutenant as the station commander. I glanced at him as I finished the report I was working on. "Something?"

He nodded. "We have several reports of pickpockets at the train station. My constables have tried to find them, but so far they have had no luck."

I blew on the report and then set it in my out box before standing. "I will go hang around and see what I can find."

He grinned. "Thanks, Ashton."

I nodded and glanced at the tiny window to see it still raining. I stopped to put my long coat on before I left. It was not very far, so I walked, greeting people along the way. Inside the station a crowd was starting; some held cases or had travel trunks. I leaned against a back wall and watched as a train pulled in. I saw a woman moving through the crowd and bumping people.

I pushed away and started toward her and saw a young man moving to her and glancing at me. I reached her almost at the same time as he did and pulled my weapon. The young man looked smug as he started to turn, and I growled, "Take a step, and I shoot you in the spine."

I gestured to the woman. "You put your hands on your head."

The man turned, I cocked my pistol, and he froze. I took a step as the crowd backed away and reached around him to take the pistol from his hand. I gestured. "Move to the back."

I froze as I saw a young woman step off the train. She was looking straight at me and carrying a single travel case. I shook myself. "Hands on your head."

I moved around them and closer to the woman. "Madam, please do not leave and stay close."

She smiled. "Of course, Inspector."

I nodded and gestured to the man and woman. "To the back wall and put your hands on it."

I kept glancing back as the crowd around us moved away and the station master pushed through.

I glanced at him as the two reached the wall. "Go call for a street constable."

He nodded and turned to push back through the crowd. I shifted the long coat as I reached to my back and took out a set of restraints.

I touched the barrel of my weapon to the back of the man's head. "Hands behind your back."

I put the restraints on him and pulled my second set of restraints as I moved to right behind the woman. I was putting the restraints on her when the street constable arrived.

I glanced at him. "I witnessed her taking three wallets. The man is her spotter and bank. He was carrying a pistol and pulled it. Charge her with petty theft and him with conspiracy and public endangerment."

I gave him the weapon.

"I will write my report and send it to the magister's clerk. Make sure you have them searched thoroughly and log everything as possible evidence. Notify the station master to send anyone reporting a theft to the station."

He nodded and grinned. "I will leave your restraints with the desk sergeant."

I turned and glanced at the two large travel cases by the train steps. I smiled at Her Highness. "Let me get a porter, and I can take you to..."

She smiled as she slipped her arm around my left one. "I have not decided yet."

I put my weapon away and gestured to a station porter. "Perhaps we can go to the station, and I can make a few calls. Where is your security?"

She sighed. "I gave them the slip."

A station porter arrived, and I gestured to the bags. "A couple of silvers if you bring them to the new constable station by the courts building."

He grinned and nodded. "No problem, Inspector."

I paid him and turned and looked around as I led the princess to a side exit. "So why have you come?"

She smiled and hung on my arm. "I needed to get away for a while, and after reading all your reports...you do know Mother has them copied and sent to her?"

I shook my head as I stopped just inside the door and paid a vendor for an umbrella. I stepped out as I opened it and looked around before we started walking. "I was not aware of that. She is still traveling around the country?"

She nodded. "Off and on and loving it. She has a team of former detective inspectors who teach all new guards for her traveling using your guidelines."

I closed the umbrella when we walked into the station and crossed to the desk sergeant. "Andrew, a porter will be bringing some travel cases. Set them behind your desk for me please."

He nodded and turned back to the woman complaining of her neighbor peeping at her. I led the princess around and up to the next floor and into my office.

I gestured to a chair. "I have a report and a few calls, and then we can find you someplace to stay."

She smiled as she took off the long travel cloak. "Tea?"

I moved to the side and started the single gas burner and put on a pot of water. I went around my desk and sat and picked up the call-box handset. "Mary, I need the city operator."

A moment later the operator answered, "How may I help you?"

I glanced at the princes. "I need the imperial city operator."

I waited, and another voice came on, "How can I help you?"

I hesitated, "I need the palace operator."

"Sir, the palace line is restricted."

I growled, "My name is Detective Inspector Knight. Now patch me through to the palace."

It was several moments before another operator came on. "Sir, you are not an authorized party to speak with—"

I looked at the princess and shook my head. "My name is Detective Inspector Knight, and I need to speak with Her Majesty's head of security."

The operator cleared her throat. "Of course, one moment."

It was a lot more than one moment before the captain answered, "Inspector Knight?"

I smiled as I looked at the princess. "Captain, I have the princess here. Would you let Her Majesty know she is safe. I would very much appreciate her guards—"

She cleared her throat. "I do not want all that attention and—"

I smiled and held up my hand. "Excuse me. When you send her guards, could you have them wear civilian clothes like an inspector? I will be calling the constable commissioner to get a few men until they get here. If you can ask Her Majesty for a moment so she and her daughter can talk?"

He sighed. "She was very worried. Give me a minute."

The princess went around my desk and checked one of the cups before she started to pour hot water to make tea. It was several minutes before the queen came on. "Inspector Knight?"

I smiled. "One moment, madam."

I held out the handset, and the princess leaned against the desk and accepted it. "I am fine, Mother."

I ignored her while they spoke and pulled out a standard form and started my report on the pickpocket. She grinned as she watched me and finally handed me the handset. I accepted it. "Madam?"

The queen chuckled. "Watch her. She came there to see and meet you. I believe your new house has a guest room?" I agreed, and she sighed. "Put her up, and her guards will be there tomorrow. Thank you, Ashton."

She disconnected, and the princess returned to her seat as I disconnected and then lifted the handset. "Mary, I need the constable commissioner."

I looked at the door as the lieutenant stepped in. The commissioner answered, and I held up my hand to the lieutenant. "This is Detective Inspector Knight, sir. Remember the visitor we had at the Gilbert House?"

He growled, "I am busy, Knight."

I waited, and he sighed. "Yes, I remember."

I nodded. "Her daughter is here now. Her...protectors have not arrived with her. I would like to ask Stern to help me and maybe get six street constables to assist."

He growled, "Use whatever you need."

I relaxed. "If you could stop by my house later, I should have more information."

He cleared his throat. "Your house...very well."

I disconnected and looked at the lieutenant smiling at the princess. "Sir?"

He blushed as he looked at me. "You have a case?"

I nodded. "If you need an inspector, call the chief of inspectors, and he will send someone."

He nodded and glanced at the princess. "I will."

He left, and I went back to work on the report. "It will only be a minute."

I called Stern, and luckily he was in and not busy. Next was a couple of calls to some sergeants. I stood when I was done and went to the gun cabinet in the corner. I took out my revolving shotgun and several cylinders. I put the single-point lanyard on and let it hang under my arm. "Ready?"

The princess set the teacup down. "I always wondered how the guards got the shotguns to hang like that."

I went to get her travel cloak and held it for her. I grabbed my long overcoat and put it on and slipped the extra cylinders into the pockets. I grabbed the umbrella and looked around the office before I stepped out. She held my arm again as we went down to the front desk. I grinned as Stern stepped in, looking wet. "You get the umbrella?"

He shook the water off his long coat while looking at the princess. "I flagged down a carriage."

I moved her hand on my arm and tossed the umbrella and went around the desk sergeant to get the two travel cases. "The other constables will meet us at my house."

When I turned and started carrying them, he shook his head and held out his arm. It was only a few steps to the carriage, and I went to the back and put the cases into the trunk. I told the driver the address and got in, and the driver started the horses moving.

I looked out at the street. "So why me?"

The princess smiled. "You have—character."

I snorted as Stern laughed, and she grinned. She held out her hand. "I am Catherine."

I took her fingers and bowed my head.

She looked out the window. "I also wanted to see what you do."

Stern shook his head. "That is not safe."

She smiled at him. "You could teach me. I was wondering why there were no female constables too."

I looked at Stern, and he sighed. "Being a constable is not safe and not for every man who wants to be one. There are requirements to be a constable, and women do not meet those requirements."

She lifted an eyebrow. "You might be surprised."

I smiled as I kept looking at the street, and Stern snorted. "No, I would not. I know women who would meet some or most. The problem is they need to meet them all. A constable must be able to fight and lift and carry a man. They must be able to use a knife, billy, pistol, rifle, or shotgun. Those are just the basics, and they have to be able to walk long distances every day."

I nodded. "And they must know something about the laws."

She sat back, and I could see her thinking about it.

When the carriage finally stopped, I stepped out and looked around before I gestured back inside. "Clear."

I waited and watched as Stern got out and then the princess, and he led her to my door. Once they went in, I went to get the travel cases and paid the driver. When I stepped into the house, she was looking around and grinned. "Neat and clean."

Stern laughed as he looked out the window, and I blushed. I moved to the stairs. "The spare room is upstairs."

I took her travel cases, and she followed and looked at the neat room. I left and went back downstairs and looked at Stern. "Her guards will be here tomorrow."

He nodded. "And what are we going to do…"

She cleared her throat as she came down the stairs. "Teach me to shoot?"

I frowned, and Stern was shaking his head. I finally shrugged. "Once the other constables get here."

I walked to a case against my living room wall and opened it. I looked at the dozens of weapons before I picked a Gem five-shot ten-millimeter pistol. I checked the draw and pulled out two spare cylinders and pouches for it and the holster.

I turned to the princess. "Madam."

She smiled as she crossed the room. "Catherine."

I looked at her clothes and turned her and took off the vest-like short jacket. I slipped the shoulder holster on and then pulled out a leather punch and cord. I cut out a section in the back strap and made holes before sewing it together. I adjusted it and then showed her how to load the cylinder and talked her through removing it to load the others.

I put the short jacket back on. "It will move around since there is no belt."

She kept checking the pistol until Stern cleared his throat. He gestured to the door, and I moved her behind me. He pulled the door open and six constables in civilian clothes stood on the porch. Each was carrying a bag and had a revolving shotgun in one hand.

He let them in, and I knew all of them and nodded. "This is Princess Catherine. We will be protecting her until her guards get here tomorrow."

Stern gestured to the side of my gun case. "Set your bags there and put the slings on the shotguns. Wear them under your long coat."

Five minutes, and we were stepping out and heading toward the city. I kept looking around as we walked and finally waved down a carriage. We crowded in with two men riding with the driver. The shop we went to sold pistols, rifles, and shotguns and had an indoor range to one side. I smiled at the old man behind the counter. "Jess, we need to use the range and borrow ear muffs, a revolving rifle, and shotgun."

He frowned as his eyes went to each of us and stopped on Catherine. They widened slightly before he bowed his head. "Of course."

To say we were a little surprised at her accuracy would be an understatement. She had a smile that seemed to brighten the room and infect everyone. Once she got the hang of changing the cylinders, she became faster. She enjoyed the rifle but not the shotgun; she did not like the kick or how loud it was. I showed her how to clean the weapons and paid Jess before we started to leave.

The rain had stopped, but it was still wet out. We stepped out the doors to see several men from a gang I knew. They had barely avoided the work farm a few months before. One saw me and growled to the others, and they all started for us. Stern moved forward with two of the constables as I pulled Catherine behind me. One man pulled out a thick club and another lifted a double-barrel shotgun and pointed it in our direction.

Stern shook his head. "You need to move along lads before you get in more trouble."

The leader sneered. "You reach for a weapon, and someone dies." His eyes went to mine. "We are going to teach you about street—"

I started to pull the shotgun when there was a shot from behind me. The man with the shotgun spun, and it went flying. We all lifted our shotguns, and the men froze as their faces went white. Stern gestured, and the two constables with him moved forward and yanked the men around and shoved them to the wall. They put restraints on, and I lowered my shotgun and looked at the pale princess.

I glanced around before I gestured. "Two of you take these in and do a report. We are going to Mrs. Johnson's and then the Pink Lotus."

I caught Catherine's hand and uncocked her pistol and put it back in her holster. I pulled her after me with the other constables around us. Down the street I led her into a bright shop and smiled at the older woman. "Mrs. Johnson, I need help."

She walked away from bolts of cloth. "With—"

Her eyes widened when she saw the princess, and I turned. "Catherine needs a suit. Think a white silk blouse with a pearl vest, a dove-gray coat, and long skirt; also she will need a gray long coat. The skirt needs loops for a belt, and she is going to need calf-length walking boots."

She snorted. "That is not what—"

I sighed. "Mrs. Johnson as much as I object, she wishes to step into our boots and learn what we do. To do that she needs to dress differently and more like us. The skirt and belt are to secure the holster with her weapon as well as restraints."

She looked at Catherine who was grinning again.

I glanced at Stern and the constables. "Two on the back door, and the rest watching this one."

I went to a chair to sit as Catherine and Mrs. Johnson went to the curtained booth. Stern sat in another chair. "You sure about this?"

I snorted. "No, but I needed to get her off the street before she fell apart." I looked at him. "Would you call the chief of inspectors and see if he has something easy?"

He grinned and then chuckled as the two constables by the door joined him. We waited and waited, and Stern returned and sat. "Pickpockets working the nobles' garment area."

I grinned. "Sounds easy."

More than once Mrs. Johnson or her husband had come or gone into the back. Finally, the princess walked out, and I stared before I stood. "Very nice."

I went closer and bent to lift the hem of her skirt to see the boots. "Treads on the soles?"

Mrs. Johnson snorted. "Of course."

I moved the coat to see the holster and pistol and checked it. I undid the belt and threaded the two cylinders on in front of the holster. I added my own restraint case in the small of her back and fastened the belt. "Now you are ready."

I called the men in the back and paid Mrs. Johnson who protested. I checked the time, and we headed to a restaurant called the Pink Lotus. The other two constables were there and waiting, and we sat to eat. When we finished it was time to take a carriage across the city to the nobles' garment area. Stern and I spoke with the constables who spread out a little.

We led the princess to the street constable who was walking around the corner. He glanced at my badge as I opened my coat and then answered our questions and gave us what he knew. I moved down the street to a shop while Stern and the others split up. I borrowed a ladies' bag and wallet from the shop owner and handed it to Catherine. "Carry it loosely and look in each and every shop window and take your time."

She nodded, and we left, and I moved away. I did not go far as she began to move down the street and gaze into shop windows. I watched the street and the windows and roof and slowly drifted after her. I saw the pickpocket a dozen minutes later. I kept searching and saw the lookout and the bank and another two who could be the distraction.

I was right as they started pushing each other and yelling. The princess turned to see what was happening just like everyone else. The pickpocket moved through the few watchers and paused at the bank. I started moving, and the other constables swept in. Stern and one constable caught the bank and pickpocket. Another constable caught the spotter, and two broke up the two boys creating the distraction.

Catherine looked surprised when she found the wallet missing. I led her to Stern and gave her a nudge. "Put the restraints on them."

They struggled and cursed, and Catherine grinned. I let the street constable return the borrowed ladies' handbag and wallet. Of course when we got to the station, I made the princess sit to write the report. Stern and the constables gave hints and facts until it was done. Instead of turning it over to the desk sergeant, I led her to the back hearing room.

The magister looked up as we stopped to one side and looked at each of us. "Yes?"

The princess blushed as she gave him the report, and he frowned. He read it and nodded. "Good job. I do not know why you brought it to me personally. Send them in, and I will listen to their plea."

I snorted. "This is Princess Catherine, and she wanted to see what we did."

He sat up and looked at her before bowing his head. "Your Highness."

I gestured. "Explain the next step in the process."

He did, and she listened and asked questions he answered. After that we led her back to the front, and I called the chief of detectives to give him a report. We left, and this time we caught a streetcar and rode it most of the way home. We walked the rest of the way, and I let Stern and the constables check the house. One watched out the front window, and one the back, while the rest relaxed.

Stern and Catherine sat in the kitchen while I made tea. I pulled out a few steaks and cut them up to make a stew. We listened to her talking about what happened and then explained what we look for and why. I made enough to feed everyone and half expected the princess to say something about the food. She did not and even seemed to enjoy it and talking with us and the constables.

The constable commissioner arrived and was let in. We were in the common room, and the princess was looking at all the weapons and asking questions. She was still holding a book on mage detection spells. She nodded to the commissioner when he bowed. "I am sorry to disrupt your city, Commissioner."

He grinned. "From what I heard you have already arrested a gang of breakers and another who were pickpockets."

She grinned. "More like I was along to watch and learn."

He chuckled. "Which is more than most nobles, my lady."

He spoke with Stern and nodded to me before leaving. As it grew dark, the rain started again and came down hard. That was good and bad, and I hoped the good would outweigh the bad. With the heavy rain, most people would not be out. I showed her to the upper bathroom and let her change and relax. When she went to bed, I leaned a chair against the wall and sat with the shotgun in my lap.

An hour later I heard her get out of bed. She opened the door and looked at me before she smiled. "That is not comfortable."

I smiled. "At least I am dry."

She left the door open and went to lie on the bed. She started talking softly, and I listened and answered when she asked questions. It was several hours before she became quiet, and I glanced in to see her asleep. In the morning we took turns washing and shaving. I dressed in a new suit and put on an old set of restraints. When the princess got up, I waited for her to wash and dress before we went downstairs.

She greeted everyone with a smile, and we had tea and pancakes Stern had made. The rain had stopped, but we kept our long coats on to hide the shotguns. We walked to the busier area of the city and caught a streetcar to my first station. I checked the time and led her into the briefing room. The sergeant was still there, but the street constables were already out.

I went over the warrant and watch boards with her and then went to the docks and shadowed two constables. I nodded and greeted people I had not seen in a while, and Catherine looked at me and then grinned. When I saw the dock-workers arguing, the street constables blew whistles. I hesitated before moving forward. "Stay behind me."

The two constables had moved between the two groups who kept pressing forward and shouting. I yanked several back and away until I was between the two dock-crew leaders. "Enough!"

They growled, and the princess cleared her throat. "Excuse me?"

They looked at her and snorted until she pulled the pistol. "I said excuse me. Now either shut up, or I will shoot you in the knee."

They shifted and looked at each other as I got ready to be attacked.

She smiled. "Much better. Now my name is Princess Catherine, and I am not too bad at negotiating. Tell me what this is about, and perhaps I can help."

They had gone from being reluctant and surly to amazed. They pulled caps off and bobbed their heads and looked at each other with red faces. Finally, the two dock-crew leaders started talking, and she listened and nodded. She put the weapon away and kept them talking and suggested a solution of switching shifts so both crews could see what the other did.

By the time we were done, a dozen street constables were to one side, watching. The princess went through both sides to shake hands. The dock-crew leaders were already whispering together before we left. I shook my head and looked at her. "Pulling a weapon in a crowd is a good way to get them to attack. Next time borrow a billy or just slap one of the leaders."

Everyone laughed, and she blushed and then grinned. "Yes, sir."

We caught several streetcars that took us to my station and found the royal guards waiting. The lieutenant was red faced when he walked to the princess. "Madam."

She blushed again. "Sorry." She looked around. "We need to find an estate. I plan to stay here for a few months."

I looked at Stern as the royal guards shifted. "The city clerk?" He nodded, and I turned. "Come along constable cadet."

The princess looked back and grinned as they started following. The city clerk did have a couple of estates that had been seized, but I saw a large manor listed that was not far from my house.

I touched it. "We need to go look at this one."

The manor was huge and furnished and even had gardens around the building. It had a small barrack-type building in the back with a stable and carriage house. It had high walls with only one large iron gate with two small gate houses. Catherine liked it, but I looked at the lieutenant, and he grinned. "It is secure."

A day, and her things were moved in. Somehow I found myself visiting her a lot after I finished for the day. She always made time or sometimes even tracked me down and walked with me. The nobles and city lords tried to draw her into their crowd, but she refused. I took her to the restaurants I had found that had good food. I also took her to plays and once to a farmers' fair.

# CHAPTER 18

# Blackmailed Nobles

I WOKE TO the dawn light in the window and looked at the young woman snuggled against me. I was not sure this had been a good idea. She rubbed my chest. "You need to go wash. I am sure someone needs your help."

I shifted and turned her and gave her a kiss. "Dismissing me?"

She smiled. "Want me to come with you?"

I grinned. "I would not mind, but your lieutenant might."

She giggled and rolled away and out of bed. "In that case come help me pick my uniform."

Her uniforms were a couple dozen sets of clothes made by Mrs. Johnson like the first. I looked out the window before following her. After that we went to wash, and I slipped out so her maid could come help. I dressed and left and went home to change. By the time I returned, Catherine and her guards were at the gate, waiting. We stopped at a small café not far away and had breakfast.

I had heard of a river race and asked her if she would like to see it. She blinked. "With yachts?"

I snorted. "Of course not. They push a pole through several barrels end to end. Most of the time, they paddle, but the fun is when they try to use a sail. The barrels can turn and roll, so it is not always easy staying on."

She grinned and then giggled. "Now that is something I want to see."

The lieutenant chuckled and nodded. "Me too."

We walked when we left, and I searched the street before I shifted and the guards moved. Catherine looked around. "What?"

It was one of the street gangs leaning against a building. Her eyes finally caught it, and she slowed and then grinned and started toward them. I sighed as I caught her arm, but she gestured. "Excuse me."

The young men looked at her and sneered.

She smiled and moved forward. "Have you heard of the river races?"

They looked at each other, and one straightened. "Yeah."

She nodded. "I am offering a purse of ten gold to the winner and the chance to become an officer in the army."

They looked at each other, and the speaker cleared his throat. "Why would we want to be in the army?"

I shook my head, but she looked at him from head to feet. "Have you seen their uniform or the ladies who chase after them? Do you know how much they make?" They all straightened, and she looked at them. "Tell you what. I will give you a gold crown to buy what you need for the race if you spread the word."

They grinned, and the speaker chuckled and held out his hand. "Deal."

She pulled out a gold coin and tossed it, and he snatched it out of the air. He looked at her. "How do we know you can get us in as an officer?"

She smiled sweetly as she turned and started walking. "I am the princess Catherine."

I glanced back to see the gang staring after her in shock. I grinned as I looked around. "Want to bet that gets spread around to every gang in the city and grows with the telling?"

We walked into the station, and I nodded to the desk sergeant as he stood and bowed. Catherine waved, and half the guards moved to the door into the back. We started up the stairs and found the lieutenant in the hall outside my office looking anxious. He saw me and relaxed and gestured. "Ashton."

When we reached the door, I looked in and saw the five duchy baronesses. They did not look happy as we came in and Catherine smiled. "Ladies."

I saw a package on my desk and went around and looked before I sat while Catherine went to make tea. I gestured to the ladies. "How can I help you?"

They looked at each other and then at the royal guards. One cleared her throat and looked at Catherine. "My lady, could you have your guards wait in the hall?"

She glanced at the lieutenant who was frowning. I sighed as I pulled my pistol and set it on the desk. "Go ahead, Lieutenant."

He glanced at the weapon before nodding and gesturing. They moved out, and Catherine came to lean on the desk. "Well?"

The same one who spoke before bent and pushed a note across the desk. Each of the others copied her, and I picked them up. Catherine tilted her head to read with me. They were almost exactly the same and demanded money, or they would tell a secret. I sat back and looked at the ladies. "So someone is blackmailing you. Was it a crime?"

They all reddened, and Baroness March cleared her throat. "Adultery."

I ignored Catherine as I nodded. "And that is all?"

I was watching all of them, and they each nodded. I turned to look out the window to think; adultery was a very minor crime and one the constables almost never enforced. I picked up the phone. "Mary, I need the city operator."

A moment later the operator answered, "How may I help you?"

I looked at the five noble ladies. "This is Detective Inspector Knight. I need to speak with Magister Green on her estate."

A male voice answered, "The Green estate."

I sat up. "This is Detective Inspector Knight. I need to speak with Magister Green."

A couple of minutes, and she said, "Inspector Knight?"

I smiled. "Madam, I find I need your counsel. I have five noble ladies who have admitted to adultery. They are being blackmailed, but before I can begin I...what type of sentence are they looking at?"

She sighed. "They have turned themselves in to you. I would be lenient and give them community service for a month."

I grinned. "Say promoting the city charity events?"

She chuckled. "That would qualify. Write it up and send it to me, and I will approve it. About the other matter, find the blackmailer and use the normal duty magister."

She hung up, and I set the handset down. "The magister has given you thirty days of community service promoting the city charity events. Now I can act without restraint."

I pushed a blank parchment across the desk. "I need the names of the gentlemen and the date and time and location of the—tryst."

They each took a turn writing until the last. I pulled the parchment back. "Now how did the blackmailer contact you?"

One had the note left on her desk in her study. Another had it slipped into her carriage. Two had a runner deliver it, and the last found it on her bed. The first and last told me a lot, and I stood and bowed. "I will find and catch whoever is doing this."

After they left I sat and pushed the package to Catherine before I lifted the parchment to read it. She grinned as she started unwrapping it. Two of the names had the same last name, and the other two had similar first names. The locations were all the same, and I shook my head. "Time to take a walk."

Catherine grinned as she held up a badge in a leather case. It was in the shape of an elongated shield with wings that grew out of the top and went around the sides and came together in a point at the bottom. In the center was the royal coat of arms. Above and below there was a scroll: the top read, "Inspector," and the bottom, "Catherine."

I put my weapon away and gestured. "It goes on your belt. Your mother approved it, so you are officially a knight inspector now."

I stopped to shut the burner off on the way out, and her guards fell in. The Gilbert House was not that far, so we walked. When we walked in, the manager hurried around the front desk. "Your Highness."

She smiled. "I am here working a case with Detective Inspector Knight."

He frowned as he slowed and looked at me. "How may I help?"

I gestured to one side, and we moved that way. I glanced around. "Someone who works here is either providing information or using it to blackmail some of your customers."

He reddened. "None...of—"

I held up a hand. "I know they have. Now if you like, I can have a magister issue a special warrant that will allow us to bring in a mage to—compel all of them to speak the truth. I am sure the city news will find out, and that will not be good for business."

His face went white, and he shifted and looked around. "The day porter Mr. Janis."

I looked around the large lobby. "And where is Mr. Janis now?"

He shook his head. "He has not come in this morning."

I sighed. "I will need his address."

He nodded and went to his office and returned a few moments later.

I accepted the paper and looked at the address. "Do not call him."

I glanced at the manager, and he shook his head. The address was to the northwest on the edge of the city. This time we caught a streetcar most of the way and then walked the three blocks. The house had three stories with outside stairs and wrapped-around porches. I checked the address before I started up to the third floor. I gestured Catherine back before I reached the door, and she stopped.

I knocked on the door. "Constable!"

I listened but did not hear anything and moved to the side and looked in a window.

I saw a body on the floor and moved back to the door and stepped back. "We have a body."

I kicked, the door crashed open, and I stepped in. The young man's head was bloody, and from the look of things, a club had been used. I pulled my weapon and carefully moved around the body and began to check the other rooms. When I returned, Catherine was in the doorway and had a white face. I stopped at a desk and looked at the few pieces of paper.

The writing did not match the writing on the blackmail notes. I squatted beside the body and looked at the wounds and the blood around him. "Whoever did this kept hitting him after he was down. It was not in defense and shows premeditation."

Catherine cleared her throat. "How do you know?"

I stood. "If it was anger or spur of the moment, the blows would be all over. From the look of things, these are all in the same area. Not only did they kill him but they also wanted it to take a while to find him. They used his key to lock the door when they left, and there was no blood outside, which means they cleaned up or changed."

I gestured her out and followed and started for the stairs. "We need to call for the constable doctor."

I used a corner call box and then returned to the room. A couple of minutes, and we had a street constable there, and fifteen minutes after that, the constable doctor arrived. I had the constable knock on all the doors to ask questions.

I was thinking and led Catherine out. "We have been assuming it was Mr. Janis, but there is another person who knew."

She looked at me as I turned and started for the stairs. "But he was the best."

I shook my head. "He was a puppet. I saw papers with his handwriting, and it was not even close to the notes."

She followed me down. "So where do we go now?"

I smiled. "Back to the Gilbert House. This time we will do what I should have done before. The ladies did not check in, which means the—gentleman did. That means we have a sample of his handwriting. We also have his description and where they met."

We walked back and caught another streetcar headed back into the city. She sighed. "This is not like I expected."

I glanced at her. "Being an inspector means solving puzzles and answering questions that are not asked."

Her guards chuckled, and she grinned. "So I need to start thinking."

I squeezed her hand. "You are always thinking. What you need to do is keep remembering all the facts of the case and think of questions they present. Why kill Mr. Janis? If he was not involved, what motive to kill him would they have? It could be someone else, but the blackmailer has been very methodical, and so was his killer."

She nodded and then smiled. "He saw the men with the ladies, so he knew what they looked like."

I glanced at her. "Remember the names they used?"

She looked at me, and then her eyes opened. "It could be one man."

I nodded. "Which means he was hunting the ladies and planned this."

When we walked into the Gilbert House, there were a few more people. I led the way to the desk and smiled at the clerk. "We need to see your guest book."

She stared at Catherine and quickly turned it and pushed it across. I checked the dates and the names where they had signed in.

I nodded when I saw the first. "Think of the notes and compare the writing to the way he signed his name."

Catherine looked and grinned. "So he is our blackmailer."

I checked each signature and closed the ledger and pushed it back across the desk. "Thank you."

We turned and moved away while I was thinking. I nodded to myself. "The Golden Crown."

Catherine looked at me. "You think he will be there?"

I started for the door. "We have three locations to check. They did not pay, which means he might be still hunting or looking for someone else. Since two of the ladies met him at the Golden Crown, that is our first stop."

The Golden Crown was a restaurant, but it was also a type of club for the wealthy. The doorman looked at me and then Catherine, and his eyes went wide. He stammered while trying to open the door wider. I stopped as I realized all the ladies would have left with the man, and the doorman would have seen. I glanced around before I gestured and opened my jacket to show my badge. "I have a few questions."

He glanced back and forth before nodding. "Anything, sir."

Catherine touched his hand. "I know you would never consider telling what you know, but we are looking for a murderer."

She told him the ladies' names and asked if he had seen them with the same man at any time. He looked around before he cleared his throat. "They did not leave together, Highness, but…I did see Mr. Glassglow meet with them and take a carriage."

She looked inside. "And is Mr. Glassglow here today?"

He nodded and turned, and I caught his arm before he could point. "Just tell us."

He swallowed. "He is the one in the far corner speaking with Baroness Bryan."

I let him go and started in and across the room. The man was speaking to a woman, but his eyes kept moving and stopped on us. He froze, and the baroness turned to see what he was looking at. We were almost to them when he moved and grabbed her while pulling a knife. He held it to her throat. "Stop, or I kill her!"

Everyone stopped talking and turned, and I shoved a couple of people out of the way. I pulled my weapon. "You are not going anywhere, so give up."

He shifted to the left while pulling her with him. "Get back, or she dies."

I shifted as I lifted my pistol. "Let her go."

He was slowly moving to the left while trying to keep her between us. I ignored Catherine as she slipped back. People were moving back as the man continued to move and I followed. He kept glancing left and jerking the woman back against him as she whimpered. He was almost to the door into the kitchen when Catherine extended her pistol and touched his head.

He froze as she cocked it, and I moved in and reached out and yanked the knife out of his hand. I dropped it and pulled the baroness away and then holstered my pistol. I grabbed him and spun him before I shoved him to the wall. I pulled an arm back as I pulled out restraints, and that was when he shifted and spun and lashed out. I slid to the side and caught the wrist and twisted it until his arm was locked.

I turned and brought the arm to my right, and he shifted and lifted a foot to kick. I yanked, and he staggered and almost fell before I slammed him face first into the wall. I twisted his arm the other way until it was behind his back. I pulled it up, and he screamed and went to his toes. Catherine caught his other hand and locked a set of restraints on.

She twisted it behind his back, and I brought his other hand down. I held his arm while she locked the restraint on his other wrist and then I began to search him. I found two keys, one with spots of dried blood on it, and turned to push him toward the door. "You are under arrest for murder and five charges of blackmail."

He struggled all the way back to the station. With the blood on the key, I asked the magister for permission to question him with a mage using a truth spell. With that we got his confession of killing Mr. Janis and blackmailing the baronesses. The magister looked at me over that, and I nodded. "Magister Green has already heard the case and issued her findings."

He nodded and turned back to Mr. Kennsaw, which was his real name. He was sentenced to hang for the murder and would have gotten fifteen to twenty years for the blackmail. We returned to my office, and I let Catherine help write the report. She also sent a runner to the baronesses to let them know we caught the man. We left early and headed to an eatery she liked.

The river race had hundreds of entries, and the shore was packed thanks to the baronesses. The purse had also grown much larger, and street vendors were making a lot of money. Even the city rich and the nobles were there. It was like a fair or festival, and more than one street-gang member had stopped to bow to Catherine. There were two categories for the race now, paddle and sail.

Photos were taken during the races while people yelled and laughed as barrels rolled and men fell into the river. With two categories there were two winners, and Catherine presented ribbons and a purse to both. I was not surprised they were both from a gang. True to her word, she had a colonel from the army there and a navy captain.

The winners were given a choice of service and commission; she even got the second- and third-place winners in. Even after the races were over, the people stayed and enjoyed the day beside the river. The whole city seemed to brighten and enjoy the celebration and the afterglow that stayed for days.

# CHAPTER 19

# Smugglers

THE NEW SUIT had been expensive, and I was more than a little nervous as I moved through the dance with Catherine. I knew many of the nobles who were here now and a lot of the wealthy merchants. When the music stopped, Catherine sighed and lifted her head from my shoulder. I led her off the dance floor and to our table. The duke for the territory smiled and leaned away from his wife. "You move well, Inspector."

I held Catherine's chair as she sat. "Since Catherine has been teaching me, she gets the credit."

He grinned as his wife laughed, and Catherine squeezed my hand. The ball was almost over, and it was late. I was trying to think of a way for us to leave. The duke leaned toward me as I sat. "I was going to see the constable commissioner about an issue. Perhaps I could come by and speak to you tomorrow?"

I nodded. "Of course."

Catherine stretched and finished her drink. "It is late, and tomorrow is not far off. I think it is time we leave."

The duke was quick to stand with his wife as I came to my feet. It still took several minutes to get out of the manor and into her carriage.

Once we were moving, she shook her head. "Another nosy noble who will tell you to stay away from me."

I smiled. "That is for you to say."

She smiled as she squeezed my hand. "Tell him Mother has given you her support."

I grinned and kept watching the street. "You are taking the train tomorrow morning?"

She sighed and nodded. "It is only for a week, and then I will be back."

We turned in at her manor, and she glanced at me. "Stay the night?"

I ignored the guards and her lieutenant. "Only if you leave a note for your maid not to walk in on us."

She laughed, and I heard the guards chuckling. I smiled and squeezed her hand as the carriage stopped. "I am going to miss you."

Our morning was rushed as she got ready to leave and I pulled out a set of clothes. I had learned to keep a set here in case I stayed over. I went to the train station with her to see her off before I walked back to my station and office. I started heating water and reviewing a few cases of constable-abuse reports. Most would be unfounded and from a criminal they had arrested, but a couple could be excess use of force.

I glanced up when the duke stepped in and stood. "Your Grace." I moved to the hot water. "Tea?"

He nodded as he sat in front of my desk. I made his tea and set it on the edge of my desk. I was ready for his speech or order, but he sighed and picked up the tea. "We have a problem. I have spoken to the constable commissioner this morning, and he agreed to let me use you."

He took a sip and sat back.

"Normally this would be a job for the imperial customs inspectors, but I do not think it is happening at the docks."

I blinked. "What is happening?"

His face reddened. "Sorry. We have been getting a lot of reports of merchandise smuggled into the duchy. Merchandise that has not been taxed or inspected."

I nodded as I thought of places smugglers could use. The last place they had been was no longer available. I sat back and turned to look out my window. "Smugglers—if you are getting reports, that means it is not small items slipped in."

I stood and went to look at the city map beside the door.

"Across the river was the last place, but the flying squad are constantly checking the coast now."

My eyes went to the east edge of the city and the swampy area beyond the few isolated estates. I touched one estate I knew had been empty and abandoned for at least a decade due to tidal flooding.

"I have a few ideas on where they could be bringing them in."

I looked at the other side of the swampy area where a ship might unload.

I turned and smiled. "I will look into it, sir."

He stood and set the teacup on the desk. "Thank you, Inspector."

After he left I looked at the map again before I cleaned cups and hesitated. If I was going into those areas, I wanted something with more range and went to the gun cabinet. I grabbed my revolving rifle and a few extra cylinders. I left a message on where I was going with the desk sergeant before I left and took a streetcar. It got me to the edge of the city, and I walked from there.

The roads were a little overgrown, but I saw a lot of signs of recent wagon traffic. I slowed when I got close to the estate I was looking for. The gates were closed, and the bars rusty, but I could see someone had oiled the hinges. I moved to the side and climbed the wall before looking at the manor. I dropped and shifted the rifle as I began to walk.

I glanced at the drive to see a lot of wagon tracks. When I reached the manor, I tried the front door, and it opened. I stepped in and looked at the large entrance hall. There were crates stacked around the room and in the great room beyond I could see more. I went down the hall to the rear of the manor. In the kitchen the stove was rusty and unused.

Through the kitchen window, I could see a wide path someone had made to a dock going out into the swampy flood plain. I moved to the door and had to force it open. I stepped out and looked at the estate stable and carriage house. Six large wagons were parked behind it, and I could see draft horses in the corral. I had seen enough and turned to go back through the manor.

As I stepped in, I heard a man shout from the stable. There was a shot, and the bullet struck the doorframe. I spun and lifted the rifle as I knelt and aimed. The man fired again, but it was high and wide, and I squeezed the trigger. My bullet struck him in the chest, and he staggered and went to his knees. I cocked the rifle and came to my feet to go to him when a dozen men ran out of the stable.

They were all carrying revolving rifles, and I spun and ran into the house. I ran to the other door into the kitchen and turned and knelt as I aimed at the open back door. I did not have to wait long as the men reached the porch and started to run in. They were still carrying rifles, and I did not hesitate. "Constable!"

I fired into the chest of the first and cocked the rifle again as he staggered and fell. The others tried to stop and back out, and one fired into the floor while lifting his rifle. I fired into the next man and shifted to the one beside him to shoot him too. They both went down as the rest finally got out the door. I spun and ran toward the front of the house.

I heard someone kick open the door and changed hands on the rifle and pulled my pistol. I brought it up as I reached the entrance hall and fired into the men in the door. I kept thumbing the hammer and firing as they went down. I crashed into the last two, and shot one in the belly and shouldered the other into the wall. I ran for the gate and shoved my pistol into the holster.

I was almost to the gate when they began to fire at me. I ignored the gate and angled to the wall and leaped. I caught the top and pulled and swung up and rolled over. I dropped to the ground on the other side and knelt while changing the cylinder on the rifle and then the pistol. I moved to the gate and peeked and yanked back as several men fired.

I turned and came to my feet and began to trot down and across the road. I did not go far and stopped at a small group of trees. I knelt behind one and aimed back at the gate. When the smugglers came out searching for me with their rifles up, I fired and one went down. The others spun and ran back through the gate, and I nodded. "Two can play this game."

I knew sooner or later someone in another estate would report the shots and constables would come. I watched the gate and shifted to keep an eye on the wall. Four men came over the wall almost straight across from me. I did not give them a chance to use the rifles and shot one in the chest and a second in the gut. The last two dived for the ditch on the other side of the road.

I managed to cock and fire and shot one through the body. The other was out of sight, and I shifted as three men ran out the gate again. I aimed and fired, and one went down, and the other two ran back in. I spun as the man across the road and in the ditch rose up with his rifle. I saw the muzzle flash and felt the burning pain as the round went through my right thigh.

I aimed and fired into his chest, and he went down. I stood and limped across the road while looking at the gate. I stopped at each of the four men and took their rifles. One was still writhing around and screaming as I went back across the road to the trees. I checked the rifles and knelt slowly and leaned them against a tree. I changed the cylinder in my rifle and waited and watched.

I saw the head and shoulders of a man peek over the wall by the gate. I shifted and aimed as he brought his rifle up and pointed. I fired, and he jerked and fell, and I heard a few men cursing. I heard horses and the jangle of a harness and the sound of wheels and the creak of a wagon. When I glanced back down the road, I saw two constables on horses trotting toward me.

I stood and moved into the road. "Constables!"

I started limping and kept my rifle up and ready. A team of horses ran out the gate pulling a wagon. It turned the other way while several men bounced around in the wagon bed.

I aimed but did not have a shot and limped to the gate faster. "Stop!" The two constables on horses reached me, and I growled and gestured, "Go catch them but be careful—they are armed."

They had their rifles in hand and nodded as they kicked their horses into a run.

When I reached the gate, I saw another wagon heading toward the road and aimed at the driver. He yanked back on the reins and lifted his hands, and the men in the wagon bed rose up slowly. They copied the driver, and I gestured. "Out of the wagon and lie on the ground."

I heard a shot from the road and had to hope the constables were okay. I watched the house and the sides as the men climbed out of the wagon and lay down beside the drive. I moved to each to take weapons and then backed away. It was ten minutes before the other wagon was led through the gates. The constables had the men walking in line behind it.

They looked sullen, and I gestured to the men on the ground. "Take these."

I started limping toward the house and shifted the rifle and pulled my pistol. I searched the house and then moved to the stable. It looked like the men were using it as a large bunkhouse.

When I returned to the front, another two constables were there. I showed them my badge. "One of you go call for a couple of wagons and the doctor. Someone else go down the road to see if the man I wounded is still alive."

I looked at the men.

"Who wants sixty days instead of twenty years on a work farm?"

They shifted but did not speak, and I nodded.

"Very well."

I looked at the constables.

"Charge them with smuggling and attempted murder of a constable. The magister can decide if they spend the next twenty years in the mines or on a work farm."

The men protested, but the constables had played this game before. They growled and cuffed them, "Quiet!"

One shifted and cleared his throat. "I will talk."

The others growled and turned on him, but the two constables shoved them against the wagon and pulled the one who had spoken out. I pulled him to the road and turned him. "It better be good."

He licked his lips. "Luke Clayton is a merchant broker. He gets the orders from other merchants who have no idea how we are bringing the stuff in. That way he can mark it up and make more money. Once he has the order, we take the merchandise to the merchant's warehouse and let them ship it elsewhere."

I nodded. "You will have to tell this to a magister under a truth spell."

He nodded. "I have a family and—"

I shook my head. "And could have lost them doing this."

He reddened and looked down. "Aye."

Thirty minutes, and I had a dozen constables with a sergeant, two prisoner wagons, the doctor, and an ambulance. Luckily for me the bullet had gone through, and the doctor only had to sew it up and give me a very large shot. I left the prisoners to the constables and sent the one who was going to give testimony back. I borrowed one of the horses and rode to the closest station.

I had the horse sent back to his rider and got a carriage into the city. The office for Luke Clayton was only a couple of buildings down from the commissioner's. I contacted a magister and got a warrant and brought a couple of street constables with me. When we walked off the stairs, three men in the lobby of a large corner office were waiting. They were holding revolving shotguns, and I lifted my rifle and aimed.

We were still at the stairs and not close to the men. "Put the weapons down!"

The constables had moved to the side and pulled their pistols. The men looked like they were still trying to decide, and I cocked the rifle. That was enough, and they quickly knelt and set the shotguns on the floor. I moved forward with the constables who put them in restraints. I lowered the hammer and slung the rifle and pulled my pistol.

I was not going to take chances and walked to the door and opened it. Several men turned, and one shifted toward his desk. I lifted the pistol as I moved toward them. "Constables! Stay where you are."

Of course the merchants who had been with Mr. Clayton denied knowing anything about the smuggling. Mr. Clayton tried to claim the same thing until he found out one of the men was talking to a magister under a truth spell. Then he was trying to say we had no authority over him because he was not a citizen of the duchy or kingdom.

With a constable being wounded and all the men I had to shoot, the magister was not going to be lenient. Mr. Clayton got life in the mines, and the men still alive got twenty years on a work farm. The one who had testified got sixty days but was put on notice. If he was caught breaking the law again, he would join the other men. The customs coastal patrol caught two ships at a new set of docks on the other side of the tidal swamp.

The duke was extremely grateful I found the smugglers so fast. Of course not everyone was happy: Catherine was upset that I had been shot. She even returned a couple of days early to help me recover.

# CHAPTER 20

# Home Invasions

SINCE MY SMUGGLER case, Catherine and her guards had been with me almost every day. She had been very protective, and more than once she had actually pulled her pistol. Of course the other side of the coin was that she made me exercise to strengthen my leg. That had led to evening walks and a more physical love life. There had also been a lot more parties with dancing.

Plus I had almost three dozen internal cases of excessive force I had to finish. Those were simple really and only involved speaking with the constables and the suspect. A few constables were not happy with the reprimand, but the constable commissioner and their commanders were. Unless the excessive force was extreme or prior to the suspect's crime, they were still sentenced according to their crime.

I hated all the paperwork involved in the internal cases and the number of people it had to go to. Catherine was as confused as I was. For example, in one case I had to send a copy of the report to the constable, to his sergeant, to his shift lieutenant, to his station commander, and to a magister. Plus I still had to send a copy to the constable commissioner and all with copies of the witness and constable statements.

The monthly meeting of inspectors with the chief of inspectors was more subdued because Catherine was there, but she brought up a few things. Like why did we have to write multiply copies of reports instead of using a courier to send the report and have it signed for. If they wanted a copy, they could write it themselves since inspectors had better things to do then spend a day writing.

Why did we go to isolated places alone instead of contacting the nearest station and arranging a constable just in case we needed help? Why did we not send out a summery of cases to all inspectors in case they had one that was similar. That happened several times, and neither inspector knew the other case was part of what he was working on. The last thing she brought up was weekly or monthly weapons practice.

Many constables and even inspectors rarely used their weapons and needed to remain capable. This was something she had brought up when she went home, and her mother agreed. She was slowly adding shooting ranges for the constables in each city. The meeting took a little longer than normal, but I felt we had accomplished something.

All her attention on and for me made me think about her, and I more than enjoyed her company and missed her if she were not there. The thing I worried about was the fact that I was a commoner. She did not seem to let it bother her, and the nobles here had finally stopped making veiled threats or remarks. The rich merchants on the other hand thought I was their way in to sell Catherine something.

It was the end of fall and had rained for several days. We went out to my old estate that I had given to Harris and Mrs. Miller. It was changed a little more, but we were here for a celebration. They were expecting a child, and Harris was more than happy. There were three dozen constables and half as many inspectors and detective inspectors.

I had spent most of my savings on a set of very old rings for Catherine and proposed the night before. She was clinging to my arm when we got out of the carriage. She waved Harris and the others up when they started to bow. "None of that here."

I started to lead her to the manor, and everyone fell in, and Harris cleared his throat. "Um…the party is around back."

Catherine grinned as we turned. "So, Constable. Are you ready for a child? Ashton says your wife has a son, but this is your first."

He grinned. "Yes and no. Raising a child is not hard. It is raising a baby that is hard and something I have never done." He shuddered. "Dirty diapers and everything else that comes out. They start out eating, pooping, and sleeping, and sometimes all at once."

Everyone laughed, and Catherine with them. "Very true."

The women stood, and Catherine let my arm go and started toward them.

"Ladies. What are these beasts having us make?"

I grinned as she switched sides in a blink and headed for a wooden bench.

"So who brought the cards, and where is the cider?"

It was a very nice party and almost over when Stern leaned away from his woman and whispered, "Is that an engagement ring Her Highness is wearing?"

I glanced around before answering, "Yes, and do not say anything. She has not spoken with her mother."

He grinned. "I hope you spoke with her father first."

I blinked and then blushed. "No, but as soon as I get home, I will."

He laughed, and we both looked at the messenger who arrived. He looked at everyone. "Detective Inspector?"

When a dozen lifted their hands, he reddened.

"Detective Inspector Knight?"

I sighed and stood. "That would be me."

He moved to me while pulling off a satchel. "It is from the chief of inspectors and the constable commissioner."

I opened it and pulled out a couple of folders and glanced at the reports inside. It was not pretty, and I nodded and turned. "I have to leave. Congratulations, and I hope it is a girl."

Everyone laughed as I grinned and turned to leave. Catherine hurried to catch up. "Ashton, wait for me."

I sighed. "This case is very dangerous and gruesome."

She caught my arm while her guards appeared. "Partners, Ashton."

I shook my head as I started walking again. "Have your guards get the shotguns out from under the carriage seat. You do what I say when I say it. No going off on your own or getting in front of me. I go though the doors first, and you will listen to the lieutenant."

She grinned. "Of course."

I snorted as we reached the carriage. "That is not what I heard."

The lieutenant chuckled as he opened the door and climbed in. He lifted one seat and began handing out revolving shotguns and belts with cylinder cases on them. I gave the driver the address, and finally we were in and moving, and Catherine looked at me. "So?"

I looked out the window. "So someone or a gang of *someones* is invading homes. They are very violent, and eight people are dead so far. They have robbed three homes and raped four women." She growled, and I nodded. "Exactly."

The house was a manor with no yard, wall, or even a fence. Steps led straight from the street to the door, and we stopped behind the constable doctor's wagon. I let the lieutenant and his men get out before I followed. I was waiting for the lieutenant to give the all clear, and Catherine got out. She walked with me, and I nodded to the constable at the door as the guards peeled off.

He cleared his throat. "The lady might want to wait out here."

Catherine smiled as she moved her coat to show her badge. The constable stared and looked at me, and I shrugged. "She is a knight inspector."

I went in with her following but stopped to look at the door carefully.

From the look of things, it had been kicked in. "Constable, could you call for Constable Mage Norris?"

He nodded when I looked at him. "Yes, sir."

I turned and started toward the large common area where I saw the doctor. "Hopefully Norris can get something from the footprint on the door."

Catherine cleared her throat. "The footprint? They can really do that?"

I smiled and nodded to the doctor. "Constable mages are different than other types of mages."

The doctor's helper looked at Catherine, but I gestured, and he bent to pull the sheet back on the first victim. Her clothes were torn and disheveled, and I squatted to lift it more to look lower. I saw her dress pulled up and signs she had been assaulted. I dropped the sheet. "Leave her for now. I want Norris to do a spell."

I moved up to look at the brutal wounds on her face and head.

"Most of these were after she was dead?"

The doctor nodded and gestured to another sheet-covered body.

The helper lifted it, and I bent to look and shook my head. "It looks like a club or some type of bar."

I straightened and looked around before I began to search the house. Catherine watched and followed in my footsteps. Mostly what the thieves took was jewelry and silver. I marked a couple of places, and we came back to the entrance. The lieutenant was talking to Norris, who smiled when he saw me. I gestured, and the lieutenant allowed Norris to come in.

I led him through the house and pointed out what I needed him the do. At the door Catherine cleared her throat as he used chalk to mark the print. "What can you do with a footprint?"

He smiled as he kept working. "Besides telling what size the foot is? I can find out what type of soil was on the shoe or boot. That can sometimes tell us where it came from. Like the river or the farms or even the center of the city."

She grinned. "That makes sense."

I was sitting on the stairs while she followed him and watched. I read all the files and tried to create a map of each location that had been robbed. I knew Norris would be able to create an image of the man or men who had raped the woman. From the list of things stolen at all the homes I knew they would be using a fence for the jewelry if not the silver.

I pulled my notebook and made some notes and stood when Norris returned. He handed me a small crystal orb with the image of two men in it. Catherine looked over my shoulder. "What are we going to do with this?"

I smiled and nodded to Norris. "Thanks. Anything on the footprint?"

He nodded. "The soil was from the west area of the city. Probably on the edge of the business district." He glanced into the common area. "The weapon was the handle of a sledge hammer." He hesitated, "There were slight traces of coal and steel with a hint of a train."

I straightened. "Train? That narrows it down."

He nodded and headed for the door. "Be careful, Ashton, and make sure these bastards are caught soon."

I followed him out with Catherine behind me. I glanced at the lieutenant. "We are going to the train yard."

He nodded, and I took Catherine's hand, and we went to the carriage. I was thinking as we rode and studied the two images in the crystal. The men were workers from the evidence and without mercy. If the jewelry and silver was not turning up in the city, it was being taken somewhere else. The trains could explain where and how, so at least one was traveling on the trains.

The carriage stopped next to the yard office, and the lieutenant got out. I followed and stood looking around at the few men I could see. When Catherine stepped out, we headed for the office. The lieutenant looked in first and stood aside. I walked in and nodded to the two women at desks as I showed my badge. "Detective Inspector Knight. I need to see the yard manager."

One cleared her throat and looked at the door to another officer. "He is in his office, Inspector."

Catherine followed as I crossed the room and knocked before I opened the door. A slightly balding man looked up from the papers on his deck. "Yes?"

I showed my badge again. "Detective Inspector Knight. I was hoping you might help me."

He sat up and gestured, and I crossed to the desk. I held out the crystal so he could see. "Do you know these men?"

He leaned forward and peered at the crystal before nodding. "One is Henry Adarson, and the other is Malcom Dean. They are workers in the repair yard. What have they done?"

I put the crystal away. "Rape and murder."

He was shaking his head as I turned and started for the door.

I stopped before I reached it and turned. "Are they friends with any of the conductors or car breakers?"

Breakers were a type of security who rode the trains and made checks to keep men from sneaking aboard. He shook his head. "Not that I know."

I nodded and left, and when I stepped out, I looked at the lieutenant and showed him and the other guards the images. From my time in the yard guarding the silver train, I knew where to go. I led the way through the yard and across several sets of tracks to a tall and very long building. We heard the men working before we saw them.

They were to one side working on the undercarriage of a train car. The supervisor turned as we approached and opened his mouth, but the two men I was after spun and started to run. I pulled my pistol and fired into the ground. "Constables!"

They stopped and shoved their hands into the air as I walked to them. I yanked the first man's hands behind his back and started to put restraints on him. Catherine had followed and was reaching for the other when he spun. He was reaching for her when she cocked the hammer on her pistol and fired. He screamed as he folded and fell to the ground.

The other man yelled, and I yanked up on his wrists. "Do not move."

Catherine knelt and shoved the man onto his stomach. "You will not need those anymore."

She yanked and pulled his arms back and put him in restraints. I sighed as the lieutenant bent to roll the man over. "Did you have to shoot him there?"

She smiled as she stood. "I thought it was a good place. He will not need them, and he will live to hang."

I shook my head and looked at the lieutenant. "Would you send for the constable doctor?"

He grinned. "Of course."

The other man gave up a breaker who was taking what they stole to other cities to sell. Both men were sentenced to one hundred lashes and then to hang. The breaker was caught in another city and sent back to join them a week later. I took Catherine with me to inform the families of those murdered that the men responsible had been caught.

That evening I made a call to the queen's consort. I was very nervous, but he sounded calm and even cheerful when he gave his consent and support. Then Catherine and I spoke with her mother, who sounded very happy. Of course we spent an hour talking and discussing dates and appointments. Following that I had to take a leave to go to the capital with Catherine for the formal announcement.

She was already planning two parties, one in the capital and the other when we got back with the constables.

CHAPTER 21

# Random Killers

THE LAST MONTH had been filled with evening parties. I also had a dozen visits from nobles to invite me into their private club or circle or—those I always gave to Catherine's lieutenant to check. I or we had also spent a week on a train, visiting major cities in other duchies to greet and let the people see us. There was only one incident, and the baron who made the threat was very drunk.

I refused to attend separate parties or functions without Catherine. I did attend a few meetings with her and sat reading a paper to one side while she spoke or heard issues. Mrs. Johnson had been very busy making new clothes for her, almost all that would conceal the pistol she wore. Finally, Catherine had invited every constable in the city to her manor for our party.

It started at nine o'clock in the morning and went to nine o'clock that night, so men from every shift had time to come. And they did, at any one time, there were several hundred men. Most were armed, which made the lieutenant and his people very nervous. Of course, the fact that every man who came would have thrown himself in front of a bullet for the princess helped.

There was also a minor rash of thefts on the docks. Most were single kegs of whiskey or rum. There were also a few cases of tobacco from the south stolen. I got to watch Catherine work the case and advised her only if she asked. She did not do bad, and we caught the six lads who had been responsible. I did not tell her the street constables had already solved it a few hours before.

I turned to look at the new suit in the full-length mirror, and Catherine chuckled. "Not bad."

I nodded. "Mrs. Lee has been my tailor since I became a constable."

I pulled my wallet and moved to Mrs. Lee. "You can make the other suits in a week?"

She smiled. "Of course. I even have silk for the shirts."

I paid her. "You are a lifesaver."

Catherine glanced at her lieutenant. "Your men could use a few new suits, Lieutenant."

He grinned. "We are on a budget, Your Highness."

She snorted and looked at Mrs. Lee. "Could you do something with them if I paid?"

Her eyes brightened. "Yes, Your Highness."

Catherine grinned as she slipped her arm around mine. "Send your men to see her when they have time, Lieutenant. I will stop to withdraw money today, and she can let me know when she needs more."

Mrs. Lee bowed, and we started for the door. Outside she glanced at the guards. "You men really do need new suits. Get the silk shirts; they feel better and are more comfortable."

They chuckled as we got into her carriage. When we walked into the station, it was chaos. People were yelling, and more than one news person was demanding answers. The desk sergeant was trying to restore order, and a couple of constables were trying to help. I caught one of the constables. "What happened?"

He growled, "Two men pulled weapons just down the block and shot a couple."

I stiffened. "Did we catch them?"

He shook his head. "They slipped through when everyone panicked and ran."

I got the location and turned, and we left. The doctor was still with bodies when we got there. He pulled the sheet back on the man when I squatted and examined the wound. Catherine was beside me and cleared her throat. "Explain what you see?"

The doctor glanced at her, but I ignored it. "See the black powder all around the wound and how the edges are burned?"

She nodded, and I touched the suit collar.

"The gun was only a foot away when fired. Look at the size of the hole."

She bent and then straightened. "So?"

I smiled. "A normal handgun is ten to twelve millimeters, but the entrance wound is much larger. It could have been a small shotgun using solid slugs or one of the old dueling pistols. They use sixteen-millimeter bullets."

She looked at me as I stood and moved to the woman. "A dueling pistol?"

I squatted and moved the sheet to look at the wound on the back of her head. "There is a market for them. Lately companies have been making a lot of replicas. They are cheap, and people mainly use them as decoration, which is dumb."

I dropped the sheet and stood.

"I will need the bullets, Doctor."

He nodded as he stood, and I slowly turned and looked around. Besides the ducal exchange bank, there were several of the larger merchant offices. Just down the street was the mint, and I saw the commerce-exchange building on a corner.

I glanced at the street constable keeping the crowd back. "Did we get a description?"

He snorted. "Two short, tall, skinny, fat men with black, brown, blond hair and a shaven, beard, and mustache."

Catherine grinned, and I nodded since I half expected that. I turned and gestured, and Catherine and her guards fell in as I headed back to the station. She looked at me. "What are you going to do?"

I sighed. "Make a lot of calls. First to the paper."

She kept looking at me, and I smiled.

"People do not use decorations they have on their wall. I will see if there have been any recent dueling pistols sold or estate sales. I will have to contact the solicitor for information about the pistols."

After a dozen calls and three sheets of paper used as notes, I had a name or alias. A cased pair of engraved dueling pistols had been sold at an estate sale three days before. I stood as the station runner peeked in. He cleared his throat. "There has been another random shooting."

Two minutes, and I looked down at the two bodies of a baron and a rich merchant. They had been on the way into the station from the commerce exchange. Both had been shot in the head from behind at close range. I turned and looked across the street at the exchange and then at the much smaller crowds on the street. Constable Mage Norris arrived with two more detective inspectors.

I nodded to the other inspectors and looked at Norris. "You are going to think I am crazy."

He grinned as Catherine snorted. "I already know you are crazy, Ashton."

I smiled and nodded to the bodies. "Can you remove and re-form the bullets and get a resonance match with the weapons used?"

He blinked and rubbed his chin while the two inspectors squatted to examine the wounds. "It is possible, but I would need the weapon to make sure of the match."

Catherine sucked in a breath, and I cleared my throat. "Once you do the resonance, can you use it to do a finder spell?"

The two inspectors looked up, and he grinned. "Of course, but the magister might say we need a warrant."

I snorted. "Let me worry about the magister."

I turned and gestured to Catherine and the lieutenant and walked into the train station and to the station master's office. I smiled at the assistant and used the call box. When we walked back out, Norris had the two bullets on two white linen kerchiefs. The two inspectors were looking at him, but I was watching the street. Down by the ducal exchange bank, two men were loitering, but I saw the way they kept looking at us.

Norris finished and looked up and then turned, and I saw the waist of both men begin to glow. I started running, and they spun and ran into an alley on the other side of the bank. When I reached the alley and ran in, they were gone, but I saw the two pistols halfway down the alley. They were still glowing as I slowed to a walk and cursed.

Street constables ran in behind me, and I turned. "Put out an all-station wanted notice. Two white men, one average height with short brown hair wearing a dark long coat and black trousers. The other is above average with light hair, a short brown jacket, and dark-blue pants. Both are wanted for questioning in four murders."

Catherine appeared and slowed as her guards looked around with their shotguns out and ready. She glared at me. "Ashton Knight!"

I grinned as the two inspectors who were following her laughed. "Catherine Elizabeth Marie?"

She strode toward me. "You were just shot, and now you are chasing killers into an alley."

I caressed her face. "I am a constable, and that is what we do. You know what I am, and I am more dangerous than two cowards."

I turned as she sighed and looked at Norris as he arrived.

"Now we have the weapons. Can you do a trace spell on them to find the men who were using them?"

He grinned as he continued down the alley. "Yes, and you will not even need to ask a magister."

I nodded and looked at the two inspectors. "I think this has a purpose. The first killing was in front of the ducal exchange bank, and the second across from the commerce exchange."

They nodded, and I gestured to the mouth of the alley. "They were in front of the ducal exchange bank."

Their eyes widened, and Catherine cleared her throat. "I do not understand."

I caught her hand. "That is because you do not think like a criminal. I think they were trying to clear the street. When the escort from the commerce exchange takes the day's trade currency to the bank, they will have a clear street to shoot them, take the money, and escape."

I grinned at the constables around us. "We need a few men to volunteer."

The two inspectors went with Norris to try to follow the trace. I sent two constables to get body armor and street clothes. I led Catherine and her guards to the commerce exchange and went in to speak with the exchange manager. We arranged for the constables to take the place of his guards and for the day's currency to be held. We would replace it in the normal escort bags with paper.

I called the station to get a few street constables with rifles into the other buildings using the back doors. Catherine and I ate in the train-station café with her guards and made room in the unclaimed-baggage storeroom. Word of the four killings had the streets almost empty. By the end of business, people were hurrying to leave and constantly looking around.

Through a hole in the wall, I saw the six men who appeared and spread out. They were wearing long coats and began to loiter, but I could see them watching the commerce exchange. Under the bottom edge of the long coats were rifle or shotgun barrels. I nodded and looked at the lieutenant. "Six men in long coats, and they have long guns."

He nodded, and I looked at Catherine.

"You do not come out until it is clear."

She frowned, but I did not look away until she nodded. I checked my pocket watch and turned to leave. I pulled my weapon and held it down beside my leg as I walked out. I went out the side door and checked both ways before I moved toward the backs of two of the men. Before I reached them, the two constables in the commerce exchange stepped out.

They looked both ways before starting toward the ducal bank. All six men began to move, and the hidden rifles came out. Unfortunately for them all the constables in the other building emerged. As the two in front of me lifted their rifles, I lifted my pistol and cocked it. They froze and shifted, and I growled as I moved closer, "Move, and this is where you die."

The lieutenant appeared a moment later as I touched one of the men in the head with the barrel of my weapon.

"Squat and set the rifle on the ground."

All the other men were kneeling or lying on the street while constables put them in restraints. I waited as the lieutenant made the other man kneel and then put my weapon away.

Catherine appeared as I yanked the first man's hands behind him and put him into the restraints. She did the same to the second man, and I pulled the first up and turned him. "Which one of you killed the four people?"

He glared but kept his mouth closed. I searched him and took the two pistols he was wearing. Catherine searched the other man and handed the weapons to one of her guards. I turned and looked down the side street to see the two detective inspectors with two prisoners. They were also leading eight horses—well, Norris was walking and talking to the horses around him.

I grinned and then nudged Catherine. "You still have business in the ducal bank."

She looked at me confused, and I caught and pushed the two prisoners.

"Funds to pay Mrs. Lee?"

She grinned as I kept the prisoners moving to the station. The magister sentenced the two killers to hang and the other six to ten years in the coal mines. The constable commissioner also began a six-man escort from the commerce exchange to the ducal bank. It only took a few minutes, and the station was not far, so it was not really that much trouble.

He also began to recruit and hire more constables with the duke's approval to enlarge our station. Mostly to increase the constables on the busy streets during the day. The two engraved dueling pistols would have been destroyed, but Catherine bought them. She keeps them on the range and loves to fire them when she practices.

Chapter 22

# Tracking Train Robbers

The last few weeks had been filled with petty thefts all over the city. At least four times a week, I had gone with Catherine to one event or another. Most were fun with music and dancing, but a few had been—annoying. One of the barons would use the party or event as an excuse to pull me aside to try pushing his idea, plea, or agenda.

That last had actually been to pass a law to prohibit constables from arresting a noble for any crime. There were also the ones who wanted me to support them in their plea to raise taxes so they could make more money. Or the ones who wanted me to support the return of serf laws. Those were the nobles I put on my black list, which Catherine laughed at.

We had been doing a lot of talking because Catherine had to return to the capital and her mother soon. It meant leaving the constables and my job and friends. Of course she had done that to come here. We had even called her mother and talked with her for over an hour. She was not pushing, but I knew it had to come. I was the one to ask her to marry me, and I had known who she was and where she would have to be.

Catherine was on my left, and her guards were behind her and very nervous. To my right were a dozen detective inspectors. We were in the newly finished firing range and here for weekly practice. I drew and fired and cocked my pistol to do it again. I did it fast because you do what you practice, and in a gun fight, you do not want to take your time.

The other men were doing the same thing, and so was Catherine. She was very smug because we had done this every morning with other inspectors or constables, and each time she scored the best. I checked my weapon and returned it to the holster and waited for the last to finish. When he did I removed the ear muffs and started toward the targets. "I am betting she missed at least one shot."

The other men chuckled, and Catherine stuck her tongue out. The lieutenant and his guards laughed, and we stopped to mark the bullet holes. Mine were all in the drawn heart or near it, and I shifted to look at Catherine's. I sighed as I looked at the five holes touching each other in the center of the heart.

She laughed as I shook my head and pulled down my target. "Dinner is on me—again."

For someone who had not known how to shoot a few months ago, she was extremely good. We cleaned the weapons in the front area of the range and turned in the targets. I glanced at the range master as he answered the call box. He shifted and turned to look around before holding out the handset. "The chief of inspectors."

I moved to the counter and accepted the handset. "Inspector Knight."

"We have a train robbery. They stopped it on the edge of the city and then escaped after robbing the passengers. They tried to force their way into the mail and currency car, but the guards stopped them. I have Detective Inspector Blaine on the way from the docks and a team of street constables to help track them. I want you to go to the train and start there."

I looked at Catherine before I nodded. "Is the train still stopped, or has it been moved?"

The chief sighed. "Moved. We had to clear the tracks for two scheduled freight trains. It is on the side track at the station, and all the passengers and crew are being kept aboard."

I nodded to myself. "I am on the way."

I handed the handset to the range master and then walked to Catherine. "I have a priority case."

She nodded. "I have to attend the duke's open court this morning and then the tour of the orphanage and—"

I smiled. "And a dozen other places. I will meet you at the Golden Crown at six o'clock."

I gave her a kiss, and she smiled since I was not supposed to do that in public. I nodded to the lieutenant and headed for the door, and my mind went to the ways someone could rob a train. The first thing was they had to get or be aboard it. That was step one. Step two would be to hold up all connecting passenger cars at once or risk someone escaping or pulling a weapon.

Step three involved how they took the passengers money and/or belongings. If they took belongings, those might be traced to a fence. Did they show any indication of violence while robbing the passengers? Since they tried and failed to force their way into the mail and currency car, they were new at this. Step four would be how they got away—on foot, or did they have horses?

I went to the closest station and got a horse and rode to the train station. I tied it and gestured to a constable beside the main entrance. "Would you watch the horse for me?"

He nodded, and I strode in and across. I jumped off the platform and walked across the tracks to the train on the far side.

I nodded to the constable standing with a conductor. "Was anyone hurt?"

He shook his head. "No one was armed, so they did what they were told. According to the reports, there were six men, one for each of the six cars. I think there might have been more. The engineer had to slow the train and stop it, and if there were six in the passenger cars—he did not report anyone stopping him or boarding his engine."

I looked to the front of the train. "Pull him aside and put him in restraints. After I finish with the passengers, I will talk to him. Let him know he is going to prison as one of the robbers."

He grinned and spun to walk to the train engine. I climbed aboard the train and found all the passengers in the one car with two street constables.

I gestured as I pulled out my notebook. "Send them to me one at a time."

I was finishing the sixth, when Detective Inspector Blaine arrived. He stood at my shoulder and listened, and when I was done, I sent the passenger off the train.

I glanced at him. "So far it has been the same. They wore long coats that were buttoned, with kerchiefs covering their faces. They took cash and left everything else."

He shook his head. "Smart for them and bad for us."

I nodded. "Nothing to track back to them."

I glanced at the door.

"I had one of the street constables take the engineer into custody. If there were only six men, how did they get the train to slow or stop? The engineer did not report one stopping him. If you could interrogate him while I finish here, we might get something."

He grinned and turned. "Sounds fun."

It was an hour before the last witness left and I went to find Blaine. The engineer was talking fast as a street constable looked at me and shook his head.

Blaine finally slapped the engineer. "Enough. That is the tenth story, and it still sounds like a lie. I think we will just take you in and charge you. Train robbery will get you twenty years on a work farm or in the mines."

The man shook his head. "I did...not—"

I snorted. "Just arrest him. Conspiracy is the same as robbery. Since he will not give up his partners, he can rot and do their time."

He shook his head. "But I did not—"

I took a step. "The train did not stop on its own. If one of the robbers did not board your engine and make you stop, then you are involved. You are no different than the men who held weapons and robbed the passengers."

I grabbed him and turned to shove him to the street constable.

"Take him in."

He stammered and then broke. "Okay...they...paid me...one hundred gold pieces!"

Blaine snorted. "They paid you?"

The engineer nodded and then shook his head. "They gave me ten, and I was to get the rest later."

I let Blaine take over as the engineer started talking and gave us a couple of names. We got the name of a sidewalk eatery they were to meet and pay him at. Somehow I doubted the names were real, but Blaine sent them out to every station. We sent the engineer to the station with the street constable to be held, and I walked with Blaine to the eatery.

I was sure the robbers had no intention of paying the engineer. What I was hoping was that one or two would be waiting at the eatery to kill him. We bought coffee and sat at one of the tables. Blaine shook his head. "Unless one talks or brags, we are not going to catch them."

I sipped my coffee as my eyes looked around the area. I saw the two men down the street leaning against the building. They wore long coats buttoned up with wide-brim hats tilted down. I smiled and looked at Blaine. "Relax. Do not be obvious, but I think the two men down the street to the left are a couple of our robbers."

He shifted and turned a little while lifting his cup and sipping. He turned back. "You could be right."

I gestured. "We drink a little more and then turn in the cups and leave."

He nodded. "And take a walk around the block and come up behind them."

Five minutes, and we returned the cups and walked away. Once around the corner, we trotted to the alley and turned to follow it. I caught Blaine when we were halfway and stopped to knock on a back door as I pulled out my badge. It was a few moments before a woman peeked out and I showed her my badge. "Mind if we slip through your store?"

She looked at Blaine before she opened her door. "Of course."

I smiled as we started in. "Thank you."

We went through to the front door and peeked out, and the two men were to our right. I pulled my pistol and stepped out and started toward them with Blaine beside me.

I stopped behind one of the men and touched the barrel of my pistol to his head. "Slowly take your hands out of the coat."

The other man started to move, and Blaine growled, "Try it, and I shoot you in the spine."

I shifted and yanked my man into the building and pulled his arms back. I put my pistol away and pulled out restraints. As I began to put them on, the man twisted and yanked on his arms while trying to stomp back and onto my foot. I slammed him face first into the building, and Blaine kicked the other man behind the knee. I caught my man's head and smashed his face into the building, and he went limp and fell.

The other man was cursing as Blaine ground his face into the stones of the building. I looked before I knelt and rolled my man onto his stomach. I pulled his arms back and picked up the restraints I had dropped and put them on him. I glanced back at a street constable trotting toward us and stood and moved to help Blaine, and he put restraints on the man.

When we were done, I showed the street constable my badge. "Call in. I am Detective Inspector Knight, and this is Detective Inspector Blaine. We need the street constables assigned to the train robbery and a wagon."

He nodded, and I bent to search my man. I took a pistol from a coat pocket, one from his belt, and two more from shoulder holsters. Blaine was shaking his head as he collected even more from his man. I slapped mine awake and then pulled him to his feet. He spit and struggled, and I slugged him. "Keep it up, and I will make sure it is the mines for you."

He glared. "You have nothing."

I tugged on the large kerchief around his throat. "Want to bet?"

He looked away, and I nodded.

"Now we want the others."

He smiled. "Sorry."

I nodded and moved to Blaine's prisoner. "I will offer you the deal. I will speak to the magister and have him take five years off the sentence."

He snorted, and I shrugged.

"Fifteen years is better than twenty."

He smiled. "Armed robbery is only fifteen."

I gave his face a pat. "But train robbery is twenty to twenty five."

He shifted and glanced at the other man as he growled. I shrugged and turned.

"We can go the other way. Since you tried to rob the mail and currency car, we will add special circumstances and make it thirty."

The man gasped. "Wait!"

My man lunged. I kicked his feet, and he went down. I bent and grabbed him and pulled him up and turned. The street constable was on the way back, and I gave my man a shove. "Hold this idiot."

I turned and looked at the other man.

"Well?"

He swallowed and looked at Blaine. "Away from the others on a work farm."

I nodded, and he started talking and gave us names and the location of the other four men. When the wagon arrived, we put the one man in and took the other with us. At the station we logged all the weapons and put the other man in an isolation cell. The team of street constables were waiting, and they had revolving shotguns. We grinned and went to draw out a couple from the station armory.

We took a wagon and went out to the west edge of the city. A block from the house we stopped, and I sent two street constables down the narrow dirt alley behind the houses. Two of the others would watch the sides while the last two plus Blaine and I would enter through the front door. We started down the street with me and Blaine on the other side.

We went ahead as the other four constables strolled and talked as if nothing was happening. We crossed the street as they reached the house. Two split off and moved to each side as we headed straight for the door. I fired into the dead bolt, and Blaine shot the door handle. We both kicked, the door burst open, and we walked in. "Constables!"

A man with a gun in each hand ran toward the back door, but we heard the two street constables yell. Another man appeared at the top of the stairs with a double-barrel shotgun. I had moved left into the small common room, and Blaine went right. The two constables who followed us in fired, and the man on the stairs went down. I had my shotgun to my shoulder as the man with two pistols spun.

I had already cocked the hammer back and shifted and fired, and he folded and screamed as both legs were hit. The two pistols fell and bounced away as I moved to the man. I heard Blaine fire as I knelt and yanked the man onto his stomach. I twisted his one arm back. The two street constables arrived, and one helped me put him into restraints.

The two constables by the stairs went up, and I could hear them yell, and a man was yelling back at whom he surrendered. I let the constables search my prisoner and went to check on Blaine and the other constables. I heard a shot from outside, and Blaine met me by the door. He grinned as he followed me out. "Mine is down and in restraints."

We found the constable putting restraints on a man he had shot in the shoulder. We returned to the inside; the man on the stairs was dead. The two street constables who went upstairs had the only man who had surrendered. I sent one to call for the constable doctor and to have the prisoner wagon driver bring it to the front of the house.

Of course now it was time to write it up and see a magister. We brought the one who had spoken in first and let him repeat everything to the magister. The court clerk wrote it down, and he signed it, and the magister sentenced him to ten years on a work farm. He made a call to have him serve it on a farm in another ducal territory. He also gave the train engineer ten years on a farm.

The others got twenty years in the mines, the ones who had been wounded were sentenced in the prison hospital. The chief of inspectors and the constable commissioner liked the way we had worked together and began a new program for special crimes. I went across to the ducal courts building and up to see the commissioner as soon as I finished all the paperwork.

I had written up my resignation and gave it to the commissioner. He had expected it and accepted my badge. "We are going to miss you."

I had to return to my station and box up all my things and take them home. I walked into the Golden Crown at six o'clock on the dot. Catherine was already at a table in the corner, and I crossed to her. I nodded to the lieutenant and the guards as I passed them. I slipped into the chair across from her, and she grinned. "You made it."

I nodded. "We caught them around noon, but the paperwork took longer."

She gestured to the waiter, and he moved to the table.

After we ordered and he left, I took a breath. "I turned in my badge."

She looked at me and then smiled. "So now you are mine?"

# CHAPTER 23

# Knight Inspector

CATHERINE HELPED ME crate up everything I owned. She also called and made a few inquiries in Ambrosia with the city clerk and arranged a house that had been seized. Her maids and servants were already busy packing her belongings up. It was a week before everything was shipped, and we followed a day later. It was a little strange not having the badge.

We stayed on the train each time it stopped, and finally we were crossing the wide Green river. I looked out as the train slowed and crossed the bridge. We could see barges and river ships and even sailboats. Further upriver was the royal palace and docks. I stood when the train stopped and turned to grab my travel bag. The servants were trying to collect their things. I sighed, and Catherine grinned.

She caught my hand and pulled. "They know where they are going."

I pulled her back to slow her so the lieutenant and her guards could exit before us. They pushed people back and made room, and I looked around as I stepped out. I turned and held up my hand, and Catherine took it as she came down and stepped onto the platform. People were calling her name and asking questions. I had heard and seen it before and started for a side door.

A royal carriage was waiting with a whole platoon of guards. Another lieutenant held the door as we approached. "Welcome home, Your Highness."

She smiled as I helped her in and followed. Both lieutenants followed and sat across from us. The carriage started moving, and I looked out the window, expecting to see that we were headed to the palace. I shifted and looked at the new lieutenant. "Where are we going?"

He smiled back. "Her Highness wished to go to your estate first."

I looked at Catherine, and she grinned. "It is a small estate to the west of the palace."

I cleared my throat. "I thought you said a house?"

She caught and squeezed my hand. "The house is on the estate. At one time someone planted grapes and an orchard of peach trees. It was a farm, and they built walls so…"

I grinned. "A farm that was turned into an estate?"

She nodded, and I looked around outside. "Sounds interesting."

It was, and I had the carriage stop at the gates. We walked through together, and the grounds were very different. Grapes were between rows of trees with vines on trellises that smelled like vanilla. I grinned when I saw the old farm house and went to look at the peppercorn trees across the front. There was a wide covered porch across the whole front.

Catherine caught up and pulled me to the door. It was unlocked, and inside were the crates with my things. The house was not fancy and looked comfortable. The guards had not followed, and I kissed Catherine. "Thanks."

She smiled and pulled out a flat leather badge case and held it out. "So you do not have to start over or feel lost."

I looked at the case and accepted it. When I opened it, I saw a badge like the one I had given her, only where her name had been, mine took its place. She laughed and hugged me. "You can go see the chief of inspectors tomorrow about taking cases."

I did not know what to say, but she caught my hand and pulled me to the door.

"Mother wanted you to come to dinner tonight."

It did not take long to settle in although I was still unpacking a crate every day. I loved to walk the estate and had spoken with a couple of the street constables. They made a few calls, and I ended up with a man who could take care of the trees, grapes, and the rest of the grounds. Mr. Mack was newly married and loved gardening and really liked what he saw on the estate.

I was a little hesitant to go see the chief of inspectors but did. At first he was a little sour until I gave him my record. I spent the first week going to the stations to meet the station commanders and the inspectors. Catherine was busy catching up with her mother and the court. Every other day I was visiting her, and either she would stay over with me or I would end up spending the night with her.

It was two weeks before the chief of inspectors sent a street constable to contact me. I was collecting peppercorns and sorting them and glanced at the constable who rode in. He grinned as he stopped and looked at me. "Inspector Knight?"

I straightened and nodded, and he swung down.

"The chief of inspectors sent me. Well, him and the constable general. Someone has fired shots through one of the windows at the palace. The royal guards searched the area it came from but did not find anything. They shrugged it off, but the chief of inspectors and the constable general think it is something to look into."

My mind was already turning and spinning. "Go to the palace right now. Tell them not to allow the repair person in until they and everything they have are searched. That includes their wagon and underneath it."

He spun and swung up into the saddle. "You think they could be assassins?"

I started for the front door. "I do not know, but someone shooting windows randomly could be something else."

I changed and put my pistol on and hesitated before grabbing my revolving rifle. I went out and found Mr. Mack and asked him to cover my work and saddled a horse. I left at a trot, and when I reached the palace, I found the constable still arguing with the gate guards. I swung down and growled as I started through, "Enough! Has the repairmen come in?"

The guard corporal scowled. "You do not—"

I spun and looked at him. "I have had more than enough experience, Corporal. Now if I find these men have weapons, I will bring you and your men up on charges for incompetence or treason."

He stiffened, and I turned and pulled my horse after me. An attendant met me at the front, and I handed him the reins. I pulled the rifle and started for the door, and he called after me. I was barely through the entrance hall when palace guards caught up. I looked at them and kept walking. "Which windows were shot out and where are the workers?" They looked at the rifle I was carrying, and I snapped. "Now!"

The lieutenant for Catherine appeared. "They are on the west side."

I looked at the intersection of halls. "That is the royal apartment wing."

He nodded, and I started running and ignored the royal guards when they yelled and ran after me. I saw the open door into the queen's suite, and the single guard was standing outside the door. I slowed. "Are workmen inside?"

He had his hand on his pistol and nodded, and I pushed past him. I saw the large broken window and one man cutting the frame. I shifted my grip on the rifle.

"Where is the other worker?"

He shifted and glanced at me, and his eyes went to the closed door into the bedroom. I saw the bulge in his coveralls and brought the rifle up.

"Do not move or make a sound."

He opened his mouth, and I cocked the rifle. He licked his lips, and I growled to the guards, "He has a weapon."

They had followed me in, and the lieutenant moved to the man while pulling his weapon. As soon as he pulled him up, I spun and moved to the door. I lowered the rifle and pulled my pistol and opened the door. A man was kneeling beside the large bed and looked at me with wide eyes. In his hand was a package and what looked like a spring.

I aimed at his head. "Set it down and stand up."

He smiled. "Shoot me, and we all die."

I shrugged. "Since I am in the doorway, I can move out."

His face paled, and his eyes flickered around the room.

I gestured. "Set it down and stand up. Make a sudden move, and you die."

He did as I told him.

I moved closer and held my rifle back. "Hold this."

One of the guards was following and took it. I moved around and turned the man and put my pistol away. I put him in restraints and spun him to face me.

"Who ordered this?"

He glared, and I nodded.

"You know attempting to assassinate the queen means death. What is your family going to say when the papers print your name as a traitor and coward?"

He reddened and looked away. "You cannot make me talk."

I looked at the guard. "Call the constables. Tell them Inspector Knight needs a constable mage. Also get me the number for a magister."

I looked at the device he had set down.

"Also ask for a bomb specialist and keep the royal family out of here."

He nodded, and I pushed the man to the other room.

"I need a room."

I had the constable and a dozen guards with me as I pushed the two men out. The constable looked at me with wide eyes as I looked around in the hall. At the end I saw Catherine arguing with her lieutenant who would not let her pass. We pushed the two men down the hall, and I gestured to the guards. "Search them thoroughly."

I looked at Catherine.

"You should not be this close. They were planting a bomb."

She looked at the men. "Why?"

I shook my head. "I do not know yet. Go stay with your mother. Keep her away from any window and close the curtains."

She nodded and turned to hurry away, and the lieutenant smiled. "Nice. I will have to remember that."

I nodded and followed as he led me to a study. The guards pushed the two men down in chairs, and I sat on the corner of the desk. "This is what is going to happen. I am going to call a magister and get a warrant for the constable mage to use a truth spell."

They shifted and looked at each other. I waited until they looked at me.

"You will tell me everything, beginning with who is behind this and why you were doing it. You will tell me who else is involved and where they are. When I finish you will be taken to one of the stations and processed. You will go before a magister, and the constables will visit your whole family to question them."

I stood and looked at the constable.

"Do not let them harm themselves or each other."

He shook his head, and I went out into the hall. The lieutenant handed me a note with the number to a magister and took me to a call box. The palace operator put me through, and I waited for the phone to be answered. It was several moments before a woman said, "Magister Quinn."

I relaxed a little. "Magister, I am Inspector Knight. I responded to the palace for someone firing shots through a window. I caught two men, who were supposed to be repairing the window, planting a bomb under Her Majesty's bed. I am asking for a warrant to use a truth spell on them and another to search their homes and/or business."

She sucked in a breath and then hesitated, "You caught them in the act or suspect them?"

I smiled. "In the act, madam. One was still holding the arming spring."

She growled, "Your warrants are granted. I will write them up and send them to…"

I grinned. "To the chief of inspectors."

She chuckled. "Of course. Call me if you have problems."

She hung up, and I set the handset down and looked at the lieutenant. "Two things: first make sure the constable mage can get through the gate, and second, detain the corporal who is working the main gate. I do not know if he is just incompetent or a traitor, but we are going to find out."

He hesitated, "Her Majesty's guard commander will need to know."

I nodded and gestured. "Make it happen but watch his reaction."

He nodded and strode away, and I returned to the room. It was thirty minutes before a young woman stepped into the room. She wore a suit coat like Catherine, and her eyes flickered around and settled on me. "Inspector Knight?" She smiled. "Constable Mage Abigail Green."

I bowed my head and gestured to the two men. "I have a warrant by Magister Quinn for a truth spell for these men."

She moved to them. "That is easy enough."

Twenty minutes, and I had six more names and a location. I also found out Ms. Green was a friend of Catherine. She was new to the constables but seemed competent. I looked at one of the guards. "Would you call for a prisoner wagon to meet us at the gate?"

He nodded, and I gestured to the constable.

"Take them in and do an initial report for Magister Quinn. Also send a runner to the chief of inspectors for the warrants."

He nodded, and I started for the door.

"Mage Green, thank you for your help."

She smiled. "You are welcome."

I looked at the lieutenant as I walked. "Where is the corporal?"

He growled, "Being held in the main guard office."

He led the way, and we walked into the large room with weapons in racks on the wall. The corporal was with a tall man I recognized. He sneered when he turned. "This is the arro—"

I grabbed him as I pulled my pistol and put it to his temple. "Say good-bye, traitor."

He gasped as his face went white. "Wait!"

I cocked the pistol. "I do not need to wait. They gave you up while being questioned under a truth spell."

He went to his knees. "It was—"

I pushed against his head and then stepped back. "Say your last words."

He sobbed and began to plead and try to explain. The captain, now a major, touched my hand and shook his head. "Smith, Derrick. Take him and lock him in a cell. I will speak with the army magister and have the gallows readied."

Two guards moved forward and pulled him up and took his weapon. They walked him toward the back corner of the room and through a door. The major shook his head. "Again you have shaken up the royal guards." He gestured to the door. "Her Majesty wants a word."

I nodded and walked with him. "I have six more names. It has something to do with Her Majesty's importation law on certain trade items. The ones behind this are waiting for the men they sent at someplace called the Alganiun Gentlemen Club."

He snorted. "A fancy name for a whorehouse."

Two guards were outside a door, and when I stepped in, another two were across the office beside another. To one side was a desk with Her Majesty's personal assistant, and to the other was comfortable chairs. I ignored both as we crossed to the other guards. One turned and opened the door. "Inspector Knight."

We walked in, and the queen looked up as Catherine turned from peeking out the curtain. I shook my head. "I said stay away from windows not look out."

She grinned and stuck her tongue out, and her mother smiled. "So what have you found?"

I bowed my head. "Madam."

I looked at the guard behind and to one side. "So far we have arrested two men and one of your guards. They were planting a bomb under your bed. I have the names of the other six men involved. Three are barons, Shay, Porita, and Korick. The other three are merchants, Accord, Donnick, and Kraig. It has something to do with your importation law on certain trade items."

She snorted. "Not trade items, Ashton, slavery or, as those morons want to call it, the resumption of serf laws. Take them and do not give the barons special treatment."

I bowed and turned to leave as Catherine hurried to catch me. "Lieutenant, would you call the station closest to the Alganiun Gentlemen Club? Ask them for a dozen constables with shotguns."

He grinned and turned at the assistant's desk while I kept going. One of the guards outside the outer office held up my rifle, and I nodded as I accepted it. I waited for the lieutenant before we headed for the front gate. Guards were falling in as we walked until we had a dozen around us.

I shook my head, and Catherine grinned. "Just think of them as extra help."

I snorted as we reached the front and I found Catherine's carriage and looked around at a couple dozen more guards. The lieutenant chuckled as he held the carriage door. "This is our honor they attacked."

I followed Catherine in. "Just remember they need to be alive when they hang."

Our ride through the streets was not a run, but it was not a walk either. When the carriage stopped, the lieutenant and his men were the first out. The other guards had ridden horses, and constables were just arriving. I stepped out and held up my badge to a constable commander. "I have information six men who attempted to kill the queen are inside."

He was not the only one to growl, and I gestured. "I need every door sealed and men to go in with me."

He turned. "Split the men, Lieutenant."

I looked at our lieutenant. "Surround the building."

He yelled, and sergeants barked orders, and I started for the door with Catherine following. Guards ignored the doorman and shoved the door open. It was like a flood as men poured in and spread out. I caught the doorman and shoved him inside. "Point out Barons Shay, Porita, and Korick and merchants Accord, Donnick, and Kraig."

He nodded quickly and looked around the main common area and then pointed to one corner. The men there were on their feet and started to reach into their coats. Luckily a constable was close and fired his shotgun into the floor at their feet. They shoved their hands into the air, and guards and constables rushed them. They were slammed to the floor, and their arms were twisted until they screamed.

I looked around the room at the white faces of men and women. "Anyone else trying to kill the queen?"

They were quick to shake their heads, and one of the women spit, "You should shoot them."

Catherine grinned. "Hanging would be much better."

Their eyes went to her, and the next thing I knew they were bowing and taking a knee. I gestured while bumping Catherine to one side. "Get them up and out. Take them to the station and call the magister. I want a mage to use a truth spell to make sure there are no more. Constables, could you get the names of everyone here please?"

I looked at Catherine.

"Time to play the princess and meet the people."

She sighed and nodded and started gesturing to some of the women. The magister was more than willing to issue another warrant for a truth spell, but we did not get any more names. The barons were single with no immediate family. Catherine seemed to delight in bringing three of the women from the club to meet her mother. They were granted the three barony patents and given the lands and property of the three merchants.

That made me grin especially when they brought the other women and workers away from the club. All the men including the corporal of the guard were judged and sentenced to hang, which they did together. I also convinced Her Majesty to select some of her guards to attend the constable academy. I added a constable call box to the gate and arranged for warrants, reports, and paperwork to be dropped off there.

Of course on Catherine's next night over, she teased me with ideas the new baronesses had told her about.

# CHAPTER 24

# Mouse in the Treasury

I SHIFTED AS the target slid aside and fired and then glared at Constable Mage Green. She acted like she had no idea what happened, and Catherine smirked as she aimed. "You missed the center."

She fired, and I cocked my pistol. "If Abigail keeps cheating for you, I will have to arrest her for violating the royal corruption law."

They laughed as I aimed and fired, and the lieutenant laughed. "Except that would only apply if something of value was involved."

I looked at him as Catherine aimed. "Something of value is involved. If I lose I have to cook dinner for them tonight."

The guards laughed, and Catherine fired, and I cocked my pistol.

"Of course Mr. Mack has made vanilla and peach brandy, and his wife put a dozen steaks into a small barrel to soak sooo…"

I aimed and fired just as the target hopped. I sighed, and everyone laughed as Catherine smirked. "That makes three misses."

I removed the cylinder and replaced it with a full one before I put the pistol away. "Okay, you win. Next time I am bringing my shotgun."

We went out front, and the shop owner grinned. "Another win, Your Highness?"

I snorted as I sat on a stool to start cleaning my pistol. This was one of the main gun shops in the city that the constables used. We could have used the range under the palace, but it was being rebuilt. Plus the city constables got to see and meet Catherine and her guards. There were also the new weapons the owner kept letting her try. She was also gossiping with the street constables to find a new seamstress and eateries.

The chief of inspectors had been keeping me busy on theft cases since the attempted assassins. Mostly it was kids, and the street constables caught them when I pointed them out. I was paid by the cases I solved, so I was doing well. An off-duty constable, Mage Green, and one of the guards were talking when a palace servant entered.

That made me pay attention since servants were not allowed weapons inside the palace. Catherine cleared her throat as he looked around and then headed straight to us. I glanced at her as she smiled. "Mr. Sorinson."

The man bowed, but his eyes stayed on me. "I am sorry to intrude, Your Highness, but—"

She touched my arm. "But you are not here to see me."

He shook his head, and she smiled.

"Ashton, this is Mr. Sorinson. He is the palace vault guardian."

I bowed my head. "Sir."

He shifted. "I have heard you are very good at solving mysteries."

I glanced at the lieutenant and Mage Green when she moved closer. "I have solved one or two."

He bit his lip. "It might be nothing but...when I opened the vaults this morning, I found a mouse."

I blinked. "A mouse? Your mystery is a mouse?"

Mage Green cleared her throat. "Perhaps someone left a crumb in the vault?"

He snorted and then shook his head. "You do not understand. Once the doors close, all the air is pumped out."

I looked at Catherine and then began to put my pistol together. "Mage Green, I might need your assistance. Lieutenant, would you please call the central station and request a hound at the palace?"

He cleared his throat. "Hound?"

I nodded and stood as I put the pistol away. "A hound."

Catherine finished putting the other pistol together and turned to hold it out to the owner. "Thank you, Markus. It is an excellent weapon, and I am sure since I used it, you will get an extra something for it."

He grinned and inspected it, and we started for the door. The guards moved out first and then the lieutenant. We waited for his signal and followed, and I gestured to Mr. Sorinson. "Come along, sir. We are going to need access to the vaults."

We rode back on the horses we had come on. Catherine of course was smiling and greeting people. At the palace gates, I swung down. "Corporal?"

The new corporal stepped out of the small building. "Mr. Knight?"

I looked at the palace. "How many ways in and out?"

He blinked and turned to look at the palace. "Five."

It was my turn to be surprised as I helped Catherine down. "Five?"

He shrugged. "This one. The servants' gate, the vendors' gate, the…garden gate, and the dock."

I hesitated, "What is the garden gate?"

He reddened. "Mostly it is where manure is taken out."

I smiled. "Of course. Are there guards?"

He nodded. "One man."

I looked toward the river. "And someone is at the docks?"

He grinned. "Patrolling it and on the river. Everyone coming in or going out that way is checked and searched."

I thanked him and let him know a constable would be bringing a hound and to send them to the vaults. We walked to the front of the palace, and Catherine caught my hand. "What are you thinking?"

I smiled. "Looking for pieces of the puzzle. I knew of the servants' gate, and they are checked. I knew about the vendors' gate and what they leave with is checked. I was not sure about the docks and did not know about the garden gate."

She shook her head. "That is not answering my question."

I grinned as I looked at Mage Green. "Well, constable?"

She smiled. "Always think like the criminal."

I nodded as we reached the door. "So what do we know?"

Mr. Sorinson caught up as we started down the hall, and he directed us the other way. I looked at Catherine. "Come on, Inspector."

She grinned and then stuck her tongue out. She looked ahead. "We know there was a mouse in a vault and the air was removed."

I shook my head. "Wrong. We know there was a mouse and that the air was supposed to have been removed."

She nodded and hummed. "So if a mouse could get in, maybe the air is still there and a person can get in."

I nodded as we went down a set of stairs. "And if a person got in—"

She squeezed my hand. "They could steal, which was why you were asking the corporal about the gates."

Mr. Sorinson moved ahead to a set of metal doors with two guards. He used a key to unlock the door, and the guards helped open it. I stopped to look at it, and the steel was at least a couple of fingers thick. Inside was a large room with desks and tables. On the other side was another steel door that was locked. When it was opened, we saw a hall with sturdy carts.

On each side were three more steel doors. Mr. Sorinson went to the last on the left and covered a dial to enter the combination. This time when the door opened, I stopped it and looked at the edge. It was a hand-span thick and had a waxlike material on it. Thick metal rods came out, and I could see where they entered the doorframe. I felt and looked at the entire door before entering.

I looked back as a constable and guard with a hound hurried in. I stood and looked around and ignored the contents. I looked at Mage Green as the hound went to the back wall and then to shelves on one side. "See anything?"

She shrugged. "I deal in magic and…"

I smiled and gestured the constable and hound out. "Learn to pay better attention. Right now I know we have a crime. I know someone who works here is involved, and I know there has been a theft."

Catherine sighed. "Okay, so teach us so we will know."

I turned and pointed to the door. "Someone made cuts through the seal so the air would leak back in."

I moved past Mr. Sorinson. "Probably because they knew if they broke in with the air sucked out, they knew the wall or stones would explode into the room."

She blinked and nodded. "I did not think of that."

Mage Green was looking at the walls. "So they needed to break in and have it go undetected."

I looked at Mr. Sorinson. "Do you have anyone new?"

He nodded. "Two bookkeepers."

I thought of how to narrow that down. "Do you record which vaults they enter?"

He nodded. "Mr. Michaels has this one."

I looked at the lieutenant, and he nodded and turned to whisper to one of the guards. I went to the right-side set of shelves where the hound had smelled and opened a bag and turned so they could see the pebble-like rocks. I slapped others on the shelf and felt the way they shifted. "This whole side has been exchanged."

I gestured to the other side. "That side still has coins in the bags. You can see the way they press against the sides."

I moved to the rear and looked at the base of the wall where the hound had first gone. I gestured to Mage Green. "The entrance is to the right but…"

She moved after me. "But you need to know how it is opened."

I nodded. "More than likely they pull it straight out on some type of sliders."

She put her hand on the wall and chanted, and one section glowed and grated as it slid into and then through the wall. I pulled my pistol and crouched and moved into the hole. It went right a few paces before I saw a cross tunnel going left and right. It was dim and hard to see, but to the right, it looked like the tunnel stopped or turned.

I hesitated and then looked back. "Wait."

I had to stay in a crouch as I went right and then looked into the short tunnel when it turned to the right again. I nodded when I saw the work on the section of another vault wall. This one would be across the hall from the one they had already broken into. I turned and moved back to see Catherine and the lieutenant. "They are working to break into another vault."

She nodded, and I looked to the left. We could see a dim light, and judging from the distance, I was sure I knew where the tunnel would come out. I started moving again and went slow and listened. The light was coming from the edges of stone blocks. To the left was a small cut out in the tunnel. I looked down to see rails and a large screw in the ring between blocks.

I grabbed and slowly pulled the blocks back until there was a gap. I moved into the cutout and lifted my pistol as I stepped out and stood up straight. I was at the end of the old palace range, and along the walls were sacks of earth and debris. I heard voices as everybody followed me out and stood. I moved down the range and lifted the counter gate on the left side.

I glanced both ways before I walked to the partially open door to the range issue lobby and the weapon lockers. I looked back to see all the guards holding their weapons. I shoved the door open and walked out, and a dozen workers spun. Their eyes widened, and the supervisor cleared his throat. "How did you get in there?"

Several moved toward the door, and I aimed. "Move away from the door and face the wall!"

The supervisor puffed up. "Listen here! Her Majesty—"

Catherine moved up beside me. "Did not give you permission to break into the royal vaults or to steal. Now face the wall, or I will shoot you in the knee."

The guards flowed around us and into the room as Mage Green murmured and the other door suddenly slammed close. The workers jerked, and the supervisor turned white. They were slow to turn but did, and guards quickly slammed them to the wall. They searched them and looked around, but I was the only one carrying restraints. I gestured to the work boots the men were wearing. "Use their laces to tie them."

I felt or heard something and looked to the right at the range-office door. My left hand caught and yanked Catherine back and behind me as I shifted and began to bring my pistol up. Two men were in the door with pistols they must have gotten from a range weapon locker. One fired as I stepped between them and Catherine, and I felt the searing pain rip through my left shoulder.

It jerked my shoulder back, but my right arm was up, and I squeezed the trigger. The pistol fired, and the second man staggered back. His pistol went off and fired high into the ceiling, and I began to shift as the first man fired again. This time I felt the pain explode into and through my left thigh. I aimed and fired, and his head snapped back, and he began to fall.

Catherine fired over my right shoulder, and three more guards fired from where they stood. The second man had managed to stay on his feet and bring his pistol up. Now the rounds struck his body, and he jerked and twisted before falling. Guards were rushing the office, and I turned and aimed as the workers spun and started to attack. I fired into the chest of one, and they froze as he fell. "Back!"

Constable Mage Green shouted, and they were spun, lifted, and slammed into the wall with force. A couple of minutes, and the door was open, and more guards ran in. The workers were tied, and Catherine finally looked at me and gasped. "Ashton!"

I smiled slightly as she caught my other arm. "Would you see if a runner could find a doctor?"

She was looking around frantically. "You need to lie down and—"

I looked at Constable Mage Green. "Since I had already put you back on duty, would you see that they are taken to the station and charged? The lieutenant should have found the bookkeeper and taken him. Get with Mr. Sorinson for a statement and arrange a full audit of the vault by one of the constable bookkeepers. Also you will need to check all vault doors to make sure they have not been tampered with."

She smiled as one of the guards returned. "Anything else?"

I was pushed down on a range chair. "Yes. Question them and find out where they took the money and how they got it through the gate."

I looked at the lieutenant, and he nodded and turned to speak to one of his men. I opened the cylinder of my pistol and dumped it on the floor and held the pistol out to Catherine. "You need to hold this until a constable inspector comes."

She took it but passed it to a guard. "I am going with you."

I smiled. "The inspector will investigate the shooting, but he will need statements from you and me so he…"

She sighed. "Stubborn man."

Ten minutes, and I was on a bed upstairs with a mage doctor helping strip me. The bullet in my shoulder stopped against my shoulder blade. She was able to remove it and use magic to weave and knit the tissue back and close the wound. The bullet in my thigh struck the bone, which had began to hurt like hell. She removed the bullet and had to mend the cracked bone before she could work on the tissue.

Long before she started, I was put to sleep. When I woke, it was Catherine speaking softly to someone. I shifted and opened my eyes, and Catherine leaned over the bed. "Do not try to get up."

I shifted and looked past her. "How bad was it?"

She shook her head. "The shoulder had a lot of muscle and tissue damage. Mage Delila removed the bullet and knitted the muscle and tissue back together. The leg was harder; the bullet hit and cracked the bone. She had to remove the bullet and mend the crack before she could work on the tissue. You lost a lot of blood, and she said there would be shock and muscle weakness but time and exercise would cure that."

I nodded and relaxed, and a man moved up beside her. "Inspector, I am Detective Inspector Glenn. I need to get a statement about…"

The workers and bookkeeper went to the mines for fifteen years. The guard at the garden gate was disciplined for not checking the workers and the bags of debris they took away. The money they stole was found in the supervisor's home. It took three months to repair the damage and the range with guards watching and checking everything.

New procedures went into place for the bookkeepers so they switched vaults each day. Also Mr. Sorinson began inspecting the doors each morning and night to make sure the seals were good. My class in the vault for Catherine and Constable Mage Green caused Abigail to begin learning from constable sergeants and inspectors. It also brought investigations and how we did them to the constable general's attention.

That led to someone being with inspectors while they did cases to write down how they did things. The idea was to collect them into a text to teach new inspectors and constable supervisors. For me it meant more strange cases that required attention, and I was required to have a constable with me. I think that was from Catherine, but she did not say.

# CHAPTER 25

# Sinister Cousin

I DIVED INTO the cold water and started swimming as Catherine sat in a boat while two men paddled. Her guards and a lot more followed as I swam out and then up the river. This was my exercise to strengthen my shoulder and leg. Catherine watched and talked while I swam, and after a half league, I stopped and tread water. I grinned. "Do you know what this city needs?"

Her eyes narrowed. "And what would that be?"

I laughed. "A river race."

She laughed and then giggled, and I started back. Before we reached the dock, she was already plotting how to make it happen. I struggled out of the water and up the ladder. I ignored the servant and grabbed my new larger towel and wrapped it around me while shivering. "Maybe you should wait for next summer."

Catherine grinned as she got out of the boat. "But if I start now, everyone has time to prepare."

I shook my head. "But the last minute entries are the best."

She laughed. "You mean they crash or roll over and make the people laugh."

She gestured, and the servant bowed. "Her Majesty asked you to breakfast. I believe Sir Richard has returned to the city and she would like a word. Your father has left for his trip through the kingdom."

Catherine stopped laughing and looked at me. "You need to wash and dress."

I looked at the servant. "Who is Sir Richard?"

She caught my hand and pulled as she started off the dock. "A second cousin. Every time he comes, things happen."

She looked at me.

"Bad things, Ashton. Two years ago it was six tortured and murdered girls wearing silver-plated crowns. They were always left just outside the palace where the guards could not see who left them. Constables suspected Richard but could not prove it was him. As a boy he used to torture and kill the cats on his family estate."

I remember reading a book. "Sounds like the development of a disturbed man with no conscience."

She nodded and looked at me. "If he is back to start something, Mother is not going to be happy."

Luckily for me since I had started using the river to swim and exercise, I always brought clean clothes and washed in the palace. Thirty minutes, and I was escorting Catherine into the small private dining room. Her mother smiled when she saw me. "How is the exercise coming?"

I bowed. "Cold but at least it seems to be helping."

She chuckled and gestured, and I held the chair for Catherine and sat beside her. I glanced at the servant when she appeared. "Just coffee."

She nodded and turned to Catherine as I looked at her mother. "Sir Richard? What happens if he is caught?"

She sighed and leaned back. "First we must take care. I do not want us at any party or function where he is going to be. If he does something and is caught—I will judge him as the nobles' law requires. If he takes a life and is caught—he will hang."

I nodded and accepted a cup of coffee. "I will pay a visit to go over the old files and speak with the inspectors. If he is killing people, he will not stop until he is caught."

She sighed and looked at Catherine. "Do not answer his notes."

Catherine shook her head. "Why has he returned? His lands and duties are to the west and not even close to this duchy."

They talked more, but I was thinking of what files and reports I would have to look for. After breakfast I took my horse and rode to see the constable general. He was not happy and sent me to the central constable station. In the annex behind it were dozens of boxes of unsolved cases. While I was going through them, inspectors and detective inspectors came by.

They were the investigating inspectors and talked me through everything. In the cases of the murders, the victims had all been washed before being re-dressed. They had not been able to trace anything back to the killer. When a clerk arrived, I looked at him as he sat. "Yes?"

He smiled. "The constable general asked me to stay with you and record what you do."

I sighed and should have expected it. An hour later I glanced up when a young constable walked in. I shook my head and pointed to a chair. Slowly things caught my eye, and I had to go back and forth while explaining to the clerk what I saw and was looking for. I glanced at the interested constable. "Know anything about magic?"

He shook his head, and I gestured. "Call and find Constable Mage Green. I also need to speak with Detective Inspector David."

A year before the dead girls, there had been dead dogs hung on the palace wall, all bitches. One thing I noticed was the collars had all been the same. The dresses on the girls were different but had been the same type for all the girls. I started notes as I thought of what I needed checked out. "How many seam-stresses are there in the city?"

The clerk shrugged, and the constable had left to make calls. I sat back. "And how many places make collars for dogs?"

The constable walked back in and shook his head. "We have a woman wear-ing a silver crown found hanging from the palace wall."

I stood and gestured to the clerk as I put the records back in a box. "I hope you have horses."

When I arrived back at the palace, it was to stop constables from moving the woman. She was hanging from a rope and was not a girl but much older. There were several palace guards and a sergeant. There were half a dozen street constables and a detective inspector. I swung down and glanced at the inspector. "I will be working this case."

He shifted. "The—"

I held up my hand. "Before we argue it will be as partners. First we need a constable mage and then the doctor. I want a drawing or picture of the body, and I want the rope cut and not untied."

I looked at the ground under the woman and gestured.

"We need a cast made of the prints too."

I looked at the guard sergeant.

"Get a man wearing gloves to cut the rope on the other side when we are ready."

He shifted. "It is tied to a bar pushed through the small crenel."

I frowned. "Use gloves and, once we remove the woman, bring the bar and rope around to us."

He nodded and turned to issue orders to a guard. I looked back to see Constable Mage Green and Detective Inspector David. "That was fast."

She swung down. "You sent for us, and I had to do a trace spell."

I turned to the victim. "Try a trace spell on the prints under the body."

She moved closer and began, and I moved back to Detective Inspector David.

"When you investigated the dogs hanging on the wall, did you find out who made the collars?"

He blinked and shook his head. "I had constables check all the shops, but no one sold that kind."

I still watched Abigail. "What about outside the city? Did you send a notice to the flying squads?"

He shifted and frowned. "No."

I looked at him. "Do you still have one of the collars?"

He nodded, and I smiled. "Send it around to the flying squads and see if anyone recognizes the work."

He grinned and turned. "I will let you know what they report."

Abigail moved out to the street as if following someone or something, and then she stopped. The detective inspector had followed and was frowning as I walked to them. Abigail shook her head. "It stops here, which is impossible."

I squatted as I looked at the street. "Not if he removed the boots and put them in a bucket of water or..."

She sighed and shook her head. "So it is another dead end."

I stood. "We are just getting started. Once the doctor arrives and we cut her down, I want an association spell on the dress. I want to find the dressmaker. If the killer is still using the same one, we might find out what he looks like from her."

I gestured to the prints. "Can you create a mold?"

She did, and ten minutes later, the doctor arrived, and the body was cut down. Of course Abigail could get nothing about the killer from her body, but she did mark a location on a city map with strong association. That was probably the dressmaker since she would have touched and kept the dress longer than the killer. She tried an association spell on the knots on the rope, but the killer probably wore gloves.

The bar was one cut from an axle, and with the grease from all the dead animals, we would get nothing. I walked with Detective Inspector Christian, the clerk, my guard/constable, and Abigail. At the closest station, we waited for Christian to saddle a horse and then followed the map through the city. In a small street off the main business street was the dress shop.

When we walked in, several women turned to look at us. I smiled and bowed. "Ladies."

I looked around.

"Would one of you be the seamstress?"

One nodded, and I described the dress. She hesitated before answering, "I think that is one I sold a week ago to a servant."

I nodded. "Did he give a name or have a crest on his uniform?"

She shook her head. "He just said it was for his lady's maids."

I frowned. "Maids? How many dresses did he buy?"

She grinned. "Six."

Abigail cleared her throat. "Would you mind if I touched you and performed a spell to create an image of this man?"

Her eyes went wide as she put her hand to her throat. "A spell?"

The other women were whispering, and I smiled. "Think of all the ladies who will come to hear about this after we leave."

She blushed and nodded to Abigail, and I moved as she stepped up. I felt the tingle of magic as she touched the woman's temple and murmured. She held her hand out with a small crystal in it, and slowly the image of a man appeared. When she finished I thanked them, and we left. Outside I looked over Abigail's shoulder at the image. "We have a suspect from before."

I looked at Detective Inspector Christian. "We need to find out where Sir Richard is staying. We check the image against him and his servants or anyone around him."

He nodded. "Sounds good."

I headed for my horse. "First we are going to see a magister. We are going to get a warrant to check the image against Sir Richard's servants. We do not rush things; if he is the killer, I want the bastard to hang."

It took twenty minutes to see the magister and go over our suspicions and what information we had. Abigail had another call, so we had to wait for her to return. Most senior nobles or those with money always stayed at a hostel called the Golden Crown. When we reached it and went in, the manager tried to keep us from seeing Sir Richard. At least until Detective Inspector Christian yanked him around and put him in restraints.

That was when he was more than eager to assist us. He led the way up the stairs to the third floor and then to a corner suite. I moved him to the side and knocked, and a moment later, a maid opened the door. I nodded to her. "I am Inspector Ashton Knight. We need to speak with Sir Richard."

Her eyes were wide as she nodded and turned and hurried into the other room. I looked at everyone and nudged the door so it would open more. We saw the other open door and heard voices before a tall, slim young man walked out and crossed to us. The face did not match the image we had from the seamstress. He smiled politely, but I saw how tense he was. "How can I help the constables?"

Detective Inspector Christian held out the warrant. "We have reason to believe one of your servants purchased dresses found on a dead woman."

He stiffened. "How many times do I have to tell you people I did not kill anyone?"

I cleared my throat, and he looked at me. "We did not say you did. Right now we are searching for the man who bought dresses he put on a woman he killed."

I gestured to Constable Mage Green. "Show him the image."

She held out the crystal, and it cleared to show the image. He hesitated before he looked and then blinked. "That is Daniel."

I looked at Detective Inspector Christian. "Daniel who?"

Sir Richard looked at me. "Daniel Markson. He is my groom. He has worked for my family since I was a boy."

174

I nodded. "Is he here?"

He gestured. "I believe the hostel has servant quarters beside the stable."

I looked at the manager. "Well?"

He nodded. "He brought two servants. His maid is in room six, and his groom is in room seven."

I bowed to Sir Richard. "Thank you for your help."

He shifted and returned my bow. "My pleasure."

I led everyone out and to the stairs. "Let the manager go with a warning."

I stopped at the stairs and turned. "Does the hostel supply kennels for hounds?"

Detective Inspector Christian was removing the restraints, and the manager nodded. "On the back of the stables."

I looked at Christian. "And would your stable master or kennel boy make or buy collars?"

He looked at us and nodded again. "We even dye the leather."

I smiled as things began falling into place. I turned to go down the stairs. "Anyone want to bet we can match the rope used to hang the women to the stable?"

We went through the back of the hostel and headed to the building that was the servants' quarters. I slowed and looked at the stable and turned.

"We need to get a warrant to search his quarters. Right now we can detain him."

I looked at the manager, who looked a lot more cooperative.

"Would you allow us to search your stable and kennel?"

He growled and gestured, "Please."

I gestured to the clerk. "Go back inside and use the call box. Call the station and have the station commander get a warrant to search Daniel Markson's quarters. Let him know he was identified as the man who bought the dress put on the dead woman."

He nodded and spun and ran back to the door, and I led the way into the stable. The stable master was an older man who met us. He looked from his manager to us. "How can I help you?"

I looked down the aisle. "I am Inspector Knight. We are here for Daniel Markson."

He turned and opened his mouth to yell, and I grabbed his arm. "Quiet."

I looked down the aisle again and started walking while I pulled my weapon. Detective Inspector Christian caught up with his pistol in his hand. He looked calm as we started looking into stalls. The constable was following, but he had the stable master and the hostel manager stay at the door. We reached the last stalls, and I did not see anyone.

On the wall beside the stall was a saddle and tack with a ducal crest. I moved to the stall door and reached out to open it, but Christian was there first. He opened the door and then jerked back as an older man suddenly appeared and slashed toward his hand. Christian jabbed into his chest, and I brought my pistol up and cocked it. "Another move, and you are dead."

He spun back into the stall, and I started after him. I jerked back as a weapon went off, and the round splintered the stall doorframe. The horse in the stall screamed and reared, and I moved to the left with my weapon up. "Drop the weapon and come out!"

I reached the open stall door and the opposite wall. I still could not see the man, and the horse was still screaming. I gestured, and Christian moved and cleared the door. The horse raced out and ran toward the main door into the stable.

I looked at the constable. "Call for the hounds."

The man inside the stall cursed and a moment later ran toward the door with a double-barrel hunting rifle. I aimed low as he swung the barrel at Christian and the constable, and I fired into his leg. His leg was knocked out from under him as he screamed and fell. The rifle flew out of his hands when he hit the floor, and I moved in and put my boot on the back of his neck.

"Do not move."

Christian reached us and knelt to yank his arms back and put him in restraints. He was cursing and spitting when we pulled him up and I gestured to the constable. "Find a feed bag and put it over his head."

I had him go call for a doctor and take the prisoner to the street. Christian and I went out back to the kennel. We checked, and the collars they made matched the ones from those hanging on the wall. Next I went into the stable tack room and work area. That was where we found the small furnace he had used to plate the crowns.

When the warrant came, it was the station commander who brought it. I let Detective Inspector Christian and the constable search the room while the commander and I waited in the hall. The room was almost tiny, so there were not a lot of hiding places. They found the dresses and the crowns that had not been plated yet. There was half-melted silver eating utensils and a coil of rope with one end cut off.

I was sure that would match the piece we had from the dead woman. When we walked into the detention area at the station, the prisoners shut up. I looked at our suspect. "We have everything. Anything to say before we take you to see the magister?"

He glared. "You damn nobles think you are so much better than us."

I smiled. "Except we are not nobles, and the women you killed were not nobles. As far as I can tell, you are a pervert who likes to play with dead women."

He stilled. "I was sending a message to the bitch queen."

I ignored him, but Christian growled, and I touched his arm. "So you killed seven women to send a message to the queen. What did the girls do to make you pick them?"

He looked away and kept his mouth shut, and I smiled.

"They refused you."

He glared at me. "They were stuck-up bitches!"

I gestured to the jailer, and he unlocked the door. "Time to see the magister."

The room had the constable commissioner and the constable general as well as three dukes and two off-duty magisters. We presented the charges and our supporting evidence and then repeated his statements to us. That made him rant at the magister for almost twenty minutes before he was ordered gagged. There was no evidence anyone else was involved, and the magister ordered him hung.

I wrote up my report and turned it in before heading to the palace. I found Catherine in her office studying a trade agreement. She smiled. "I will be finished soon."

I ignored the others in the room. "It was not your cousin."

She looked at me and sat back. "Who?"

I gestured to her desk. "Finish, and we can go tell your mother so I only have to tell it once."

The next day Sir Richard was invited to the palace for breakfast. Of course I still had my morning exercise before we joined him.

CHAPTER 26

# Army Supplies Missing

THE CASE DREW a lot of attention, and more than a few people tried to claim the groom had been set up. At least until he got to say his last words on the gallows. After that everyone felt sorry for Sir Richard, and within a couple of weeks, he was engaged. At least he was no longer shunned or ignored. He was the one who spoke with the queen and the constable general about an inspector school.

I looked past Catherine and down the line of constables. She grinned and stuck her tongue out, and I sighed. "On the line—ready—aim—fire!"

Ten men and one woman fired with Catherine and kept it up until their weapons were empty.

I waited and then yelled again. "On the line—clear your weapon!"

I waited and then finished.

"Okay, bring me your targets."

The lieutenant snorted. "They are constables; why make them qualify each month?"

I snorted as I walked the line to check each station. "Thirty did not qualify last month. The constable commissioner thinks monthly qualifications will change that. If they asked me, I would say have them practice after each shift on one of the constable ranges."

I returned to the back table and accepted Catherine's target. "At least I know one inspector who does not have problems with qualifying."

She grinned at the small group in the center of her target. I circled the group and marked it and then signed it. She moved around me as I took the next target. "So you were asked to do the hands-on inspectors' course and exams."

I nodded as I scored the target and reached to the next. "The constable general and all constable commissioners want a hands-on course with an experienced inspector to teach new inspectors how to investigate. Everything from scene examination to how to read evidence. I even managed to get Abigail assigned to help."

She grinned as I looked at the only other woman. I took her target as she stood defiantly as if expecting me to scold her.

I scored the target and nodded. "Nice shooting."

I looked passed her, and she hesitated before moving to join the others who were done. She was Lady Megan Fiera and a duke's heir. She had gone through the constable course and passed. She had only been on the street for a few months. She had an outstanding record, and both her sergeant and commander recommended her to be an inspector.

I finished the last target and walked to the firing line. "My turn."

I checked to make sure everyone was behind the line before I looked at my target, pulled my pistol, aimed, and fired and kept firing until I was done. I cleared the pistol as I looked at the target. The lieutenant chuckled as he sent one of his men down to bring it back. "Abigail was not here to make it harder for you."

I reloaded and holstered my weapon as I turned. "You have one hour to clean your weapons and meet me at the central station. You have the list of things I told you to wear and bring. Make sure you have a horse in case we have to go to another area in the city."

They nodded and left, and I sighed as I accepted my target. Catherine took it away and checked the tight group in the center before circling it and signing it. We waited for her guards to leave and followed, and Markus met us. "How was your new pistol, Your Highness?"

Catherine grinned. "You were right about filing the trigger sear. It is a dream now. Thank you."

His shop had turned into an unofficial inspectors' range, so he was getting a lot more business. He was also carrying much better weapons than most gun shops. I made sure the constables had paid him, and we left. Catherine slipped her arm around mine. "I am free today, so I might tag along."

I grinned. "You just want to gossip with Abigail about her new boyfriend."

She grinned. "And she has a few ideas for our wedding."

I looked up at the dark clouds at a loud grumble. "You might want to send for your rain cloak."

We walked to the station and cleaned our pistols in the constable briefing room. A runner arrived from the chief of inspectors with a case, and I looked it over. "Stolen army supplies?"

Catherine snorted. "More like sold by the supply clerks."

I glanced at her. "Not even going to investigate before you declare it solved?"

She sighed. "Okay."

I checked the time as the constables arrived and picked seats. I nudged Catherine toward Lady Fiera and walked to the front. "It looks like our case is going to start at the army depot on the south edge of the city. They have reported a large theft of munitions and medical supplies. Before you assume it is a clerk, think. Who is the first person their leaders look at and suspect?"

I looked around the room.

"Next is how was it removed? It went missing over a single night, and there was more than one wagon could carry; that means wagons and horses. Last is the clerks were the ones to report the supplies missing or stolen. Enough to start thinking on the way. Everyone to the stable and the horses; because of the area, I would suggest bringing a shotgun or rifle."

I started for the door and caught Catherine's hand.

"Want to partner Lady Fiera?"

She smiled. "Sure."

Fifteen minutes, and we were riding through the streets. They were talking and making guesses about who or how the supplies had been taken. When we reached the depot, we found Abigail waiting at the gate. The guards were expecting us and let us in. The depot was a large area with warehouses surrounded by a tall stone wall. In the back was a wagon yard, a large stable, and a horse corral.

A constable and an army lieutenant were waiting when we reached one of the back warehouses. I swung down and tied my horse to a hitching post. I nodded to the constable and looked at the officer. "We will start with where the missing supplies were stored."

He nodded and turned to the warehouse beside us. "The medical supplies were in here."

I gestured to Abigail and started following the officer into the warehouse. "Have the gate guards been questioned?"

He snorted. "All six, and they said nothing went out. Someone is lying, and it is either the clerks or the guards."

I looked at the high windows as we turned left and headed to the end of the warehouse. "The warehouse was locked?"

He glanced back at everyone following and looked at me. "According to the clerks, it was when they left, but it was unlocked when they came in."

We stopped in a large empty space on the left side of the warehouse. I could see where pallets had been and slowly looked around. "This would be where the medical supplies were?"

He nodded, and I turned.

"All right. This was where some of the supplies were. Everyone look around carefully and tell me how it was removed."

They murmured and whispered as they spread out, and I touched Abigail.

"See the marks on the beam next to the windows?"

She looked up and then grinned. "Sneaky."

It was Lady Fiera who caught it. "It looks like someone used a set of ropes over the beam to lift the supplies. From there they could open the window and lower them outside."

Everyone looked, and I nodded. "If you look closely, you can see the inner window latch is unlocked."

I glanced at the officer. "Show us where the munitions were kept."

He turned to lead us out, and I stopped and looked at the door lock. On the outside there were tiny scratches that were fresh. I let everyone look before we went straight across to another warehouse. I checked the door lock, and it too had scratches. This time we went right and all the way to the end of the building. I looked at the empty space while everyone looked up at the rope fibers on a beam.

I glanced at the officer. "Do you have a list of what was taken?"

They had taken one whole pallet of rifle ammo, which was a lot. The medical supplies were mostly dressings and water-purification tablets, muscle relaxants, and pain pills. The ammo was specifically for military rifles. I passed the lists around and then headed back to the door. Outside I led the way to where they would have lowered the crates of ammo.

There were no signs of wagons or even horses. I looked around and crossed to look at the area outside the other warehouse. I turned to look at everyone. "Okay, so what do you see or see a lack of?"

They shifted and looked at Abigail, but she was shaking her head. Catherine and Lady Fiera were whispering and turned. Lady Fiera cleared her throat. "They did not use horses or wagons."

I smiled and nodded. "Correct."

I turned and started toward the wagon yard beyond the warehouses. When we reached the yards, I slowed and moved back and forth while looking at the ground.

"If they did not leave through the gate or were not seen by the gate guards, they left another way. Look at all the footprints in the dirt. Does anyone notice how much deeper those entering are compared to those leaving?"

Everyone nodded, and I looked at Abigail.

"Could you make a solid mold of these?"

She nodded, and I started toward the other side of the yard.

"So either they put the supplies in the wagons or…"

I stopped beside a wagon that had been lifted and moved until it was against the wall. "Or they went over the wall."

I gestured to one of them.

"Climb up and hang a kerchief over the wall."

He nodded and climbed onto the wagon first and then peered over the wall. I turned to head for our horses.

"Back to the horses."

Once everyone was in his or her saddle, I turned to head back to the gate and then started following the wall. When we got to the back wall, there was another very large walled compound for the army. This one for troop barrack and training fields. The guards looked at us and refused to let us enter. I swung down and walked to the guard booth and used their call box to call the officer of the watch.

Two minutes, and an officer was running to the gate, yelling at the guards to let us pass. I swung into the saddle and led the way around and to the kerchief hanging from the wall. I swung down and looked back as everyone copied me. "So look around and tell me where they went from here."

Abigail grinned because there were several places where a horse had shit. One of the men cleared his throat. "They had wagons here."

I nodded as I looked toward the row of barrack. "Want to bet they did not go through the gates?"

I gestured to a wagon yard and a large stable.

"We start there and speak with the night watch for the stable."

We walked and led the horses, and when we reached the stable, it was busy with men working and grooming horses. The night watch was gone and would not be back until it was dark. The sergeant for the men was not helping and ignored the supply officer. I grinned at Catherine as everyone looked frustrated. "Tell me, Sergeant, how long would you like to spend in prison?"

He smiled smugly. "You are on an army post and have no power here."

The stable hands were grinning, and I pulled my pistol and pointed it. "One of you put him in restraints and any other man who wants to continue protecting thieves."

The sergeant shifted. "You will not get off the post."

I snorted as two new inspectors yanked his arms back and put the restraints on. "I am not taking you off the post, Sergeant. I am going to turn you over to the provost and let an army officer judge you. The charge is going to be disrespect to an officer and conspiracy to steal from Her Majesty. Just so you know, the law applies to all, even on an army post."

I looked at the other men. "Who else would like to go to prison?"

They shifted and looked around, and I nodded.

"Now I will ask again. Who took the horses out and moved wagons from the wall, and where did they take them?"

It was quiet, and one cleared his throat. "The major for the Forty-Third Combat Battalion ordered the horses readied and harnessed to the wagons."

Several hissed or growled, and I nodded. "And where did they take the supplies?"

The sergeant shifted. "They were supplies and needed, and it is none of your business!"

I looked at him. "The commander of the supply depot made it our business when he reported the theft. If it was issued, we would not be here and hunting real thieves and criminals. Now where was it taken?"

He looked away and after a moment sighed. "Forty-Thirds supply building."

I glanced at the lieutenant and gestured to my horse. "Go ask your commander to join us."

I pointed to another man as the officer swung up into the saddle.

"You go to the post provost and tell him Inspector Knight is about to arrest the commander of the Forty-Third Combat Battalion."

His eyes were wide as he spun and started running. I pointed to another man.

"You go to the post headquarters and inform the commander that we are going to arrest a battalion commander."

He ran off, and I looked at the sergeant before I gestured.

"Release him. For the record, Sergeant, any constable has Her Majesty's authority to investigate and arrest soldiers even on a post. If you like, you may ask Her Highness why."

Catherine cleared her throat; his eyes widened, and he stammered and then went to a knee. The soldiers copied him, and she sighed. "Stand up, men."

Her guards were finally grinning, and I turned. "Okay, we have tracked the evidence out of the warehouse and over the wall. Now we know who ordered the horses and wagons and where the stolen supplies were taken. Someone tell me what your next step would be?"

Several spoke and said arrest the major, but it was Lady Fiera who said, "Confirm the location of the supplies and detain the battalion supply officer. Interrogate him and find out if he was acting on orders and if so whose. You sent notice to the supply commander, the provost, and the post commander so they would have to act and come to us. That way the battalion will not interfere, and we can get the why."

I grinned as I started walking. "Very good. Most of the time we have to arrest thieves, but sometimes there might be reasons behind it that can change the charge or even make it disappear. Now if this major did order the supplies taken, we could just arrest him, but the why could make a difference."

I led everyone to the street with the row of barrack and turned in at the Forty-Third Battalion and then went to the supply building. They were loading wagons and getting ready to leave when I saw the supply officer. He was watching us as I started for him. "Guards!"

I glanced at the two soldiers with rifles as they trotted toward us. I looked at him. "My name is Inspector Knight, and I will only say this once. Her Highness princess Catherine is here. You will lay down your weapons now, or her guards will consider you traitors."

He froze as his face went white, and the two guards did not hesitate and knelt to set the rifles down. All the men knelt, and Catherine shifted. "Please stand."

I nodded and looked at the officer. "Now we are here about stolen supplies. Would you like to talk to us or wait for your commanding officer and a court?"

He shifted and glanced at Catherine. "We are going to the southern border. The supply depot would not let us draw enough ammo or medical supplies. If we have to fight, men will die. The commander was only getting what we needed."

I sighed. "Which wagons have the supplies?"

He pointed them out, and I gestured to one of the new inspectors.

"Check them."

I looked at everyone.

"So now we have the stolen items and a statement of why. It seems we have our suspect, but the motive is something to consider. Anyone want to say just put him in prison?"

They looked at each other, and I smiled. "Okay, so what are our options?"

Lady Fiera grinned. "Make the big boys play well together. We put the case before the post commander, the provost, and the supply commander."

Everyone laughed. I nodded. "Sounds good."

I turned and started for the battalion headquarters. The staff tried to block us when we entered, but I gestured. "Move, or go to prison."

They shifted and slowly moved, and the major stepped forward with his head high. "I am responsible, and not my men."

I nodded and gestured to the others. "Everyone out."

I looked around the outer office and gestured. "Everyone find a seat. We are going to wait for the rest of the party."

It was not long before a captain wearing the emblem of the provost arrived. He growled, "This is—"

I held up a hand. "We are here for a case of theft. If you have a problem, talk to Colonel Porter. If you would like to talk about our authority, you can talk with Her Highness."

He froze and then shifted. "What do you have?"

I sat on the corner of a desk. "Evidence collected from the two warehouses the supplies were stolen from. Footprints left by the thieves leading to the wall between the supply depot and the post. Witness statements that the battalion commander ordered wagons and horses to the wall on this side and sent them to his supply. Last we have the supplies."

He sighed and nodded. "Then—"

I held up my hand. "Now we are going to wait for Colonel Porter and General Givins. They can hear the case and decide what actions to take."

He grinned and moved to sit beside me. "Sounds good."

It was not long before the two senior officers arrived. I explained the case, which the colonel knew, but he did not know the battalion had requested the supplies and the request was turned down by one of the junior officers. The general looked pissed, but the colonel shook his head. "He should have talked with his regiment commander or gone up the command to me."

I looked at the major. "That is a good question but not one we need to hear. Now we only need to know if you still want us to arrest the major and his men."

The general sighed. "No. Thank you for your hard work, Inspector, but we can take it from here."

I stood. "Perhaps your officers need a little cross exposure. Have a good day." I headed for the door. "Time to write up the report."

We rode back, and after we put the horses away, I had everyone meet in the briefing room. I started with a review and with how many had thought it had been a clerk when we started. I talked about how we examined the scene and why we look at everything, even if it was in the air or on the roof. Why even the absence of evidence was sometimes important.

I talked about interviewing witnesses and suspects and when to change from being polite to firm. How to always watch the whole situation and not just what was in front of them. Last was to learn all the facts of the case before bringing it to the magister. I had one write the report and sent it to the chief of inspectors before I released everyone for the day.

Lady Fiera looked smug as she left, and Catherine was talking with Abigail when I slipped my hand into hers. "All that and still in time for lunch, and it has not rained."

The classes helped the new inspectors a lot when we finished. Lady Fiera even learned something about how to act as an inspector and was not as defensive. I heard through the royal guards that changes were being made in the supply depot so the soldiers would be able to get what they needed. They also made sure it was put out that constables could enter a post and arrest soldiers.

CHAPTER 27

# Missing Maid

SEVERAL NEW GUARD posts were built around the edge of my estate, including a small guard building at the gate. Unlike the palace with its many ways in, there was only one way into my estate. The three squads who were stationed on the estate rotated in shifts, so one was always there. I even had three sergeants who were more than helpful to Mr. Mack or his wife if they needed it.

I grinned as I kept shaking the screen so the peppercorns would fall through. Catherine was sipping tea with Mrs. Mack and gossiping while we sacked up the peppercorns. She had stayed over and loved the peach jam on her pancakes that Mrs. Mack had made and left. So did her guards, and they had made sure Mrs. Mack knew how much they liked it.

Our wedding was only a month away, and the whole city was preparing. The fall was fully on us, and all the trees had lost their leaves. Mr. Mack had already pruned the grape vines and prepared the peach trees. I had done research and found the perfect wedding gift for Catherine. Foreign nobles were beginning to arrive and fill the richer hostels.

The higher nobles or the rich merchants were also beginning to show up since the fall harvest season was coming to a close. That meant there were parties every night, and that brought in more money to the city merchants. Catherine and I were both getting constant invitations, but so far we had only gone to a couple. I set the last bag down and stretched. "Finally."

Mr. Mack grinned as he began to rake and clean up the debris. I sat beside Catherine.

"So how is the midwinter festival planning coming?"

She grinned. "We were thinking of planting evergreen trees for next year, but for now the city lords have planters of holly trees for each corner. We have almost one hundred entries for the parade and twenty volunteer caroling groups practicing. You and I are going to be on one, so start preparing."

I smiled and looked at her lieutenant. "As long as I do not have to wear one of those tiny costumes."

She laughed and shook her head, and I sighed.

"Three weeks before you are hidden away."

She smiled. "It is only for a week until the wedding. Mother promised you could send notes."

I looked up at the touch of something wet on my cheek. "It is starting to rain."

I stood and held out my hand to pull Catherine up and then bent to grab several bags of peppercorns. Besides the peach and grape harvest, we had vanilla beans. Mr. Mack also had a dozen beehive boxes placed around the outer wall, but they were dormant now. In the kitchen we set the bags down while Mrs. Mack heated a large pot of water for more tea.

She added a little diced, dried peach to it, which made the whole kitchen smell nice. I went to wash and change and returned to the kitchen. Catherine was teasing the clerk who normally accompanied me. The constable assigned to me arrived and nodded to the lieutenant. He had a lot more experience now and was more relaxed. Catherine smiled and looked at me. "So what case do you have today?"

I shrugged and looked at the clerk, but he shook his head. "Nothing yet."

She stood. "Well I have a meeting starting in an hour, and then Mother and I have a fitting."

She started for the door, and I caught up. "Dinner?"

She turned at the door as her guards slipped out. "With Mother. Do not forget you have exercises tomorrow morning with Duke Kelvin's sons. You also promised to take them to buy hunting rifles after."

I kissed her and caressed her face. "And tonight?"

She grinned and then laughed as she turned to the door. "Dancing lessons, and if you pay attentions, we will see."

I grinned as I watched her leave and get into her carriage. I grabbed my long coat and looked back. "Time to go see what the constable general has for me."

The clerk and constable put on long coats as they followed me out. The ride in was wet and only got worse as the rain came down harder and colder. I was sure it would be ice by morning or maybe snow. The stable at the city lords' building was full with several small heaters going. I noticed three horses, one with a side saddle with noble tack waiting beside the side door as we crossed to enter.

We climbed the rear stairs and walked the wide hall to the front of the building. The constable general and commissioner had offices next to each other. The constable commissioner was in charge of all constables in the city, but the general commanded all constables in the country. I think they were still trying to decide where I fit in.

We stopped in the general's outer office. His secretary was a little red faced as someone next door was demanding action from the commissioner. I smiled and moved down the hall and started through the outer office. Two guards stood beside the inner office door, and the assistant stood. "Inspector Knight, he is in with someone. If you wait, I will let him know you are here."

I kept going. "That is okay, Tamara. I wanted to ask him about the security for the wedding."

The two guards shifted to block me, and the constable with me moved forward and growled, "Move, or you go to jail."

They hesitated, and I touched the constable. "Relax. They were just moving."

They looked at each other and moved, and I pushed the door open. A woman spun from leaning on the commissioner's desk. "Get out!"

I ignored her as I crossed the office and looked out the window. "The general does not seem to have a case for me, Commissioner. I was going to speak to you about the security for the wedding and the review route after. Do you think we could perhaps invite constables from other cities and duchies to participate?"

He blinked and looked from the woman to me as she glared. "Um...I could speak to the general...if the general does not have a case I could use a discreet inspector."

I looked at the woman. "Something to do with Her Grace?"

She straightened. "And who are you?"

The constable commissioner cleared his throat. "Pardon me. Lady Bethany, this is Inspector Ashton Knight. Ashton, this is Duchess Hollywine."

I bowed. "Lady. Her Majesty has spoken of you."

She frowned. "Mr. Knight…um…you would be the one who is marrying my husband's niece."

I nodded. "I am afraid she captured me fair and square."

Her lips quirked before she sighed. "Mr. Knight, my maid is missing…and this…person is not being helpful."

I ignored the red face of the commissioner and gestured to the chair behind her. "If you would sit and explain?"

She glanced back, and I moved to lean on the desk. She hesitated and then sat. "We have taken rooms in the Golden Crown. They did not have a servants' room available for my maid, so she took a room at the Devinshire down the street. Last night she left and was to be back this morning. She did not come, and I sent one of the armsmen. She was not in her room, and the hostel staff refuses to check the room."

I nodded. "I assume they knocked on her door, but she did not answer?"

She snorted. "Of course they knocked."

I looked at the clerk and constable and did not say anything about the maid finding or having company. I shrugged. "I will find her."

The duchess stood. "I will need her back before noon."

She turned, and I let her go and looked at the commissioner and waited until she closed the door. He sighed. "I tried to tell her I would send a constable, but she demanded I go. She can be…very…high minded."

I started for the door. "So Catherine warned me."

I gestured to the constable and clerk once we were out of the office. "Hopefully this will not take long, and we can return and see the general."

It was a cold, wet ride through the streets with people hurrying from shop to shop. I swung down in the stable yard of the hostel and handed the reins to a lad. "Put them inside until we come out."

He grinned at the constable and nodded, and I headed for the door. Inside there were nobles and rich merchants, and they were all looking out the windows. I moved through them and stopped at the desk. "Is your manager here?"

A young clerk smiled politely. "He is helping a guest."

I opened my coat and showed my badge. "We are here to check on a guest. She is the maid for Duchess Hollywine."

He frowned. "Like I told her guards, we are not going to disturb a guest."

I tapped the counter. "You saw the badge, and you see the constable with me. Now either you come open the door or give us the key. If you do not do either of those, you go to jail for interfering in an investigation."

He looked at the door into the office behind him. "The manager gave me an order not to give that key out or to open the door."

He licked his lips and turned to take a key from a box and hand it to me. I looked at the number and turned to head for the stairs. "Now why would the manager not want to check on a guest?"

The constable snorted. "Maybe the maid invited him into her room?"

I glanced at him. "Or?"

He grinned as the clerk chuckled. "Or he did something to her."

I nodded as we stopped on the third floor and headed down a hall. At the end I examined the door carefully before I unlocked it. I pushed the door open but did not enter and looked around the room. It was empty, but a chair was turned over, and someone had turned back the covers on the bed. On a dresser I saw a handbag. "Okay, now I am prepared to think something happened to her."

I moved in slowly and walked to the open door into the bathroom. Water was all over the floor, and the tub was half-full. A towel was off the rack and thrown against the wall. "It looks like she was taken while she was in the bath. See the water on the floor and the way the towel has been thrown against the wall? The maid's clothes are folded on the counter, so she was here."

I moved back and aside and knelt to look at the floor between the two doors.

"There are dried boot prints from the bath to the door."

I stood and started for the door.

"Time to go question the manager."

I glanced at the constable.

"Call for Constable Mage Green. Maybe she can get something from the bathroom."

It was no longer just a case of a missing maid. Now it was possible something had happened to her. I glanced at the window as we came down the stairs and saw hail. We crossed to the desk, and I looked at the clerk. "Where is your manager?"

He shrugged. "He just said he was going to help a guest."

I kept looking at him, and he blushed and looked at the office door again. I started around the counter. "Watch this one."

I pushed him out and to the constable and then started for the office door. I pushed it open and found the manager looking dazed and a packet of drugs and a syringe on the desk. I moved in and caught his head and looked into the eyes before yanking him up and shoving him to the door.

I followed and looked at the clerk. "Call Constable Mage Green again."

The manager finally began to struggle. "Do you know who I am!"

I slammed him over the counter and pulled my restraints. "My prisoner on the way to the gallows. You kidnapped a maid in her bath. You are a drug user and a thief."

He struggled. "No! She was just a common maid!"

I slapped the back of his head. "If I do not find her in the next day, I will assume you robbed her and dumped the body in the river."

He jerked on the restraints and whined, "I...sold her to the Scarlet Jay."

The constable growled, and I glanced at him and pulled the prisoner to the call box. I called the central station and requested a constable for the prisoner. I looked at the white-faced desk clerk and the crowd in the lobby watching us. I requested the constable commander get a warrant for Abigail to do a truth spell on the clerk. I also requested a few street constables meet us at the Scarlet Jay."

It was not long before Abigail walked in and shook off the rain. She pushed her coat open to show the badge and started toward us. "Trouble, Ashton?"

I nodded and pushed the manager around the counter. "I need a room checked to identify those involved in taking a maid. I also asked for a warrant for a truth spell for the clerk."

Two constables wearing long rain coats pushed the doors open and walked in.

I handed the room key to Abigail. "Keep a constable with you and watch your back."

She nodded, and I gestured to the constables and pushed the manager.

"This one goes in. Lock him in the drunk tank for now. He is on a drug he injected in the office. The charge is room breaking and kidnapping. There might be other charges later. Take the drugs in the office, and one of you stay with Constable Mage Green."

They nodded, and I headed through the room and the side door.

I glanced at the constable with me when we were outside. "You know of this Scarlet Jay?"

He growled as we headed to the stable, "An upscale whorehouse we suspected of selling women to foreign lords."

I grinned as we swung up into the saddle. "In that case we get a warrant on the way and close it for good."

We stopped at the central station and went in and back to see the duty magister. He listened and granted us a search warrant for the Scarlet Jay on the testimony of the manager even though he was not there yet. I think the constable had a few words with the commander or lieutenant. When we left, there were a dozen constables accompanying us.

If anything the tiny hail had grown larger. The horses did not like it and kept dancing and bucking. At least we only had a few streets to travel. We stopped at a tavern a few buildings away and paid for the lad to keep the horses in the stable. We walked down the street and found a few more constables waiting. I sent half around to the back and a couple to search the stables.

I walked to the front doors and knocked. It was a couple of minutes before a woman opened the door. She smiled. "We are closed until—"

I pushed her back and walked in with the constables following. "I am Inspector Knight, and we have a warrant to search for a missing maid. When we find her, you are going to prison or the gallows."

She sneered. "You will not find her here."

I smiled and moved closer. "If I do not, I will have a mage use a truth spell on you. We will find her one way or another."

I turned and gestured.

"From the attic to the basement."

The constables poured in as two very large men came out of a room.

I pushed the woman ahead of me. "Let us start with the rooms down here."

One of the men growled and reached inside his shirt, and I brushed my coat back. I pulled and cocked my pistol as I saw one coming out of the shirt. I pointed and fired, and he jerked up and spun. I shoved the woman to the wall as I brought my pistol all the way up while cocking it and aimed. The other man was pulling a pistol as the first went to his knees. That was when four more men holding pistols rushed out the door.

I fired, and the second man's head snapped back. Even as I shifted to aim at another man, the constable with me fired. One of the four new men folded and fell, and the other three panicked and fired. I felt the bullets crack as they missed and then constables on the stairs and those rushing in from the back fired. The men jerked and went down, and I turned and grabbed the woman. "Now you go to the gallows."

She screamed and struggled, and I pushed my weapon back into the holster. I kept her pinned against the wall. "I need restraints."

The constable with me held a pair out, and I took them and put them on her.

I glanced at his bloody shoulder. "Someone call for the constable doctor."

I yanked her back and pushed her to another constable. I pulled my pistol and moved to the room the men had come from. Four constables were already checking the men as I stepped into the room. It was a study and looked empty. I looked at the men on the floor of the hall and shook my head. I started to move around the room and looked at the other three walls.

The one on the right was between the study and the front parlor. The side wall had windows looking out at the back of the stables. I slowed at the back wall and realized it was a couple of paces short with no back window. The house extended a long way to the left and had three floors, but it was not very deep. I looked at the floor along the wall and saw scratches. "We have a secret door!"

Several constables moved into the room as I started searching for the way to open the door. It had to be on the wall, and I found a tiny cord tied to one corner of the frame of a painting. I tilted the painting to one side and pushed, and part of the wall swiveled.

I saw a set of stairs and looked around. "We need a lantern."

While I waited I replaced the cylinder in my pistol and held up the lantern and peeked in and down. I jerked back when I saw a man with a gun, and he fired. I shoved in with my pistol leading the way and fired and cocked my pistol again. The man jerked back as the round hit his shoulder, and he began to curse. I kept my weapon up as I moved down the stairs with three constables following.

I reached the bottom and spun around the doorframe and fired as the man lifted his pistol. He folded as he was struck in the belly, and I moved into the narrow hall. On the left were several cages, and each held a girl. I moved to the man and kicked the pistol away as he writhed around. I let one of the others put him into restraints and finished checking all the cages.

Only one had a girl with a sheet wrapped around her. Since I had not asked the maid's name, I smiled. "You are Lady Hollywine's maid?"

She looked terrified but nodded, and I started searching for keys to unlock the cages. There were six girls in the cages and another three hidden upstairs in a secret room inside a closet. Eight of the twelve women working in the house had been forced. The man downstairs was a foreign merchant here to buy girls and sell them to foreign lords before the wedding.

We also found a major drug supplier thanks to the hostel manager. The clerk was innocent if a little on the naïve side. When the duchess found out what happened to her maid, she was shocked and appalled and clung to her as if she would break. The madam and those men still alive were sentenced to hang. The owner of the Devinshire hostel was shocked his manager had been a part of what happened and came to run it himself.

I had found the madam's client book and sent out a notice. Before the day was over, Catherine had several hundred new donations for the midwinter festival. I also asked for and got the magister to seize the large building and spoke with the city orphanage about moving. It had twenty bedrooms and a large yard, which was more than enough for the orphans.

I also visited the constable who went around with me and had been wounded. I had spoken with the commissioner and his commander. I gave him a constable-inspector badge. "You start the course next Monday."

The constable general had been more than a little surprised. He had also spoken with the commissioner and agreed to ask for constables from every city to come help during the wedding. It was a chance for constables from the whole country to be involved and be part of what was happening. All that, and I still made it to dinner on time and enjoyed the dance lessons.

# CHAPTER 28

# Dead Minister

I SHIFTED AND reached for the small man's wrist and tried to yank my hand back. It was too late; he caught my hand, and I felt pressure from his thumb. My hand and wrist were bent and twisted, and my body started to go with it. I stepped and snapped a kick around and up and yelled as my arm was lifted. I went down and slammed onto the padding and rolled to my feet.

Before I could stand, the small man was there and kicked into my chest, and I went back and down again. This time I ignored not being able to breathe as I rolled over and came to my feet. I turned and brushed another kick to the side and lifted the foot and cursed to myself. The small man was already in the air and rolling as he snapped a foot around and out.

I leaned back, and the foot missed as he fell. Before I could act, he was coming to his feet and striking again. I was angry and snapped as I caught and yanked the hand passing me and kicked down and across into the back of his knee. My other hand grabbed the back of his neck, and I turned and twisted and threw. He went into the wall as I followed and brushed a kick aside and grabbed his shirt and yanked.

He was thrown across the room, and I followed as he laughed. He rolled and came to his feet and turned and bowed. "Much better. You finally stopped thinking and acted."

I finally took a deep breath and bowed. "It only took you beating me for an hour to do it."

He moved forward. "But now you know in your heart what to do. Your wounds are healed, and your body sound. Your grandfather will be proud."

He glanced at the smirking constable to one side.

"Now if only you can get these lazy bones to exercise."

I smiled. "Thank you, Joseph."

He nodded, and we moved to the side of the room to stretch. Joseph was here with my grandfather; he had been the one to teach me years ago at the shooting-and-fighting gallery. I grabbed a towel when we were done and led the way out of the room. I glanced at the corporal and his men and shook my head as I headed for the bedroom.

I had to wash and then dress before I came out. "We are going to the palace before I head to the city lords' building."

The corporal nodded and gestured to the two guards waiting by the door. With two weeks left before the wedding, the three squads guarding the estate were joined by a three-man detail to guard me. The constable with me was new but thought everything was funny. Of course no one thought the constant falling snow was funny. I shifted the small package I was carrying and ignored the horses and started to walk.

The guards grumbled as they led the horses and followed. It was a refreshing walk with more than a few children out playing in the snow. The guards at the palace nodded and let us pass and went back to the small stove inside their guard building. My own pretty much did the same thing. I found Catherine in the small private dining room with her mother and father.

I ignored the guards around the wall and the two ministers eating with them. I bent and kissed her and set the package in front of her. She grinned. "That time already?"

I pulled a chair close and sat. "I had to do a lot of hunting for that."

She tore the wrapping and looked at the slim wooden box. She opened it and stared at the elegant silver-and-gold necklace lying on velvet. "Oh, Ashton!"

I smiled. "This was the wedding gift of the first queen by her husband. It was passed to her youngest daughter who passed it to—let us just say it has been handed down. The last owner was a baron who died childless. The estate solicitor had the letters certifying most of the linage, and I tracked it the rest of the way using the description."

Her eyes were bright as she took it out and caressed it. "It is perfect."

Her mother chuckled. "Put it on and kiss him."

I put it on her, and she kissed me hard and then turned and reached for a small package a servant held out. "Mother and I have been speaking to the constable general. We have decided that every duchy needs at least one knight or royal inspector. They will investigate crimes involving nobles or capital crimes if that is all they have. They will report to the constable general only."

She held out the package.

"You have more than made a name for yourself. We have approved this as the second step our inspectors should strive for."

I opened the package and then the small box. Inside was a badge like the one I wore, but in the scroll at the top, it read, "Royal Inspector." I grinned and used a finger to follow the lines in gold. "It is beautiful."

She grinned. "I thought you would like it."

I shifted as a runner came in out of breath. I slipped the badge into my pocket. His bow was brief, and then he blurted, "Minister Foxe is dead."

I straightened as the queen answered, "Dead. How, lad?"

He reddened. "They just found the body in the snow by the corner of Woodrow and Dye Streets. The street constable recognized him and sent me."

I glanced at the queen. "Minister of what?"

She sat back. "Interior trade."

I bent to kiss Sabrina. "I will go look into it."

One of the ministers at the table stood. "I better summon the others."

I did not hear the rest as I walked out. The constable caught up. "Horses?"

I nodded and glanced at the corporal. "Keep your men back when we get to the body."

He nodded. "The lieutenant told me what to do when you are working."

Outside we swung up onto the horses and started for the gate. I stopped there to have the guards call the city lords' building to send the clerk to the scene with the body. The corner was not that far and located on the edge of the estate and commerce districts. I saw several constables together by the call box, and the body was to one side.

Only two sets of tracks went to it, and one came to the call box. I swung down as I looked around. On the corner was a herbalist shop, and beside it a café that was not open yet. Across the street was a bakery; the front was not open, but I knew the baker would be working. I gestured to the bakery. "One of you go knock and ask the baker if we might use the front of his shop to stay warm."

I looked at the body and moved to it but stayed to one side as I looked at the snow. There were many old tracks under the fresh snow, but it would be hard to see any new ones.

"One of you call and see if Constable Mage Green is available."

I stayed close to the building as I moved to the body and knelt.

I looked at Constable Donny since he was following me. "What do you notice?"

He was not laughing now and squatted. "He was murdered."

I nodded and gestured to the disturbed snow around his body. "If you look hard, you can see blood frozen in and under the snow. Look at his hands."

He leaned. "One has a cut on it."

I nodded. "Defensive wounds."

I saw the constable doctor wagon and the clerk who was supposed to follow me coming down the street. I remember seeing the ministers a lot, and they all had satchels. I looked around and saw where it had fallen, but it was gone now.

"His satchel is missing. We will need to see if his assistants knew what was in it."

The ambulance wagon with the constable doctor stopped, and he climbed down. "Inspector."

I gestured. "Permission to turn over the body?"

He snorted. "Go ahead."

I shifted and leaned and caught the far side and lifted and pulled. The body was completely stiff, so it had been there long enough to go into rigor and freeze. I looked at the front of his body, and we could see multiple stab wounds. I shook my head. "It was not professional. By the number I would say it could be personal if it were not for the missing satchel. The blade was very narrow, maybe a penknife or stiletto."

I gestured to hilt marks.

"The hilt mark tells us they were strong enough to drive the blade all the way into him. I might even think it was anger."

I checked down his body and saw lots of blood splatter.

I stood. "Thanks, Doc."

I moved back the way I had come and headed for the bakery. By the look he had opened the shop, and the constables were inside.

I walked in. "Our suspect will have gotten bloody. Check trash containers for a couple of blocks. One of you stay, and when Constable Mage Green arrives, see if she can track the blood trail that should be under the snow."

They nodded, and I smiled at the baker as I pulled out a few silvers and set them on the counter. "Are the pastries done?"

He grinned and turned to bring a tray of pastries to the counter.

I took one and looked out the window and said to the constables, "Have a pastry and then let us get back to work and find the killer."

It was the satchel that stayed with me as I ate the pastry. The constables went out to start searching, and I saw Abigail arrive. I went out and watched as she tried to use a spell to follow the blood. With the falling snow, it was very faint.

I sighed and then grinned. "You see where the satchel was dropped?"

She nodded, and I looked down the street. "Can you use a resonance spell to the minister to identify and find it?"

She blinked and then grinned. "Sure."

She chanted and moved to where it had fallen.

She knelt and drew a rune and then stood and looked down the street. "It is not far."

We walked through the snow and slowed at an alley with trash cans. A constable had already searched them, but she nodded to a snow drift beside some steps. "There."

I walked to it and knelt and carefully brushed layers of snow away until I saw the satchel. It was open, and I used my knife to tilt it to look inside. "Open."

I looked at Constable Donny.

"That means it could be personal, but they searched and maybe took something."

I glanced at Abigail.

"Can you track or identify the one who touched it?"

She whispered and then shook her head. "Falling snow is like running water."

I picked up the satchel and started out. "So now we need to go to his office and speak with his assistants. Thanks, Abigail."

She chuckled as she wrapped her cloak around herself and started for the bakery. Constable Donny and the clerk followed as the corporal and his men fell in. I let them lead the horses as I walked and thought. I did not think the killing had been passionate, but it had been personal. We returned to the palace, and I nodded to the guards and headed around to the ministers' entrance. "Put the horses away for now."

When I walked into the large entrance, it looked like all the other ministers were in. Mostly it was the number of assistants and clerks who told me. I caught one as she hurried toward a side hall. "Where is Minister Foxe's office?"

She had stiffened and then pointed. "There, but he is dead."

I nodded as I headed for the hall. "Thank you."

I checked a couple of offices before I found one with interior trade ministry on the door. I opened it and walked in, and a well-dressed man turned. "We are closed."

His attitude and appearance were not one of mourning. "I am Inspector Knight."

He looked me over and turned back to sorting through the papers on the desk. "You are not needed here."

I gestured to Constable Donny. "Put him in restraints."

The man spun, and his eyes went wide. "I…"

I smiled. "I am here on royal business. Since the minister is dead, no one touches his work."

Donny moved to him and reached for his arm. The man jerked it away. "I will have your badge!"

I smiled and held it out. "Since it was given by Her Highness and the queen, I doubt that is going to happen. What *is* going to happen is you will go before a magister for tampering with evidence in a murder and threatening a constable."

Donny grabbed his arm and spun him and slammed him over the desk. He yanked his arms back and put the restraints on as the man cursed us. I turned as the corporal growled at someone in the hall.

"Who is it, Corporal?"

He glanced at me. "A couple of assistants."

I gestured. "Send one in."

He moved, and a young man stepped in, and by his bearing, he was probably the son of a noble. He sniffed and looked at the man being put into restraints. "The queen will not allow this."

I smiled. "What is your business here?"

He looked at me like I was something he stepped on. "The foreign trade minister wanted us to collected everything in the office and bring it back. You need to leave so we—"

I had heard enough and gestured to the corporal. "Get him out of here before I lock him up for stupidity."

The corporal grinned as the young man stiffened. He caught his arm and pulled him out. I looked at Constable Donny and his prisoner, who was now glaring at me.

"And now what is your story?"

He sneered. "I am the personal assistant to Minister Foxe and a personal friend of Her Majesty."

I nodded. "And you knew he was dead?"

He nodded, and I gestured.

"Take him in, Donny. He has just admitted to tampering with evidence. Let the magister know I will come by this afternoon to fill out the charge sheet. Make sure you search him and log everything you find. He can wait in a cell until I get there."

I looked at the desk.

"Where is the minister's day calendar?"

Donny yanked and pulled the man to the door. "On the floor behind the desk."

Before they were out of hearing, the assistant was pleading with Donny. I smiled at the clerk as I looked around the office. I moved around the desk and bent to pick up the calendar. I thumbed through the days and went back and found the one before minister Foxe died. It was torn out, but I could see the imprint of writing on the next page.

I set it on the desk and used a piece of graphite. I shaved it into a powder and then blew it across the page while explaining to the clerk what I was doing.

The writing from the page was visible, and I pulled out my notebook to copy it. "It looks like Minister Dodley authorized an agreement between two duchies."

I began to sort through the papers on the desk. I pulled up a list of trade goods written down with the annotation of the Kistler duchy and a question mark. I blinked and then realized what it was and collected all the papers and the day calendar. I checked my pocket watch and started for the door. "Corporal, call one of the palace guards. I want the door locked and guarded."

He moved in and to the call box as I waited in the doorway. A minute, and a guard appeared, and I led the clerk and my bodyguards out. "No one enters until I give permission."

I walked through the wing, and we were passed through into the royal wing. In the queen's outer office, I stopped and smiled at one of her assistants. "I need a few moments. Let her know it is about Minister Foxe."

She nodded and stood to cross and enter the inner office. It was a minute before she was back and gestured. The clerk and my guards stayed as I crossed and entered her office. Five men I recognized as ministers were in the room, and so was Catherine. I bowed and crossed to the desk and set the papers and calendar down. "Why would the duke of Kistler grow a restricted-drug plant?"

The queen frowned. "What does this have to do with Minister Foxe?"

I saw one of the ministers shifting as I adjusted my coat so I could get at my weapon. "Parts of the trade agreement between merchants in Kistler and Hollywine were in the office. The part with the trade minister's signature was missing. Only in his day calendar he wrote that Minister Dodley had signed the agreement."

She turned to look at the man who was shifting around. "Harold? Why would you sign an agreement between duchies?"

He looked at me hard and then smiled at her politely. "The inspector must be mistaken."

I looked at his clothes, but they were clean. What was not was the tiny spots of dried blood on his shoes. I used a tiny hand gesture to Catherine. "I am not mistaken, Minister. I am sure when I go look up the authorized trade-import records for the Kistler, I will find your authorization. Just as I am sure I will find the merchant who accepted it is the same one on the interior-trade agreement."

He shifted, and one hand moved to a coat pocket. "It is a legal drug to import."

Catherine had moved until she was beside her mother as I drifted closer to the minister. I nodded. "And used in several distillations in that duchy to fight spring and summer illnesses. What I am betting is the amount brought in was a lot more than needed. When distilled with a couple of other things, it makes a powerful euphoric that also causes—"

I shook my head.

"I am betting I also find the other raw ingredients being brought in through other duchies. You must have used Minister Foxe's assistant to get it past him. Too bad—he is on the way to prison and is already talking to a magister."

Minister Dodley shoved his hand into his pocket as he growled, "Noisy bastard!"

As he yanked his hand out, Catherine was pulling her mother up and away while the guards beside the door reacted. My left hand snapped out and caught his hand holding a small pocket pistol. I twisted it up and away from Catherine and the queen while stepping in and bringing my knee up. The minister screamed as his other hand brought up a stiletto and he jabbed.

I twisted, turned, and leaned but did not let go of the hand with the pistol. I yanked as he came down and started to bend forward. I jerked up on the hand and arm with the pistol, and he screamed as I dislocated the arm. He went down, and the pistol went flying across the room. I continued to turn and step and went to a knee on his back. "Drop the knife!"

I twisted the arm, and he kept screaming, and finally time sped up, and the guards reached us. The doors had burst open, and more guards were pouring in. The knife was yanked out of his hand, and his other arm pulled back. I shifted and pulled my restraints and put them on. I moved and let the guards pull him up as he cursed them and me.

I searched him, and in an inside pocket, I found the signature page of the trade agreement. I went to get the stiletto. "I am sure this will match the wounds in Minister Foxe."

I accepted the pocket pistol and used a kerchief to wrap both weapons. I nodded to the corporal of my guards since he was holding Minister Dodley. "Time to go to the magister."

I went to give Catherine a kiss. "Nice reflexes."

Her mother shook her head. "Anything else to disrupt my day?"

I kissed her cheek. "A suggestion to have minister assistants spend a day each month as housekeepers or manual laborers. They are more than a little snide and conceited."

She smiled as I headed for the door. "I will consider it."

Our walk in the falling snow was filled with Dodley whining and complaining about his dislocated shoulder. The clerk talked about what I had seen and noticed. When we reached the station, Constable Donny was just leaving. He blinked and turned to follow us in. "I found a torn page in the assistant's pocket."

When we brought the minister in and the assistant saw, he started talking. I was right about the other agreements and shipments. Even before I pushed the two in front of the magister and gave him my report and the charges, I made calls to the duchess of Hollywine. She was incensed that the minister and merchants would dare make drugs in her duchy.

She made several calls to the constable commissioners in her cities, and the merchants were picked up. Raids in a large warehouse turned up the drug lab and smugglers who were going to bring the drugs into other duchies. In a matter of one day, a new and unknown drug ring was destroyed. Even when he was before the magister, Dodley had no remorse for killing Minister Foxe.

He was sentenced to hang, and the assistant ended up with fifteen years on a labor gang. It took another week for the queen to appoint two new ministers. That night my grandfather walked to the palace with us for dinner with Catherine and her mother. He had met Catherine, but her mother and father and my grandfather hit it off like old soldiers and spent the evening talking about the past.

CHAPTER 29

# Raiding Lords

I was more than a little nervous—the wedding was only a day away. Thousands of people had flocked to the city until every house and shop was filled. Outside the city farmers had tents lined up in fields. My wedding suit was finished, and everything else done and just waiting. The weather had cleared, but there was still snow on the ground.

What I needed was a distraction. I could not see Catherine until the wedding, and for the last three days, I had no cases. Looking at my estate and watching the guards was feeling a little closed in. I decided to slip away and take a walk in the country or at least in the outer suburbs and estates. I dressed warm and slipped out the back door when no one was looking.

I went straight back and looked at the wall before I jumped and pulled myself over at a spot free of snow. On the other side, I found myself in a pasture full of tents and headed to one side and a low stone wall. I looked both ways and jumped over and turned to walk north on the narrow path. I took a deep breath and smiled as I looked ahead and watched people leaving tents or farms.

When I reached an intersection, a cart was having problems with one wheel that had slipped off and into deeper snow. The farmer was struggling to help his horse, and I moved to wade into the snow. I caught a spoke of the wheel and pulled, and slowly the horse moved forward and pulled the cart out. I grinned as I stopped and nodded to the farmer. "You should be okay now."

He smiled and waved as he kept leading the horse down the small track. I looked both ways and then crossed to continue down the same path I had been on. There were no more fields of tents, and after a quarter hour, I turned off the path and onto a wider road. I waved to the few country people I saw and enjoyed the fresh air. I caught up to a constable walking his horse. "Everything okay?"

He smiled. "Just taking a break to warm my legs."

I nodded. "I know the feeling."

He looked at me and then around. "You live around here, sir?"

I shook my head. "Closer to the city. I just needed to get out for fresh air."

He grinned. "The city is a little crowded right now."

I chuckled as I looked that way. "And loud."

I looked ahead to see a fancy carriage at the intersection of roads. The one it was on was large and more traveled. "It looks like something happened."

The constable shook his head. "I bet it is the damn raiding lords again."

I looked at him as he turned to swing up into the saddle. "Raiding lords?"

He glanced at me. "Nothing to worry about."

I shifted and opened my coat and pulled out my badge. "Inspector Knight. What raiding lords?"

He blinked. "Knight? You are…"

I sighed. "Bored and nervous. I wish we could have just slipped away to have a magister marry us."

He grinned and shook his head and then sobered as he looked at the carriage. He sighed. "So far we have two dozen cases of young lords raiding fancy carriages and outlying estates. They never stay long and take jewelry and bank notes. From witnesses we know they are using engraved weapons and horses in very good shape. We have not been able to track them because of the traffic into the city."

I turned and started walking. "Maybe I can help."

He caught up. "It would to dangerous, sir."

I snorted as I kept going. "I am sure as soon as my security finds me, we will have more than enough protection."

We reached the carriage and found the driver beaten and two women crying inside. I let the constable deal with the women while I helped the driver. I looked at the trampled snow and shook my head as I moved to put him into the carriage. "We need to get him to a doctor and contact a few people."

The constable nodded, and I moved to tie his horse to the back of the carriage. I climbed up onto the driver's box and shook the reins. It was a few minutes before we reached another crossroad and another constable. I gestured, and he came closer as I kept going.

"There has been a robbery. The constable is inside, and we have an injured driver."

He nodded, and I looked at people walking on the road in front of us.

"I am Inspector Knight. We are going to need a doctor and a constable mage. Ride ahead and use the closest call box. I will drive the carriage to the Saints Hospital and wait there."

He kicked his horse into a trot, and I watched him turn in at a farm with several tents in their yard. I was careful as the carriage reached the outer streets, and I got the horses to trot. Once we reached the cobbled streets, I slowed in case the horses slipped. I turned in at the hospital and slowed and then came to a stop at the main doors.

"We need help!"

I swung down as a nurse and orderly came out. The constable opened the door, and the orderly brought a litter. We moved the driver onto the litter and carried him in with the two women following. Once the driver was on a gurney and doctors were moving him to a treatment room, I started back out to the carriage. I looked into the carriage and saw the driver's long coat.

Blood was on it, and I was careful as I turned and spread it out. I saw a reversed image in the blood and left it as the constable returned. I glanced at him as I moved around the carriage. "Did you get a statement from the ladies?"

He followed. "Yes, but the men had part of their faces covered. They took jewelry and bank notes like always."

I found where one climbed into the carriage and left a snowy boot print. I marked it and kept going and checked the bridles of the horses. In one I saw where someone had grabbed it and marked it. "Make a note. The constable mage needs to try to lift the image on the long coat. There was a boot print on the far side door. Maybe she can get a resonance. There are also minor signs of someone grabbing the front-left horse's bridal."

He grinned as he started making notes. I went to the rear of the carriage and opened the boot. There were horse blankets, but that was it. I glanced at the street as the corporal and Constable Donny rode in. The guards looked very— determined, and Constable Donny was not smiling. I ignored them as I finished my walk around and gestured to the constable. "As soon as we can, let us move the carriage to the central station stable."

He nodded, and I turned. "I apologize, Corporal, but being shut in the house doing nothing was…"

He sighed. "Sir, you are our responsibility. We have been looking everywhere. You cannot just run off."

I smiled. "Actually I can and did. I was having a nice walk, and no one had any idea I was out. Now I have a case, which means danger, and that means you and your people get to do your jobs."

I turned when I saw Abigail riding up. She frowned as she swung down. "What are you doing out, Ashton?"

I grinned. "Escaping to do something before I went crazy."

I gestured and led her around to the carriage door.

"So far we have three things for you. There is a boot print I am hoping you can restore and get a resonance and cast we can match to a suspect. Next is a long coat with an image in blood. If you can bring up the image so we can see what it was, I would be grateful. Last was one of the men grabbed a bridle, and maybe you can get something."

She sighed as she gestured me back and moved into the carriage. She looked at the print and whispered, and the hair on my arm stood up. There was a chill, and the print shifted and became very clear and solid. She opened her satchel and pulled out a powder and sprinkled it on the print until it was covered. Next she mixed two small bottles and poured the mixture over the powder.

She turned and looked at the long coat. She frowned and murmured, and again I felt the magic. I glanced at the two constables who were watching intently. Abigail leaned closer as the image lifted into the air. "It looks like a crest from a ring."

She pulled a crystal and murmured, and the image moved to the crystal and seemed to sink into it. She held it out to me and then looked at the blood and chanted, and the image of a fist appeared. I accepted the crystal and looked at the hand and saw a scar. "See the scar?"

I looked at the constable and Donny, and they nodded, and I gestured. "Notes, gentlemen."

Abigail bent to lift a solid cast mold of the boot print, and I helped her out. She held it out. "There is a bootmaker's mark."

I led her around and to the front horse. She looked at the bridle and pat the horse. She grinned as she pulled another crystal. "Actually I think I can do something better."

She put her hand on the side of the horse's head and chanted. I watched the crystal and a face slowly appeared.

She finished and gave the horse another pat before handing me the crystal. "That should help."

I grinned as I accepted it. "It will. Thanks, Abigail."

She nodded and started for her horse. "Do not miss the wedding, Ashton."

I grinned as I gestured to the constable. "Let us move the carriage."

Since the corporal had brought my horse, we rode. We put the horses in the constable stable and the carriage in the hay barn. I had been thinking and led everyone back to the palace. The gate guards frowned, and I smiled as I leaned forward. "I need to see the librarian."

They blinked and gestured, and I led the way in and to a side door. I let one of the palace-stable boys take my horse when I swung down. I led the way in and to the back where the large royal library was. I opened the door and stepped in and looked at the tall shelves of books before the old librarian moved to me. I smiled and bowed. "Sir, I was hoping you could help us identify a noble crest."

He turned and gestured to a corner. "New or old?"

We followed him, and he stopped and looked at me. I pulled out one of the crystals. "New."

He nodded and touched a thick book, and I pulled it out. We moved to a table and set it down, and I showed him the crest in the crystal. He frowned and then turned to open the book and turned pages before stopping. I looked at a crest and then the one in the crystal. "It is missing…"

The librarian smiled and turned the page. "That was the crest for the baron. This is for his heirs."

I looked at the crest on the next page and then at the crystal. I nodded and looked at the constable. "If you would copy the information, Constable Harris."

I turned at a throat clearing and bowed. "Your Majesty."

She smiled. "Working?"

I grinned. "Well, I went for a walk to get some air and found something." I turned. "Your Majesty, this is Constable Harris. He is one of your flying-squad constables. Apparently we have young lords raiding carriages on the roads. They were not having any luck catching them, so I decided to help."

The constable bowed, and she moved closer. "Lords? As in one of my nobles?"

I sighed. "Their children, most likely."

I turned to the book.

"I had the image of a crest from a ring. The lord beat a driver, and it was from his clothing. This is the crest that matches."

She looked at the open book and nodded. "Baron Stills. He is a bully, and his child probably takes after him."

I pulled out the other crystal. "And would you know this lord?"

She leaned closer and then sighed. "That would be Baroness Tereance's son; she is very strict, and he is very spoiled."

I smiled. "Thank you."

She turned and started for the door and her guards. "We have caught Catherine attempting to sneak out several times. It is good the wedding is tomorrow."

I grinned as she left and then took a breath. "Right. Does anyone know where we might find the young lords?"

Donny snorted. "The Chesser House."

I looked at him, and he shrugged.

"We have responded to a few calls for minor assaults. There are always young—ladies available to the lords."

I started for the door and glanced back. "Thank you, sir."

The librarian bowed as we left and strode back outside to get our horses. I swung up and waited and gestured to Constable Donny. "Lead the way."

He nodded and turned his horse, and we started for the gate. I was thinking while we rode and let the constables and the corporal watch. I looked up when we stopped at a large establishment just outside the banking district. I swung down and moved to tie the reins to a post.

I glanced at the doorman as we approached and opened my long coat to show my badge. "Inspector Knight."

He snorted. "Do you have a warrant?"

I smiled. "This can go easy or hard."

He looked me over as if I were a street beggar. "Bring back a warrant."

I nodded and turned to Constable Donny. "Go use a call box. Contact Magister Simon and tell him what our evidence is. Tell him I am asking for a warrant to search the Chesser House and to detain and search all patrons and their employees. Next you contact the constable general and inform him the Chesser House is involved in armed robbery and I am suspending their business license."

He grinned as he looked at the doorman. "Sir."

He trotted down the street, and I looked at the doorman. "Constable Harris, place this man in restraints for conspiracy after the fact in armed robbery."

The constable moved forward, and the pale-faced doorman gasped. "You… cannot."

He squeaked as the constable caught his arm and spun him and shoved him into the door. He yanked his arms back and started putting restraints on. I looked at the corporal. "Just out of curiosity, how many guards will I be getting after the wedding?"

He grinned. "A full squad."

I shook my head, and we waited until Donny returned. I was not surprised to see a half dozen constables with him. He grinned. "I told the magister that Her Majesty identified the two lords and we were here to find and detain them. He was more than willing to issue the warrant. He even sent his clerk on a horse so it should not be long. The constable general made a call, and it seems the Chesser House has not been issued a license."

Twenty minutes, and the clerk arrived, and we shoved open the door. Two constables had gone around to the back while we went through the front. The very large and lavish common room went silent, and I looked around. I recognized a few people as a servant hurried toward us. The servant hissed. "We do not allow—"

I held up the warrant. "This says you do. I am looking for Lords Stills and Tereance."

He sniffed as if we smelled. "I have no idea where…"

I gestured to a constable. "Arrest him."

I took a step as he gasped and the constable grabbed him.

"I am Inspector Knight! I am looking for Lords Stills and Tereance!"

Several nobles turned to look at a back corner. Five men with as many fancy women around them stared back. I started toward them and made sure my long coat was open. My guards knew not to move in front of me, but they did spread out to the sides and pushed people out of the way. Donny and the other constables followed quickly.

The five lords looked at each other as the women moved away, and one shoved a hand into his coat. I brushed my coat open and brought my hand up as I stopped. I pulled my weapon as the lord was pulling his and the other four were reacting. The lord lifted and extending his arm, and I fired as I pointed my pistol. The pistol kicked as I brought it up, and the lord spun as he was hit in the chest.

His pistol went off toward the ceiling, and I cocked the hammer and shifted. The four lords were bringing their weapons up, and there was a crash as the corporal and his men fired and then several constables. They staggered and fell, and I moved forward to the first one. He had gone to his knees and dropped his weapon. "It was…just a bit of fun—"

He coughed up blood and slowly fell, and I looked at the other four sprawled out on the floor. I knelt and turned his hand to see the ring and scar. I looked at the constables as I stood. "Search them and the women they were with. Someone call the constable doctor, and a couple of you go search the tack for their horses."

I turned and looked around the shocked room. "It was fun robbing people? Is that how young nobles think they should act? Do you believe it is okay to brutally beat people or threaten women?"

I was angry and started for the door.

"Detain everyone, and search them. Use the stolen item list, and if anything is found, charge them with possession of stolen goods. Close and seal this place; arrest the owner for operating an illegal saloon. Harris, get warrants, send constables to their homes, and search for other stolen property."

The corporal and his two men hurried after me, and I shoved out the door and took a deep breath. I looked at the corporal. "Home."

He nodded, and we moved to our horses. All I could think of was all these people coming here to watch Catherine and I marry, and these nobles thought it was fun to rob and beat someone. It had not been for money or power but fun. I rode in a daze and did not realize where I was going until I looked up to see the palace. I stopped and stared and then swung down and started through the gate.

I ignored the guards and kept walking, and when I entered the halls, the servants tried to stop me. I shoved them aside as I continued until I reached Catherine's door. I moved the guard and knocked but held the knob. "Catherine!"

I heard her step and touched the door with my forehead. I kept her from opening the door as I poured my heart out in frustration. The guards moved away while we talked. It was an hour before I left and went home. It was my grandfather who sat with me, and we drank peach brandy and talked. He snorted and shook his head. "It is not just sons of nobles, boy, and you know it."

I looked at him, and he shrugged.

"Idle hands and no conscience for the welfare of others, boy. You remember the gallery and those who walked the street outside. It is why you wanted to be a constable. What you do is prevent others from doing the same thing by showing them what happens when they are caught. If they fear what happens, they do not break the law."

It did remind me, and finally I went to bed. The wedding was huge and took hours to get ready, and then suddenly Catherine was walking toward me, and all I saw was her. I did not care what was around us only that she was there. I remember little of the actual wedding once her hand was in mine. Once we walked out of the huge cathedral, I held her hand, and she waved to the cheering crowd.

Next was the long carriage ride through the city and then back to the palace. We changed, and there was the huge reception and ball and...

CHAPTER 30

# Murdered Guard

THE PARTIES AFTER the wedding had lasted for several weeks, and then once more Catherine and I traveled the kingdom. In every city we always stopped to see and speak with the army and the constables. There were hundreds of events and parties we had to attend. It was three months before we returned home, and I was more than tired of traveling.

It was the beginning of spring, and flowers were everywhere. We had slept on my estate for a change and left the window open. The perfume of flowers filled the room as I turned my head when Catherine got out of bed. She was reaching for her robe, and I frowned when I saw the slight bulge. I sat up. "Catherine?"

She was headed for the door and smiled back at me. "I have to wash."

I moved off the bed and after her. I caught her in the hall and pulled her back against me for a kiss. "You have gained weight."

She frowned as I moved and caressed her pelvis. I smiled and she giggled. "It only took you three months to see."

I grinned as I swept her up and twirled around. "You are with child!"

She laughed as she kissed me and her maid appeared with one of the guards.

I set her down. "Sarah, use the call box and make an appointment with the royal doctor for the first thing this morning. Also request a moment of Her Majesty's time later this morning. Next Her Highness will need to make an appointment with her dressmaker."

Catherine laughed again and pulled me after her to the washroom. An hour, and we were in her carriage and on the way to the palace. Once we got there, I held her hand as we walked in and went to see the doctor. The guards were all grinning as I closed the door. Thirty minutes, and Mage Delila was smiling. "Pregnant, and everything looks good."

I squeezed Catherine's hand and thanked the doctor. We left and walked through the palace and stopped outside her mother's outer office. The lieutenant returned from speaking with the door guards. "She has time now."

He had a straight face as he gestured, and the guards moved to the walls, and we walked to the doors. I opened the door and held it for Catherine and looked at her mother. She was sitting back and smiling, and we crossed the room. Catherine went around the desk and bent to kiss her mother's cheek. "He finally noticed."

Her mother chuckled. "The notice will be sent out this morning."

I grinned as I looked at Catherine. "And she gets to go shopping for new clothes."

They laughed, and we talked, and then I took Catherine out in her carriage. It was interesting to shop with her and let the seamstress and others know she was pregnant. She made the decision to move away from her skirt suits to dresses. She also made arrangements for a few more fittings over the next few months. We had lunch in one of her favorite little diners.

We started back and reached the gate into the palace, and I saw a lot more guards. I gestured, and the lieutenant slipped out while we waited. He stuck his head back in the door a moment later. "The guard at the garden gate is missing."

I straightened. "How often do they get checked?"

He shrugged. "They have to call in every quarter hour. The sergeant of the guard or officer do a check each hour."

I looked at Catherine as I thought and then looked at him. "How much time lapsed before the gate was covered?"

He turned and went to speak to the corporal in charge of the gate. He came back and shook his head. "It just happened, but there was a twenty-minute gap."

I moved to the door. "Take Catherine to my estate and double the guards."

Catherine snorted as she started to follow, and I spun and caught her. "No."

She frowned, and I shook my head. "You are pregnant. When you get to the house, go to my weapon case and get the revolving shotgun. You wait there until I send for you or come."

I stepped back and closed the door.

"Get her out of here and protect her."

The lieutenant caught the running board and barked orders as I started for the main doors into the royal wing of the palace. The corporal and his men fell in, and he looked at me. "You think there is a threat?"

I nodded. "First we speak with the queen and her consort, and then we send them to safety. Next we let the guards search the grounds and palace while we begin investigating."

The guards were checking everyone, but I noticed they were not looking or checking each other. It was like the guard uniform made them invisible. We reached the queen's office, and I stopped to gesture to the sergeant by the door. He moved out. "Sir?"

I looked at his other guards. "I would like to see Her Majesty. I would also like to speak with the guard commander."

He nodded and turned to speak with a guard and then slipped through the doors. A moment, and he was back. "She has a moment."

I nodded and gestured to the corporal and started walking. In her office were several guards and their commander. Both the queen and her consort were there, and I nodded to them as I came closer. "You have been told about the missing guard?"

The queen looked to the side at the guard commander. "Missing guard?"

The major had been promoted to colonel since the wedding. He nodded. "It is nothing. We are still searching for him."

I shook my head. "You are missing the point. The guard is missing, and the gate was left unguarded. Not only is there a chance assassins are in the palace but one could also be wearing the guard's uniform. There is a serious threat to Her Majesty. I have sent Catherine to my estate until everything is searched and I have answers."

He blinked and looked at the queen, and she and the consort stood. "What do you suggest?"

I looked at the colonel. "I would suggest you move her to her country estate and have supervisors check and confirm every guard. Let the palace detail sweep the whole place looking for intruders, poison, or bombs."

He nodded and bowed to the queen. "Your Majesty?"

She hesitated, "You think it is necessary, Ashton?"

I nodded. "Even if the guard walked off his post, which I doubt, we need to be sure and make sure you are safe."

Her consort took her hand. "Actually we can go to his estate, and you can sit with Catherine and talk about the baby."

I looked at the colonel. "Check every guard, and if you find one you do not know—"

He strode to the door. "Sergeant!"

A few minutes, and a full company of guards surrounded them as they left the palace. I took a breath and nodded to my corporal. "Time to find the officer of the watch."

He turned and led the way toward the back. "He will probably be in the office."

The office was in what looked like an armory. Several guards were by a series of desks with a lieutenant looking at a map of the palace. They turned as we came in, and several looked at the lieutenant who frowned. I nodded to them. "You know me. I am investigating the missing guard. I would recommend a few things before I start."

The lieutenant shifted. "Such as?"

I turned to look at the map. "The queen and her consort are gone. I would call the chamberlain and the ministers. Man the exits and stairs and start at the top and bring everyone out through one place and identify them, including guards. After everyone is out, search for hidden assassins, poison traps, or a bomb. Once the floor is clear, you can send the people back, but they will need to remain until the palace is completely searched."

He nodded. "And then do the next floor and so on until we have done the whole palace."

I agreed and turned. "Meanwhile no one enters. I will investigate the guard and see what I find."

I started for the door as the lieutenant began issuing orders. The corporal chuckled as we left the building. "Nothing like a nudge to point them in the right direction."

I was already thinking as we headed for the garden gate. If the guard had left on his own, he would not have returned to the palace, and if something happened—well they would not bring him inside the grounds since they would be searched. That left the area outside the gate to hide him or his body. There was a whole squad moving along the wall and searching the gardens as we approached.

The guard at the gate looked at us as we walked up. I looked out. "Has anyone left since the guard went missing?"

He shook his head.

I gestured my guards back as I walked to the gate. "Keep your eyes open."

I opened the gate and examined the ground as I slowly walked out. Unlike the main gate that had cobblestones, this one was dirt, and I was looking for footprints. There were more than a few since the many gardeners entered and left through this gate. They all went in or out from the dirt lane that went left along the wall. I stopped as I saw two sets going the other way toward the river.

I did not think they would go that far and started to follow them. A hundred paces, and the lane intersected another lane going north. It was a little overgrown with bushes growing up on each side. A dozen steps, and they left the road, and I followed and looked around a bush. I turned to the corporal after seeing the naked body of the guard. "Dead and stripped."

So at least one man inside the palace was wearing the uniform of a guard. I led the way back to the gate and used the call box. The sergeant of the guard answered, and I did not wait. "You have at least one assassin wearing the uniform of the guard. He was killed and hidden outside the grounds."

I hung up and looked around inside the grounds.

I looked at the few garden carts close to the gate and blinked. "How many garden carts are there?"

The corporal frowned, and the guard on the gate shrugged. I turned to look around the grounds and saw a few gardeners with carts.

"Someone get me the head gardener."

I was thinking they could kill more guards and use the carts to hide the bodies or even pretend to be a gardener. Of course that did not make sense—why pretend to be a gardener? They could not move around in the palace without being seen. The guard could, but why in the middle of the day? The queen had more guards around her then and…

I remembered the case in the vaults and spun. "The vaults!"

The guard could get them into the outer vault area, but more importantly the inner vaults would be unlocked.

I started running with my squad of guards chasing after me. We had to go around and in and then down, and I slowed when I saw the guard. I looked at him carefully as he touched his weapon and then relaxed. "Has anyone been down here in the last hour?"

He shook his head. "No, sir."

I looked through the open door to see Mr. Sorinson and his clerks. I turned. "Well…"

The corporal smiled and then straightened. "Except there is the ministry vault, and today is the quarterly government funds transfer."

I blinked. "Funds transfer?"

He nodded. "They take the budget funds for every duchy to the train and send them out."

I looked at him. "When?"

He looked into the vault at a large clock. "Now I think."

I turned and gestured. "Show me where they come out of the palace."

The corporal turned and strode back the way we had come. When we came out, he turned and headed around to the ministers' entrance. I thought he would go in, but he kept going, and I saw a guard by another door with an empty garden cart to one side. The first impression I got was the uniform did not fit, and there was a stain on his side. It hit me as I realized no guard would wear a uniform with a stain or that did not fit correctly.

I pulled my weapon. "Impostor!"

My squad of guards copied me as the corporal knelt and pulled his pistol. The guard beside the door yanked out the pistol he wore as I aimed and fired. Several more echoed mine, and the man jerked and twisted as he fell. I moved forward and past the corporal and kicked the weapon away from the man. I looked at the door and moved to the side and yanked it open.

Shots ripped the doorframe, and then two of my guards stepped out and fired into the hall. I spun and squeezed past them to see two men dressed like gardeners down on the floor. They had been at another door that was armored but open, and I kept my pistol ready as I moved toward it. "Someone yell for more guards."

The corporal growled as he moved after me, "Damn it, sir, we are supposed to protect you."

I grinned as I kicked a weapon away from one of the men. "I will try not to get shot."

I peeked in the door and ducked back as several men in the counting room fired.

I glanced back. "It looks like four more with one wearing another guard uniform. There are bodies on the floor, and it looks like they have broken into the vault."

The corporal nodded as the guards moved along both walls. One shifted, leaned, and fired before pulling back, but the men inside fired, and the door-frame was struck several times.

I shook my head as I remembered what I had seen. "In and left is a desk, and to the right is another."

There had also been another steel door to the left, but it was closed and locked. I looked at the corporal, and he shook his head, but I spun and rushed in and left. I extended my pistol, pointed, and fired into one of the men as they reacted. Before they could fire, the corporal and two of the guards were firing as the corporal rushed in and to the right. I dived and slid behind the desk and turned, so I was fully behind cover.

The three men left back into the vault with a cart loaded with chests block-ing the door. I leaned out and aimed but did not have a shot. I rolled the other way and ran for the wall as the rest of my guards entered. They split up and moved to each side, and more guards were following. I stopped beside the vault door. "There is no way out; surrender."

One yelled back, "And hang! Come and get us!"

The corporal leaned out and pointed his pistol but jerked as one fired. He spun and staggered back, holding his shoulder. "Damn."

I gestured. "Someone get him out and call for the royal doctor."

I thought and moved back and lay down as the guards looked at me like I was crazy. I rolled onto my side between the cart and the door while extending my arm and aiming. The three men were behind an overturned cart and shifted while changing their aim. I fired, and one's head snapped back. I rolled back and away. The two men fired into the floor where I had been, and I stood.

I shook my head as more guards arrived and started thinking. The vault door was too narrow to rush through and to the side with nothing to protect us. I looked at the cart and moved out and caught the handle and pulled. One of the guards quickly came to help, and we moved it to the side and out of the way. I looked at the vault and then the guards on the other side. "Close the door. We can suck the air out and open it tomorrow."

They grinned as the two men in the vault cursed. The guards moved and slowly pushed, and the heavy door swung around and started to close. When it shut, there was a loud clang, and I moved to spin the locking wheel.

I gestured to the two large wheels on the walls. "Pump the air out."

Basically there were pipes in the vault with one-way valves. They went to a set of bellows that the wheels operated, and another set of pipes with one-way valves sent the air into the counting room. Above the vault door were several valves to open pipes into the vault to let air in so it could be opened. I made sure those were closed as the guards began to spin the wheels.

I gestured to one of the guards. "Go find someone with the vault combination. A half hour with little or no air, and we can open it and bring them out."

The palace duty officer arrived while we were checking the bodies in the counting room. Their throats had been cut, and from the look of things, it had been a while they had been held. It had started to get hard to turn the wheels, so I was sure there was not much air left in the vault. The guard lieutenant ordered the dead removed and went to the vault and used a combination.

When we open the door, the two men were right inside but dead. I checked each of the dead thieves, and one of the guards recognized one as a former gardener. That was probably how they got the idea and information. Altogether we had two dead guards, three clerks, and the ministry treasurer. That was without the seven dead thieves.

I did recommend a few changes to man the gates with more than one guard. I let the guard lieutenant handle the clean up and went to check with Mage Delila to see how the corporal was doing. He had been shot in the shoulder and would be out for a few days. I waited to see if the search in the palace turned up anything else, but there were no more imposters or bombs.

I led my squad of guards out and to my estate and found the estate crowded. The consort was with Mr. Mack as he checked the grape and vanilla plants. He actually seemed to be enjoying himself too. I walked in to Catherine and her mother in the kitchen with Mrs. Mack. They were talking about strange food cravings and making a large peach cobbler.

I moved the shotgun and sat beside Catherine and took her hand. "Two guards, three clerks, and the ministry treasurer were killed. It was not assassins but thieves trying to steal the money from the ministry vault. Why they would think to enter the palace grounds to do it, I have no idea."

The colonel was leaning against the counter sipping tea and snorted. "Because on the way to the train, it is guarded by a dozen guards who are looking for and expecting them. If they used the guard uniforms and pretended to be gardeners as my lieutenant reported, they could have gotten away with it."

He looked at me.

"If we did not have a suspicious *royal inspector* finding out, they could have."

Catherine grinned and then hit my arm. "And he reported that you were in the gun fight and the corporal was wounded."

I caught her hand and squeezed it. "Once a constable always a constable. It has given me an idea for a new type of firing range."

She laughed as her mother smiled, and I stood.

"I need to go wash and clean my weapon."

That was the first time the queen and her consort visited, and they seemed to relax and enjoy their visit. They stayed most of the day and even ate dinner with us before leaving. New procedures at the minor gates were put into place to protect the guards and ensure what happened would never happen again. I made a few calls, and constables went to the homes of the thieves to make sure no one else had been involved.

CHAPTER 31

# Hunting a Fugitive

I HAD BORROWED from Catherine and bought an estate on the west side of the city. The manor had burned down, and the estate was long abandoned and overgrown. That was fine because I brought in workmen who built the walls taller and made hardwood walls with windows and doors. I made spring-loaded target frames that turned suddenly to show the target.

The shooter walked down a hall and stepped into a doorway, and a target would appear, or they were on a street, and the targets were in windows. Catherine helped when she could, and my guards were more than interested, and so were any and every constable who found out. We only built one real building, and it was more a large lounge with weapon cases.

I walked behind Catherine as she held her pistol and stopped at a doorway. She jerked and brought her weapon up and fired and then fired again. "Damn!"

I grinned as she turned to continue down the hall. "I told you each target is exposed only for a few seconds. The floor plate activates the timer to turn it, which starts another to turn it back."

She glanced back and grinned as she moved to the next door. "It is still a surprise."

The floor plates were in the hall in front of each door. The hall had four turns and six to ten doorways in each straight section, so we had to change cylinders. The guards following us had all been through the course. I heard them chuckling, and Catherine spun and fired. She smirked as she looked at me and then jerked her weapon up and to the side as she fired again. "Hey!"

I laughed. "And some targets are on a delay, so they do not all turn at the same time."

The guards laughed, and she shook her head as she removed and replaced the cylinder. When we finished and headed back to the lounge, she slipped her arm around mine. "Now that was fun."

I nodded. "And it is going to help constables and your guards."

I had six retired constable sergeants working for the range. One followed each person to make sure it was safe. The targets were one-inch plate, so they stopped the bullets. The walls and outside were also armored. The day before I had almost a hundred guards and constables test the course. This was the opening day, and there were already three dozen men waiting.

I grinned when I saw the old constable sergeant Jones following Lady Fiera. "Good luck."

She smiled. She had loosened up a lot since she made inspector. We walked into the lounge and crossed to the tables for cleaning weapons. Beside the lounge building was the beginning of a large gun shop Markus was building. He was going to move his shop, and there would be a regular range in it. I nodded to the constable general and the constable commissioner as they sipped tea.

They grinned, and I reached for Catherine's weapon. "So what do you think?"

She smiled and accepted a cup of tea from a guard. "I think you need to expand the idea."

I blinked, and she gestured to the constable general. "What do you think of having ranges like this in every city, sir?"

He chuckled and nodded. "I went through it twice yesterday and still missed a few targets."

The constable commissioner nodded. "I think it is going to help officers learn to react to threats. I did have an idea to put targets in rooms that were nonthreats like women or children."

I thought about it and smiled at Catherine. "And the constable who shoots the nonthreats gets to buy the ale."

She laughed as I went to work cleaning her weapon and the empty cylinders. The constable general sighed and then leaned closer. "I have a case for you. I know royal inspectors are supposed to do capital cases or cases involving nobles but—yesterday we had an escape of a prisoner. He was sentenced to ten years for passing counterfeit gold crowns."

We looked at the door as Lady Fiera came in looking frustrated. I grinned and gestured and then turned back. "How did he escape?"

He snorted. "Slipped the chains and ran when they were moving the prisoners to the train."

Lady Fiera reached the table and sat. "That is a wicked course."

I grinned as Catherine giggled. "The commissioner just gave me ideas to make it worse."

She groaned as she set her pistol on the table and began to take it apart. I looked at the constable general. "I will need the inspector's case file."

He shook his head. "He was caught by a street constable."

I smiled and put the pistol together. "I would send him or her to the inspector course. Okay, let me get the case file, and I will see if I can find the fugitive."

I looked at Lady Fiera. "Have you ever done a hunt for a fugitive?"

She shook her head, and I smiled. "Well, since Constable Donny is going through the inspector course, I could use a shadow to protect me."

She snorted at the same time as Catherine. "How many times have you used your weapon?"

I knew she was not talking about the range and shrugged. "A few."

She nodded. "And how many times have you been wounded?"

I reddened. "Several times to many."

Catherine covered her hand. "That is why I do not want him alone, and his few is more like a lot. He does not know when to wait for help."

I snorted. "Okay, it was only a couple of times I probably should have waited, and I still finished before help came."

Lady Fiera smiled and nodded. "Okay, I will come with you."

I turned to the corporal. "Use the call box and have the clerk meet us at the central station."

He nodded and moved across the room, and I began cleaning the cylinders. By the time I was done, half the men waiting had gone through, but another couple dozen constables had arrived. I reloaded the cylinders and slipped one into the pistol. I accepted the pistol case from a guard and put everything in it and closed it. I stood and nodded to the constable general and commissioner.

Catherine stood and smiled. "I have a dozen meetings with Mother today, but it was nice to get out before they started."

I handed her pistol case to a guard as I slipped my hand into hers, and we started toward the door. "See you at the central station, Lady Fiera."

Our guards slipped out, and I waited for the lieutenant to turn and nod for us to come out. We took Catherine's carriage to the palace, and I walked her in and turned her and gave her a kiss. "Remember the doctor's orders and your diet. I will try to be back before dinner."

She smiled and gave me a push. "And you are bored and ready to be a constable again."

I grinned as I turned for the door. "Yes."

I walked out, and the corporal and my guards were waiting with horses.

I swung up on mine and turned. "Okay, time for exercise. Try not to get shot again, Corporal."

He chuckled as we headed for the gate. "I will try, sir."

The colonel had wanted me to accept another corporal, but I had refused. It was not that the corporal had failed, but until he was fully healed, he was not 100 percent. We took our time and rode through the street and turned in at the station and went around to the constable stable. I dismounted and let one of the guards take the horse as I headed for the door.

I was reading the file when Lady Fiera came in. "This is not going to be easy. The man refused to give his name, and there was no known address for his home. The only thing we have is his description and the store where he was caught."

She shook her head as the clerk walked in behind her. "So…"

I closed the file and stood. "So we start at the store and then begin checking the others in that area. We use the street constables to check the stores for counterfeit gold crowns. From those we get Constable Mage Green to do an association spell to find where they were created."

She nodded. "And from that we find something to track him."

I returned the file, and we walked out to the desk sergeant. I asked him to call and have the area sergeant meet us at the mercantile store and to call

Constable Mage Green. I gestured, and the corporal moved to the door with the guards. A minute, and we were walking and then caught a streetcar. Lady Fiera grinned as she stood beside me in the car.

The guards were around us and searching for threats, but the corporal seemed relaxed. Finally, I gestured, and they moved off, and we followed. We walked down another street, and I saw a constable sergeant standing on the walk outside a store. He blinked when he saw us, and I nodded. "I have need of your people, Sergeant."

I pulled out the drawing of the escapee and showed it to him.

"One of your constables caught him passing counterfeit gold crowns. I would like all the stores in the area checked for more counterfeit gold crowns. Have them ask about our man, like which way did he come from and which way did he go. If you find any counterfeit gold crowns, have them call out."

I looked back to see Mage Green riding toward us.

"We will see if Constable Mage Green can use them to locate where they were made and maybe our man."

He nodded and used his whistle to call his street constables as I walked into the shop. I went to the shopkeeper and showed the drawing. "Remember him?"

He looked and nodded. "I remember."

Lady Fiera smiled. "Do you remember which way he came from?"

He looked up and finally nodded. "From the right. He walked past my display window."

We checked his gold crowns before leaving. Abigail smiled as we came out. "You needed me, Ashton?"

I nodded, and we looked around as constables began arriving. "We are hoping to find counterfeit gold crowns that may have been passed at stores. If we do, I wanted to see if you could do a trace spell to find the place they were made."

She nodded and turned. "Possible."

I looked at Lady Fiera. "So with no name and only a description, we can only try to back track. If this does not work…"

She smiled. "We see if the counterfeit gold crowns in evidence will help."

I grinned. "Or…"

She frowned. "Or what?"

I turned as the constables split up and headed for shops. "Or we get the restraints he slipped and try to trace him using them."

She nodded. "That makes sense. I think I will call and have them brought here."

She moved to the corner call box. A minute later a constable came out of a shop and crossed to us. "We have a dozen counterfeit gold crowns. The owner said he came from the south and went the other way when he left."

He had them in his kerchief, and Abigail reached out to use her finger to separate them. "Hold still."

She murmured, and the notes began to glow. When she stopped, the glow shifted to one side. "The side that is glowing is the direction where they were made."

Lady Fiera came back and looked at the counterfeit gold crowns. "The restraints are on the way with a runner."

I smiled. "Time to divide forces. Wait and see what Abigail can do. If she can get a trace, take a few constables and send word before following it. I will follow the counterfeit gold crowns to the printers and then search for our man."

She nodded, and I gestured to the constable holding the glowing gold crowns. "Lead on, Constable."

He grinned and turned to head down the street, and my guards fell in as I followed. We made a few turns until we were in a quiet area with large shops and a few factories. The constable slowed and looked back before nodding to an empty-looking factory building. I glanced at the corporal. "Would you like to knock?"

He grinned and strode to the door and kicked it open. I gestured to the constable as three guards followed the corporal. He grinned and led the way in as we heard men yelling. When I walked in, it was to see three men backing away from a printing press while holding pipes. My guards all had their weapons out, and I shook my head. "Gentlemen, I would drop the weapons before my guards get the idea you are a threat to me."

They shifted and one by one let the pipes fall. I nodded to the constable, and he strode forward and turned the first to put him in restraints.

I waited until he was finished and then came closer and held up the drawing of the escapee. "Do you know this man?"

They looked away, and I sighed. "Gentlemen, I already know he was part of your little—enterprise. He was caught and sentenced to prison. Now he has escaped, which brought us here. Now I need a name and information. If you cooperate, I will let the magister know you helped, and he may be lenient."

They looked at each other, and one sighed. "James Gilbert. He lives at the Sorrinson boarding house on Rosewood Street. We thought he just took off with…"

He reddened, and I nodded. "Thank you. Constable, please let the magister know they were helpful. My case is the escapee, so these are yours."

He nodded. "Thank you, sir."

I turned. "Corporal, the Sorrinson boarding house on Rosewood Street."

He turned and gestured as he started for the door. The guards moved out, and I followed with the rest around me. I had memorized the streets, and if I was right, Rosewood was a dozen blocks away. It was a nice day, so we walked. I nodded to people or slowed to wish them a good day. At first it was workers and then people in front of large rooming houses.

The corporal stopped a street constable to get directions, and then we were moving again. When we reached the corner of Rosewood and started to turn left, Lady Fiera, Abigail, and a half dozen constables appeared. I grinned as she shook her head. "It looks like we are back on the same path."

She nodded as they fell in beside me.

Two blocks, and we saw a sign in front of another rooming house. It was the Sorrinson, and I gestured to a couple of the constables. "Around back."

They nodded, and we waited to give them time before I nodded to the corporal. We walked to the door, and he stepped in and jerked back as a shotgun ripped into the doorframe. Everyone pulled pistols, but it was Lady Fiera who leaned out and aimed before firing. She cursed and moved in, and I followed as my guards yelled and charged after.

The man had pulled back, and Lady Fiera moved to the stairs as people in other rooms kept yelling. I turned to back up the stairs along the wall to let my guards see the landing. Lady Fiera was against the stair banister as she backed up with me. We saw the barrel of a shotgun as a man shoved it up and over the rail. We knelt as it fired, and I fired into the solid banister twice.

We heard the man curse and then running steps and started moving again. We reached the landing, and Lady Fiera moved left and across while I moved after her and to the rail. The guards came up and around behind us with two between. We moved up together and ducked as two more shots ripped into the wall over our heads. I took three quick steps to see the man reloading the shotgun and fired.

He jerked back into the doorway he was in while cursing us. I held my aim as Lady Fiera and the guards moved forward and then moved right to the far wall. I nodded, and we started down the hall together. "You might as well surrender!"

"To hell with you, copper!"

I gestured to Lady Fiera and then ran across in front of the door to the other side. Two blasts struck the wall across from the door. She spun with her weapon up. "Freeze!"

The man turned and dived through the window. She blinked and spun. "Stupid bastard!"

We ran for the stairs, and the other four constables who had been following were in the lead. We came through the front door and leaped off the porch. When we ran around the corner, it was to see the man hanging in midair with Abigail sitting on a planter. He was upside down, and his shotgun was on the ground below him. She smiled. "Is this your man?"

Lady Fiera laughed as she started walking. "Yes."

I shook my head. "So Abigail gets the credit."

I gestured to the constables.

"Let him go, and they will put him in restraints."

She gestured, and he dropped to crash into the ground. They moved toward him, but he rolled and leaped up and tried to run. They caught him, and he twisted and struck, and one constable staggered back cursing. I shook my head as I moved to sit with Abigail. "That was dumb."

The constables tried to use their billies, but he was twisting and kicking; Lady Fiera walked into the fight, and the next thing we heard was the man screaming. The guards took him to the ground and held him as she bent and twisted one arm back and put a restraint on. Another guard fought the struggling man and got the other arm back, and the second restraint went on.

I nodded. "Well done. Now one of you go up and search his room, and someone call for a wagon and make sure they have leg restraints."

They nodded and pulled him to his feet while he continued to curse.

I stood and moved to him and touched the wound in his shoulder. He jerked and yelled, and I nodded. "He is on a drug. Someone add a second set of restraints and search him for a hidden blade."

One moved behind him, and then they held him while he was searched. Lady Fiera sat with Abigail while we waited, and the constable who went to search the room returned. He grinned as he held up a sack. "Packets of gold crowns and drugs."

He went before the magister again, and more charges were added, including the escape and drugs. This time instead of a work farm, he was on the way to the mines for twenty years. They were also using waist-chain restraints and leg shackles when he was moved. The rest of the counterfeiters got five years on a work farm, but the magister specified early release in three if they behaved.

It gave Lady Fiera an idea, and she sat down to make a list of ways to track escapees. My new range was extremely popular, and I began making calls to other cities. First I looked for distinguished constables who were ready to retire and then the type of land and protections needed. Before a month was up, six more were being built, including one by my former training officer, Constable Sergeant Harris, and Detective Inspector Stern.

We had the six constables visit to go through our range before they returned to their city. We did add a few more targets and mixed in nonthreats like men, women, or children.

# CHAPTER 32

# Gunfight in the Nursery

IT TOOK ONLY three months to pay Catherine back and get the range in the black. The first six ranges were up and running, and nine more were being built in other cities. I was also busy helping the constable general with selecting the new knight inspectors. I had mostly moved into the palace with Catherine, but we were spending a couple of days each week on my estate.

I think it was to relax and get fresh air. Plus she was being pampered by Mrs. Mack. At over seven months pregnant, she was not doing a lot of walking and only rode in her carriage. Each week the mage doctor visited to examine her and the baby, and everything was fine. Of course, there were the strange cravings in the middle of the night.

I ignored the other boats following and around us as I kept rowing up-river. Catherine was grinning as I kept pushing harder. "You are not going to win."

I snorted as slowly the boat pulled away from the ones following us. I was not worried about the guards, but the dozen boats filled with young women and their men irritated me. Each time I tried to take Catherine out alone, they always showed up. Being on and around the water helped keep Catherine cool, so once each day we came out onto the river.

When I saw the sailing skiff, I grinned. "Tomorrow we are escaping."

She laughed as she followed my look. "By sailing?"

I stopped rowing and used an oar to turn the boat. "Okay, Lieutenant, back to the dock."

I waited for them to turn before I started back and let one of the guard boats lead and scatter the following boats. We went slow, and the boats tried to move in closer until the guards yelled. Halfway back Catherine giggled, and I followed her look. I grinned. "I see we have contestants for the river race."

It was three sets of barrels on poles with a small sail through a middle barrel. The young man waved and kept shifting as the barrel he was on turned. Catherine shook her head. "Three days before the race, and we have two hundred entries. I also received an invitation to the one in Honore next week."

I smiled as I kept rowing. "I would not mind a visit. I hear Stern's wife just had a little girl."

She chuckled. "Then we will schedule the train."

I turned to head for the dock, and the followers were warned off. "Perhaps I should call Stern to let him spread the word. I heard your officer candidates are doing extremely well."

She laughed. "When they are not getting in trouble for chasing women."

I let a guard catch the boat and stood to help her up and onto the dock. I tied off and climbed out and took her hand, and we started for the palace. "Abigail has time off coming, and I know of a certain constable mage who might enjoy meeting her."

She laughed. "Norris?"

She nodded.

"Come to think of it they might hit it off. Plus he has been training a couple of new mages for the constables there."

I nodded. "I was thinking of that, and perhaps we could speak to the constable general about a constable-mage school. We have the academy and the inspector course, so it would make sense to have one for mages who want to join the constables."

She squeezed my hand. "I have checked, and Norris is one of the more experienced constable mages. Perhaps we should speak to him about running the school."

We entered the palace and headed to her mother's office. She smiled when we came in and stood. "Time for lunch?"

Catherine grinned. "The cook promised flavored shaved iced after."

I glanced at the corporal whispering with the queen's assistant. He looked at me. "Sir, the constable general is requesting your help."

I looked at Catherine, and she smiled and gave me a push. "We have months; go arrest someone."

I gave her a kiss and gestured, and the corporal strode for the door with half the guards. I followed with the rest around me and ignored the wait for horses and walked to the gate. The guards sighed, and I grinned. "Exercise is good for you."

After we walked out, I hurried to catch a streetcar. We rode all the way to the city lords' building before we got off. We went in through the front and climbed the stairs. We entered the outer office for the constable general, and his assistant smiled. "Just in time, sir."

She gestured, and I touched the corporal and walked to open the door. The rest of the guards waited, but the corporal followed me in. The constable general looked up, and I saw his look of relief. "You needed me?"

He sat back and nodded. "I have a report from Duke Terrence of an attempted break-in."

I frowned as I tried to remember. "The queen's cousin's son?"

He nodded. "Normally he and his family would be in his duchy. His new wife had their third child over the winter, and he has had more than a few threats."

I nodded. "And with the attempted break-in, you want to be sure it is not something more serious."

He shrugged. "I would like it checked out."

I turned and headed for the door. "Since I do not have a clerk or constable, I will..."

He chuckled. "A constable is waiting at the estate. Get the address from my assistant."

I did, and then we left and caught another streetcar back toward the palace. We changed cars before we got there and headed east. For an estate for a duke, it was actually small. We reached the main gate, and I saw a constable speaking with two guards. The guards straightened when they saw us. I nodded to them and looked at the street constable as I moved my coat to show my badge. "Royal inspec—"

He grinned. "Knight. I recognized you, sir."

I blinked and then nodded and looked at the guards. "Yes. Well, let us go see about this attempted break-in."

One of the ducal guards was using the call box as the constable turned and gestured. My guards fell back except for the corporal, who stayed beside me. The constable started walking toward the side of the estate manor. "One of the guards heard someone and walked in to look. Several men were on ladders at a second-floor window. He yelled, and they slid down and ran to the wall."

He gestured to a side wall, and I saw another ladder. "They left the ladders?"

He nodded. "There is another on the other side of the wall."

We came around the side of the building, and I saw the tall ladder. "Any footprints?"

He pulled his pad and handed it back. "Four sets. I tried to draw them and marked the sizes."

I stopped by the ladder and looked at the prints and the ladder. I pointed to a dropped pry bar. "Those are used on the docks to open crates."

The constable gestured up to the window. "There are marks on the window. The lock held, but I would not trust it to do so again."

I turned and backed up as I looked at all the other windows. "So—why this window? There are eight on this side of the building."

I looked at the constable.

"What is in that room?"

He reddened. "I have not gone in yet. I went up the ladder to check the window, but that was it."

I smiled as I turned to head around to the front door and handed his pad back. "Right. First we call Constable Mage Green to see what she can get from the ladders and prints. Next we see what is in the room they were trying to break into."

When we reached the door, it was open, and a man older than me was waiting. He smiled and held out his hand. "Consort Knight."

I took his hand. "For now it is royal inspector, Your Grace. I would like to see the room the intruders attempted to break into."

I gestured to the corporal, and he nodded, and the guards turned to wait. The duke glanced at them and then at me before turning. "Of course. I have heard a lot about your career as a constable and inspector."

He led the way with me, the corporal, and the constable following.

"Tell me, do you really think these new knight inspectors are necessary?"

We were climbing the stairs, and I smiled. "Knight and royal inspectors—yes. Nobles tend to be an…"

He glanced back and grinned. "An arrogant lot?"

I chuckled as we turned down a hall. "Yes, and I have had a few cases where they were corrupt. That is not why they were created; they investigate crimes involving nobles as well as capital crimes. I have had more than a few cases involving nobles. Sometimes constables or inspectors might miss something in the crime aimed at the noble because they are nobles."

We turned into a room with a bed that had been made. There was a rocking chair, standing closet, a dresser, and another door. I moved to the door and opened it to look into the nursery.

I turned as I thought. "Were any of the threats in writing?"

He nodded. "Several. It was the usual threats for revenge over the death of children. I burned them."

I shook my head. "Did they name the child or children?"

He shook his head. "I have strict orders in the towns and cities in my duchy. The threats concerned the children starving, and I created aid sanctuaries to feed the homeless. I have orders that any child in need of food is to be fed first. I thought…"

He shrugged, and I turned to look at the window. "I would contact the constable commissioner in the city the threats came from. Have him contact the knight inspector and check the morgue for the record of the deaths and then the sanctuaries and the managers. If it was more than one threat, then several people are involved. Something is wrong if the children did starve."

He stiffened when I looked at him. "I would—"

I held up a hand. "Clerks and managers steal, and it could have just been a mistake. First have the knight inspector investigate, and then if he does find someone negligent in the deaths, then let the magister judge."

I started for the door. "Constable, please note the room belongs to the nanny and connects to the nursery. Your Grace, while you contact your constable commissioner, we will try to find the men who attempted to break in."

He followed us out and to the stairs.

I glanced at the constable. "Constable Mage Green."

He nodded, and when I kept going through the front door, he stopped to use their call box. It was almost an hour before she arrived and found us at the corner of the house.

I led her around and to the tall ladder. "Anything you can tell us about the ladder or the footprints."

She moved to the ladder and murmured as she touched it. She shifted and looked around. "It is a roofer's ladder, but the last ones on it were not roofers. I cannot get any more detail on them."

I waited as she made a mold of the prints.

She glanced at me. "The boots that made the prints are old. You can use the mold to get a match if you have a suspect. I might be able to follow them, but once in the streets, there will be too much relation to other streets."

I sighed and shook my head. "It was worth a shot."

I gestured to the pry bar.

"What about that?"

She moved to it and touched it while murmuring. She looked at me. "A dockworker?"

I snorted. "More like stolen from a dockworker."

The only thing I could think was that these men were determined and would try again. I shook my head and gestured to the constable. "Call and have the ladders removed. Send a notice out to all stations about missing or stolen ladders."

I looked at the corporal.

"I will speak to the duke. I think I will stay here and keep watch from the nanny's room. You might as well send half the squad back for the horses."

I grinned at Abigail.

"I was speaking to Catherine about taking you with us when we went to Honore for their river race."

She laughed as she headed for the gate. "Sure."

I looked up at the window the ladder was at and turned to head around and in. Four guards followed me, and I went in and up to the nanny's room and stepped in. The guards waited by the door as I looked around the room. I walked to the nursery door and smiled at the two children. I watched them for several minutes and turned when I heard voices through the open door.

When I heard shots, I moved quickly and caught the two young boys and went to the far wall and a bed. "Under the bed."

There were more shots from the hall as the two children scrambled under the bed and I moved back across the room. I turned to look into the nanny's room, and motion at the nursery window caught my eye. I dived toward a dresser as the window shattered from a shotgun blast. From the shots in the hall, there were at least several gunmen firing at the guards.

I spun and rolled behind the dresser as another blast ripped into the dresser. I pulled my pistol and rolled and lifted it as I saw a man moving through the window. He held a revolving shotgun and pointed at me, but I fired first. He jerked, and the shotgun went off, and I felt the shot pass over me. He started to turn and cocked the shotgun as I cocked the hammer and fired again.

This time he fell, but a second man was climbing in and aimed another revolving shotgun. I rolled back behind the dresser, and he fired. The shot ripped into the floor where I had been. I leaned out and jerked back as he fired again while moving to the other side of the room. I leaped to my feet and spun as I brought the pistol up and fired into his chest.

A third man was already in the window, and I saw a fourth following him. I spun back behind the dresser as the man I fired into staggered and he and the man just inside the room fired. I felt the shot as it hit the dresser and went passed, and I leaned out and fired into the man again. This time he went to his knees but was still cocking the shotgun again.

I pulled back as the other two men fired and felt the shots ripping into the dresser. I leaned and shot the man on his knees in the head as he lifted the shotgun. His head snapped back, and I pulled back as he fell. I removed the cylinder, dropped it, and slipped in a loaded one. I cocked the pistol and turned and fired as I leaned out.

I hit the next man moving to the door into the nanny's room. He twisted and cried out as I cocked my weapon and fired into his chest again. He fell, and

I pulled back and knelt as the other man fired over the dresser, and the shot hit the wall. I spun while cocking the pistol to see him rushing me. I fired into his chest and cocked the pistol as he spun.

He fired the shotgun, but it went into the wall as he staggered. Before he could recover or fall, I aimed and fired, and his head snapped back. I pulled another cylinder as I moved to the window and looked out and down. No one was there, and there were only a few shots from the hall. I put the cylinder away as there was a burst of firing and then quiet.

I moved to the nursery-room door and opened it and peeked out and into the hall. My four guards were behind two overturned tables and a single chair, and one was in the doorway of another room. One turned and looked at me and relaxed. "Glad you are okay, sir."

I nodded as I looked at the stairs with the duke climbing them and holding a double-barrel shotgun. I turned and moved to the bed as I put the pistol away and knelt. I looked under the bed and smiled. "Ready to come out and go to your dad?"

The little boys nodded, and I reached under to help them. I took their hands, and we walked out, and in the hall, they saw their father and ran to him. I went to look at the stairs and found another four men with revolving shotguns. One was still alive, and I moved around and down to yank him onto his stomach and put him in restraints.

I searched him while he cursed me and all nobles. I looked up at my guard as they moved to the stairs. Two had bloody shoulders, and I gestured. "Go call the constables. Tell them we need a doctor and a detective inspector."

One nodded and moved around the bodies and down the stairs.

I left my prisoner on the stairs and went to open the uniform shirt of one guard. I checked the five wounds from pellets, and they had not gone through. I stripped the shirt off and used the under shirt to cover the wounds. "Hold it."

I knew he was in pain, but he held the shirt, and I moved to the other man. I glanced at the duke. "Sir, if you would take your children downstairs, I would be grateful."

He nodded and moved around us as I checked the other guard. Two minutes, and we had street constables walking in. It took twenty minutes for the constable doctor to arrive, and the detective inspector was with him. My corporal and the rest of my guards rode horses in at a trot. I wanted answers on why the men had done this but waited.

The doctor worked on my guards first, and they went to the hospital to remove the shotgun pellets. The doctor checked the wounded man but did not move him yet. He checked the dead and pronounced them in the spot they died. I was not surprised when Abigail showed up. When Catherine and two platoons of royal guards arrived, I glared at the corporal, but he ignored me.

I gestured at all the guards. "Out of the house before you destroy evidence."

The lieutenant was shaking his head as Catherine walked to the stairs.

I moved down to meet her. "What do you think you are doing here?"

She looked passed me and up the stairs at the bodies. "They said you were in a gunfight in the nursery and that two of your guards were wounded."

I held her arm and walked her into the parlor where the duke was with his children. His nanny was there, and so was his wife and the baby. I sat Catherine down. "And you know I can take care of myself."

She snorted as she shifted. "Like the last time when you were shot?"

I smiled. "I stepped in front of you when that happened."

She nodded. "And the time before that?"

I gave her a kiss and stood. "We could discuss every time I have been wounded, or we could discuss all the people who have tried to kill you or your mother. I have guards now, and they are very good at their jobs."

I turned and nodded to the duke and his family.

"This time I was protecting two very brave boys, and I would do it again."

She looked at the boys and the duke, and he bowed. She finally sighed. "Okay, Ashton."

I smiled. "Now I have a detective inspector to see and a suspect to interrogate. You could perhaps speak with Her Grace and look at their baby."

She leaned to the side to look and grinned. "That sounds good."

I turned and headed for the door and glanced at the lieutenant. "Lock her in the closet next time."

He grinned. "She is armed and would shoot the lock or me."

An hour, and we had a warrant for Abigail to do a truth spell. The man told us everything, and if it was true—I would be following the other knight inspector's case. According to the man, his wife and child had starved to death, and he had barely survived. The other men had similar stories from what he said, and the weapons and everything else they used had been stolen.

To me the men had been as much victims as their families, but to use children to get revenge was just…

I let the constables take him and wrote my statement and report. I knew he was headed for the mines or a work farm for life. Because of his story I doubt he would hang. I used the call box and then let the constables clean up as I led Catherine to her carriage.

I looked at the lieutenant. "The palace."

He nodded as she climbed in.

I leaned in the door. "I will be home as soon as I speak with the constable general."

I stepped back and let the lieutenant get in as I headed for my corporal and the horses. I swung up on mine and glanced at him as Catherine and her guards left.

"New rules."

The corporal stiffened, and I looked at the guards.

"Every other man carries a revolving shotgun, and the others carry a revolving rifle."

I turned and got my horse moving, and the corporal chuckled. "And we bring the horses if we walk."

I nodded but kept going, and we rode to the city lords' building. I had a private word with the constable general. It was that evening when I got the report relayed from the knight inspector. There was not just the death of the men's families who tried to kill the duke's children but over thirty others. I was in our sitting room and growled and wanted to hit something.

Catherine came to read the report while I paced. I finally sat and started writing, "Okay, criminal neglect in the death of forty-five people. The shelter manager fired the staff because he claims they did not have funds to buy food. I want his books audited and the books for the other shelters. Also I want an audit done on the ducal finance clerk. When you catch the bastard responsible, let the magister know they starved women and children." I looked at Catherine as she looked over my shoulder before I continued, "Notify all constable commissioners to have constables begin checking the homeless shelters once a week and, if there are shortages, to notify you. You let me know, and I will have Her Highness follow up to help those who need it."

I gave it to a guard to be sent to the constable general first thing in the morning. The man who had been wounded did get life on a work farm. The knight inspector caught the ducal clerk, and he had stolen the funds for the shelters. He was going to the hangman, and I made sure the man I caught was told. Duke Terrence was furious and began having each and every shelter manager personally send him weekly reports.

For my work the queen brought me to her court and granted me the title of knight commander of the constables. It was an honorary title, but if I ever needed to direct constables…

# CHAPTER 33

# Duke of Knight

I HELD THE baby while Catherine swam after Joseph, and two guards rowed. I had already done my laps, and now it was her turn. Sometimes we did them together, but our son was either sleeping, eating, or getting his diapers changed. Two full platoons of guards kept the river clear each morning while we exercised. I had even convinced her mother to build an indoor pool beside the river.

Catherine was determined to get her shape back, and I had even talked old Joseph into visiting and helping her. Each time she looked at me, she glared, and Joseph would chide her into swimming faster. She reached the dock after he was already out, and he bent. "Want to give up?"

She growled as she climbed out, "No."

He grinned and gave her cheek a pat. "Time for your stomach exercises."

She groaned and followed as he trotted off the dock, and she staggered after him. A guard held the boat, and I got out and shifted the baby to grab the bag with his things. At the end of the dock, the nanny was waiting and took the baby and bag. Catherine was on her back, lifting and swinging her legs to each side. More than one guard had made a mistake and commented and ended up trying to do the exercises.

I did not say anything as I lay beside her and started to copy them. Joseph called the cadence, and finally he came to his feet. "Enough for today. Tomorrow we walk and work on the arms."

Catherine sagged to the ground, but I rolled and came to my feet and bent to catch her hand and pull her up. She leaned against me, and we started walking toward the palace.

Joseph fell in beside her. "You are doing well. Slowly your muscles will tone, and it will be easier. The first couple of months are always the hardest. Even your lazy guards could use more exercises."

The lieutenant grinned as he reached us. "After you shamed the whole platoon yesterday, the colonel thinks you might be right. After you break your fast, he would like to speak to you."

I laughed, and Catherine giggled and moved away to walk on her own. Joseph nodded and looked at me. "Your grandfather has decided to sell the gallery."

I grinned. "To come here and run the shooting range?"

He laughed. "And visit with your Mr. Mack to make more of that brandy."

Catherine laughed, and we continued in and went to wash and dress. I had a meeting with the queen at breakfast and another with the constable general about a found body with a noble's signet ring. According to the note, the man had been dead at least a decade. An hour, and I was carrying our son while the nanny followed. In the private dining room, her mother and father were having breakfast.

Catherine took William and sat behind a screen to feed him while I fixed her a bowl of warm cereal. The nanny would help her as I went to get a cup of coffee and sat at the table. The queen smiled as the consort chuckled. "Ashton, you are a very strange man."

I took a sip of coffee and relaxed. "So—how may I help you today?"

She looked at the screen. "I understand you wish to continue as an inspector."

I nodded, and she took a breath.

"We would have you spend more time with Catherine. There are many meetings and appointments that she is not able to attend. As her consort you—"

I sighed. "Your Majesty, I am not a noble, and I have not been trained to govern. Half the bull...nonsense...she listens to would probably make me punch someone. To be blunt you allow too much of that. Like that group last week that insisted you grant them title to the entire southeast gulf waters. All so they would have the right to tax shipping and fishermen."

I snorted.

"If they had told me that, I would have slapped them and sent them to work on a fishing trawler. You baby and pamper the rich and nobles instead on making them stand up straight and do their own jobs. One out of every ten has legitimate reason that needs your intercession. One out of ten nobles is actually doing his or her job."

I looked at Catherine as she came out from behind the screen.

"A noble earns his or her rights and privileges by serving the people. Half believe their right is for the people to worship and serve them. If you want me to go to these meetings, I am not going to bow and scrap. I am not going to play nice with morons and assholes who are wasting my time."

The queen shifted, but Catherine grinned. "I told you. I would not mind; it will wake a lot of the…it could cause a lot of the idiots to stop bringing nonsense to us."

Her father grinned. "And cause an uproar with the nobles' council."

I finished my coffee and stood. "Besides half of the meetings you take should have been handled by one of the ministers. They are still an arrogant bunch of stuck-up…"

Catherine laughed, and the queen smiled. "Okay, Ashton, just think about it."

I bent to kiss Catherine before I strode out, and the corporal fell in. I glanced at him as we walked. "I heard you are up for sergeant."

He grinned. "Yes. The colonel has been surprised I have not requested another assignment or struck you."

I laughed as we walked through the halls. "There is always my biweekly fighting exercise you could volunteer for."

He chuckled. "No, thanks. I get enough bruises."

We walked out, and he gestured to a guard who brought the horses. My squad had been waiting by the door, and we swung up and turned to ride toward the gate. The constable general was just arriving when we got to the city lords' building. He smiled and looked around as I swung down. "Early but welcome."

I smiled. "So you have a body with a noble's signet ring."

He gestured, and I started walking in with him as my squad fell in around us. "The body was found in an old sealed room. The building had been abandoned for at least a decade, so there was nothing to track the killer."

I nodded. "True unless we use science. Who was the victim?"

He shook his head. "The only clue we have is the ring."

We climbed the stairs and walked into his outer office. His assistant was not in yet, and my guards stopped as we kept going. In his office he crossed to his desk and picked up a ring and turned. He held it out.

"I was hoping you would be able to identify it. We can at least let the family know we found his body."

I pulled a kerchief and accepted the ring and looked at the seal. "Just from what I see, it is related to the royal family."

I looked up.

"The body and the building it was found in?"

He smiled. "The body, or mummy really, is with the medical examiner. The building is Five Emerald Way. It is off Sanders Street and used to be an exclusive hostel for nobles before it suddenly closed."

I nodded and wrapped the ring and turned for the door. "I will look into it and let you know what I find."

I left and gestured to the corporal as the squad surrounded me again.

I handed the ring to him. "Have one of the men return to the palace. He is to go to the royal library and see the librarian and look up the noble's crest. When he is done, he is to return to us at Five Emerald Way with the ring."

He nodded and reached out to catch one of the men. He gave him the ring and told him what to do as I stopped at a desk on the ground floor. I called the central constable station and left a message for Constable Mage Green. After I was done, we left and took the horses, and I let the corporal lead. The house or building was at the end of a small lane.

It would have been impressive if not for the weeds and overgrown ivy smothering the building. Signs of age and neglect were everywhere as we rode through an arch and into a stable yard. The stable was stone like the house, but the roof was faded and needed repairing. To one side was another building that looked like a long barrack.

Through the stable we could see a disused corral that was overgrown. I swung down and shook my head. "Now this is as much of a mystery."

The guards were looking around and frowning as I moved to look at the other side of the stable. There was a large herb garden, but like everything else, it was overgrown. I turned and moved to the stable-yard door into the house. It looked like someone had forced it open, and the corporal cleared his throat.

I grinned and stopped to gesture. "After you."

He nodded, and two guards slipped in ahead of me, and he followed. A minute, and he was back, and I followed them in.

"We are going to have to search for the sealed room."

Actually all we had to do was follow all the footprints in the dirt and debris. They led us around and then up to the next floor. At a set of double doors, someone had forced them open. I looked at the doors carefully, and more than age had sealed them.

"Do not touch the doors."

In the room was a large parlor with another door. That led to a bedroom, and I could see where the body had lain on the bed. I gestured the guards back as I moved in carefully. Most of the things in the room had rotted away long ago. What struck me was the old shoes the person had left to one side of the room. Very old clothes lay folded, and I found an old jewelry box for a man.

I pulled out my gloves and put them on before I opened it. I looked at the rings and a few necklaces before lifting a tray. I know I put important papers under my top tray, and I lifted out a very old letter. I was extremely careful opening it and silently read it. It was from a woman breaking off an engagement. I looked at the name it was addressed to but did not recognize it.

I set it down and moved to the bed and started to look at everything. There were lots of signs of blood, which made the linens decay faster in those areas. I looked at the door when a guard cleared his throat. He smiled. "Abigail and another constable mage."

I nodded. "Send them in."

Abigail and Norris walked in and stopped to look around.

I smiled. "Two for the price of one. You are not going to get a resonance. From the signs in the bed, the victim was killed there. First, we do not know who he was. Second, we do not know when this happened. Third, we do not know who killed him. I will get with the medical examiner to find out how he died."

Norris nodded as his eyes searched the room. Abigail moved to the bed. "I should be able to find out the when by examining the signs left by the blood."

Norris followed. "You could try a relation spell to the blood to look for the weapon."

I moved to the door so they could work and ignored the tingle and bumps on my arm from their magic. A guard strode in, looking grim, and handed me the kerchief. "The librarian says it belongs to the duke of Derry."

I looked at the others. "I have not met him."

The corporal shook his head. "He is a recluse. He only issues orders through his manservant and has not been seen out of his manor in a long time."

I looked at him and then at the bed. "Or he is dead, and his manservant has been pretending to be him."

Norris pulled a pair of glove on and reached onto the bed and folded crumbling piece of sheet back. He lifted a straight razor. "He was killed with this."

I moved to take it, and the blade was pitted and rusted with age. "Most high nobles born to the rank do not shave themselves, and they sure do not do it in bed."

I pulled a small bag from an inside pocket and put the razor in it. I put down where it was found, when, and by whom. I also noted that Norris was a constable mage, and it was identified by relation to blood found at the scene. I closed it and looked at Abigail, and she shrugged. "Ten years and two months is as close as I can get."

I nodded and headed for the door. "Thanks for coming."

If this was the duke, I needed to make a few calls, and I needed to see the queen. She would have some memory of him I might be able to use. I still needed to see the medical examiner and look at the body. The medical examiner did not take long. The man had his throat cut, which was not how someone would commit suicide.

I logged the razor as evidence and made a call to Derry City. The switchboard put me through to the knight inspector. "Knight Inspector George."

I was thinking and trying to ignore the minor chaos in the station. "Inspector this is Noble Inspector Knight. We have a body that was wearing a signet ring bearing the crest of the duke of Derry. I understand he is a recluse, but you need to see him and confirm he is alive. Find out where he was ten years and two months ago. That was when the man was murdered."

I could tell he was interested as he cleared his throat. "I might need a warrant."

I snorted. "With the signet ring, that will not be a problem. Give me an hour, and I will have the duty magister notify the court there."

I disconnected and looked at the desk sergeant.

"Do me a favor and have one of your constables stop in at the ducal clerks and find out who owns Five Emerald Way. He can call the palace and leave the information with soon-to-be sergeant Thompson."

I grinned at my corporal, and he shook his head. I went into the back and waited for the duty magister. He was more than willing to issue the warrant to question the duke on the basis of the evidence. Next we rode back to the palace, and I left my guards at the door when I went in to see the queen. She was in with two rich merchants who glared at me.

I had looked at her appointment calendar and moved around her desk. I ignored her guards as I pulled out the kerchief and opened it. "Recognize this?"

She frowned as she looked at it. "It is very tarnished, but I believe it is the signet for my cousin William Derry."

One of the merchants cleared his throat. "Your Majesty, the trade items should not be—"

I looked at them. "Leave now. Go to the trade minister and speak with him. I saw the items you are trying to bring in. I am sure the foreign trade minister can explain the raw ingredients are used for more than medicine. In fact they can be used to make explosives and illegal drugs, which is where you would make a profit. I will be notifying the customs people to check any and all your cargo for related ingredients."

They paled and stammered, but I looked at the guards.

"Show them out."

The queen had sat back and looked at me as her guards moved to do as I asked. She shook her head. "Those two merchants can cause a lot of problems."

I snorted. "Those two are smugglers and should have gone to your foreign trade minister. I will speak with customs and the constable commissioner in Honore since that is where they are bringing their cargos in."

I tapped the ring.

"My problem with this being the duke's ring is that it was found on a ten-year-old body. Now the reports I have is that he is a recluse and no one has seen him."

She blinked and looked at the ring again. "Now that you mention it, I have not seen him in...well, ten years. I have always gotten an excuse from one of his servants, usually that he is sick and unable to attend me or the court."

I looked at the door when the corporal stepped in. "Well?"

He nodded. "It is owned by the duke of Derry."

I looked at the queen. "That is strike two. The place we found the body was his."

She looked at the small desk in the corner where her private assistant sat. "Mary, send someone to the Derry ducal office. I want to know if any documents they have received in the last ten years had the ducal seal."

The assistant nodded and stood to walk to the door. I took the ring back. "I will let you know what I find."

The queen smiled. "Thank you, Ashton."

I headed for the door. "I might even look at the few...people here to see you."

She laughed as I opened the door and stepped out.

I looked at the dozen people waiting and moved to the secretary behind her desk. I turned the appointment book to read it. I looked across the room. "Baron James, it is not the queen's job to get your son into the navy. Go see Admiral Kennet about accepting him into the navy cadets. All you need is your endorsement and for your child to have a decent record."

He stood slowly. "But—"

I shook my head. "No one enters the navy as an officer without training. That gets people killed, and it could be your son. See the admiral and enroll him as a cadet."

He nodded. "Thank you."

I nodded and looked at several merchants. "You go see the interior trade minister."

They reddened, but I ignored it and gestured to a guard. I looked at a small man constantly squeezing his hat. "Sir, as much as I would like to let you see the queen, she is not the one you need. If you go down to the office of court review, see Senior Magister Sarasota. Let him know it is about a military court review concerning actions under fire. More than likely he will move your son's case to their case load." I smiled. "With his awards for valor, there should not be a problem with returning his body for burial."

He blinked and stood slowly. "But—"

I gestured. "Tell the magister that Ashton Knight sent you."

I looked at the other men. "Now who wants to guess what I am going to say next?"

Several stood and left, and I nodded to the secretary.

"Much better."

I headed for the door as the guards chuckled. We left the palace and rode back to the city lords' building. I stopped at the constable general's assistant and asked her to make the calls to Honore regarding the merchants. I knocked and stepped into his office, and he sat back. "Well?"

I crossed to sit in a chair across from his. "It could be Duke Derry. It is his signet ring, and the building he was found in belonged to him. I sent Knight Inspector George to question him. It was murder, and we do have the weapon and time, ten years and two months."

He grinned. "Excellent."

He reached for the call box when it rang and answered. He nodded and looked at me. "Get the full confession and send me the report."

He hung up. "Speaking of Knight Inspector George. He went to question the duke, and the manservant tried to send him away and then keep him from seeing the duke. Only there was no duke, and when the manservant said he had gone out, he refused to say where. Inspector George told him we had found his body, and he broke down."

He shook his head.

"He admitted killing the duke and trying to cover it by pretending he was still alive. Apparently it had something to do with a woman."

I stood. "I will write up my report."

He nodded, and I headed for the door. I rode back to the palace and sent my guards to take a break. I went to see Catherine, and my first order of business was to look at her appointments. I canceled three and sent six to one of the ministers. I redirected two nobles to see the librarian to look up imperial law on slave labor using prisoners.

I sent the queen a message about the duke and went in to sit with Catherine while I did my report. My little redirecting and examination of those seeking appointments changed how the secretaries and assistants did it. A week, and the queen and Catherine's daily appointments had been cut back by two-thirds. Of course the ministers screamed during the weekly meeting until they made the mistake of doing it in front of me.

I smiled politely at the one glaring at me. "In that case, Minister, I am sure Her Majesty will accept your resignation."

He sputtered. "I am…not going too—"

I leaned forward past Catherine. "Listen to me, you self-important clerk. You will do your job, your entire job, or I will bring in a dozen men who not only need the work but would also be more than willing to do it. You are a trade minister, and it is your job to speak with and handle merchants. You do not send them to Her Majesty to decide the issue—that is your job and one with duties and responsibilities."

He reddened, but the queen and Catherine did not say anything until the consort chuckled. "Especially when you know the trade items are illegal or for gray markets that are not good for the kingdom."

The ministers looked at each other and shut up. It was another week before I was summoned to the nobles' court. Catherine would not tell me why but kept covering her mouth. Before I knew what was happening, I was giving my oath of fealty as the new duke of Derry, or Knight as the queen called it.

CHAPTER 34

# Wizards Do Not Die

I SMIRKED AT Catherine as I watched the two young mages following Norris away from Abigail—they had just married the day before. She shook her head as we entered the servant quarters. Since Five Emerald Way was owned by the duke of Derry, it was mine now, and I contacted Norris. He wanted to start the mage school for constable mages, so I made him the headmaster.

A new mage he trained had replaced him in Honore, and the house and grounds on Five Emerald Way became the school. He was still cleaning it up but had made the servants' quarters into labs for the mages. They already knew magic and how to use it, but using magic for the constables was not the same. I had donated my large collection of books on science or magic.

There was everything from science and religious spells to sorcery or witchcraft. If it dealt with forensics, I had a book on it. We stopped in the doorway as he created a ward and looked at one of the young men. "What is first?"

The young man smiled. "First I use a spell of discovery to find—"

Norris was shaking his head. "I told you a hundred times. First, you put on gloves. Second, there is a poison somewhere in the room, so you protect yourself. It could kill by breathing it or by touch, so before you try a spell, look around and use your eyes. Also the constables are the ones to call you, so listen to them first."

He nodded to the other young man who grinned. "I am Constable Parris. I found a bloated body in this room. It was holding a flower, and the victim's lips were blue, and the fingertips looked burned. There were no signs of violence or a struggle."

It was like he was reading a script, which he was. It was actually from a case file from another city. The young mage shifted as he looked at the corner. "A flower, blue lips, and burned fingertips."

Norris was quiet as the mage put on gloves and murmured a ward. In the corner was the flower, and he knelt while looking at it. He started to reach out and then stopped and looked back at me with a grin. "Caution."

He pulled a set of tools from inside his light jacket and a ball of cotton. Next he bent and scrapped the stem of the flower. He whispered when he was done, and flames flickered and seared the tool. He held the cotton ball and murmured a spell, and tiny glyphs appeared in the air over it. He grinned and whispered, and they separated. "Two chemicals. One to make it absorb faster and the other a very deadly poison."

He looked at Norris.

"From a serpent."

Norris nodded. "Now you need to seal the evidence and—"

The young mage grinned. "And completely identify the chemicals to exactly what they are and from what, for the court records."

I turned and held Catherine's arm as we left. "I think this is going to work. The constable general has two dozen requests for mages and three dozen who want to learn. Teaching them using examples from past cases is going to help them learn. Right now we do not know how long before they will be ready, but Abigail thinks they should also spend a period watching a constable mage for probation."

She nodded. "I agree. I mean I knew the law and thought I knew what you did until I was with you and doing it. I still remember my first case and those pickpockets."

I smiled. "True, but you were not trained like a constable going through the school. Lady Fiera did, and even with her training officer, she made mistakes, which is why we have training officers. That was what I was thinking."

As we left the servant quarters, our guards fell in, and she nodded. "You want to assign the young mage to a constable mage."

I nodded. "For six months until the training officer clears him or her."

She nodded. "Makes sense, but why tell me?"

I smiled as we reached her carriage. "Because the first would be here in your duchy with Abigail, and it would set a precedent. The school is technically in my domain, which is…anyway since the school is in another duchy, you need to agree. I was hoping, between us and the constable general, we could get your mother to change the law."

She smiled. "Sure. Right now each duchy has its own constable academy, but it is evaluated by the constable general's office."

I nodded. "And there are not enough mages to create a school in each duchy."

She turned and caressed my chest. "I will speak with Mother."

We both turned as a rider came in and slowed to a walk before dropping off the horse. It was a royal page, and he strode to us. "My lord Knight, the queen has directed you to join the constable general at the Willingham estate."

He took a breath and looked toward Abigail.

"We have a report the wizards' council is dead."

I turned. "Abigail!"

I looked at Catherine. "See you when I am free."

She nodded and squeezed my arm. "Be careful. Just being around a true wizard is dangerous, and there are five on the council."

I grinned as I gestured to Sergeant Thompson and my guards. "I will be careful."

I waited at my horse for Abigail. "I am going to need your help. The queen received a report that the wizards' council is dead."

She snorted. "Wizards do not die."

I shrugged. "Get your horse and follow."

She nodded, and I turned and swung up. "The Willingham estate, Sergeant."

He turned his horse and nodded, and two guards spun theirs and started moving. We followed, and the rest fell in around me. I glanced at the sergeant. "Make sure your men do not speak or touch anything when we get there."

He opened his mouth, but I shook my head.

"Dealing with mages or wizards is not like being in a crime scene. If it is a place they gather or frequent, there could be traps or enchanted items."

He blinked and nodded as he looked around. "Of course."

When we reached the estate, there were constables outside the gate. Two men wearing black guarded the gate, and the constable general was arguing with them. I swung down and moved to him, and he turned. "They refuse to allow us in."

I pulled my weapon and aimed at one. "Kill them."

The two gasped, and their eyes went wide, and their faces paled. One sputtered as I cocked the pistol and quickly yanked the gate open. "Wait!"

I looked at the constables as I put my weapon away. "Put them in restraints. If a wizard is dead, they could be conspiring."

They moved forward and grabbed the two guards as they protested. I smiled at the constable general and turned to walk into the estate. "Leave the constables. Someone send Constable Mage Green in when she arrives!"

I was thinking if the queen got a report but the guards did not know or were refusing entry, how did she get it? I reached the large front doors and pushed them open. To one side an ancient-looking man appeared and moved to me. "My masters do not wish to—"

I touched the badge on my belt. "Royal Inspector Knight."

I turned and looked around the huge entry.

"And this is the constable general. We are here on orders from the queen."

He shifted, and I looked at him.

"We need to speak with the council."

He shook his head, and I sighed. "Or I set the damn manor on fire."

He blinked and then shook his head. "Leave the others and follow."

Of course he walked very slowly, which gave me time to stop my guards from following. By the time we reached a grand staircase, Abigail was there. We went past the second floor and turned to cross another entry-type room on the third. On the other side was a set of huge double doors. The servant stopped and lifted a hand to knock. There was no reply, and he turned. "They do not wish to be disturbed."

I snorted and moved forward and tried the handle. It was locked, and I stepped back and kicked. The doors flew open as Abigail started past me. "I could have opened them."

I caught her. "And if the doors were spell warded? Remember your training constable."

She stopped and blinked before she nodded. I walked in with her following and then the constable general. The room was impossibly large and stretched into the sky and seemed a hundred paces across. Either it was an illusion or the manipulation of space. I put on my gloves as I continued across to a strange pentagon-shaped table.

Four men were frozen in chairs at each of the points, and the fifth was sprawled out on the floor in a small puddle of blood. I ignored the others and moved around and knelt by the body. First I looked and caught Abigail's hand when she reached out to check it. "Not yet."

I looked at the eyes and then stood and moved to one of the others. I looked at him very closely and removed a glove and held it in front of his mouth and nose. There was a slight feel of breath, and I checked each of them before I moved to the empty chair. I looked at what was on the table and took a breath and sat and reached out with the hand that did not have a glove on.

I covered a glowing plate of crystal like each of the others. There was pain, and the world vanished, and then I was in a huge work room. I looked around without moving and saw five old men. "Excuse me?"

They spun, and one glared and lifted his hand, and I shook my head. "That would be very bad."

He froze, and they looked at each other before one moved to me. "Who are you, and how did you get here?"

I held still. "Royal Inspector Ashton Knight. The seat I am in is at the table you used to get here. One of you was shot, but the spells to transfer you hold it as if frozen, but it is slowly dying unless something is done. I do have a mage with me, but I do not know if she can remove the bullet and heal the body."

I nodded to the angry one.

"You are the one shot and dying."

They growled and shook their heads, "If one dies, we all die, and there is no way back unless it is together."

I sighed. "Gentlemen, you are wizards. Think. I am here, so the seal has been broken. Now what do I do?"

They hissed, but one moved closer. "Think of your real hand and lift it. If you can return, have your mage remove the bullet and place the body at the table.

Stand beside it and cover the hand when you place it on the crystal plate. You will return, but we will be able to leave."

I nodded and did not look at my hands as I thought and imaged my hand on the crystal and struggled to lift it. It was like it was being held down, but slowly in my mind, I saw it lift, and then I blinked as my hand jerked into the air, and I was at the table. I nodded and moved. "Help me lift and move the body back into the chair. Abigail, I will need you to pull the bullet straight out the way it went in without affecting the body."

The constable general moved to help as I lifted and moved it into the chair. I leaned it back and looked at Abigail, and she covered the wound and murmured. The wound bulged, and then she caught the bullet.

I nodded and gestured them back. "Watch for me."

I stood beside the chair and took the hand in mine and placed it on the crystal. A moment, and I felt the pain, and then I was back in the room. Only this time the other four were sitting across from me, and the last moved and placed his hand under mine. The room spun, and there was pain, and then I was catching the wizard as he grabbed his chest.

I moved to lay him on the floor with the constable general while the other four wizards chanted. The one I was helping stiffened and froze, and I looked at the other wizards. One came and knelt and covered the wound. He murmured, and the wound closed, and a moment later, the wizard was moving and taking breaths. I relaxed and stood as I put my other glove on. "Okay, now I can get to work."

I nodded to Abigail.

"Now if you can get a relation to the bullet, we might find the weapon."

The constable general cleared his throat, and I grinned.

"Sirs, this is Constable General Stone and Constable Mage Green."

The four wizards who were standing nodded, and the fifth moved to the chair. I looked at the constable general. "I think you can return to your office, sir. Send a messenger to Her Majesty that the wizards are alive."

He nodded and glanced at them before walking out. Abigail touched the bloody bullet and murmured, and one of the wizards snorted. "That is—"

I looked at him. "Excuse me, sir, but unlike Constable Mage Green you are not trained as a constable mage. She must establish any and all relations to the evidence, which means the victim and the weapon that fired it. Constable mages are trained in forensics, from resonance from victims to suspects and identification of poisons and objects."

I glanced at her when she finished.

"She has an entire city of constables who call on her to help find thieves and killers. Sometimes it is easy to trace the person, and sometimes she must use the elements found at a crime scene."

They were shifting around as I looked at them.

"Take a blackmailer who leaves threatening notes. For the magister she must prove they wrote the note and identify the person. She must show how she found the relation; it could be in the paper or the ink or the handwriting."

I moved to accept the bullet back.

"Well?"

She grinned and ignored the wizards. "The weapon is close, and the relation is going to be the powder."

She drew a slightly glowing glyph in the air. "They are using Kelm six twenty-one, which is ground finer than other powders. The weapon should be a Gem ten millimeter, probably with a short barrel."

I nodded and pulled a small envelope and placed the bullet in it. "So we follow the trace of powder."

She turned and gestured, and I fell in beside her as we crossed the huge room following a faint glow in the air. We walked out the door and turned toward the stairs. She glanced at me. "You realize you just insulted five wizards."

I grinned as I looked at every table and painting in the hall. "Even the great need someone to whisper in their ear."

She gestured down, and I led the way and saw the sergeant at the foot. I gestured for him to come up and looked back at the wizards following us. I shook my head as Abigail stopped on the second floor. She looked down a wide hall, and a glowing trail in the air appeared. I nodded as I started moving. "I wonder how many servants there are."

Halfway down the hall, the trail turned and vanished at a door. I moved Abigail to the side of the door and knocked. "Constables!"

I looked at the wizards and tried the handle before I stepped back and kicked. The lock burst open as my sergeant pushed through the wizards. "Sir!"

I was moving to the other side of the door, which was good as branching lightning exploded out. I dropped and rolled away with the tingling feeling of being too close. I growled as I rolled, and a young mage stalked out. Lightning was reaching out and cascading over the walls up and down the hall. Abigail was on the floor like me, and the sergeant had his weapon out as he dived.

He quickly flung it away as a small arc touched it, and he cursed. The wizards were together chanting as lightning kept striking what looked like a ward around them. From the occasional flare around the young mage, I was sure he had a ward shield also. I looked at Abigail and then the sergeant, and he was staring at me and shook his head.

I reached to the small of my back as I came to my feet behind the mage. "Hey!"

He spun as I took long strides, and he reached out to point at me. Only I was too close, and my left hand crossed my body and came up through the ward shield. I brushed his hand to the left and across his body while I stepped. My right hand was pulling a leather-wrapped sap as the mage turned with his arm. My foot came down as I turned and lashed out, and the sap struck behind his ear.

As fast as that it was over as the mage dropped. I followed him to the floor and looked at the sergeant. "I need something to blindfold him."

He came to his feet. "You know—"

I snorted. "A blindfold, Sergeant."

I rolled the mage onto his stomach and yanked his arms back to put him into restraints. I turned his head to look at his eyes, but they were closed. Abigail chuckled as she finally came to help me. "I thought you would shoot him."

I looked at the wizards as I sat up. "He had a ward, which meant nothing magical or metal would pass through."

The sergeant disappeared into a room and returned with a pillow case. I rolled it and used it as a blindfold and relaxed. "That was interesting."

One of the wizards cleared his throat. "So you have your man."

I stood. "No, we have a suspect; we still have to prove he is the one who attempted to kill you."

I looked down.

"Who is he?"

The wizards looked at each other, and one finally shrugged. "A nephew."

I kept looking at him, and he shook his head.

"He has been trying to get us to force the queen to pass a law."

I thought I knew where this was going. "Let me guess. He wants mages immune from the kingdom law and governed by a mage council."

They shrugged, and I shook my head.

"Sergeant, watch him."

I moved into the room and looked around before I began to search. He had not even hidden the weapon, but if he was trying to threaten the queen, I would not expect him to. I checked it to see if it had been fired and then used a sheet to wrap it.

I carried it to Abigail and pulled out the small envelope with the bullet. "Was it fired from this weapon?"

She touched both and murmured before nodding. I put both away and knelt and slapped the mage until he groaned, and I smiled. "Head hurt?"

He struggled against the restraints. "Let me go!"

I caught him and pulled as I stood. "I am Royal Inspector Knight, and you are under arrest for—"

He twisted and tried to jerk away, and I shoved him into the wall. "You are under arrest for attempted murder with a deadly weapon and assault on a constable. There could be other charges later, and anything you say will be heard in court."

He cursed me and kept struggling. "When I can see, you will suffer!"

I pulled him back and pushed him down the hall. "First, mage, since you have been threatening and used magic, plan to wear a black hood for the next dozen year or more. Second, if you continue, the magister could order the wizard council to perform a block to keep you from ever touching your magic again. And last—if you piss off enough people, they just might use coals to burn out your eyes."

He shut up as I kept him moving down the hall. I looked back at the wizards.

"I will need statements, gentlemen. I will send a constable if you would write them up."

Abigail followed with the sergeant and chuckled. "I cannot wait for when he explains this to Catherine."

He was an angry arrogant mage, and the magister read everything and even used the call box to speak with the wizard council. The mage was the one to send the message to the queen that her wizards were dead. He wanted to be caught so he could use his magic and prove we could not enforce the laws against mages. Of course now he was belligerent and demanding.

The wizard council made the decision. Two arrived and kept him between them as they reached in and bound his magic so he could not use it. The magister sentenced him to twenty years on a work farm. Something else happened, and that was the wizard council came to the constable mage school. At first it was to observe and then to improve it.

The queen did submit the request for a kingdom-sponsored constable mage school to the full court for a vote. When they heard the facts of how our mages were overworked and how few there were, it was passed. Of course I was called before them and asked about policing the mages. I snorted and looked at the dukes. "You are asking me as if what I did in capturing a mage was exceptional."

I shook my head and looked around.

"How many of you know what your constables are required to learn? Do you know facing a mage is taught? They are dangerous, but so are gangs with access to weapons. Breaching a ward is as simple as reaching through it. They are meant to stop weapons and magic and not an organic object like a constable's billy."

They looked at each other, and more than one grinned.

# CHAPTER 35

# Death of the Constable General

WE HAD EXERCISED and even gone to the range. It had been six months since the case with the wizards. It was fun when we got to watch Joseph helping and teaching the guards. I had to admit they were a lot better after six months of practice. I was spending at least half of each day with Catherine in her office. Most of the time, I had stacks of reports from my duchy.

I had recalled my constable commissioner for the capital city to speak with him. Now he was doing the same for the two other major cities. I was also making calls to six of the nine barons. I had twelve baronies, and three were vacant. They had been neglected after the duke died, and now I was playing catch-up. I had only a dozen cases from the constable general, and they had all been easy.

I bumped Catherine as our son walked on shaking legs, and Joseph moved his arms. She giggled and shook her head as William tried to go faster to catch him. Of course he turned and kept moving the arms. "Three months, little monster, and we will start training."

I laughed but knew he was serious. He was here in the mornings, and then he went to help grandfather. My grandfather took over the range, and somehow he was now teaching classes on weapons for those going through the constable academy. I moved forward and bent to pick my son up. "And when does he start exercising?"

Joseph stood up. "On his birthday."

I looked at Catherine. "In the pool."

Joseph laughed as he headed for the door. "Of course. All children love water, and it will be easy to teach him to swim like his parents."

She smiled as I walked back with William on my hip. "The pool will be finished by then."

I think he was walking now because of Joseph, but he was also speaking words that could almost be understood. Catherine slipped her arm around, the one not holding our son. "I saw the doctor yesterday while you were chasing Baron Wilson's rebellious daughter."

I looked at her, and she smirked.

"I am pregnant again."

I grinned and turned as I shifted William and pulled her close. "So that is why the herbs are missing."

She laughed and kissed me. "This time I want a daughter."

I glanced at the door as the lieutenant stepped in. "Let your people know she is pregnant again."

He grinned. "Congratulation, Your Highness."

Catherine reddened but nodded, and I turned as William squirmed. "What is it?"

He smiled. "Lady Fiera is here. Her father sent her about one of his new knight inspectors."

I looked at Catherine, and she sighed and let me go. "The constable general sent Mother notice of his appeal. The duke wanted the son of a baron to take the position, but he has not been an inspector."

I nodded as I started walking, and we stepped into the hall. Lady Fiera was striding toward us, and I smiled. "I am sure Lady Fiera will be the first to tell her father there is more to being an inspector than the course we started. They need a training officer to direct and guide them, which is another inspector. That is why I suggested only seasoned inspectors be offered the position of knight or noble inspector."

She smiled as she stopped and nodded to Catherine. "Which is what I told Father. Even now that I no longer have Detective Inspector Kerns as a partner, I am still learning new things."

I kept going while Catherine turned to go the other way with Lady Fiera. "Send the baron's son here to go through the inspector course and train under Megan as an inspector!"

They laughed, and I smiled as I turned in at the nursery. I set William down and watched him head straight for his toys. I nodded to his nanny and left; I promised myself I would return early to take him to the estate. Even in the cold of winter and with snow, he liked it there. At least this year, the snow was not as deep. I headed for the door thinking of going to see the constable general.

True, I was bored, but I wanted to know what this baron's son was like. I was not sure why the duke of Fiera would want to push it; they normally do not get involved with the constables. I peeked in the guard room and gestured to my sergeant. He stood and called the others while walking to the door. I waited and let him move in front of me. "The city lords' building."

We rode through the light covering of snow on the streets. The street sweepers had been doing a great job in keeping them clear. A lot of people were out and seemed happy. More than a few lads were playing in the snow or throwing snowballs. We turned in and swung down and led the horses back to the stables. The sergeant looked at me as I headed for the door. "You know someone has made a steam car that does not need rails."

I grinned as we entered the building. "Think the steam will keep you warm? What happens in the summer?"

He chuckled and shook his head as we climbed the stairs. "I was thinking of new horseless carriages filling the street."

I shook my head. "Maybe in twenty years or when everyone can afford them. Now I read about new weapons that use a brass cartridge. The cap, powder, and bullet go into the cartridge, and you load the cartridge without removing the cylinder."

He nodded. "The captain has one we are testing. The army has new rifles that use the brass cartridges, but they are single shot."

We walked into the outer office for the constable general, and his assistant looked up. "He is not in yet."

I frowned. "He is never late."

I looked at the sergeant and turned. "I think we will head for his house and meet him along the way."

Five minutes, and we were back in the saddle and riding out. I had talked with the constable general enough to know where he lived, which meant I was sure of the streets he would take. We took our time since the air was clear and it looked like a nice day. That ended when I glanced at bushes beside and in front of a house. There were drag marks in the snow, and someone had covered them, which left more.

I pulled the horse to a stop and frowned before I swung down. The sergeant cleared his throat, but I had a bad feeling and ignored him. I moved to the side and walked in unmarked snow until I could see into the bushes. That was when I saw the body and moved quickly. I knelt and reached out to feel for a heartbeat, but he was already beginning to get cold.

I sat back on my heels and looked around. "Sergeant, send a man to the corner call box. I need constables, the doctor, and Constable Mage Green."

I looked at him.

"Have him call the palace. Notify the queen her constable general has been murdered."

He nodded and gestured, and one of the guards spun his horse and rode back to the corner. I stood and moved back to the street, looking at the tracks the killer had made while trying to cover them up.

I looked at the snow and frowned at the way it was melting. I leaned closer to look and then cursed. "Salt."

From the outside temperature and the feel of the body, he had been killed a couple of hours ago. I moved back along the walk toward the constable general's home. I saw the killer's prints blurred where they emerged from behind a bush. From the look of things, he had shot the constable general in the back and then moved the body. I searched behind the bush and blinked when I saw where something very small had sunk in the snow.

I went the other way until footprints in the snow appeared out of the mess thirty steps away. "Lazy."

This had not been a robbery or crime of passion. Someone had waited and killed him and covered it up before walking away. I looked at the house and climbed the steps to bang on the door. From the look of things, no one had entered in a long time. I turned and looked across the street, but there was an empty lot. To each side were houses with tall, bordering snow-covered hedges.

Most of the street was the same, which made this an ideal place to ambush someone. Constables trotted down the street as the guard rode back. His face was set as he stopped and looked at me. "The queen has demanded you find his killer. She wants them brought before her senior magister. She said to tell you she considered this an act of treason to her and the crown."

I nodded and looked at the constables. "The constable general has been killed. Block off this side of the street and go to every house to question them. Find out if anyone heard the shot or shots."

They nodded and moved away while I walked back to my horse to wait for the doctor and Abigail. More constables were coming down the street, and I finally saw Abigail trotting her horse toward us. I was sure the doctor would not be far behind. She came to a stop and swung down. "Is it true? The constable general was killed?"

I nodded and gestured. "Until the doctor gets here, there are a few things you can do."

I led her down to the bush the killer had hidden behind. "The bastard used salt on the snow to cover his tracks."

She hissed, but I pointed to where something had sunk into the snow.

"Something melted and sunk into the snow there."

She murmured and moved closer, and the wet end of a cigarette rose up and out.

I put on gloves and pulled a small bag and set it on the bag. "Can you get an image?"

She pulled crystal and chanted, and the unlit end glowed. In the crystal the image of a man appeared. I nodded and looked down the street when I heard a wagon. Beside it were the constable commissioner and a constable commander. I pulled my notebook. "Can you copy the image so we can send it to all officers?"

She looked at the image and then at me. "I do not need to. That is Constable Wertholm from the Fiera duchy. He was here to see the constable general about becoming a knight inspector."

I scowled and turned to walk to the doctor as he climbed down from the wagon. I watched him check the body and give us a time of death. From there Abigail pulled the bullet from the body and tried to get a resonance, but everything was blurry, so the killer has rubbed salt on the bullet.

I had her try to get an impression from the prints as the killer walked away. Even though it looked like the killer had stopped, using salt on the soles was enough to make using magic impossible. I remembered something from one of the science books. "Freeze the print and then use plaster to make the mold."

She grinned and moved to her horse and the saddle bags. "And we can roll the bullet to get the bullet marks and match it to a weapon."

I looked at the constable commissioner. "I need a wanted notice put out for Constable Wertholm."

He nodded and turned to the commander as a couple of constables returned. None of the neighbors had heard the shots, but one held up a milk bottle with the bottom cut out. The inside was filled with cotton fibers that looked burned. "I found this in the snow at the end of the block."

He was wearing glove, and I gestured to Abigail. She touched it and murmured and shook her head. "More salt, but I do see finger marks."

I nodded. "Use graphite powder and make a mold."

I turned and looked around as constables helped moved the body to the wagon.

I looked back. "Bag the bottle and molds. Everything goes to the central station. Constable, I need your statement with the bottle. Abigail, I will need the crystal and your report as soon as possible."

I took the small evidence bag with the cigarette and accepted the crystal.

"Wait at the station. I need to see Senior Magister Gold, and then we are going to find Constable Wertholm. With the cigarette I should be able to get a warrant for a truth spell."

I strode to my horse and swung up and looked at the constable commissioner.

"Have your people check every hostel or boarding house for Wertholm."

He was watching the wagon as it pulled away and turned. "We will find the bastard."

I turned, and the sergeant did not try to stop me as I kicked my horse into a trot. My mind was calm, but beneath I was very angry—the constable general had been a friend, and I respected him. I slowed to a walk when we reached the palace and turned in. The magisters there were all senior and mostly did appeals and case reviews.

I swung down and started in at the ministers' entrance. To one side was a hall, and I ignored the few clerks as I stopped at a door and opened it. Senior Magister Gold looked up from a thick file and blinked. "Um...Lord Knight?"

I strode to the desk. "I am here as Royal Inspector Knight."

I set the small envelope on his desk with the crystal.

"The constable general has been murdered. The queen has directed the case to you. The killer will be charged with murder and treason. At the scene, I saw where something fell into the snow. Constable Mage Green retrieved the end of a cigarette. It had been smoked, and she was able to get a relationship image."

I pushed the crystal across the desk.

"She identified Constable Wertholm from the Fiera. I am asking for a warrant for her to use a truth spell on the constable when we bring him in."

He looked at the evidence bag and then picked up the crystal. "Her mage rank?"

I blinked. "She is a certified mage trained to assist constables."

He looked at me, and I smiled.

"If she were not certified, she would not have received her badge. If she were not qualified, she would not have lasted this long. She would not have been able to impress the relationship image into the crystal."

He smiled and nodded as he turned to open a drawer. "True. Very well, I will grant the warrant."

I watched as he wrote it out and accepted it when he was finished. "The case will be at the central station, sir. The other evidence is being sent there, and Constable Wertholm will be brought there when he is found."

He nodded, and I turned and walked out. The sergeant was waiting in the hall and headed to the door with me. He looked at me carefully. "Calmly, Ashton."

I looked at him, and he smiled. "Do the job, and if you prove he did kill the constable general, you can punch him before he is hung."

I smiled as we walked out and then nodded as I caught the reins for my horse. I swung up and waited for the guards before I turned to head for the gate. "Central station."

It was a quiet ride through the streets that seemed a little darker. When we got there, several constables were getting ready to ride out. The commander was with them and gestured. "We found Wertholm. He was seen entering the estate of the duke of Fiera's, but the duke is refusing us entry."

I shook my head. "Have a constable wait. Senior Magister Gold should be on the way. Have him give us a warrant both to enter and to search since Wertholm is there."

I turned with my guards and rode out while thinking. There was something between the duke and this constable Wertholm. When we reached the estate, a dozen angry constables were outside the gate. Inside were another dozen estate guards. I swung down and did not wait for the sergeant, but he caught up. I strode to the gate and gestured to one guard, who ignored me.

I nodded and turned. "One of you go notify the palace the Fiera duchy is rebelling."

A guard snorted. "We are not rebelling. We are just not allowing constables in without a warrant."

I nodded. "Which is on the way; however, I would like to speak to the duke or Lady Fiera if she is here."

He shook his head. "The duke has said he does not wish to speak to constables."

I waited and shook my head. "And Lady Fiera?"

He looked at me for a moment before he walked to the gatehouse and used the call box. He returned a moment later. "She will be out."

I waited, and finally she came out the front doors and strode to the gate. She looked angry and stopped to glare. "All this because we refuse to accept a knight inspector?"

I looked at her carefully. "No. We are here looking for a suspect in the murder of the constable general."

She blinked, and her mouth opened, and then she closed it with a frown. "What suspect?"

I looked back as the constable commissioner and more constables arrived. "He was shot in the back, and the person waited behind bushes. A cigarette was found there, and we got a relationship image of Constable Wertholm."

She stiffened. "And you think he murdered the constable general?"

I sighed. "We have him as a suspect. The killer used salt on the bullet and his person and the snow. We do have a mold of a boot print and bullet marks to match to a weapon. I do have a warrant for a truth spell to compel him to speak. I need to know if he was there and if he was involved. I will need his weapon to have it checked against the bullet marks and his boots against the mold."

She looked at me and then turned to look at the manor. She finally shook her head. "Father will refuse unless you have a warrant."

I glanced back when the constable commissioner swung down from his horse. He looked at Megan. "Open the gate."

She shook her head, and he straightened.

"You are a constable inspector."

I caught his sleeve. "That would be a conflict of interest."

He growled, but I turned. "We will wait for the warrant but send constables around to the back."

He nodded and did as I asked, and I looked at Abigail as she came closer. It was almost an hour before a constable rode toward us and swung down and held out the warrant. I took it and turned to walk to the gate and held it out. "Open the gate."

The guards did not look happy but unlocked and pulled the gates open. One pointed to my guards. "They will have to stay here."

I snorted as I started through the gate. "They are royal guards and could have entered without a warrant unless you want us to arrest you for treason."

Lady Fiera fell in behind me with Abigail, and as I reached the main doors, they swung open. Her father stood in the door and glared. "This is an act—"

I slapped the warrant on his chest. "Of the courts. This is a warrant to search your grounds for a person wanted for questioning in the murder of the constable general."

He stammered as I pushed past him and saw the man from the crystal. "Mr. Wertholm, I have a warrant to detain you for questioning."

He sneered. "That is Knight Inspector Wertholm to you."

I reached him and grabbed a wrist and twisted and lifted it. "Not here, asshole."

He struggled and lifted one foot to kick, and I yanked the arm up. He screamed, and several constables surged forward and grabbed him and helped me put him in restraints.

I spun him around and pulled a new pistol he was wearing concealed. I smelled the barrel and unloaded it and held it out to Abigail. "Please note this was on his person. It smells like it has been fired recently."

I pushed him to the door.

"Since it was on his person, we do not need a warrant to compare it to the bullet that killed the constable general."

He snickered. "Good luck using magic."

I kept pushing him. "We do not need magic. We have bullet marks and can fire one from your weapon and match it."

He shifted and looked back. "But—"

I pushed him out the door. "But I also found the cigarette you left and have a warrant for a truth spell."

The duke moved out. "Stop!"

I turned. "This involves the laws of the kingdom."

He glared. "I refuse to allow my subject to be removed from ducal soil."

I looked at him as he looked at all the constables. Megan was staring with her mouth open. I held up the warrant. "This—"

He growled, "Does not allow you to remove a subject from another duchy."

I kept looking at him. "Why are you protecting him? I am sure you know he killed the constable general. He was never qualified to be a knight inspector and should never have been recommended. Why are you doing this?"

He snorted. "That is the business of my duchy."

Megan stiffened. "Then it is my business."

He looked at her, and I could see contempt. "No."

She started toward him. "I am your heir."

He looked at Wertholm. "Not for long."

Now things were making sense. "Baron Wertholm is very influential both in your duchy and throughout the kingdom. You are trading favors—this pathetic moron for the removal of your heir. You would move your wastrel son and make him heir."

He looked at me in contempt. "You have no understanding of being noble."

I nodded and turned and pushed Wertholm. "Maybe not."

He yelled. "Guards, stop them!"

I turned. "First, the warrant you did not look at was signed by the senior royal magister Gold, which means I do not need a warrant to remove him from your duchy. Second, interfering with us is treason."

His face was pale, and he looked at Wertholm and then me. "Take him, and you will bring the kingdom to civil war."

I stopped as everyone stopped moving. "Take it back."

He straightened. "Take him, and I will declare war."

I let Wertholm go and pulled my weapon and aimed at the duke's head. "Duke Fiera, you are under arrest for treason. Sergeant, take him, and if his guards attempt to interfere, you will kill them. Constable Commissioner, take my prisoner and escort him to the central station. Have Constable Mage Green conduct a truth spell in the presence of three witnesses and Senior Magister Gold."

The duke opened his mouth, and I cocked the pistol. "Do not speak, traitor."

Megan moved and shifted, but I did not look at her.

"Pull your weapon, and you will hang with him."

My guards moved forward and grabbed the duke, and Wertholm struggled and yelled. The constables surged to pull him away, and I held out the warrant and small evidence envelope.

I finally looked at Megan. "Lady Fiera, I must formally ask you to accompany us to see the queen. As heir, you are required to witness my charge of treason before her and the court."

She was white faced but nodded, and I turned to follow my guards as they pushed the white-faced duke. Constables were thinking ahead and disarmed those by the gate before we reached it. One of my guards led the horses, and we walked, and more than a few people were out to watch. I sent one of the guards ahead to call, and when we reached the palace, all the guards were out.

The duke had recovered a little and walked stiffly. When we walked through the gate, nobles and their representatives were still rushing in. A guard slipped in beside me and whispered. "The throne room, sir."

I nodded and changed directions, and we entered the grand entrance a minute later. It was very large, and guards in formal uniform lined the way to the large double doors. I stopped at the doors and moved to Duke Fiera. "One attempt against the queen, and I will break your back."

I undid the restraints.

"This is my only courtesy, and it is for your daughter."

I gave him a nudge.

"Walk."

At least he had not lost all reason and knelt three paces from the queen. His bluff did not work, facing her or the other nobles. True, only half the other dukes were present, but when I told the full story, the queen took over and questioned him. She seemed calm, but I had no doubt he could not lie to her. He admitted threatening civil war, and then the whole thing came out.

Baron Wertholm wanted and demanded that his youngest son be a constable. When we began to create knight and royal inspectors, the duke was looking for support to remove Lady Fiera as his heir. He went to his strongest and most influential baron. He agreed to help but only if his youngest son was made knight inspector. Then the duke began to rant and made the mistake.

He told the queen and court that females should not rule or command. Never mind that his son was a drunk and had arrests for attempted assault on women. She let him go on until he glared. "I renounce my daughter and"—he looked and spit at my feet—"your pet."

I struck before he could act and knocked him to the floor. I stalked after him as the court broke out in talk. I bent and grabbed his hair and pulled him up and slapped him. "You better pray this court takes care of you because I will challenge you and cut your throat."

I pulled him back before the throne and kicked behind his knee.

"Kneel."

I let him go and stepped back, and the queen stood. "My lords."

The court went silent, and she looked at Duke Fiera.

"Duke Fiera, I find you guilty of treason against the crown. You have already told this court you have betrayed your sworn oath to me and them. I take from you your lands and title and bestow them to Lady Megan Fiera. You will be taken to the Takadi Monastery, where you will live out the rest of your days."

He came to his feet with his face red in anger. "Never! I will—"

I struck behind his knee and grabbed his hair and slammed him to the floor. I stepped on his throat and looked at the queen. She sighed. "If you refuse my grace, so be it. Master at arms, remove him and prepare the gallows."

I moved as a very large guard wearing a scarlet uniform strode forward. He bent and yanked the former duke to his feet. Megan stepped forward. "Wait!"

The queen sighed and gestured, and Megan took a knee. "Your Majesty, I know he deserves it, but I would beg for his life."

The queen held up her hand, and the huge room quieted. "If he goes to the monastery and accepts his fate."

Megan looked at her father coldly. "He will."

The queen nodded and gestured and Megan came to her feet.

She spun and looked at her father and slugged him. I think it stunned the whole court, but I grinned as she stalked after him. "You are a yellow coward. You will do as you are told, or I will use a whip and have you hung myself."

He was marched out of the room, and I bowed to the queen. "I thank you, Your Majesty."

She nodded, and I turned and headed for the door. The sergeant was waiting, and we took the horses to the central station. They had done the truth spell, and he had admitted killing the constable general. It had been in spite for refusing to make him a knight inspector. With that and the match with his boots and the bullet marks, he was sentenced. It was three weeks before he was hung.

His father had tried using all his influence to get him off, and the queen had summoned him and his heir. His patent and lands were given to his son, and he was warned against speaking to any noble. Over five thousand constables from all over the kingdom came for the burial of the constable general. Many stayed to watch his killer hang. It took a month for the queen to select a constable commissioner to replace him.

It had made me think. I was a good inspector, but—now I was a noble and the consort of the princess. I spent the time after the killer was hung thinking and talking with Catherine, and finally I covered my badge and retired. Catherine did have a daughter and another after that. I still keep an eye on the constables and have helped them develop and train for new things, including women constables.

The queen made it very clear to all nobles: the constables were her guardians, and the royal and knight inspectors do not answer to any but her.

The End

94321589R00157

Made in the USA
Middletown, DE
18 October 2018